ADVANCE PRAISE FOR *BORR...*

"Snappy, snarky, an... ...... *Borrowed So...* shelf! It's the stella... ...at makes this book a standout hi... ...ta this s#*t!'"

—...Darynda Jones

"*Borrowed Souls* is ... not miss ...ba... ...s..., ...ique world for readers hungr... ...r... ...something awesome."

—*New York Times* bestselling author Lauren Dane

"Fun, heartfelt, and wildly creative, *Borrowed Souls* packs a new brand of punch in a debut urban fantasy with a soulful twist on magic. Chelsea Mueller brings a new and exciting voice to the UF genre."

—Kelly Meding, author of the Dreg City series

"Dark, fun, and edgy, *Borrowed Souls* sucked me in from the very first page and didn't let go."

—J. C. Daniels, author of the Colbana Files

"Gritty realism, pitch perfect characters and a heavy dose of red hot sex. What more could you ask for?"

—Shannon Mayer, author of the national bestselling Rylee Adamson series

"Fast paced with tons of great action, snarky dialogue, and just enough steamy romance. If you're a fan of the Alex Craft series by Kalayna Price or the Mercy Thompson series by Patricia Briggs, you'll love *Borrowed Souls*!"

—Kate Baxter, author of the Last True Vampire series

"The perfect urban fantasy cocktail. Spectacular world-building and a badass heroine."

—Shawntelle Madison, author of *Coveted*

borrowed SOULS

borrowed SOULS

A Soul Charmer Novel

CHELSEA MUELLER

Talos Press
New York

Talos Press books may be purchased in bulk at special discounts for sales promotion, corporate gifts, fund-raising, or educational purposes. Special editions can also be created to specifications. For details, contact the Special Sales Department, Talos Press, 307 West 36th Street, 11th Floor, New York, NY 10018 or info'skyhorsepublishing.com.

Talos Press® is a registered trademark of Skyhorse Publishing, Inc.®, a Delaware corporation.

Visit our website at www.talospress.com.

10 9 8 7 6 5 4 3 2 1

Library of Congress Cataloging-in-Publication Data

Names: Mueller, Chelsea, author.
Title: Borrowed souls : a Soul Charmer novel / Chelsea Mueller.
Other titles: Soul Charmer novel
Description: New York : Talos, 2017.
Identifiers: LCCN 2016039123 (print) | LCCN 2016055614 (ebook) | ISBN
  9781940456829 (paperback) | ISBN 9781940456836 (eBook)
Subjects: LCSH: Brothers and sisters--Fiction. | Loyalty--Fiction. | Threats
  of violence--Fiction. | Immorality--Fiction. | Spirits--Fiction. |
  Paranormal fiction. | BISAC: FICTION / Fantasy / Urban Life. | FICTION /
  Fantasy / Paranormal. | GSAFD: Fantasy fiction.
Classification: LCC PS3613.U365 B66 2017 (print) | LCC PS3613.U365 (ebook) |
  DDC 813/.6--dc23
LC record available at https://lccn.loc.gov/2016039123

Cover artwork by Jeff Chapman
Cover design by Rain Saukas

Printed in the United States of America

For my parents
(Sorry for all the swearing.)

CHAPTER ONE

Callie Delgado needed a soul.

Her brother had been kidnapped, his captors were blackmailing her, and here she was, outside one of the most unusual pawn shops in all of Gem City, about to rent one. She just needed to force herself to walk the twenty steps to the Soul Charmer's front door. The one wedged in a dirty, rundown building on a dirty, rundown street in the dirty, rundown part of town. It was the last place she wanted to be, but the one place she had to go.

Fate was kind of a dick like that.

Downtown Gem City rolled up by 6 p.m.; she was alone with her thoughts. She batted an empty soda can with the tip of her shoe. It skittered along the concrete, banging into a nearby dumpster overflowing with the rotting remnants of life. The kind of life her brother would cease to have if she didn't walk in that door and let the Soul Charmer put another person's soul into her body.

What was she doing here? She knew the answer, of course, but pride—well, that and a healthy dose of fear—swelled at the base of her skull anyway. What she was about to do was something she'd sworn she never would. It was dangerous, morally corrupt, and maybe worst of all, made her feel like if she went through with it, she wouldn't be any better than the junkies and criminals she'd spent her entire life trying to run away from. The thought made her queasy, like she was covered in a coating of grease she'd never scrub away.

But Josh needed her, and family came first. So Callie walked up the steps to the front door of the shop. A faded, gold "Charmer" was painted at eye-level. Flecks of peeling black paint stuck to her damp palm as she pushed the door open. The musk of rotting wood found its way to her nose, along with the warm decay of day-old fast food and cheap beer.

It didn't smell any better inside the tiny shop. The Nag Champa burning in a glass tray near the door couldn't cover the stench. It was a reminder of what happened here—dirty, dank things, ones she'd been avoiding all of her life.

The thin carpet squelched beneath her boots. The sound sidled along her skin to spiral up her spine. It was almost enough to make her turn back, walk out the door, and hope everything with her brother turned out for the best on its own.

Dark wood beams peeked out from between tapestries, their gold and burgundy threads muted by the years. If a seedy pawnshop were to set up in a bankrupt church, it would probably look a lot like this, she thought. All that was missing was the "CA$H 4 SOULS" sign. She stepped up to the front counter, which was as dilapidated as everything else in the room. The only thing on it was a small, tarnished bell.

Callie clamped her teeth on her tongue as she reached out. A flash of pain centered her. She had to do this. She had no choice. The bell chimed out loudly when she hit it.

Almost immediately a tiny man, barely five feet tall, emerged from a rear doorway covered in heavy velvet. Words like filthy, dangerous, and wicked rumbled in the back of Callie's mind. She'd heard plenty of warnings about this man. His eyes narrowed upon seeing her, then lit up like lights on a Christmas tree. He looked like the type of man who would lie about his height, claiming he'd shrunken over the years. Just like everyone said: the Soul Charmer was a sketchy fuck.

"What can I do for you, sweetheart?" His grandfatherly looks—the guy wore green pajamas—didn't disguise the prurient way his mouth cradled the pet name.

Telling him off and storming out of the store sounded damn appealing, but Callie knew she needed what he was selling a whole lot more than he needed her business. So she swallowed her retort and replied: "A soul."

He laughed, and it made her stomach pitch. She swallowed the fear-and-bile cocktail. She knew the shame of what she was doing would come later. "You're going to have to be more specific."

Moving her weight to her right foot didn't make the words come any faster than shifting back to the left did. She opened her mouth, only to close it again. Her good sense held the reply hostage. "I need one for just a day or two."

She needed to sound confident, like this was no big deal, a business transaction she did every day, even if the opposite were true. That would be a good start, right?

"A short timer, yes. Not a problem." His lips parted, revealing two shiny silver teeth in the front. The rest were missing. "The question is: Do you want something *pure*?"

The way his tongue curled around the word made her skin crawl. Every individual sin weighed a soul down, if you believed the Cortean Catholic church—and there were a lot of believers in Gem City. If a pure soul had been pawned to the Charmer, it meant horrible things for its original owner. Callie wasn't about to pile on extra shit for that person to shovel. No, she didn't want to taint a clean soul, even if it was a borrowed one. She was after the non-celestial perks anyway. "Purity isn't an issue."

He cocked his head to the side until his ear nearly grazed his shoulder, staring at her. The shop was quiet, long enough to make her think she'd blown her shot at a soul already. "Purity is always an issue. Your soul, for example, would fetch a nice purse. I could arrange—"

"I'm not here to sell."

He lifted his hands in faux supplication. "I meant no harm."

"Fine. I need an average soul for a couple of days." *Average* soul. She shook herself. What did that even mean?

"That's understandable. If I were you, I wouldn't want someone too tainted curling up in that little body of yours either."

"Are we going to do this or not?" she almost spat at him. Was this how he treated all of his customers? Callie's irritation was boiling up inside her, but as disgusting as the Soul Charmer was, she couldn't afford for him to say no. She had to bite her tongue. She looked around the dank room, avoiding his gaze.

"I don't see a rate menu," she finally said, gesturing toward the counter between them, careful not to touch it.

"How much do you have?"

Great. Renting a soul was just like buying pot for the first time. Now, though, wasn't the time to negotiate; she couldn't risk not getting the goods. Her savings were minimal, but she could only hope the offer would be fair. "$200."

He shook his head. "Not enough. What else you got?"

What *did* she have? A car with a hole in the muffler, an apartment with an inconsistent heater, and a brother who fucked up so royally his baby sister had to do a job for some hustler in order to keep his stupid ass alive. A job that required this soul. A soul that wouldn't raise questions, one that could cover her crimes, and one that could withstand the taint of the filthy things she'd have to do to save Josh.

She shrugged. "Not much."

"You could pawn that pretty soul—"

"We already covered that." Irritation, and her need to get the fuck out of his shop as soon as possible, steeled her spine.

"No need to get testy." His tongue darted to wet his lips, and in that moment Callie swore his green pajamas sprouted scales. Nothing like doing business with the cold blooded.

"Unless you've got layaway, I've got $200."

"You can work off the extra."

The list of things she wouldn't do to help her brother was short, but renting a soul was already on the outer limits of her comfort zone. She aimed for Zen breathing, and waited for him to take the offer back, shooting him a death glare.

He rolled his eyes. "Not like *that*. I can see your soul, remember?"

He was bored. Too bad. She was roiling with fear, guilt, and an extreme need for a shower, but she wasn't getting all preachy about it.

"Then what?"

"A collector."

"Like I'm supposed to know what that is."

"Not everyone is good about returning the souls they barter for in this shop. I employ people to retrieve them for me."

"Employ? You mean like a job."

"Yes. It's a common term."

She didn't need a job; she needed a soul. "Either you want my money or you don't."

"You don't have money."

If only that weren't true. Defeated, Callie turned and strode toward the door, realizing as she left that she was about to fail Josh. She'd do almost anything for him, but this? Working for the Charmer was too much—too terrifying, if she were being honest—and too close to hitting rock bottom.

The Charmer called after her but she was already out the door, into the alleyway. The wind whirled around her, cold and unforgiving. Her hair whipped her face. Lashes she'd earned. Five minutes earlier, she'd expected to leave the shop loaded down from the guilt of having rented a soul. The weight of *not* renting one was turning out to be worse.

"Okay, I'll give you a partner," the Charmer's voice called out behind her, his tone hardened, like it really was his final offer.

Sometimes people say something so idiotic it nearly stops your heart, and all you can do is wait for your brain to recover and jumpstart the whole operation. That was Callie: a statue in denim. She stopped walking, and turned slowly to face him. "Do I look like the enforcer type?"

"I didn't say anything about collecting funds. Or injuring anyone."

"Yes, because I'm sure a polite 'Please return that soul' is all it will take."

"You're lucky I can see your soul," he muttered loud enough to avoid losing the words to the wind.

"Not interested." She shuffled forward again. She'd find another way to save Josh, she told herself. There had to be another way than this, right?

"I'll give you a partner who can handle the—ahem—heavy lifting. Your soul intrigues me. I think you might have a knack for this work."

"I don't *want* a 'knack' for this."

"It's an easy job. You can keep your $200, *and* you'll get your soul."

Follow around some collections guy and she'd get the soul she needed to save Josh? The Charmer eyed her—and her soul, Callie suspected—with too much leering interest, but he wasn't the first creep she'd met. She'd had worse offers before, and besides, deep down she knew she had fuckall in the way of options.

"How long?" she asked, like it mattered.

"You collect with the partner of my choosing for six weeks, and I'll let you rent a soul for one day."

"Six weeks? No." She could probably earn the money in a legit way in six weeks. Plus, Josh didn't have that kind of time.

"You need me for the soul." He wasn't wrong.

Before Callie knew what she was doing, she began haggling.

"Two weeks." It was her final offer. This was it or she was out.

The Soul Charmer sighed, and gave Callie one last hard look. "Agreed. Two weeks of work for a one-day rental. You get it after your services are finished."

Fourteen measly days. A fortnight. Hopefully Ford wasn't going to do anything to Josh between now and then. And anyway, he was the one who'd ordered her to specifically use the Charmer's services in the first place.

Making the deal felt like the aftermath of downing a shot of bottom-shelf vodka. "Two weeks, and then I get a soul."

The edges of the Soul Charmer's lips curled up slowly, lasciviously. Somehow, Callie managed to keep down her lunch. He gestured back to the store's front door. A flash of gold on his hand drew her attention. How had he managed to get bulky gold rings over those knuckles? They looked like tree trunk knots.

"C'mon then. . ." he started, then trailed off. "I should probably know the name of my newest employee?"

"Callie," she said, uneasy about him having even *that* much of her personal information.

She re-entered his store, but held back as he shuffled toward the worn black curtain he'd parted to enter the room through. He held the curtain open, but didn't repeat his earlier request. The low ceiling, slathered with a cheap black lacquer, closed in as Callie met his gaze. Guess the job had already started.

The air thickened in the doorway. The step through was like wading in tar. She pushed herself forward, but suddenly her breath locked in her chest. She cleared the doorway, gasping, only to be blasted by a wall of pure heat. It was as though her coat had been incinerated and electricity danced on her bare skin. Callie all but fell into the next room, forcing her hands to stay tight to her side, avoiding the temptation to reach out and grab onto some unknown surface for balance. She finally found her footing, and staggered to a stop. *What the hell was that?*

The Soul Charmer looked back curiously, but a momentary brightness in his eyes was gone before Callie could be sure she'd even seen it.

"Don't mind the door," he said, making his way across the anteroom and opened another door—this one made of a honeyed wood. Warm light began to spill into the chamber.

"The door?" Callie's voice was distant as she focused on the rows upon rows of picture frames hanging on the walls at her right and left. The glass panes were cloudy, but her gut told her she probably didn't want to see the obscured faces anyway.

"Keeps other magic from my workspace," he explained. "Come, come." He waved his gnarled hand at her. She didn't flinch this time.

Other magic? The only known magic was soul magic, she thought.

"The pictures do that?"

"Part of the pawn process. Those who choose to lend their souls for my services are recorded in there. They depart when their term is complete." Eight lamps filled the two-hundred-square-foot space in the next room, their brightness doubled by the reflection from the pristine tile floor. Gone were the dark wood and aged tapestries pandering to the church. These walls were lined with shelves, obsidian jars stacked to the edges on each one. If she closed her eyes, the astringent in the air brought Callie back to the ICU. Memories welled against her lower eyelids, bringing up broken dreams she'd spent a long time trying to forget.

The Charmer settled behind an aged oak desk and began digging through a lower drawer. Callie shoved her hands in her pockets absentmindedly, and for a moment her coat stretched, showing off more of her figure that she ever wanted to reveal to him. She quickly removed them, hoping he hadn't noticed.

"This—" he finally said, holding up a silver flask with a rich, black stone inlay, "—you will need to take with you."

Callie reached for it, but he pulled it back at the last moment, out of her reach.

"Press the open mouth of the jar to the person's sternum, nice and low." He tapped two fingers against his own. "That will transfer the soul to the vessel. Then all you have to do is return it to me."

"So where's the 'on' button?" she asked sarcastically.

He ignored her.

"Fine, but does it have to be a flask?" She wasn't averse to booze, but it was a little closer to alcoholic territory than she cared to venture.

"This one. Yes."

"Why again do you need *me* to do this? I mean, I'm not reneging on the deal, but couldn't your normal guy touch a flask to peoples' stomachs just fine?"

"No."

Callie waited for him to elaborate, but the Charmer clearly didn't want to divulge more. She reached out her hand again. "Fine, then."

This time he obliged. Her fingers slid over the obsidian inlay on the front of the container. The cool stone didn't heat with her touch, but her fingertips tingled all the same.

The Charmer smiled, flashing silver. "Yes, you'll do. Derek will meet you at your home tomorrow afternoon."

"I'll meet him *here*."

The Charmer glared, but didn't argue. "4 p.m. Don't be late."

Did she really have a choice?

CHAPTER TWO

Callie cranked the car key in the ignition for the third time, her shaking hands more to blame for the car not starting than the vehicle itself. She tapped the gas pedal and the engine finally turned over. The lemon on wheels was running, and she still had $200 in her bank account. It was almost enough to convince her this evening had been a success.

The Soul Charmer's store was less than a ten-minute drive from her apartment, but she wasn't ready to head home yet. She needed time to accept what she'd done. Time to understand what she was *about* to do over the next two weeks. Being cooped up in her bare-bones apartment with scant furnishings would only amplify her anxiety like a Feng Shui echo. Her extended family was reliable, but she couldn't call any of them to visit. The closest cousin was sixty miles away and her brother . . . well, he was obviously unavailable as well. Wallowing and recounting her mistakes was simply safer outside of her one-bedroom. She hooked a left on Agua Fria and headed toward the Plaza.

Under the midday sun, Gem City's Plaza lived up to the town's name. The vibrant jewel tones of painted tiles set into the walls of each storefront sparkled under natural light. But the sun had set hours ago. Tourists were tucked back away into their hotels with their authentic chimineas lit in every room to counter the cool desert night air. The sparse streetlights made it difficult for the uninitiated to spot when dusk shifted to pitch black in the empty spaces. Transient men and women meandered the streets. Those who were truly homeless tucked in by store entrances to make camp for the night.

Callie drove the unreasonably slow speed limit, but still had to slam her brakes as a twenty-something woman ran out into the street. The woman's braided pigtails bounced against the woven poncho she wore, the kind sold at every rural roadside stand within a two-hundred-mile radius. She yelled out to another unseen hitchhiker friend, and then stashed the screwdriver she held in her hand in her right pocket. The hitchhiker—Callie could spot them a mile away—was why Gem City couldn't have nice things. Callie didn't need to spot the missing tile in front of Gem Jewelers to know the poncho girl had pilfered it. She might be destined to be a thief, but she wasn't about to go advertising it.

At least they didn't touch the Basilica. The church kept their grounds covered in lush, green lawn. The city didn't enforce water restrictions when it came to the Cortean Catholic church. Callie hit the adjacent stoplight, and spent the next minute and a half next to the bronze statue of Saint Catalina. Three LED spotlights revealed her soft cheekbones and flowing skirt. Others in town might have looked at the statue and thought of Catalina's story, of her martyrdom, of her quiet strength. But Callie remembered the time Josh tried to convince Father Duncan he wanted to pick Catalina as his saint name. The priest had taken on all the attributes of a turnip, vaguely purple and puffed out at the sides. A few years later Callie chose Catalina as her own saint name, in Josh's honor.

A couple blocks from home, she pulled into a convenience store parking lot. All the chaos of the day had blocked out her mundane responsibilities. She had laundry to do, but no detergent to make that happen. Her building hadn't stocked the soap vending machine in seven months. She didn't have quarters anyway. She stepped out of the car and onto a scrap of yellow police tape with the standard "DO NOT CROSS" verbiage. It fluttered in the cool October breeze.

The shop's cashier, Callie remembered from the newspaper headlines, had found a severed arm around the side of the store two days earlier. The matching body had been discovered seven blocks over, behind a street taco shop. No arrests, but the whispers that Ford was behind it were growing louder.

They hadn't bothered to remove the tape yet. Callie shouldn't have been surprised. Chalk outlines only disappeared when it rained or snowed. The locals didn't often bring out a hose to wash it away.

So much for calming her nerves before going home. She thought about popping a Xanax when she got home, about how nice it would be to blank her anxiety for a few hours. But that was something Josh would do, and she wasn't like him. Not like that. Besides, if she was going to save her brother, she needed to keep her own shit together.

Even if that meant a night of laundry, followed by tossing and turning.

Callie had been serving breakfast and lunch to the elderly at Cedar Retirement Home for eight months, and she mostly didn't hate it.

The people were all right, if you didn't mind cynical reminiscing over lifetimes of bad decisions, along with a whole lot of gallows humor. Both had been standard operating procedure for Callie since the age of nine.

Unfortunately, keeping busy chopping vegetables to help Louisa with food preparation wasn't enough to keep her mind off the deal she'd made with the Soul Charmer. She'd woken up with a wicked case of regret. Just what had Josh gotten her into?

Louisa broke into Callie's thoughts. "Father Domingo asked about you."

Her distraction must have been obvious, because Louisa didn't usually mention church so early in the morning. Callie's boss's grey hair was wound in a sharp bun, letting light catch her gold cross pendant.

"Nice of him," Callie muttered. New Mexico had become Cortean Catholicism's strongest foothold in North America more than a century ago, and now the faith had unyielding public devotion throughout Gem City. In the church's eyes, purity and piety were equal, and keeping one's soul light enough—not weighed down by sin—to "rise to Heaven" was the paramount goal of any regular churchgoer. Callie attended services with Lou once a month. It kept the general judgment levels of those around her low—she wasn't a bad person, but she wasn't a true believer either—and it made Louisa happy. Callie did what she could to make Lou happy.

"I told him you've been taking your mom to service elsewhere, and he said he hoped you were finding time for confession."

She hadn't confessed to a cleric in five years. The Charmer had said her soul was still pure, so she guessed she hadn't done anything to fuck things up too royally. Watching Josh sink to dismal depths had Callie less worried about her own afterlife than others in Gem City. Not that she'd ever admit it. "The church near my house is growing on me," she lied.

Dropping in on Father Gonzales hadn't been on her to-do list. Off the books, he encouraged his congregation to leverage soul magic. Soul magic was real, he acknowledged, which was rare enough for *any* cleric to say publicly. Confessing the use of magic was required, he clarified each time, but whenever she took her mom to his services, Father Gonzales preached reaching heaven by any means necessary. It made sense, then, that all but a handful of people in their state subscribed to a religion founded by a conquistador.

Callie wasn't too superior to say she didn't know people who had used the Charmer's services before, and she wasn't classy enough to pretend she'd never been in that neighborhood. However, in the decade since the Soul Charmer had set up shop and soul magic became known outside the back alley crowd, she'd never once thought she'd find herself using his services, let alone working for the snake. No matter what loophole Father Gonzales gave his congregation, it was no secret that bad things happened to people who borrowed souls.

Besides, a pristine soul didn't wash away consequences. Her cousin Kristi was proof enough.

She shook her head at the memory and almost sliced into her index finger with the bulky chef's knife. Kristi had a nasty husband. No bones to be made about it. She'd also had a sense of finality about marriage: once you're in it, you're in it, and there's no getting out. Callie thought it was a rather fatalistic way to look at a union that's supposed to be born of love. Then again, Callie was twenty-two and had no intention of getting married.

Callie's cousin, though, took the shit seriously. Well, the part about never leaving. She yearned for romance (or, more specifically, good sex), and when she realized she wasn't ever going to get it from her husband, she took matters into her own hands, and rented a soul to cheat on him. It wasn't staining their relationship, she'd argued. Yes, God cared about her soul and yes, she should avoid sinning, but if she committed adultery using *someone else's* soul, she was golden, right?

Callie had never seen the logic, but how could she argue when Father Gonzales basically condoned it? As far as reasons to rent out someone else's soul, Kristi's purpose was mild. From stories, Callie knew most people used rented souls for exacting revenge, violence, and murder. Still, it always ended badly. Even if one was out just to get laid.

The idea of a swapped soul might have spared Kristi the wrath of God—though Callie wasn't quite buying that, regardless of the Church's stance—but it hadn't done a damn thing to stop her husband from shattering both her orbital bones and literally caving in Kristi's face when he caught her in the act. She swore the adultery was on someone else's soul. While it assuaged her guilt, it was more than a year before the surgeons had her back solid. They didn't have the money for full reconstruction, though. Kristi had blown all her savings on souls from the rental service she'd spotted in the back pages of a free newspaper: the Soul Charmer.

Real world consequences followed soul rental. Callie's slices into the onion became forceful chops. The clack of the blade against the wooden board grew louder as she focused on making each movement a prayer she'd stay whole. Her eyes began to water from her sloppy style with the onion.

That's what she told herself.

CHAPTER THREE

What did one do to prepare for the first day as a soul collector? Pray? Drink? Sacrifice javelina? There wasn't a guidebook for things like this. Callie had convinced herself that her work for the Soul Charmer was essentially blackmail. He might not be the source of her woes, but he'd taken advantage of her need. Close enough.

She'd changed out the maroon scrubs she'd worn to work, showered to blight the remnants of kitchen work from her skin, and swiped her chestnut hair up into a simple plait. Everything needed to be casual. Pretending this was any other afternoon would help get her through day one. The jeans, black tee, and pair of Chucks she wore should have been comfortable, but even the rubber soles pressed against her feet as though they wanted to squeeze blood from her. Just another payment she'd make for family.

The phone call to Josh the night before had gone as expected: shitty. He'd been elated to hear she was coming through. The joy hadn't lasted long.

"Two weeks, sis? Two *goddamn* weeks?" The jubilation from moments before had been smashed into a hiss. At least he hadn't called their mom. She'd tried to pawn her furniture for Josh the last time he got in over his head.

"Sorry, but I don't have a stockpile of money to bail you out again." Callie had liquidated her savings account for him just nine months earlier. The smashed furniture in his apartment hadn't elicited much sympathy from her (it wasn't that out of the ordinary at that point), but the deep, wallowing welts on his forearms had convinced her to hand over the funds. She'd paid his drug debt, and drove him directly to Blue Dove Rehabilitation Center. Four-fucking-thousand-dollars later she was broke, and her brother had somehow gotten himself even deeper in danger.

"I thought I could count on you," he'd said, resorting to a familiar tactic.

The jab would have hurt last year. This wasn't the first time he'd thrown it, though. She had to remember: The highs and lows of the conversation weren't due to his fear or the stress of the situation. He was high, and twenty grand in debt to a drug dealer. He'd paid for oblivion. *Must be nice.* "I'm doing what I can, Josh." It was all Callie could offer.

Ford had snatched the phone at that point. "Did I hear I'm keeping this asshole for two weeks?"

Ugh. Even just a few words from Ford left Callie feeling like she was covered in thick tar. She'd fought through the viscous fear. "Yes, and you're supposed to keep him safe, not *high*."

His laugh had unsettled her. "He's safest around here when he's not in his own mind." There had been too much knowledge in those words. A threat had been buried in there, too.

She'd wrapped her hair around her hand and lifted it into a makeshift bun. It hadn't cooled the heat blossoming at the base of her neck.

"I need a couple weeks to get the soul secured for your job." She'd rushed the words. The sooner the conversation was done, the better.

"The Charmer running low on stock?"

"I'm low on cash, unless you've changed your mind about fronting the money." Getting the soul might cover her ass when she did a job for Ford, but that didn't make any of this okay.

"I've fronted enough cash. That's the problem."

"I know," she'd muttered, swallowing again and again as her brain had fought to keep the idiocy inside. "One of your men would be better at getting the information from—"

"Don't say that shit on the phone," he'd cut her off. Her cheeks burned from the verbal slap. She should have known better. Even a criminal rube like her knew talking about breaking into police records on the phone was dumb. "Your brother made an agreement. In my world we honor our word. You're holding up his end of the deal. No renegotiating the terms. Two weeks is enough of a change in plans."

Arguing the finer points of her involvement with a mob boss would only get her snuggled into the dirt. *That* much she knew. "Right."

"I expect results." Ford's teasing tone had then disappeared. "I'll keep your bro whole for now. He's come in handy in the past. You drag this out, though, and we'll be doing this exchange in pieces. You get me?"

She'd gotten him.

Callie shivered at the memory of her only face-to-face with Ford.

From the outside, Ford's house was like any other rich asshole's. A single-level adobe wonder sprawled in a private slip of desert. The mature juniper bushes surrounding the home made it blend into the skyline at night, but Callie doubted Ford had ever spent too much time enjoying the clear skies.

The entrance was where the peaceful façade disappeared. The family portraits inside depicted men Callie had only ever seen in courtroom reports on the ten o'clock news. The henchman who escorted her to Ford's office was short and wiry. The gun strapped to his hip was hard to miss. With each stutter-step she took, her shoes clomping against the tile, the exposed wooden beams above her seemed to drop, inch by inch, like she was living a video game from the eighties. The burnt-orange accent wall in Ford's office was a welcome distraction.

"You're Josh's sister?" Ford's back was to her. She'd seen him on the news, but in real life he was shorter, probably five-foot-seven. He wore blue jeans and a red polo shirt. His short hair was freshly cut, making it look like he was still in junior high.

"Yeah," her voice shook in a the-guy-behind-me-has-a-gun kind of way.

"You sure he's worth all this?" Ford turned as he spoke. He had a baby face—cherubic with dimples and gentle eyes. In another context, he might have struck her as the sweet boy down the street who'd offer to help the elderly woman rescue her cat. He wasn't that boy, though. She'd never convince herself Ford was so harmless when there were three severed fingers resting atop a white sheet of paper on the desk next to his hip.

Her brain shorted at the sight, as if ceiling beams had crashed down on her neck. When she came to, they were in another room and she was agreeing to whatever Ford asked. She didn't argue when he told her a different soul would be required to commit the robbery. Overlaying a second soul onto your own muddled DNA and fingerprints—the cops knew it, but the legal system hadn't yet caught up to making it illegal. That made soul renting attractive to guys like Ford.

Callie's mind returned to the present. Despite everything she'd gotten herself into over the past few days, she couldn't undo the past. What was done was done, and she had to focus on moving forward if she had any chance of getting herself and her brother out alive. Working for the Soul Charmer couldn't be that awful if it meant Josh wouldn't be returned in brown butcher paper.

She made a turkey sandwich, but it wasn't any more appealing than the chicken she'd served at the retirement home. She ate half, and then wrapped the remainder in plastic. Day-old sandwiches weren't exactly the peak of leftover cuisine, but she'd at least save a few, much-needed bucks.

The air had turned crisp while she was inside. Snow would be capping the mountains in the distance soon. She stepped out and locked the door. An autumn breeze whipped through the exposed staircase at her apartment building. It didn't cut through her hoodie, thankfully, but the blast cooled the nape of her neck and did nothing for her nerves. Better cold wind than a clammy palm on her neck, she tried to convince herself, but in that moment it was hard to tell the difference.

The drive to the Soul Charmer's storefront only took about ten minutes. Halfway there, street lamps became sparse enough that clusters of transients could take shelter against the crumbling, graffiti-tagged adobe buildings without drawing the attention of passing vehicles. Her mother had told her she'd get mugged living in a neighborhood "like that." But her mom's place wasn't any nicer. She'd just lived there long enough to know all the neighbors.

Callie debated how close to park. She didn't know how they'd be finding those who reneged on their deal with the Charmer, and even though renting souls was technically legal, the cops undoubtedly did drive-bys of the place. She didn't blame them. Criminals used rented souls. She would know; she was on her way to being one of them.

As Ford explained it to her, the first step toward making soul renting illegal was convincing local legislators that borrowing a soul was directly related to criminal activity. Even though it was assumed most congressmen were like everyone else, and enjoyed a little taste of sin without suffering the eternal consequences. Rented souls obscured the proof of the crime, and that made it easy to pass the buck. Once concrete evidence eventually emerged, the truth would be out, and it would be near impossible to change public opinion. The lawmakers would have to fall in line.

Ford had said he had it on good authority that Gem City Police were close to linking the two. They had enough hard data to bury soul renting once and for all, and making soul magic illegal would make criminal activity in the city that much harder. That couldn't be allowed to happen, he'd said, and that's where Callie would come in. Once she got her rented soul, she'd be the one stealing their research. Ford said he would take care of the researcher. She didn't want to know how. She was already too deep in this shit.

In the end, she'd opted for parking beneath a street lamp two blocks away. Far enough that she hoped she would avoid police attention—her inspection sticker was four months out of date—but not so buried in the bad part of town as to have her tires stolen. Fingers crossed.

"You're late."

Callie involuntarily stepped backward at the gruff voice. There was so much debris on this street, and so much on her mind, she hadn't looked up once as she walked to the Soul Charmer's shop. Something else to add to her long list of recent mistakes.

She corrected her gaze now to assess the new threat. He stood at least six feet tall, and the black leather of his motorcycle jacket helped amplify the width of his shoulders. Her petite form barely equaled half his muscled frame.

"And that would make you . . . ?" She didn't bother with formalities, or even to point out that she was actually two minutes early, since it mattered so much to him.

He scratched along the harsh edge of his jaw. He had a handful of years on her, making him maybe twenty-eight or twenty-nine. Old scars crisscrossed his knuckles. That bulk beneath the leather and denim wasn't borne of the gym, then.

"Derek." He said his name like he hated it. Or her. What a great way to start a working relationship. But really, what had she expected from a person shady enough to work for the Soul Charmer?

"Oh." She swallowed the 'you don't have to be a dick' lingering on the tip of her tongue, and collected herself. "Then I guess I'm your temporary partner."

She watched as he took her in, from the ponytail right down to the Chucks on her feet. She'd concealed her figure beneath the hoodie, but she'd been ogled enough times at bars to know he wasn't assessing her like *that*. She shifted her weight, unsure what to say next, and glanced around her. The alleyway they were in smelled terrible. Was he going to say something, or were they going to just stand there all day?

Derek narrowed his eyes.

"You bring the flask?" He was all business, she thought. Was that a good thing?

"Yeah." She'd tucked the onyx in her pocket earlier, and it was still chilly to the touch. Even now she could feel it through the denim of her jeans.

"Let's see it." Did he not believe her? No one said tests were part of this gig.

Then again, maybe he was as much in the dark as she was. She sighed and pulled it out. "See? All ready to go."

He grunted. Callie's gut twisted. Derek was nearly impossible to read, which meant two weeks of working together would probably be a total fucking delight. Apparently finished with the small talk, he turned his back to her and stalked down the street with silent footfalls that belied his size. She slid the flask into the pocket of her sweatshirt. The extra layers muted the icy sensation of the stone.

"You coming?" He didn't bother looking back. The Soul Charmer must have told him how desperate she was. Or maybe he'd recognized the guilt hiding behind the deep brown of her eyes when he'd given her that visual dressing down.

Callie took a few long strides to catch up to him. He stopped next to a well-loved, old motorcycle. He held out a matte black helmet for her, but she didn't take it.

"Just put the helmet on." Did he think he was talking to a toddler? Callie wasn't going to survive fourteen days of stilted orders.

"My car is just down the street." She jerked a thumb over her shoulder. "I can drive."

"I drive."

"Congrats, that makes two of us. I'll follow you."

"Doesn't work that way, cupcake." He watched as Callie stared dubiously at the twin chrome exhaust pipes. "Don't look at the bike that way. Jobs like this require nimble rides. This is it."

"Seems like a car would be better for, you know, collecting things." It was a last-ditch argument. Even Callie heard how silly the words sounded aloud.

"The flask in your pocket doesn't require a whole lot of cargo space," he pointed out.

She wasn't about to give him the satisfaction of admitting defeat out loud. Callie snatched the helmet from him and strapped it on her head.

"Thank you," he mumbled as he swung a leg over the machine. He leaned forward enough to make sure there was enough room for her.

Callie climbed on behind him. It had been a long time since she'd been on a bike. Only once her legs were pressed against the outside of his did she realize what she'd inadvertently signed up for. No doubt that she would be getting damn cozy with Derek in the weeks to come. He'd made it clear he was as excited about her involvement in his day as she was, and now she was pressing her chest against his back. A meet cute, it was not.

"Hold on tight." His words rumbled in echo of the engine firing beneath them.

Derek's muscles were hard and unforgiving, but as he drove them down the street, the wind whipped at her face, and she welcomed his warmth. A few turns later, and Callie found herself leaning toward the simple and clean scent of soap escaping over the edge of his jacket. He took a quick right and her nose grazed his neck. He stiffened in her arms, but didn't say anything. Though, she wasn't sure if she would be able to hear a grunt of displeasure over the roar of engine.

They weren't on the bike for long.

After five minutes of dodging Gem City's famous potholes, Derek pulled the rumbling motorcycle up to the curb and killed the engine. She wasn't struck by silence after the roar died—the street they were on had enough locals on stoops and kids yelling from the basic playground at the corner to fill the void—but Callie was surprised to find the cold stole her breath as she leaned away from Derek's solid frame.

She bristled at the thought, and climbed off the bike in a hurry, only to find she had nowhere to go. She didn't know the plan, and wasn't ballsy enough to ask what it was. She shoved her hands in the front pockets of her sweatshirt, her fingers finding the flask, and stared with faux purpose at the boys riding too-small bicycles up the street, doing her best impression of a tough, relaxed woman who did this shit all the time.

She had only herself to blame for the discomfort. She'd put herself in this situation. Blaming Josh would have been nice, but it was her own damn fault for lending him money. She'd never said no to him. He'd been the cool older brother who took her to concerts and introduced her to pot. But where she'd only dabbled, Josh had taken the whole gateway drug thing as a challenge. He fell deeper and deeper into heavier and heavier narcotics and amphetamines each year. When he'd come to her door, skinny as a rail and saying he didn't have money for food, she took care of him. She fed him and slapped a couple twenties in his palm. Then she did it again, and again, and again, until she lost count. And she'd lie to herself, telling herself that he was using the money she gave him for bread and meat.

But now her eyes were open, and she was done with all that. Callie put herself on the Soul Charmer's doorstep, and she had no choice but to follow through. Even if the process made her as uncomfortable as a punk rocker at a country line-dancing bar.

Derek bent forward to stow his gear, and she couldn't resist picturing him kicking up hay at a hoedown. She snickered into her fist, and it made her feel a little better.

He led her toward the street corner. His legs were much longer than hers, and as he neared the intersection with Eighth Street, he leveraged his ample stride to put a small bit of distance between them. He didn't look back once to see if she followed. His shoulders remained rounded forward, muscles tight. It was as if he could sense her behind him.

The door handle to The Fall disappeared in Derek's grip. The bar was unmarked on the street. The faint echo of the street number—a seven and, possibly, a one—were hazy on the door's window. The lone window—if one could call it that—had the look of antique brass. But she wasn't in some steampunk den, and it wasn't for looks. Time and neglect had filled the glass with green and brown fog. The picture frames at the Soul Charmer's shop, she remembered, had the same ghastly visual, and both came with a steady, unsettling sense of danger. A shiver snaked around her spine and Callie jerked forward involuntarily.

Derek, waiting just outside the doorway, caught her shoulder. His hand lingered after she'd steadied herself. "You been here before?" His rough tone softened.

She gave him a quick shake of her head. She didn't trust her voice to be steady. Worries were piling above her head, and acknowledging any of them would trigger an avalanche she wasn't prepared to deal with. At least not now. On a street corner in front of a sketchy bar. With him.

He grunted. Callie thought he sounded pleased, but she didn't speak Neanderthal. Were they going to communicate in grunts and shrugs like this for the next two weeks?

"Try not to make eye contact inside." He jerked his head toward the door. He still clutched its handle. "It'll start trouble."

Callie was trying to recover, to ignore the twist in her gut. "Do I look like trouble?"

The corner of his mouth quirked up. "Actually, yeah. You do."

The compliment washed over her, warming her a little. "Hey man, I'm just along for the ride."

"Right. You could wait—" He trailed off, his dark gaze fixed on two guys walking near his bike. When they moved past, any hint of comradery had been snuffed, and he continued with his stereotypically deep rumble. "Well, I'm not in the mood to fight."

She doubted that. The boots on his feet were made for kicking ass, and she'd bet a soul rental that he had at least one weapon hidden under all that denim and leather. She wasn't about to call him on it, though. "Kay."

He opened the door, stepping inside, and Callie followed, dropping into The Fall with him.

She hadn't been lying about never stepping foot in The Fall, but that didn't mean she was unfamiliar with the bar. Its reputation was whispered about at the places she frequented. In Gem City, there were a few different kinds of places to grab a drink. First were the "dive bars," where rich kids went to blow their parents' money and line bartenders' pockets with $2 tips on $1 Pabst Blue Ribbons. Then, there were shitty watering holes where actual poor people went. The dimly lit establishments served the same drinks as the dives, but the music was better and there sure weren't any Bentleys parked around the corner. They were places you went for cheap drinks. Callie liked those kinds of bars. It wasn't just that she didn't have money—though, that was definitely a factor—she genuinely liked the people. The patrons at her kind of bars were respectful if you didn't want to talk. They were fine if you refused a drink. They also wouldn't hesitate to warn you that there were much safer places to go than The Fall.

Callie wasn't surprised to see brick red stains on the concrete floor. The Fall was the kind of bar you went to for a fight. The blood splatters had lost their vibrant color with age, and it's not like they would be sticky, but she still did her best to avoid stepping on them, like some fucked up version of avoiding the cracks in the sidewalk. A year ago, would she have ever thought she'd be in this situation right now? She clung to the pious belief she was only here for Josh. Family was all you had sometimes, through thick and thin. This was definitely the thin.

Callie stayed close to Derek as he moved through the room. He was big enough to silently command people to step aside for him, and she took advantage of his wake. He led them to a booth pressed against the far wall, far away from the bar itself, which was fine by her. She wouldn't put a beer bottle from The Fall to her lips if she had a gun to her head. Even the cheap plastic cups she saw littering tables looked suspect. This was the kind of place where the bartender would drug you himself, and you'd wake in the alley without your wallet, or your kidney. No. Thank you.

"So, what now?" Callie did her damnedest to focus on Derek, and not the way the cushion beneath her sagged to the left.

"We wait." He had a knack for short answers. Lovely.

"For?"

He'd been glaring at the entrance, but he cut a look her way that about sliced her in half. "Too many ears," was all he said. It was enough.

She decided his silence was keeping her as safe as possible in a shithole like this. So, instead of bothering him with more questions or counting the minutes, she surveyed the room. She wasn't the only one skipping church services that night. Most people were clustered at the bar. The conversations were physical. Sharp nods, harsh elbows, fists slamming down. Callie drew in a deep breath before glancing up at the dirty ventilation system in the ceiling and shuddering. She couldn't afford to catch whatever plague simmered in here.

Derek's fingers wrapped around the edge of the table. His knuckles turned white, but he didn't move. A short, skinny guy had walked in the door a few moments earlier, and Derek watched him with an intensity that would turn most to dust. The guy sidled up to the bar, rested one elbow on the dark surface, and ordered a shot.

Callie opened her mouth to ask who he was, but Derek was on his feet. He took one step in the man's direction, and then looked over his shoulder at her. He'd forgotten she was there; the conflict in his eyes told her as much. "Stay here." The words cut through gnashed teeth. She wasn't going to argue.

Derek stalked to the bar. The recognition on the skinny guy's face was obvious. He began to fidget, tucking his hair behind his ear over and over, the length not long enough to stay put. Derek's bulk cast the type of shadow that could force someone to forget how long their own hair was.

A voice yanked her attention away from Derek. "You're new."

Callie turned, intending to let whomever it was know what a piss-poor pickup line he'd used, until she saw the man who had spat it at her. He drove his knuckles into the table, her table, and leaned close. His scraggly beard couldn't hide the worn lines on his face, or the caustic smell of three-day whiskey breath.

"You here for a good time or somethin'?" He leered even closer. Callie tried not to breathe, but the necrotic air surrounding him still found its way into her nostrils. "Why don't you have a drink, girl?"

She bolted. Callie had spent her high school years slipping under chain link fences for a variety of bad reasons, but the skill paid off now. She slid past the man, squeezing her abs tight enough to turn them to stone to make sure her tummy didn't graze *any* part of his body. She did a stiff run-walk directly to Derek.

"Give me McCabe's new address and we can be done, Mike. It's that easy." Callie barreled into Derek right as he laid into the guy bellied up to the bar. She'd meant to stop sooner, but the threat of the filthy asshole behind her overrode her brain. Derek, surprised, nevertheless turned and caught her with solid strength. He curled his fingers to cup her shoulders and held her until she steadied.

"One sec, Mike," he said, without looking back. Mike didn't move a muscle. Derek frowned, and started to open his mouth. He was pissed she hadn't stayed put, she knew, and he was about to tell her so. But then he looked over her shoulder, his eyes narrowing to slits as he noticed the man who'd accosted her. "We'll deal with him in a second." The growl in his voice was unmistakable. Mike heard it too; he twitched.

"Um, hey, gimme a pen," Mike said to the bartender. Once it was delivered, he scratched an address onto a cocktail napkin—the first Callie had seen in this place. He passed it to Derek. "We good?"

Derek held up the napkin to read it, then grunted at him. Mike must have understood its meaning because, faster than Callie thought was humanly possible, he'd slipped away from the bar and ducked out the front door.

Derek stuffed the napkin in his jacket pocket. What other secrets lined that leather? Mafia addresses? Soul IOUs? Dirty secrets about every snitch in town? In that moment, it all seemed plausible. Derek stepped around her, taking a step away, and when she didn't immediately follow, he murmured, "This will just take a sec."

He crossed the decrepit floor in four long strides. His speed startled the bearded cretin, who wagged a beer bottle in Callie's direction as she turned back to their table and caught the man's gaze. Derek didn't bother with niceties—not that Callie would have heard them over the din in the bar anyway. Derek jerked a thumb over his shoulder, presumably toward her. The biker shrugged. All's not fair in The Fall, though. Nothing is harmless or without consequence. Derek's fist shot up and out so fast, Callie wasn't completely sure she'd even seen the punch. But the biker stumbled backward to plant his ass on the table, hands cradling his nose. Derek took a half step toward him, and the biker nodded fervently.

Derek lifted his chin in response and returned to Callie's side. He took hold of her upper arm, and spoke into her ear. "Now's probably a good time to bail."

She shook her head in agreement, distracted both by the sudden violence and by how giant Derek's hand was wrapped around her upper arm. She wasn't a fragile thing, normally. But with a hand the size of Texas—one that'd just put a large, nasty man in his place—holding her steady and guiding her out of the bar, she was starting to reconsider her frailty.

CHAPTER FOUR

Callie's throat tightened, each slow-motion swallow enflaming her panic. Fiery sparks pricked her lungs. Her brain was being goddamn ridiculous, and there wasn't an easy fix. Her palms hadn't dried since leaving The Fall. Derek's presence helped at the time. Now they were alone, on his bike, and Callie was having second thoughts that she was all that much safer in his care. Was trading up to the bigger predator really an improvement? It was easy to forget that Derek worked for the Soul Charmer, and the Soul Charmer's goons couldn't be good guys. They were the kind of men who punched people in the face without fear of repercussions. They made threats and people obeyed.

Callie had just seen it up close and personal.

The shit she did for Josh. He'd dug himself in deep this time, and she was side-stepping scorpions to rescue him.

It might have been the oxygen deprivation, but she couldn't decide if she was terrified or thrilled. As scary as the whole situation was, she couldn't help admitting that being on the side that didn't cower, the side of power, provided enough of a rush to open her airways. She didn't feel safe. Not even a little. But the strength of being linked to Derek (even if technically he was linked to the Charmer) offered to galvanize her insides. If she'd let it.

The price of doing so might be more than she was willing to pay. She was already an indentured servant for two weeks. She was severely lacking in goods to trade. Now she was sitting in a stranger's apartment with a strange man she'd only met a few hours earlier, and she had no idea what they were doing here, other than waiting for the owner to return. So why was she kind of okay with it?

Derek toed at a black smudge on the floor with his boot.

"How long 'til he comes back?" she asked. *Not soon enough.*

"Tough to say." His eyes stayed glued to the floor.

"That's not very helpful."

He looked up at that. A wry smile played at the corner of his mouth. "Why should I be helpful for free?"

"Are you suggesting you'll only help the Soul Charmer then?" Irritation and humor both tugged at her.

"Not necessarily. I get paid in all sorts of ways." *What the hell does that mean?* she thought. It sounded too close to sexual.

She slapped an open palm against the top of the table between them and instantly regretted it. The Formica looked as though the last time it was clean was when it came out of the factory. In 1953. "Gross," she said to both Derek and the dirt and dust smeared on her hand.

His chuckle melted some of her ire, which was frustrating in its own way. "You're too easy, you know that?"

She'd expected to still find humor in his eyes when she met his gaze, but there was none. Instead his brows furrowed as though he was attempting to peer into her skull and see the moving cogs. Could he see the cobwebs, too? The bits of tar and dust her brain had gathered from years of taking care of her mom and her brother in the shit part of town? No. Of course not. The Soul Charmer had granted Derek the skills to reclaim untethered souls, not X-ray vision.

"How long until McCabe shows up?"

She noticed for the first time that fine stubble had grown in along his jaw since they'd first met. He rubbed his fingers across it, and Callie's fingers curled into a fist in asinine and unbidden jealousy. "Not sure when he'll get here, to be honest. If I knew, we wouldn't be sitting in his shitty apartment, would we?"

Callie shot him a dirty look.

"But I have it on good authority a girl he wants to sleep with is going to be at the bar around the corner in an hour and this jackass is going to want a shower first. I expect he'll be here in the next twenty or so."

"You're banking on a shower?"

"Even dirtbags know a lady likes it when they smell nice."

Derek smelled nice. The thought popped into Callie's head before she could stop it, and she sat up straight, clearing her thoughts. Dwelling on the clean scent of Derek's skin didn't change the fact she barely knew him. What the hell was going on with her? "Well, I could probably survive another twenty minutes. Provided I don't touch anything."

"Heaven forbid." He held his hands up in mock horror, and she let herself smile. Just once.

"That's more like it," he said, punctuating it with a grunt.

"Can I ask you a question?" They had time to kill. It wouldn't hurt to try to find out a little something about the guy she'd be spending the new two weeks working with. What's the worst he could say? No?

He smirked, and she thought he was going to ignore her. Then he said, "Fine. Ask away."

"Can you do magic, too?"

"No. That's the Charmer's deal."

"You see ads for it all the time . . . " She trailed off.

He picked up the thread. Thank God. "Most of that shit is fake. Magic is an apprentice trade."

He didn't elaborate, but Callie was good with that. It was okay with her if the details of a soul magic tutorial forever remained unknown to her. Especially if it didn't have anything to do with Derek.

"Okay, my turn." He shifted gears so smoothly. He had charisma. She'd give him that. "What's Callie short for?"

She groaned internally and looked around the apartment for a window she could jump out of. Of all the questions he could have asked . . . quickly, and as concealed by her breath as possible, she whispered, "Calliope."

"Calliope?" His belly laugh could have woken the dead. Or at least disturbed the neighbors.

"What's so goddamn funny? Maybe I should ask for your middle name and start mocking it."

"Go ahead; it's Alexander. Next?"

"No, really, why did you alert everyone in a two-mile radius to our presence over *my name*?" She'd been mocked for it since she was old enough for kids to talk. She'd grown up, embraced the nickname. She would be damned if some biker thug was going to make her feel bad about it now.

"Not laughing at you. Just too appropriate." He smiled, and even though the initial wave of defensiveness still hadn't worn off completely, she realized that there wasn't a hint of maliciousness in his tone. "It's been business as usual for six solid months. No fuck-ups. No difficult runners. The last couple weeks have been busy. You show up, and now the circus is coming to town."

"You can hardly blame me for that." Her shrug hinted at chagrin. Since he hadn't clued her in as to what they were actually doing, how was she supposed to know what was normal and what wasn't in the soul retrieval biz?

"True. And I don't. Not really." He paused, his gaze flitting to the door. After a moment he shook it off and continued. "Something's been coming. Charmer's been loaning more than usual lately."

"Really? I'd figured business would be pretty steady by now." Callie had always figured the draw of guilt-free sinning had to be irresistible to a certain percentage of the Gem City population, and the fact that there was always crime and shady shit to do meant there would be perpetual interest in his services. So why would business be any busier than usual?

"It is. It ebbs and flows like any other gig. Gets weird around full moons. You'd think the place was an emergency room the way the lobby packs up with people trying to snag a soul for the night."

"Are they good about returning the souls they rent? The full moon ones, I mean."

"Not really. It's like they're coeds on spring break, and the high they get from the freedom hooks 'em fast. They get their soul and then fully let go. I spend full-moon nights trying to keep the line of people that's gathered outside in order. Then a few days later I'm seeing them again when I'm retrieving." He said "retrieving" like it was a noble profession. Callie didn't know anyone who would think that kind of work would be honorable, but she wondered if they were in the dark about the truth. Was *she* in the dark?

"You like your job?"

He nodded. "People don't realize what housing someone else's soul inside you does. There are consequences. It's fighting with your own soul the whole time. It's wicked and leaves the host scarred, you know, in here." He tapped two fingers against his breastbone. "Do it too long and you'll go crazy."

"I didn't know that." But Callie thought it made sense. Gem City had more sanitariums than hospitals. The officials said they were the seat of the state, but maybe it had more to do with the side effects of having a local Soul Charmer.

"You're probably not supposed to." He laughed again, this time maudlin. "Never had a partner before."

"Maybe you needed one." What made her say that? Callie didn't want to be here. Derek obviously liked working alone. She was only here to help her brother and get out. Why then did she have to fight the urge to reach across the table to take his hand? Clearly it'd been too long since she'd had an honest conversation with anyone.

Derek snapped out of whatever deep thoughts had turned his blue eyes to a cold grey. "Charmer doesn't work in fate, and if he did you'd be getting the raw end of the deal. You're a time-saver, though. Usually I drag their asses back to him for extraction."

Her reply was cut off by the sound a key sliding home in the front door's lock. Derek quickly shot her a "More, later" look and moved toward the door.

It was time to retrieve a soul. Her first one. Callie crossed her fingers that McCabe would be reasonable, that everything would go smoothly, that no one would get hurt. Deep down, though, she knew the odds weren't in her favor.

Callie had already watched Derek flaunt his size and power once earlier. When he'd come to her aid at The Fall, it was the kind of thing you'd want your boyfriend to do for you, but would never admit aloud. Not that she found him lover material.

As McCabe's key clicked in the lock, Derek pressed himself against the wall next to the door. Derek hadn't suggested she move, so Callie remained seated at the kitchen table. She burrowed her hands into the pocket of her hoodie, finding the flask and pressing a clammy palm against the cool stone exterior.

McCabe leaned into his apartment. His head crossed the threshold before his feet. The smack of Derek's hand connecting with the nape of McCabe's neck made Callie flinch. Derek had ditched his jacket earlier, allowing him to move more freely. Not that it mattered much. While muscles popped and cut along his stretched arm as he guided McCabe forward, the rest of his body remained at ease. He swept a foot to the right and ghosted the man to the ground, pinning him there with only his hand and a knee.

Their target sputtered profanities and professed innocence in equal measure. Derek spoke over him, to Callie, as though the man pinned to the floor didn't exist. "You waiting for a formal invitation?"

Her head spun. He'd been way too casual about throwing a man to the ground. She took a steadying breath. "Aren't you going to give him a chance to return it?"

"He's had plenty of chances to do that already. We don't sell souls. Just rent them." That callous tone, the same one he'd leveraged back at the bar, was in his voice again.

"Who's she?" McCabe spat the question. Derek pressed the writhing man further into the floor.

Callie gritted her teeth. It was true; she didn't know the history here. McCabe's frame was lean—completely dwarfed by Derek, but then so was she—and track marks pocked his skinny arms. Junkies weren't the most reliable. Josh taught her that.

It didn't matter. Harvesting souls from meth heads while her terrifying biker acquaintance brought the muscle was now her night gig. And to think her mother worried she'd become a stripper.

Callie slid her hands out of her hoodie. She gripped the flask in her right hand. Her thumb skimmed up and down on the onyx inlay. She was ninety-eight percent sure her hand was tingling, but it could have been the lingering effects of mental whiplash from seeing Derek go from laidback to Rambo in the blink of an eye. He held McCabe so effortlessly. As if he did this kind of thing every day. Fuck. He probably *did* do this kind of thing every day.

She stood and stepped closer. "So I just touch this to the front of him, right?" She didn't recognize her reedy voice. She'd been through so much and this was what tripped her up? She ordered herself to get a grip.

"Yeah. Get over here, and I'll flip him." Derek's arm was flexed, but she didn't see strain in the rest of his body. The edge in his voice steeled her stomach. If he could fake it, she could harden up, too—at least on the outside.

Callie was still standing two feet away from McCabe. She shuffled forward until the rubber tips of her shoes almost touched his elbow. The man's skin was ashen. Derek grimaced.

"McCabe, no chance you want to make this a little easier for us?" Derek asked the prostrate man.

"Fuck, man! That's what I've been saying. Just let me explain—"

"No," Derek cut him off. "We aren't here for stories and excuses. You're going to keep your goddamn hands to yourself when I roll you."

McCabe stopped thrashing and the muscles in Derek's forearm visibly relaxed. Callie had no doubt he was still in control. "Right. Yeah. Whatever you say, man."

Derek continued as though McCabe hadn't spoken. "And if you so much as graze her, I'm breaking something of yours. We clear?"

"Y-y-yes."

"What was that?"

"Yes." His answer was firmer this time.

Derek inclined his head toward Callie. "Ready? One, two, three." On the third count, Derek moved to McCabe's side while wrenching the man's shoulder to flip him onto his back. Once McCabe's shoulder blades knocked against the worn floor, Derek snapped forward to press his forearm across McCabe's cheek and neck. It forced the man to look away from her, but she still caught a glimpse of the dark halos framing his sunken eyes. There were decent odds Callie would be heaving shortly, as soon as feeling returned to her body, that is. At least McCabe wouldn't see her. She let out a little sigh of relief. This ghastly man probably wouldn't remember her after they left. He'd remember Derek though. There was security in pretending she wasn't really a part of this moment.

Callie's fingers turned ghastly against the black flask. She swallowed her nerves and it felt like the sound of it filled the apartment. *This is crazy*, she thought.

"Hey." Derek's voice had lost its earlier nastiness. "Just press the opening to his sternum, and we're done."

Uncertainty tainted his words. Or maybe she was projecting.

She nodded twice, and then flipped open the lid on the flask. Her breath hitched when the small metal cap clinked against the side. Callie pressed the opening against McCabe's chest as lightly as she could—the metal grazing his black tee shirt.

Nothing happened, as far as she could tell. Wasn't something supposed to? The Soul Charmer had acted like any idiot could do this, but how was she supposed to know when it worked? Perhaps she was a special kind of idiot. God. She should have asked more questions.

She pressed the flask a little firmer. If she could get this done without knocking the wind out of McCabe, it would be a win.

Still nothing.

"Derek?" She whispered his name, unconcerned she was practically pleading. She just wanted it to be over as soon as possible. The whole situation was giving her the creeps.

"It should be warm." His hushed tone matched hers.

Callie's hands tightened on the flask. "It's not."

"Fuck." And with one simple word, Derek shattered her hopes of a quick, simple first night on the job.

He nudged Callie with an elbow. She rocked back onto her haunches, putting the flask in her lap. She eased her grip, and warmth spread into her hands, fingertips first.

Derek eased his forearm from the other man's face. The junkie's smushed cheek righted itself with the elasticity of pudding. A violent storm roiled in Callie's stomach. She might not wait until they left the apartment to puke.

"What did you do?" Derek's metered words were for McCabe.

"I told you that I needed to explain." Rubbing it in wasn't going to do any good, Callie thought as she watched.

Derek didn't bother repeating his question. Instead he took McCabe's hand and twisted. The man yelped in obvious pain.

"She took it," McCabe yelled. "I wanted to keep it. The fucking feeling, man, but she took it."

Derek arched an eyebrow, but didn't push further on the hand he held.

"She's the one on those flyers down in Forrest. She wears those scarves. She came yesterday," McCabe said, the words tumbling from his lips.

Callie couldn't keep up. She'd seen the flyers, though. "The chakra massage lady?"

"Yeah." McCabe's deadened eyes darted in Callie's direction. Damn it.

Derek finally released McCabe's hand. "The soul didn't belong to you. Why did you give it to her?"

McCabe scrambled backward a few feet, to a seated position on the floor. "Have you seen her? She's, you know, distracting."

"A woman gives you a hard-on, and you give over a soul that doesn't belong to you?"

"She's going to save the world, man." McCabe believed everything he read, apparently.

Derek rolled his eyes as he lifted himself up from the floor. "She's out for herself, McCabe. Like everyone else."

Then he turned and held out a hand to Callie. "Ready to leave, doll?"

Confusion clouded her mind and it was as though stomach acid had torn through most of her stomach lining.

McCabe sputtered, "We good?" but Derek ignored him. Callie did, too.

She'd hit her emotional stress limit for the day, and answered Derek definitively: "Hell yes."

—— CHAPTER FIVE ——

Callie's brain buzzed with the burgeoning pain of a low-level headache. The rumbling of the motorcycle didn't help. Questions that had been shell-shocked into submission at McCabe's house finally flitted to the front of her mind.

This was only her first day working for the Soul Charmer, and it was darker than she imagined. Would the next thirteen days bring the same darkness, the same violence? Would she sink deeper and deeper into the dives she'd told herself she'd never stoop to? Were fourteen days enough to desensitize her to crime? Her throat tightened. She'd seen her share of street fights and back-alley brawls. This was different. Being a part of this was going to change her.

Her arms tightened around Derek. He grunted in response, but remained focused on the road. She clasped her hands together, nestling them next to his stomach. It was nice to hug someone without a cost. He wasn't seeking money from her. He didn't know her well enough to manipulate her like her mom did. He just let her press her face against his back and siphon his strength.

The hug couldn't last, though. Fifteen minutes later, he eased the motorcycle into a parking space behind her car. It wasn't a full day's work. Could they already be done? She held her tongue as she climbed off the bike, hoping he would speak first, not wanting it to come off the wrong way.

But he stowed their helmets without a word. Was he angry with her for how things had gone down with McCabe? Maybe she'd imagined the rapport back at the apartment.

"Half day on day one? I like it." She exhaled the light words on shaky breaths.

The corner of his mouth began to pull up. He shuttered the smile before it fully formed, though. "I wish. We need to talk to the boss."

She couldn't give the Soul Charmer the chance to renege on their deal. "Why would he want to talk to me?"

"He will."

She glared at him. Ignoring her question stoked her anger, but at least anger was better than fear. "I don't know what happened back there. I'm along for the ride, remember?"

"You're along to retrieve souls."

"I hold a flask, Derek. That's what I do." Or what she was *supposed* to do. They hadn't explained her role too clearly, but she had to grip on to anything she could if it meant staying out of the Charmer's shop.

"That's a big part."

She choked on her instinctive laugh when she realized he was serious. "Did I screw up?" she asked, her voice barely audible.

"Tonight's screwed, but no, it isn't on you." He rasped a hand down his stubbled cheek. Then, with a painful scowl, he continued, "The boss just likes his information direct. It won't be bad."

Easy for him to say. While Derek had had her back tonight, that same protectiveness might not carry over inside that dank, mystical store. As he edged toward her with a hand out, she knew he wasn't going to let her run. She couldn't have anyway. No matter how much she was squicked by all of this, no matter how much she wanted to just get away as quickly as possible, she still needed a soul to rescue Josh. Meeting with the Soul Charmer was required.

She was going to kick her brother's ass so hard after this was all over.

They bypassed the shop's front door, and walked around to the far side of the building. Derek slid a key into a pale grey door marked with generic black vinyl numbers—731. The simplistic look couldn't hide the sinister sensation that coated the entrance, though. Callie's skin was crawling before she'd stepped past the threshold.

Things didn't improve from there.

The hallway they entered was a narrower version of the one she'd passed through the day before. Murky pictures of dead-eyed portraits hung in neat rows that covered the burgundy walls. Callie quickened her pace, unsettled, and caught Derek's heel with the toe of her shoe.

"Sorry," she muttered.

His bulky shoulders shrugged, but he didn't further acknowledge her fumbling.

He opened the next door to reveal the Soul Charmer's pristine workshop. She stepped into the doorway of the room, and every muscle in Callie's lean body suddenly yanked tight. The heaviness of the magic inside choked her. Derek saw her stop short and wrapped a massive hand around her wrist, pulling her the rest of the way in.

"It gets better," he whispered in her ear, and then strode across the room to knock on a heavy wooden door. Based on the room's orientation, it had to be the one that led to the main shop.

The weight pressing on her body eased a little, but she couldn't completely calm herself in this room. Four walls and a ceiling shouldn't have shaken her like this, but the pressure of being watched dug into the back of her neck. The coat of ick slopped on her when she entered felt like she imagined the Charmer's magic would. Heavy, thick, crude. She tried to focus on reading the labels on the dark black jars lining the Soul Charmer's shelves. They didn't tell her much. Each mentioned a gender, and presumably an age, but there was another number on each. The fraction at the bottom of the label was always out of 2000, and that meant nothing to her. She doubted the Soul Charmer cared about the average daily caloric intake of those providing his wares. Imagine if you could opt out of the soul rental business by downing a double cheeseburger. Gluttony was a sin, after all. Her lips curled up into a hint of a smile at the thought. It almost made her hungry.

"What do the numbers mean?" she asked. The hard surfaces throughout the room amplified her quiet question.

"Purity." A single word rumbled past a mouth full of marbles. Perhaps now was not the time for questions.

The Soul Charmer entered the room, and her stomach tried to cave in on itself. So much for snacks. The elderly man with the gnarled fingers moved more quickly this time. He still wore pajamas, but this time she was doubly wary of him. Even dictators could look like genial grandpas in the right wardrobe.

His bare feet squeaked against the tile floor as he scuttled to the second bookcase filled with jars. A middle-aged woman in a beige pantsuit followed behind him. Her heels tapped out an uneasy *click, clack-clack*. She and Callie avoided meeting each other's gaze.

The Charmer selected one of the jars. Its label read F37 780/2000. "This one is sure to be the right fit for you, Ms.—"

"No names," the woman snapped nervously, risking a quick glimpse at Derek and Callie. The Charmer curled his wrist toward his chest and turned back toward the customer, pressing the prized jar against his robe.

Two seconds under his cutting glare broke the woman. Callie didn't blame her. "Sorry. I just—" she cut a glance to Derek before turning her gaze to the container the Charmer held "—don't want to wait any longer. I'm ready to do this."

"I hold no ill will. You'll be eased by this." He held out his empty left hand. "Payment?"

She reached anxiously to tuck her hair behind her ear, but it was already coiled neatly in a bun. Her hand fluttered as she reached into her pocket and passed the Soul Charmer two folded hundred dollar bills. Callie glared at the paper money. Was that all it took to rent a soul? She'd offered that much. Was the Soul Charmer screwing with her?

He caught her look and flashed his gold teeth. "Sliding scale for frequent customers."

The Soul Charmer was every bit as bad as a corner dealer. A fact worth remembering.

He stashed the cash in a pocket and beckoned the woman closer. "Deep breath. You'll be able to relax in a moment."

The Charmer rubbed his gnarled fingers across the jar's lid four times before opening it. He cupped his palm over the opening and stretched forward. "Deep breath, and hold it," he instructed.

He jabbed the container squarely between her breasts. Her shoulders shook, but instead of revulsion at the cretin grazing her chest, the woman's jaw went slack. A soft light began to emanate from inside the jar, and within seconds the glow had lit the skin of her arms, neck, and, finally, her face, as well. Soul magic had given the woman the kind of healthy glow earned from all-night sex. Her posture was relaxed, a peaceful countenance had replaced her earlier scowl, and her skin was now positively radiant. It wouldn't last—no high ever did—but at this rate Charmer's store could be reclassified a spa.

The Charmer set the presumably now-empty jar on his table, and pressed his thumb against the woman's forehead. "Breath out."

As she did, he blessed her with the Holy Trinity. Callie's stomach flipped. A wink and a nudge from the church was one thing, but did they know he was acting as clergy? One more reason to limit her involvement.

If only it were so simple.

"Euphoria," the woman muttered, before catching herself and following with a more standard, "Blessed be." The Charmer sure was selling elation . . . that much was clear.

The second the woman was out the door, the Soul Charmer squeaked his way across the room to Callie. He held a hand out, palm up. He better not expect her to hold his hand. He had not even earned a handshake, and even if he'd successfully tricked people into thinking that soul-renting was the same as a spa retreat, she would much rather use a mud mask than get a facial via Charmer. He stopped in front of her, arm stretched outward, his knuckles almost grazing her navel. She stared at his hand. Studying the patchwork of lines and fading scars was preferable to meeting his gaze. Callie had just watched him perform magic. Real. Legit. Magic. And it was goddamn unnerving. He opened and closed his hand a couple times, like a small child begging for a treat on the countertop just out of his reach.

"The flask," he spat. What was she, his secretary? His irritation did nothing but stoke her own frustration.

She thrust a hand into her pocket and yanked the metal and stone container out, slowly placing it in his palm. There was no reason for her to be afraid of touching his skin, but the same part of her that locked her car doors as soon as she got in her vehicle told Callie that flesh-on-flesh with the Soul Charmer was not in her best interest.

Once he had the flask, she buried her hands back in her pockets, grabbing at the cotton fabric as though it could cleanse her skin. The flask didn't taint her—as far as she knew—but being in the shop, so close to an angry mystical man, made her skin pinch and writhe. She was going to exhaust the water heater's stores when she got home. The longest, hottest shower would purify her. It had to.

"It's empty." The accusatory tone of the Soul Charmer's statement punched her in the chest. Forget showers. She needed an ice pack and a bottle of whiskey.

Callie steeled her nerves, and lifted her gaze, expecting those beady eyes to bore into her. They didn't, because all of the Charmer's ire was directed at Derek. Callie's quasi-partner towered over the geriatric man. If he fell atop the Soul Charmer, the man's brittle bones would probably turn to dust before he suffocated him with the mass of his torso. Their size disparity didn't matter; the Soul Charmer was more than human. Father Gonzales suggested magic workers were prophets. The details were a mystery, but in this room where magic had been performed, the air vibrated with supernatural menace. The Charmer was no man of God, that much Callie knew instinctually. Her insides squeezed in discomfort. Derek had to have been in pain as well, but if he was he didn't show it; he simply locked his jaw and returned the old man's stare.

"There were complications."

"Her, you mean?" The Soul Charmer sneered in Callie's direction. He really might be part reptile, she thought.

"No," Derek answered quickly. "She did fine. I mean, the soul wasn't there for us to retrieve."

The Soul Charmer hissed.

"The POS said—" he added, and glanced at Callie, though she had no idea why he thought she might be able to help him. "He said the 'chakra massage' lady took it."

"Unacceptable." The Soul Charmer suddenly huffed, and shuffled away toward his worktable, the air in the room immediately losing its malicious edge.

Callie sucked in a deep breath, surprised to find herself a touch lightheaded. Derek gave her a slight, quick bob of the head. Nods must be like grunts to him. Eventually she might be able to decipher their meanings. For now, she simply nodded back and hoped it was the right answer.

"Well, this worked out well for you, didn't it?" It took Callie a moment to register the Soul Charmer was talking to her. His hands were busy beneath the table, doing God knew what.

"Not exactly." She glanced to Derek, but he didn't offer anything but a chiseled jawline.

"You didn't have to capture a soul yet."

"True," she said slowly, unsure of his angle.

"Have you ever seen a soul?"

Why was Derek backing away from the table? Her mind was racing. The Charmer turned his harsh gaze on her when she didn't answer quickly. "Well?"

"No." Funny how under the right circumstances, a simple question could take her rightfully earned anger and beat it down until it was obsequious fear. It made her sick the way her emotions wanted her to placate him. "I mean, I watched you with that woman a few minutes ago, but I didn't see the soul."

"Hmph. You aren't lying. That's something." He sat one of those black canisters on the table. "Come over here, please."

It wasn't a request, despite the pleasantry tacked on the end. She strode to the table with all the confidence she could fake. Up close, she could tell the jar was actually made of a smooth black glass. It was a modicum less opaque than the inlay on her flask. Scratch that. *His* flask. She wasn't about to start laying claim to the thing. She was working here for two weeks. Thirteen more days of terrifying shit, and then she'd rescue Josh and forget any of this ever happened.

"Where did those souls come from?" The eddying fear and anxiety in Callie's sternum couldn't prevent her many questions from bubbling to the surface.

"You haven't earned that knowledge. Now come here."

A jar couldn't stare at you, and yet Callie was acutely aware of the container's presence. Knowing soul magic existed, and being shoehorned into seeing it, were oceans apart. She'd already surmised the walls of the Charmer's spotless back office were lined with souls, but now it was out in the open. Her insides squeezed as though her organs were making a mad dash away from her flesh. Like they could hide from this dirty magic business if they managed to squish themselves against her vertebrae. She inhaled a shaky breath, and ignored the warm essence on the oak table. Derek was far away, across the room. She was alone now. She might be in this room for her brother, but even that allegiance faded as the Soul Charmer speared her with his dark, cutting gaze.

"Do you feel it?" There was far too much pleasure in the Charmer's voice.

"What am I supposed to be feeling?" Encasing herself in a wall of sass worked last time.

He grabbed her wrist with a deceptively quick motion, and pulled her palm close to the jar. When it was just a scant inch away, an orange flame surrounding the container flared, fire touching her fingers. Callie gasped, trying to pull away, but the old man's grip was unnervingly strong. She panicked. The smell of burning flesh should have been tingeing the air, but her tight breaths only caught clove and the muted Nag Champa from the front room. Her fingers began to tingle. The tips turned a bright white, glowing. The sensation of her hands being on fire burrowed in her gut, but no matter how warm it was, the flame didn't *actually* hurt and her skin didn't react. She couldn't tell which was more of a mindfuck: her fingers going bonfire bright or the fact that it didn't make her scream in agony when it absolutely should have.

"What the ever-loving fuck?" That wasn't her front of false confidence coming through. She hadn't even realized she'd spoken. Her jaw locked and her eyes widened.

His lips pulled tight before curling into a delighted smile. That didn't ease any of the tension in Callie's body. She didn't want the old man mad at her, but she also didn't need him excited or making her damn hands glow like a raver's party favor.

"Splendid things," he said. The brightness of her incendiary fingertips reflected and shimmered in the Charmer's eyes. He was a magpie spotting diamonds for the first time.

Like she could let him leave it at that. She pulled hard against his grip again. This time he released her. She stumbled backward, cradling her hand to her chest like it was now a mutilated appendage. Maybe it was. Her fingers continued to emit a soft light, which gave her charcoal sweater a heather tone. One. Two. Three. Four. Callie counted the seconds as the light faded. Sixteen seconds. Her hand had been lit up for sixteen seconds. "Didn't feel splendid," she snarled even though her hand didn't hurt and her skin wasn't mangled in the least.

The motherfucker just rolled his eyes. "I have no patience for dramatics. My magic protected you from pain. You aren't injured. Quite the opposite."

"What did you do to me?"

"Seeing as how you weren't able to retrieve the soul today, I wanted to ensure you'd be able to detect them from now on."

"Everyone's got a soul. It shouldn't be rocket science. Ever think that it might not be my fault?" Her bravado was returning in waves, obscuring the panic making her lungs and heart quiver.

"Oh, if only it were so simple. Most people have souls, yes." The way he emphasized *most* made Callie shudder. "Don't forget I can take the soul out of anyone, and one can live with a scrap of soul for years."

She couldn't keep up the front. The pressure of his gaze, the nonchalance of using magic on her without her consent, it was all too much. "Did you do something to my soul, just now?" she blurted out.

A moment later the scent of leather and aftershave hit her. Derek. She'd forgotten he was still in the room, perhaps thought he'd scurried away to let his boss do whatever to her. The anger wouldn't come, though. She'd stoke that fire later. For now, she would be happy she wasn't entirely alone.

"You're still untainted," the Soul Charmer said. "Only you can mark your soul. I simply made it easier for you to detect other souls."

"Why?" She kept the pleading tone out of her voice, but she couldn't completely mask the aching need to know. Just how deep had she gotten herself?

"Someone is stealing my souls. If you can detect those in possession of too many or too few, you will be quite useful in helping me recover my products much more quickly."

"Wait a second. I thought I was just the one with the flask. That was the deal."

"The deal was you'd assist Derek in retrieving souls. You will continue to do so. If that means also finding the person who thinks they can take what is mine, so be it."

Her body went rigid as she began to understand what he was getting at. "You can't force magic into people."

The Charmer glared at her, and the muscles in her neck snapped sharp like tension wire. If she turned her head, the squeal would echo for hours.

"Why don't you use your fucking skills to make everyone able to find these souls?" Hysterics were a new one for Callie, but light-up fingers could do that to a person.

"Oh, child, you've primed yourself to take magic for years. You just never realized it."

What the hell did *that* mean? The staccato beat of her heart tapped against her temples. Callie opened her mouth to reply, but Derek spoke instead. Finally. "I can handle hunting down the chakra therapist on my own."

Callie held her breath, but the Charmer's reply didn't change anything. "Of course you can. Now you have a better tool to do so."

How had her day gone from helping an underworld soul rental service to being a magical tool in a matter of minutes? The room rocked beneath her feet. Why had she thought she'd ever be able to get out of this unscathed?

Derek spoke over her shoulder, closer, as if he was trying to distract her from the fact the Charmer had just called her a tool. "We'll start tomorrow."

She wanted to argue. To fight. To be the badass everyone wanted her to be. She was Josh's savior. Couldn't she be her own, too? Derek's gigantic hands emerged from behind and cupped her upper arms in a tight grip, steering her toward the door they'd entered through. When her legs didn't immediately follow along, he whispered in her ear, "It can only get worse if we stay in here. Please."

It was the please that got her feet shuffling across the floor and through that nasty hallway, even if she still hadn't ruled out slugging him when they made it outside. The Charmer didn't say a word as they left. Whatever he'd wanted with her, he'd already gotten it.

In the safety of the alley—she'd already adjusted her definition of *safe*—Derek edged to her side. "We should talk."

Oh, so he *could* speak. With every step away from the Soul Charmer's shop, the numbness Callie had endured from the oppressive magic inside dissipated a little bit more. A fiery anger quickly moved in to replace it. "You knew what he was going to do to me in there, didn't you?"

"I've worked for him since I was twenty-two, and he still keeps secrets from me. You deserve more answers." His guilt was painted in plain stripes over his face.

Derek could stew in his shame, though. He chose to hold all his words until they didn't matter. Callie was too familiar with being tossed to the wolves and getting a sloppy apology when it was too late. She needed to quit being surprised when it happened.

"Yep. I do, but I'm done for tonight." Her car was only ten feet away. A teensy drop of relief slid down her neck as she looked at her escape, haloed in the light of the streetlamp.

Derek stepped in front of her, blocking both her progress and her view of her beat-to-shit magic pumpkin. "That stuff in there, though—"

"Am I going to die?" she cut him off.

"What? No." She'd thrown him off balance with that question. At least she could make him uneasy, too.

"Then I'm going home." She stepped around him, and he didn't move to stop her. "You have my number?"

His grunt was close to a "yeah." She hadn't given it to him, but then again, she wasn't surprised he had it either.

She didn't bother making plans with him. Derek wasn't done with her any more than the Soul Charmer was.

CHAPTER SIX

allie's fingers were no longer glowing. She'd stared at them for the last hour and a half, and zero light had shot out. If she watched them all night, she swore she could convince herself the magic-fingers shtick hadn't happened.

It might have been easier if her hoodie hadn't held on to a mix of Derek's clean masculine scent and the musky spice of the Soul Charmer's shop. She'd taken the sweatshirt off and shoved it deep in the hamper an hour ago, but the aromas still filled her nose.

She needed to get a grip. Her fingers weren't going to glow again. It was like a watched pot; it would never boil. She scrubbed her normal hands across her face, but the slight roughness of her palms against her cheeks wasn't enough to remove the grime of what she'd gotten into that day.

Callie moved into the kitchenette. She scooped some Folgers and put it in the coffee maker. Caffeine could fix anything, right? As the machine did its thing, she gathered a mug from the cabinet. The flock of little chinstrap penguins on the cup made her smile. Her cheeks ached. Letting go of her locked jaw probably had something to do with that.

The aging mug with its chipped handle was a relic of better times with Josh, a souvenir from the Gem City Zoo, and one of the best days of her life. She'd been eleven, and any school field trip should have filled her with excitement, except she'd spent much of the fifth grade hiding the fact that she didn't have much of an "immediate family." The other kids' moms dropped them off at school with kisses on the cheek and lunchboxes filled with snack packs. Her mom had missed every parent-teacher conference for the prior three years.

At the time, Zara, Callie's mother, had been working three jobs. Later, as an adult, Callie understood. Mostly. Her mom hadn't been around because she needed to wait tables or stock shelves to make sure there was enough money to cover her bills. It was normal for Callie to go days without seeing her, and the lead-up to that field trip was no different. She'd left the permission form on the kitchen table one night and it was signed the next morning when she got up. Per usual the box regarding volunteers was unchecked.

The other kids' parents had been nice enough to her. She'd grown accustomed to latching on to a chaperone and pretending no one noticed she didn't have her own. Only the trip to Gem City Zoo was different. That glorious sunny day, Josh had come through. As they stood in line to board the bus, her sixteen-year-old brother darted up beside her.

"Sorry I'm late, kiddo." Back then he'd been like a god to her. Their five-year age gap meant so much more when they were little.

"You're coming with us?" She remembered staring up at him. He'd had a growth spurt the previous month, and was already edging toward six feet tall.

He'd scuffed his knuckles in her hair. "Like I'd miss the chance to go to the zoo with you."

"Mom know?" she'd asked, scared about the answer.

"Don't start worrying on me. Your teacher's cool with it, so we're good." Even then, she'd fretted over consequences. Josh hadn't, but at sixteen he was better about coming through for her.

He had, too. She had the cool older brother who wanted to spend time with her. He'd stayed at her side, and explained how the chimpanzees' shoulders worked to let them swing. He'd then demonstrated on a lamppost to the delight of her friends, too. For once, she had family others envied. Her chances to relish in the sin of pride had been scarce at that age, and she'd reveled it. Probably best she wasn't rich. That shit could get out of control.

Josh had bought her the mug, and wouldn't let her worry about where the money came from. The penguins had been her favorite, and for the last nine years she'd used the penguin mug whenever she was sick. It was the feel-better mug.

It might not have the power to pull her out of the hole she'd dug herself into with the Soul Charmer, though. Josh was worth it, even if he'd hurt her as they'd both gotten older. His mistakes didn't negate the fact he was the one who looked after her until she was in high school, when their roles began to reverse. Committing a crime on her big brother's behalf was a new low for her. She'd said it was the farthest she'd ever go, but when she'd made those promises to Josh (and to Ford) she hadn't realized just how much this would taint her.

She poured the fresh coffee into her cup. The Soul Charmer had a reputation, but magic was still the unspoken new evil in her world. Its prevalence during the last ten years didn't make it less mysterious. She'd only spent one day as part of the Soul Charmer's team, but already felt like he had changed her. True, her fingers were no longer glowing, and her skin wasn't tingling. That didn't stop her stomach from fluttering. Two weeks of souls and magic had sounded simple. Now she knew better.

She needed to fight to stay the same Callie. She might not want to know this world, but she was a part of it now. She wrapped her hands around the hot mug, appreciating its warmth. She needed to put Derek in his place tomorrow. An ally would sure as shit help her get through the job, but he'd failed pretty miserably there at the shop, and he needed to know that. She sipped the coffee. She'd find strength to do it all, for Josh. Stubbornness had gotten her this far in life. If she could keep the steel in her spine from melting every time she was near soul magic, she might have a chance.

Callie muddled through the breakfast shift at the retirement home the next morning, dishing up the eggs, toast, and occasional slice of bacon at a pace more akin to the home's residents than her usual speed. If any of the clients complained, it didn't make it to her ears, though she wasn't exactly giving them much attention. A collective two and a half hours sleep the previous night wasn't enough, especially when it came in twenty-minute intervals.

She grabbed the list for the special diets and began filling the trays accordingly.

"You're slamming those things in the rack with some force," Louisa said, not missing a beat as she diced a handful of green onions.

Callie glanced at the rolling metal rack. It had scooted back a couple inches from when she'd started loading it, but all the food was still secured under the lids. "Sorry for my bad mood." She meant it to be a genuine apology.

"Do I need to slip a couple fingers into your coffee?" Louisa's tone was light, but Callie knew the woman was dead serious; she stashed a couple bottles—tequila and whiskey—in the drawer beneath the aluminum foil.

Callie surprised herself with a genuine laugh. At least someone was looking out for her. "Nah, Lou, I got more problems than a shot of your shitty tequila can fix."

"You underestimate just how much tequila can fix."

"It's been a rough one." Callie bit back the details. As soon as Josh had been taken, she'd needed to pluck her heart from her sleeve and stash it deep. Bottling her feelings was second nature to her. "Too bad they don't make something strong enough to make you forget how sucky your life's gotten."

Louisa put down the knife, clearly not kidding around anymore. "They do. It's called meth, and you and I both know it ain't worth it."

"Yeah," Callie whispered. Lou's son was addicted to the bathtub drug. He'd stolen from her, but hadn't liquidated her savings. Callie hoped her experiences with Josh could keep Louisa from making those same mistakes, but deep down, she knew they wouldn't. She and Lou were the same. Family came first, even if that family abused your love.

Lou grabbed a fresh batch of green onions. "You want to talk about it?"

Yes. "Not now, but thanks."

Lou's voice lowered when she spoke again. "Some of the ladies from my church have tried that soul borrowing thing. Bette said it eased her guilt. Father Domingo told me the church wouldn't look down on anyone who used it to ease past transgressions. I know you wouldn't be using it to cheat on anyone, so it's safe to try it, I suppose. Don't know what you're caught up in, but maybe it could help."

Callie stiffened. She couldn't escape her thoughts of the Soul Charmer. Last week the comment would barely have scratched the surface. Now it dug under her skin. Seven days ago, soul magic was merely an easy escape whispered among sinners or advertised next to strip joints in the final pages of *Gem City Weekly*. How quickly perceptions could shift. "Nah," she eked out, for Louisa's benefit.

Her boss nodded, and turned back to her vegetable prep. They worked quietly for several minutes. Callie prepared meal trays and Louisa chopped everything she needed for her chicken tortilla soup. It was nice to focus on the mundane. Food was security, and today, more than usual, Callie clung to it like her favorite blankie.

It couldn't last; it never did. "Trays are done," Callie eventually called over her shoulder as she wheeled the cart near the kitchen's side door and locked it in place.

"Thanks, but can you go ahead and take them on down to the ward?" Louisa was asking a big favor, and yet she couldn't have been more casual about it. Either that, or she was full of bullshit. "Jo's out sick today," she tacked on after seeing Callie's death glare.

"Fine," she muttered, as she unlocked the wheels and started rolling the metal cart out of the kitchen.

The unyielding astringent scent of the Home grew stronger with every step she took toward the psych ward. Not that anyone at Cedar Retirement ever called it such. No one needed to be reminded that getting old could make you crazy. There were plenty of things out there that caused mental health issues, but the reminder that time was one of them was simply too unnerving for the staff.

Callie neared the first set of locked double doors, and fished in her pocket for her access card. Ninety percent of the residents in the ward were dementia patients. They were the reason Callie didn't want to visit. She could handle sick. She could cope with old. She could not, however, swing sweet people whom you couldn't trust. That was the ward. She wanted to be a better person, but the wing behind the locked doors gutted her. She'd been stabbed with a pen the first time she'd visited.

She'd been in the process of setting a tray out for a kind lady, commenting on the beautiful floral arrangement on a side table.

The irises at the center were Callie's favorites. The woman, Sara, said her son had brought them, and invited Callie to take a closer look. She'd obliged. The head nurse later told her the lighting change in the room had set Sara off. The woman had become convinced Callie was her long-dead husband's mistress who had arrived to steal her flowers. That kind elderly woman had then jammed a ballpoint into Callie's thigh. A couple centimeters to the right and she could have nicked the tendon.

Trusting people was a luxury. The ward illustrated that beautifully.

"Excuse me. Can you let me in there?" A woman with a thick braid draped over her shoulder and piercing blue eyes stopped Callie outside the ward's entrance.

Occasionally family members—the ones shitty about visiting—asked for directions. Callie could put on a customer service smile when required. "Who are you visiting? I can point you in the right direction."

"I'm not visiting. I'm here to treat the residents." Saccharine sincerity bubbled over the confidence in each word. The lady was laying it on thick, and Callie didn't quite buy it.

The woman might actually need to be secured in the ward herself, despite being a couple decades younger than most residents. It wasn't the weirdest thing to have ever happened at the Home, and it didn't hurt to be a little extra careful. "Oh, I see. Can I see your employee badge?"

"Oh, honey, I don't work here. Not like that, anyway." With a sweet smile plastered on her face, the woman wiggled her fingers at Callie. "Massage."

The flowing skirt and spacey countenance she wore matched the profile of those who visited for therapeutic massage. Except for one element. "Okay. Where's your table?"

"With the elderly, it's simpler to ease them in their own beds," the woman replied.

"Oh. The others always bring tables."

"I focus on energy and overall well-being more than deep kneading." Her voice had a lulling quality. It was probably helpful in her profession.

"Like chakra alignment?" Callie remembered her cousin Jackie saying that crystals had reinvigorated her. The business cards Jackie had shown her called the woman she was seeing a healing specialist, for what it was worth.

"Something along those lines." The woman paused to offer an overly sweet smile again, the kind strangers flashed before coming in for a hug. Callie resisted the urge to step backward, and the woman kept her distance. "I ease their souls so they can improve the world."

For as long as Callie could remember, a strong undercurrent of the mystical had run beneath the smothering omnipresence of the church's religious authority in Gem City. In fact, most of the state was open to both healing crystals and Cortean Catholicism. You had to travel fairly far over state lines to find skeptics. That temptation to escape to the land of non-believers had been palpable when she was a teenager who had no interest in church confessions or having her aura read. Before she knew soul magic existed.

The woman was too woo-woo for Callie. She didn't care much about energy and chakras and hunks of rock hidden under beds. One could find a massage spa or three in every Gem City neighborhood, and the therapists were good about visiting Cedar Retirement for real work. Still, Callie hadn't seen this woman before. "Right, well, I can't let you into the locked wards. Visit the front desk and someone can escort you to the patients you're cleared to help today." She pointed toward the hallway leading to the information desk.

The woman keened her head to the right and smiled. "You could use a massage." It wasn't a question.

Her fake laugh didn't fool the massage lady.

"I could balance your energy. It would only take a moment." She took a step toward Callie.

She stepped back to maintain the distance between them. "No time. Sorry. People are waiting on lunch. I'll see you around." Her stomach twisted.

"Thanks." The other woman's gentle smile didn't falter, but relief washed over Callie as she departed.

Callie buzzed herself and the large rack of meals through both sets of doors, but stopped immediately inside the ward. It wasn't the beeps of medical machines or the soft voices that made her uneasy. Those were normal. It wasn't the too-white walls, either.

Her fingers were frozen. Not. Normal.

This was no case of shitty circulation, or someone screwing with the thermostat. She tried to let go of the cart, but her fingers barely moved. Her dark blue nail polish was chipped and peeling, but the fact her skin was beginning to take on a similar hue was more concerning. She pried a hand from the cart and lifted it closer to inspect. Her skin was turning a cool grey color. Great. She was locked in a facility with the dying, while her skin took on its own ghastly shade. That had to be a bad sign. About right for this week. Brother abducted. Shanghaied into the service of the mafia, and then blackmailed into working for the goddamn Soul Charmer. And now her fingers were turning necrotic and would probably fall off any second. Could she bail on the deal with Ford if she didn't have fingers? There was a fucked-up silver lining.

"Girl!" The shout shook Callie from her spiraling stress. She looked to find one of the residents, face red as he hollered to get her attention. Maybe he'd been at it awhile. How long had he been right next to her?

"Yes?" She did her best to bite back the nasty instinct clawing at her throat.

"You gonna stand there all day?" As he finished speaking, an orderly rushed up and corralled him.

"Sorry about Mr. Beck. He's been in a mood lately," the orderly said.

As the moody Mr. Beck moved away, Callie's fingers began to regain their dexterity, and the color lost the undead sheen. What the hell had that been all about? "Sure, thanks," she muttered, trying to hold it together.

The orderly gave her a genuine smile, and went back to his duties. Callie did the same. She tried to stay focused on getting to the end of the hallway, on finishing the task she'd come here to do. The local news was playing on a television mounted in the far corner. She'd start at the end, and work her way back to the way she came in, toward the door and her escape.

She took a deep breath, and started down the corridor, barely taking more than a few steps before her hands went AWOL, turning frigidly cold again. Callie's head was spinning. She told herself to keep moving. Another few steps, and the cold almost immediately thawed, and her hands returned to a normal temperature. A few more steps and they were back to freezing again.

The sensory overload was overwhelming, almost too much to handle. She didn't know what was setting her off, but the sooner she got out of the ward, the better.

She passed the small lounge area on the right. Usually family members joined the patients to play cards here. No one was visiting now. She glanced at the TV blaring from its corner mount in the nook, and damn near skidded to a stop when she saw Ford on the screen. He was playing up his teenage looks in a blue and white button-up shirt, even though he was nearly thirty. His blue eyes glinted as camera flashes lit the scene. He was speaking with a reporter. The ticker below read MOB BOSS'S SON IMPLICATED IN NARCOTICS RING. The time stamp said the clip was from the day before, but Callie could feel Ford in the room with her. He flaunted that genial, nice-guy charm as he spoke past the reporter and directly into the camera. "My father made mistakes. No one denies that. His Alzheimer's puts him at no risk to anyone, though. I'm just trying to keep Ford Aluminum—the business he bled to build—up and running while taking care of my family."

A shiver spiked down Callie's spine. Great. Clenching the tray did little to alleviate her anxiety. She spared another look at the screen. The camera had refocused on the reporter, but in the background, fidgeting with her overly long braid, was the massage therapist Callie had met in the hallway moments ago. She was positive it was her. Did the masseuse know Ford? Did she work for him?

The blood drained from her face as realization dawned on her. Had she been sent to check up on Callie?

This world was officially too fucking small.

Mundane work would have to be her savior. She would simply have to focus on completing one task at a time instead of letting her mind wander. She brought the first tray in. Her hands didn't freeze. Normal hands. The resident was sleeping, so that probably helped. She ducked in and out of room after room, avoiding eye contact and moving as fast as possible without sending food flying to the floor. In three of the rooms, though, she had difficulty letting go of the tray. Her icicle fingers flipped on and off faster than the residents skipped through the game show channels. Was she having some kind of a weird allergic reaction to some of the patients? Delivering food had never been so difficult before.

She'd been right last night. The Soul Charmer *had* done something to her. Derek might be quiet, and bigger than a Mack truck, but she was going to make him talk tonight. Or she'd let her icy fingers break his beloved motorcycle, piece by piece, until he did.

Hard gusts of wind shoved Callie toward her apartment building. After the frigid hands issue earlier, she was kicking herself exceptionally hard for foregoing her winter coat that morning. She tugged her sweater closer and charged up the stairs, only to be blocked from entering by Derek's hulking form.

His heavy shoulder pressed against her door. No disguising he'd been waiting. *Of course he has*, her mind growled. She'd spent half her day practicing the way she'd rail on him, and how she'd storm up to him outside the Soul Charmer's store. She would have moved with lethal grace, like she knew what the hell she was doing. She would have kicked his stupid bike if he grunted at her. She had been preparing to become someone he wouldn't deny answers to.

And he'd ruined it with his impromptu visit. Heat rushed to Callie's face. She was still angry about yesterday, and Lord knew she wanted immediate answers about her fingers going into lockdown mode in the psych ward, but right now, teetering halfway up the stairs to her apartment, her ire was singular. She was livid he'd stolen her control. Now she was cold, off balance, and—with an audible gurgle from her stomach to remind her—hungry. He was probably going to want her to make him a sandwich, too. Well, she was out of turkey for jackasses.

"You're early." His low rumble was too husky for anything other than straight from bed. Lucky bastard.

"Actually, you're the one who's early." Callie resumed walking to her apartment. "We aren't supposed to meet for another couple hours."

He shrugged, but didn't call out that she specifically hadn't made plans.

Control was slipping through her fingers, and that was not acceptable. "Look. Jobs have start times and end times. And some of us have more than one job."

He didn't reply, nor did he move when she arrived at her door.

She sighed. First Ford sent someone to covertly check on her. Now Derek had demolished her chance at even a momentary respite before whatever soul magic bullshit he had on the agenda for that night. "I can't open the door with you draping yourself on it."

"You inviting me in?"

"No."

He pushed himself off the door. Callie half expected a dent to mark the center. An unsigned *Derek was Here*. "Thought you'd want to talk, that's all."

She did want to talk, but this wasn't how it was supposed to happen. "You're going to answer my questions?" Her disbelief was blatant, but what was the point of hiding it now? Kind of hard to act aloof and badass when she'd stumbled at the sight of him moments earlier.

His tone softened. "That was the idea. Yeah."

She unlocked the door.

Derek loomed behind her.

She dropped her purse between her feet. He gave it a curious gaze when the bag made a soft *thunk*. His mind probably conjured images of weaponry. Good. He didn't need to know she'd stuffed a paperback romance novel in there for her lunchtime read. She edged her apartment door open six inches, just enough to reach around the corner to the coat hook. She snatched her grey wool coat, closed the door, and then slipped her arms inside.

"We can talk. Just not here."

Derek glanced at the closed door. His jaw flexed and Callie could tell he'd hoped to poke around her pad. No such luck. He watched her as she began buttoning up. "Where should we go, then?" He threw a silky tone over the words, like he wanted her to think of hotel rooms and not flop houses. How nice. She was a master when it came to bullshit, though. She'd reclaimed control, and somebody wasn't too pleased.

"Dott's." She named her favorite greasy spoon. The food was cheap, good, and they slathered pretty much everything in butter, including the burgers.

Tension ebbed from his face. Callie's muscles ached for him, constantly clenching and releasing. She could see trust wouldn't come easily with him, but she recognized a little too much of herself when he lowered the internal weapons. He wanted to trust her. She shouldn't have liked it or cared, but she did. On both counts. "Good choice."

"Glad you think so, because you're buying." She picked her purse up from the floor, and started down the stairs. Derek's thunderous steps followed closely behind.

He insisted on taking the motorcycle to the diner. Callie didn't bother telling him it was only a five-minute walk. He probably didn't want to leave his bike unattended outside her apartment building, and admittedly, it wasn't like her complex was going to be getting any of those renters' top picks awards or a safety seal from the city.

They commandeered a large booth at the back of the restaurant, adjacent to the Dia de los Muertos altar the diner had already begun to fill with candles and ceramic butterflies. The din of the place was more than enough to conceal their conversation, but Derek wanted the extra security. Callie hadn't argued there, either. "Pick your battles" was her motto today.

Once his coffee and her Coke arrived, and they'd both placed orders for suitably unhealthy meals, it was time to talk. Derek leaned back against the cherry vinyl upholstery and rested his hands on the table. Nothing-to-hide posture didn't sell Callie these days. Her brother had once turned out his pockets to prove he wasn't carrying meth on him. Turned out he'd hidden it in his shoe. His fucking shoe. Derek wasn't her brother, but simply not being a junkie didn't mean he was Mr. Truthful.

"Where do you want to start?" he asked.

Starting at the beginning would have been smart. Dominoes falling in a line, and all would be clear if she followed that path. Being smart would have been a whole lot easier if her fingers hadn't locked up and turned straight-up Icelandic this morning. "I want to know what the fuck that asshole did to me."

Derek arched a brow. The sugar skulls in the painting above his head may have given her the side-eye, too. Perhaps she could have been a little less accusatory.

"My hands." She lifted them, palms toward him.

His grunt said he understood. Derek closed his eyes as he hauled in a deep breath. With every Zen move he made, the volcanic rage simmering inside her edged one notch closer to exploding. She was about to slam her hands against the table when he finally spoke. "He made it so you can sense when a person has too much or too little of a soul."

She was not goddamn Goldilocks. "You're going to have to do better than that."

"You're able to sense soul magic." At her exasperated look, he held up a hand and took a hearty swig from his coffee mug. "You know people rent souls, right?"

"Yes."

"Those souls have to come from somewhere. So from time to time, people barter theirs out in exchange for money or other goods."

"Sure," her tone soured. She remembered the Charmer's original offer. No clerics winked and nodded in tacit approval at that part of business, as far as she knew. "The Charmer's souls have to come from more places than just people who want to hawk them, though, right?"

Derek's nostrils flared, but he replied, "I can't tell you where he gets the other souls from, and he sure as shit ain't going to tell you."

"What *can* you tell me then?"

He ignored the acid sprinkled atop her words. "Well, now you have the ability to sense those who have been a part of soul magic. Two souls were never meant to inhabit a single body. If someone's renting a soul, the two will fight against each other. They both want a home, and they both want dominance over the other. It's why we have so many crazies here. The longer you keep the borrowed soul in you, the more damaged yours becomes. Anyway, when your hands get hot, it means you're close to someone carrying multiple souls."

"Hot?" She remembered the burning sensation back at the Charmer's shop when he'd grabbed her hand and held it to the jar of souls. So she'd been sensing those extra souls? That still didn't explain her morning in the ward. "Okay, except this morning, when I went into a few of the patients' rooms, my fingers locked and *froze* at work. I know these people couldn't be harboring bonus souls. They're in a secured facility, and no one is letting the Soul Charmer into that ward."

He winced. That couldn't be a good sign. "That's the other side of the spectrum. Remember I said too little? People who have used soul magic and have a less-than-whole soul will make your hands cold. It's the most common reaction, and the strongest, which is why you can feel it from farther away."

"Less-than-whole?"

"Shit. I don't suppose you'd forget I said that?"

His wince worked on her. Callie replied, "Explain it, and then maybe I can promise not to share."

His grunt of appeasement pleased her. "Souls like to fuse to the same spot, right?"

She nodded, despite not knowing what he meant.

"They also, kind of, fuse to each other. So when we extract a borrowed soul from someone after they're finished with it, a little bit—really, it doesn't make a difference to the person we're taking it from, they'd never know—of their own soul, the one they were trying to keep pure, comes with it."

"He takes part of people's souls? Takes souls that haven't been pawned or whatever?"

He wasn't meeting her gaze. "It's not the same. They still have a soul. It just has a little more character."

Callie's thoughts collided like synchronized swimmers with no rhythm. People were giving away slivers of themselves to the Soul Charmer and had no idea. He'd have part of her forever. Fuck if she knew what he did with these bonus bits of soul. Fear and distrust of soul magic was legit, even if people didn't understand the real reason it was sketchy. Local priests quietly embraced soul renting—for them, upping the tally of heaven-bound souls was clearly the greater priority—but they must not have known about this. Could mangled souls even rise to heaven? Callie had never wanted to have another person's soul in her body, but she'd agreed to do it for Josh. He had no idea how much saving him would cost her. It was no longer simply working for the bad guys. It wasn't only committing a crime, which, admittedly, was bad enough. She would have to let the Charmer own a tiny piece of her.

"Close your mouth, Callie. People are starting to stare."

Her teeth clacked together and she pressed her fingers against her lips. They kept her fears from bubbling out. The metallic tang of blood hit her tongue. She parted her teeth, freeing the inside of her cheek. Licking the wound wouldn't make it better.

"What happens to the souls people rent? Do they never move on to heaven, hell, wherever?" she asked, trying to focus on the souls instead of what was happening to her.

"The magic eventually destroys them. The Charmer says they don't move on to anywhere, but I don't know if that's the truth."

Callie nodded. The Charmer was certainly the secretive type. Why would anyone give up their soul then? "How can someone live without a soul?" she asked, thinking back to years and years of Cortean Catholic classes. The importance of pure souls, so one could rise to heaven was paramount. No soul, no heaven. Could renting souls keep you out of heaven? Callie didn't know how to feel about that possibility, but she already had enough worries on her plate without celestial concerns.

"They don't live well. Technically, they have a tiny piece left. Enough to spark life, but that's it."

"Why would someone do that?" She hadn't given the Charmer's proposition for hers a second's thought, but others clearly had. "How much is a soul worth, exactly?"

He scrubbed his palm against his chin before answering, "What it's worth depends on the soul, and only the Charmer can say there. It's always at least a couple grand."

Two thousand dollars would make a difference in more than her bank account, but not that big of one. "Doesn't seem worth it."

He shrugged. "I don't pretend to know their lives, but yeah, it's usually a shitty situation. People can live without them, though. Whether they sell it outright or they keep their rented souls too long and the process mangles their soul, or—" he took another big swig of coffee before finishing "—it's stolen."

She sputtered and coughed as the fact caught in her throat. "Whoa. We'll get back to my fucked up fingers in a second—so don't think I'm forgetting. People can jack another person's soul?"

"Not normal people."

"The Soul Charmer?"

"He can, but he doesn't."

She didn't believe that. Her memories from last night sparked with new meaning. She remembered the woman McCabe had mentioned. "He's not the only one who does soul magic, is he?"

"No."

"And he just turned me into his own personal soul magic detector? Are you going to take me out to the beach to hunt for treasure, too?" Caustic words weren't enough to cauterize the knowledge that she was being used.

Derek flinched, her words like a proverbial slap to the face. Too fucking bad. "He *did* make it so you could sense these things." At least he wasn't lying to her.

"He said I'd already prepared myself for this, even if I didn't know it. What did he mean?" She'd practically choked at the memory of the Charmer's delight, and leveled a glare that dared Derek to deny her an answer.

"You're not going to like it."

"It involves the Soul Charmer forcing magic into me. No, I'm not going to fucking like it, but I didn't ask you that."

He let out an exaggerated sigh. "Fine. To take in magic, you have to be morally agnostic."

"That doesn't sound offensive, so there must be more."

He glanced away. "You have a pure soul, but you don't actually have anything against sinning."

"And?" Father Gonzales would be aghast, but it wasn't news to Callie. She attended church because it was socially and culturally necessary. Shops didn't open until noon on Sundays. Prayer cards were available at every restaurant. There were more churches per capita than there were grocery stores. Gem City was Cortean Catholic through and through. Whatever was necessary to survive,

Callie did. If God had a problem with her stealing in order to keep her and her brother fed, then he'd take it up with her after she bit it.

"Most people wouldn't like others knowing sin means nothing to them." The tremble in his voice was too personal. The sooner he let go of that shame, the happier he'd be, but it wasn't Callie's place to instruct him.

Also, she had more pressing concerns. "Why didn't he do this to you?"

"He can't."

"Bullshit. He's a scary mystical whatever, and you and me have more in common than you're going to admit."

"No, honestly, Callie." He shook his head. "He's real picky about who can do what. Says he can read it on the soul. And I don't know if I'm fucked up so he can't do it to me, or if you are so he can. I just know he's never done it to me, and I'm actually sorry he did it to you, and I don't have every answer."

"That was a lot of words for you all at once." Did she say that out loud?

His deep, rumbling laugh suggested, yes, she had. "Don't get used to it."

"Maybe my skills are detecting people screwed by soul magic, *and* getting you to talk." She was rambling, but if she didn't laugh, she was going to cry.

She was saved by the arrival of their waitress with two loaded plates. Callie wasn't done questioning Derek, especially if he was willing to keep giving her honest answers. But first she was going to ignore her shitty day by sinking her teeth into the fiercest patty melt in the whole state.

CHAPTER SEVEN

The second day in the soul business had to be better than the first. Right? If Callie helped collect even a single soul, she'd be ahead of the game. Derek had spent their meal convincing her that the more they got shit done, the less they'd need to deal directly with the Soul Charmer. That's about all it took to get her to climb onto the back of his motorcycle again, and go for round two.

"I'd like to avoid bar fights tonight, too, if that's an option," she said while handing over her helmet. He'd parked the bike near a street light with a cluster of three frosted bulbs. The Eastender District's traditional adobe buildings often made tourists think they were in the Plaza, but they wouldn't find the Basilica or the Governor's mansion anywhere nearby. The wear on the buildings and the cracked cobalt tiles near storefronts should have clued them in. It wasn't as downtrodden as last night's locale, but Callie'd bet the house they weren't going to find their first collection target in the Ritz, either.

"Don't be stealing the fun from the job, doll." His wry grin bolstered her confidence a smidge.

"We'll see," she muttered.

He lifted his chin toward a bail bondsman's office. "Can't promise there won't be brawls in there, but there should be less booze."

She followed him toward the building. "This person has a bond out on them? Isn't that, like, toeing too closely to trouble?" She thought about the job Ford expected her to complete in two weeks. The flip of her stomach almost made her regret the patty melt.

"Nah, Nicole works here."

Derek switched gears, adopting a saunter a few yards from the door. He timed it perfectly, just as he and Callie walked past the first pane of glass for Gem City Bonds. The entire storefront was covered in floor-to-ceiling windows. It might have looked nice, if not for the wrought iron bars spanning each pane. Better black bars than bricks through your windows. They reached the front door, but Derek stilled Callie's hand when she reached for the handle.

She furrowed her brows, but gave him space as he rapped his knuckles against the door. A moment later, the camera mounted above the doorframe panned toward them with a dull hum. Derek smiled up at it, oozing charm. She told herself she'd never trust a grin like that, but she also doubted her knees would remain solid if he ever turned it on her.

Inside her coat pocket, Callie took hold of the flask. Soft warmth emanated from the stone inlay at her touch, but as a short, curvy blonde came to the door her fingers began to sizzle. The heavy application of kohl around the woman's eyes didn't hide the charcoal underscores or the hollowing below her cheekbones. The blonde shot Callie a curious look before stepping out to join them on the sidewalk.

She would have given her a doubly dirty one if she'd known what Callie had been thinking. Her fingers had started to tingle as soon as Nicole had opened the door, and as the heat rushed to fill her palms and her grip tightened on the flask, Callie knew Nicole had a bonus soul wedged beneath her pushup bra. She *really* was not the bail lady's biggest fan.

"Hey, Derek," Nicole cooed. They were on a first-name basis. Great.

"Time to return it." No matter how benign the phrase was, dark menace laced Derek's words.

Callie's fingers tried to burrow into the onyx of the soul canister in her hand until they burned. If only she could make herself believe it was a lava rock and not her hand heating the stone.

Nicole brushed a hand along Derek's sleeve. A bold move when you were blocking a big man from doing his job. He shot a pleading glance Callie's way. It was so quick, she was almost convinced she'd imagined it. Still, her fingers ached and she wasn't enjoying watching the soul renter in front of her get her flirt on. Callie pulled the flask from her pocket.

"I sure wouldn't mind keeping it a little longer, help take the edge of stress off another day. I could come meet you downtown after work, you know, to return it and we could grab a drink," Nicole purred.

Callie decided it would be a good time to join the conversation. "We've got shit to do."

Nicole blinked, as though she'd forgotten Callie was even there.

"And you are—" the questioning tone was cut off as Callie smacked the open flask against Nicole's sternum. The woman's face paled, but Callie's palm immediately began to cool and feeling quickly returned to her fingers. As the magic metal-and-stone container did its thing, a fluttering sensation blossomed in her sternum. It was as though feathers were grazing the insides of her rib cage. Unnerving, but also . . . reassuring? She pulled the flask back, capped it, and looked at Derek.

He was beaming. Not the smarmy Rico Suave look he'd given the camera earlier, but a "you've got to be shitting me" grin. Heat rushed to her cheeks, and that didn't have a thing to do with soul magic. Callie averted her gaze and, thankfully, the blood rush quelled.

Derek stepped backward a couple paces, ready to beat feet. "Thanks, Nicole, but I think we're all set here. See you next time."

Nicole's cheeks regained a hint of color, but she didn't say anything as he moved away. She cast a bewildered gaze in Callie's direction, but Callie was more worried about following her ride than the spurned soul renter.

They hurried toward his bike, and as Callie neared him she heard him mutter, "Can't keep her damn hands to herself."

"Not your favorite client?" Callie asked, not bothering to hide her amusement.

"None of them are *my* clients." He scrubbed his hand against his bicep, as though to remove the memory of her touch.

"That's not really an answer." One really shouldn't poke at lumbering beasts, but sometimes the temptation was too much.

He rounded on her. "No, I don't like her. Better?"

No, his answer didn't give her enough. He was the Charmer's thug. Why would he let her manhandle him if he didn't like it?

As if he could read her thoughts, he added, "Not everyone needs a rough touch to return what's ours."

Callie bet that woman wouldn't have minded a rough touch from Derek. And he sure as hell hadn't given McCabe the soft sell the night before. Goddamn it, heat was flooding her cheeks again. Luckily, they'd reached Derek's bike and he was already strapping on his helmet. Callie put hers on as well, and willed herself to stop thinking about the pleasurable ways Derek could be rough. She'd watched him flip into violent mode in a split second, and he could do the same with charm. Maybe her trust in him was less warranted. The thought slowed her thundering heart.

Callie didn't bother asking where they were going, or who the next target was. She slung her leg over the motorcycle and scooted closer to him. She tried to take his strength via hug osmosis again, but it wasn't the same. Her mind buzzed with new questions about Derek, the business, and, most of all, its clients. What was Nicole's deal? She didn't work in the noblest profession or the nicest area, but that meant exactly jack shit. Callie made food for old people and got paid fifty cents above minimum wage. Though, her pay *was* set to bump up another quarter if she made it to the end of the year. If, you know, she didn't get arrested working for the Soul Charmer, or Ford, or Lord knew whom else.

Derek drove them to the Arts District. Banners proclaiming new shows by local painters hung from lampposts, while sandwich boards atop the brick sidewalk directed tourists to the brochure-worthy galleries. Callie hadn't been in the area, other than passing through, in years. Hell, the last time she'd visited the district she wasn't old enough to drive.

He parked the motorcycle beneath an iron street lamp. Its safety was less in jeopardy here than any of the other places they'd visited thus far. She dismounted and tried to guess their next stop. The Sofia Museum was across the street. The wide windows set into whitewashed building turned grandiose under floodlights. The twenty-four-hour security was merely a shadow at the structure's corner. It displayed local art, and served wine. She'd never been there. The Gem Museum was on the next block. The name confused the hell out of tourists. It wasn't one for fans of rocks and minerals. Instead it showcased relics from the Native American tribe on the nearby pueblo.

Callie'd visited several times on field trips as a kid. Josh hadn't attended those, so few memories stuck, but she did remember asking a teacher why they didn't name the museum after the people whose work it proudly displayed. She'd been chided for her "rude question." As an adult, she'd guess the name had more to do with city officials being dicks than anything else. If one thing was consistent in Gem City, it was that the politicians weren't the most upright folk. The fact they could partake in the Soul Charmer's services now wasn't likely to help matters. If proof soul magic facilitated crime finally made it to the legislature, Gem City would go downhill fast. How quickly would the church extricate itself?

"What's next?" Callie asked, mostly to distract herself. It was that or ogle Derek, and given their current situation, that wasn't going to help anyone.

"We find Casey." He loped off to the north, away from the Gem Museum. When Callie didn't immediately follow, he reached back to grab her hand, pulling her forward. When she reached his side, he threw his arm across her shoulders. The leather of his jacket pressed against the nape of her neck, covering the gap where a scarf would have warmed her, if she'd thought to wear one. The weight pressed down on her shoulders, but somehow it made her want to stand taller. Safety wasn't so simple for her, but on this street, right now, no one would touch her.

"She an artist? Hard to picture how borrowing a soul could help anyone be creative. It's not like injecting yourself with a muse, right?" She willed her voice to stay steady.

"First, Casey is a guy. Second, he's not an artist, though I bet he'd say he were if he could get a peek at your panties in return."

Callie's pace slowed, and she started to sputter. Before she could protest her virtues or whatever she thought would save the discussion, Derek continued. "Finally, no, souls don't make you creative or a genius or whatever, but don't tell them that. Assholes try it all the time, get addicted to the freedom, and the Charmer charges 'em double."

"Oh." She liked being in on the secret. Dopes being robbed for their own greed and stupidity didn't exactly earn her pity. "What kind of freedom?"

"When the fear of eternal consequences disappears, it opens a lot of doors. We're a fucking guilty lot."

Wasn't that the truth? "But what if you don't buy into the whole heaven thing?"

He cocked a you've-got-to-be-kidding-me brow and shook his head. "Do you really think anyone in Gem City is denying the church's truth?"

"Doesn't matter what we say aloud. I'm talking true belief."

"We have souls. It's a fact. You wouldn't be here if it weren't. I don't know what happens after death, but I do know that I've never met a person who rented a soul who said they didn't like getting to be someone else."

"Does it really make you into a different person?" Renting one of these things better not change her. Callie didn't always love who she was, but she trusted herself more than anyone else. To thine own self be true and such.

"Nah. You're still you."

"So what's the point then? Placebo effect?"

"It really doesn't mark your soul. From what I've learned working for the Charmer, the shit that makes it hard to fall asleep at night, those niggling thoughts, they don't dig in the same way as they would if you were sinning on your own soul."

He didn't elaborate further, and maybe he couldn't. She wasn't about to bulldoze the foundations of friendship they'd constructed by prying.

After a moment, Callie accepted the subject was closed. "Well, where do we find Casey?"

"His girlfriend serves bar at the cafe on the corner. If Casey isn't there, Phoebe will know where he is."

"You think she'll give him up to you?"

"Phoebe is not a fan of soul magic. You have that in common with her."

Callie shrugged.

"Why are you so bent on getting a soul from the Charmer when you hate the magic so much?" His gaze burned into her. Callie studiously focused on the cracks and poor patch-jobs in the sidewalk's aging concrete.

She opened her mouth to answer, but what was she supposed to say? There was the temptation to tell him the truth, to expose the guilt laid deep inside her gut, and to explain why she owed it to her brother to do this. But while Derek was off to a start as her safety net in this world of soul rental and magic, that didn't mean she needed to fork over all her secrets after less than forty-eight hours of nonstop trust exercises. She was trust-falled out.

"Family first," was all she said.

His brows furrowed, and he offered her the disappointed grunt. He didn't push, though. Smart man.

Callie eyed the glass case filled with pie when they entered Café on the Square, but Derek offered a dude-bro two finger wave to the bartender. He received a nod in kind from the petite woman with chubby cheeks. The café balanced 1950s diner aesthetics with a gluttonous dose of jalapenos, chiles, and fried eggs. As they bellied up to the bar, the faint lines at the corners of Phoebe's eyes became more visible, but her baby face still had to make most do a double take when seeing her sling tequila. Probably also earned her hella tips. More power to the woman.

"Casey around?" Derek's tone was casual, but the tension holding his shoulders locked back still evoked a threat. Or at least the potential for one.

"He's smoking. Should be back in a minute." Phoebe removed a table tent offering last call on Hatch chile specials, wiped the counter in front of Callie with a damp rag, and then placed a small, square cocktail napkin down. This was much better than last night's bar debacle. "What can I get you?"

Callie shook her head to decline. A clean countertop was nice, but she wasn't ready to chat with these people. Phoebe looked nice enough, but the more they knew her, the more she was truly involved. Smacking a flask to people's chests and walking away was probably safest.

"Why don't you make us both the house margarita?" Derek suggested. He then looked at Callie and, mostly to himself, said, "You take salt? Nah, you don't."

"Two margaritas, no salt?" Phoebe's gaze pinged from Callie to Derek and back again like they were pillars in a pinball machine and someone was racking up points. Callie couldn't help the girl figure them out. This dynamic was too fucked.

Callie shrugged. She *didn't* like salt, but what about her screamed anti-sodium? Their bartender moved around behind the counter and flexed her drink-making skills with tidy efficiency. When Derek's lips unexpectedly grazed her ear, Callie jumped a little. The reaction was enough to elicit a little, pleased grunt from the man.

"Figured a stiff drink would help calm some of the nerves," he whispered.

"Do I look nervous?"

He must have mulled the question for thirty seconds, but he kept his mouth next to her ear the entire time. "Not nervous. Uncomfortable."

"And you want to comfort me."

His grunt said yes, but the words that followed were more complicated. "Adjusting to the magic, this lifestyle ain't easy. It's not fair to throw you in the deep end, and hope you know more than a doggy paddle. Just want to help, doll."

Callie wasn't ready to deal with the implications. Did he sympathize or pity her? Did he actually have issues with this situation on her behalf? Was he working some sort of con on her? "Why do you call me that?"

"What?"

"'Doll.'"

He hiked his huge shoulders up in an exaggerated "whatever" move. The move made him look like a teenager, and Callie smiled. "Feels right," he said. "Plus, I figure you don't want me using your name in public."

If this was a con, it was working.

Phoebe set their drinks on the counter, and then moved to help another customer. Her diligence earned her some kind words at the other end of the bar, but Callie quickly began to suspect the hustle was more about avoiding Derek's questions than upping her tips.

Derek pulled away from Callie, and settled himself on a black cushioned stool. Callie sat, too, and gave her margarita a cursory sip. Derek had called the concoction a stiff drink. He was right. It was heavy on tequila, and Callie relished the momentary burning of her sinuses when she took a longer pull. The familiar sensation hadn't changed since she'd had her first taste of the liquor.

Josh had gone through a baseball phase when Callie was fifteen. She'd nipped out of school early to drive down the mountain for the minor league game with him. He'd placed an Isotopes cap on her head and tucked a mini-bar bottle of tequila in her pocket. She'd coughed and sputtered at her first covert swig in the stands. Josh laughed conspiratorially and slapped her on the back. Then they'd sipped their contraband drinks and hollered at the opposing team for hours. She'd felt brave and grown-up that day—more so than managing the bills had ever done. Like being an adult could be an escape, and not just a litany of responsibilities. When Josh was sober again, she told herself, she'd take him to a game. Minus the booze.

"Our man is here." Derek had flipped to his scary, gruff voice. Callie should have been more unnerved than she was that she could recognize the difference.

She would give this target credit: He didn't turn tail upon spotting Derek at the bar. His footsteps slowed, but he continued his initial trajectory. Derek stood, and indicated Casey should take his freshly vacated seat. What was Callie supposed to do, stand? They hadn't discussed protocol for this. A list of basic rules of engagement for dealing with those who didn't return rented souls would have been nice. So, not knowing what else to do, she remained seated, but put her glass back on the bar. The last thing she needed was for her fingers to go all icicle-like and drop the booze in her lap. Party fouls were much worse in mixed company, at work, and when you weren't even drunk. She'd hit the trifecta if she flubbed here.

Casey followed Derek's instructions with obvious false bravado. "Long time, no see, bro."

The whites of Casey's eyes were milky, but Derek met them without flinching.

"That's true. Usually you're better about coming back to the Charmer's." Derek sounded like a disappointed older brother. Callie was all too familiar with the tone.

"I meant to, really, but you know how it goes." How had Casey landed a girl like Phoebe with game that bad?

Callie slid her hand into her pocket and thumbed the flask. It might have hummed under her touch, but she wasn't willing to say it was anything more than her imagination yet.

"I don't, actually. Why don't you tell me?" Derek's frustration began to show. Or was that part of his game, too, like the charisma with the bail bonds woman earlier?

Casey opened his mouth to offer additional bullshit—his cheekbones threatening to pop through his too-taut skin—when

Callie realized Casey was only a foot and a half away from her, but her hands weren't heating. In fact, they were getting colder. Wasn't he supposed to have a borrowed soul inside him? What. The. Fuck.

"He doesn't have it," she said, mostly swearing to herself. She let go of the flask, which was frigid in her grip.

Derek tensed as he saw Casey's eyes go wide and fists clench. Callie rose. If this was going to get messy, she wanted to be solidly planted on her Chucks.

Casey had one foot off the floor, in an obvious attempt to scramble backward, when Derek's meaty hand grabbed him by the front of the shirt. The gingham fabric twisted into a ball of blue wrapped around the collector's fist. "Care to explain?"

"Who's she? You going to trust some rando?"

Derek thrust the arm holding Casey outward, and then yanked him in close. "I asked you a question."

Callie preened at how Derek had kept her concealed. She wasn't dumb. She wasn't exactly hidden in this half-filled café. But they didn't know her secrets or who she was or what she might be to Derek. A breath had caught in her throat when Derek had let loose his anger, but now her breath was steady again as a veil of acceptance draped over the violence. It should have been concerning, but her options for security were getting smaller by the day. Better to be on the side of the Big Bad Wolf than left meandering with all the sheep.

"He gave it to someone else." Phoebe had leaned in, her voice dropped low, without skimping on the vehemence. Callie was ninety percent sure that was because Casey was causing a scene at her work. She understood the irritation. Josh had pulled a similar stunt back when she'd still been at the hospital.

Derek didn't loosen his hold on Casey, but he did lower his hand so the guy could relax a touch. Well, as much as one could in the face of imminent bodily harm. Derek nodded toward the bartender. "Talk."

When he went monosyllabic, he was in work mode. Callie's trust in him bumped up at the realization. She'd gotten him to talk.

"Don't get involved—" Casey started to say, but Derek cut him off with a rapid shake. The soul renter's teeth gnashed together in a clank that turned Callie's stomach.

"If I do, will you let him go?" Phoebe asked.

"Depends on what you say." That was a no.

"That Tess something-or-other has been around here lately. You know the one."

Callie didn't, but Derek nodded.

"She acts like she's hawking her frou-frou massage business, but our clientele ain't much for woo-woo shit."

Callie glanced around the room. Despite being in the arts district, work boots outpaced sandals three to one in the corner café. When Phoebe didn't elaborate, Derek turned his gaze back toward Casey. "Care to add anything?"

"No," the man squeaked.

"Wrong answer." Derek stalked toward the door, dragging Casey along with him.

Phoebe hurried through the gate at the bar and rushed to block Derek from exiting. Whether she was brave or stupid, the lady had stones. Casey saw her coming, though, and finally piped up. "She wants souls."

"You didn't give her yours, though. You gave her ours." Derek's hiss conjured images of the Soul Charmer and his reptilian movements. Callie swallowed. Hard.

"She didn't want mine, man." Casey's voice grew louder, his words now clumsy yelps.

Derek frowned. Callie should have waited for him to ask the obvious question, but apparently her mouth had other plans.

"What's wrong with yours? Every soul has its uses." Fuck. Now she sounded like she was *with* the Soul Charmer.

Casey's eyes darted between Callie and Derek, unsure of who to address. "She wanted the other one."

His fear was so heavy it nearly turned the air rancid. There had to be more. "Why?"

"Fine, bitch. She wanted the Charmer's soul."

Derek sucker-punched Casey in the gut. The guy gasped and floundered as he fought for air. When he started to regain composure, Derek let go of his shirt, only to promptly throw a jab right at Casey's nose. It snapped with a soft crack, and the power of the hit sent him flying to his back.

Derek took Callie's hand. "We should go now, doll."

As they sidestepped Casey's bloody form, Callie quietly asked, "He gave us answers. Honest ones, I think. Why'd you hit him?"

"He disrespected you."

"Oh." Callie's nape heated, and she licked her lips. Yes, definitely better to be on the side of the Big Bad Wolf.

Outside, the evening air had shifted from crisp to almost-winter cold. The mountains in the distance would be capped with snow tomorrow morning. Derek kept hold of her hand. The earlier wind from the day had died, and the rich moisture in the air wasn't even close to enough to combat her simmering emotions.

They retraced their steps, walking back toward a cluster of art galleries. His motorcycle was monstrous, lit beneath the streetlight. The lamp's glow only magnified the bike's wicked black lines and feral glint. She'd never been a motorcycle person, but she'd make an exception for Derek's. She stole a glance at Derek. He'd locked his jaw, the act making his cheekbone more prominent in profile.

"What's next?"

His face relaxed when she spoke. Enjoying his reaction seemed normal to Callie. Acceptable, even. The bad guy was on her side—probably—which made him the good guy. For now. Lord, why was she so flustered?

"One more pick-up, and then I need to ask some more questions about Tess."

"You say her name like you know her." Unexpected jealousy tinged the words. How embarrassing.

He gave an amused grunt. "Not like that, doll."

"Whatever. You do know her, and how to find her, right?" Callie blustered through the words as though it would make him forget the why-not-me from the first time she'd asked.

"Not exactly. I'm familiar with her, but she's adept at only being found on her terms."

That was a question dodge if Callie had ever heard one. "What exactly does that mean?"

"She makes a point of only being around when she's expecting people, and she's not too keen on taking appointments from the Charmer's crew." The edge of his upper lip lifted, the sneer more prizefighter than blues crooner.

"You can just say it's woo-woo magic shit." And they weren't magical. Mostly.

His grin overwhelmed her. "She's very much about the 'woo-woo magic shit.'"

"Then can't the Charmer handle her?"

"Not that simple. He ran her out of Gem City a couple years ago."

"Ran her out?"

"You could say it's a territorial business." The brutal truth tiptoed between the lines. "No clue what Tess is up to, though, because last night was the first I've heard of anyone other than the Charmer within fifteen hundred miles being able to work real soul magic."

"There are lots of ads—"

"You didn't go to anyone else," he cut her off.

"True. Doesn't mean they aren't legit."

"I'm telling you. They aren't. Little shit is easy, but grappling with pulling and pushing souls requires a long apprenticeship and a whole lot of dark dealings. Neither the Charmer or I believed Tess had next-level skill."

Derek didn't have to tell Callie the Soul Charmer wasn't going to be pleased with the news. She didn't want to be the one to tell him. "Why not?"

"She sucks chi."

"Excuse me?" Was that a magic slur? Hadn't that massage therapist at the home said something about balancing chakras? If Ford's spy dabbled in soul magic, he was even more of a threat than Callie had originally thought. No wonder he wanted those police files.

"She tells people she can cleanse their bodies of toxins, purify them, shit like that, but her magic is more about siphoning their energy instead. She gives them a massage like any other asshole in town, but in the process steals bits of their souls or shoves extra souls into their bodies. From what I've heard, it's like a life force dialysis."

"Ew. What's she get out of it?"

"Same thing every magic user does: power."

A bolt of pure ice shot up Callie's spine that didn't have a damn thing to do with souls. Derek didn't miss the shudder as her hand twitched in his. He stopped walking, and pulled Callie in toward him. He'd moved so quickly she didn't lift her hands to stop her body from colliding with his. He must not have minded, as he gave her the satisfying weight of his arm across her shoulder blades. Safety. She languished in it.

"Magic?" he whispered in her ear. His breath tickled and she squirmed.

"Mmm?" So warm.

"Do you sense it, or was it too much info too fast?"

"Too much, I think." She pulled in a deep breath, simply because he smelled so good.

"I keep forgetting this isn't normal for you."

She laughed without humor. "Fucked up is par for the course for me."

His brows furrowed. "I'm sorry you got dragged into this."

"Me, too." Callie sighed, and then continued. "But I suppose there's something to be said for being on the inside."

"I'm going to keep you safe. You know that, right?" He nearly winced with the plea. This wasn't simply a placation, and Callie doubted it was totally about her. That's why she believed him. Maybe the touch of magic she'd acquired was working. They both had battered souls, and the earnestness in those grey eyes said he'd failed before and wouldn't let it happen again. She understood the need for redemption.

"I do."

Derek's sigh of relief blew a few loose strands of Callie's hair across her cheek. She watched his hand, waiting for his fingers to reach out and lightly caress her face as he moved them into place behind her ear. Instead he let her go and shook himself.

The spell was broken. He urged them along to the next stop, where there was another soul to retrieve.

──── CHAPTER EIGHT ────

Callie regretted teaching her mother how to send text messages.

Her phone buzzed against her kitchen counter. The rattle was loud enough to make Callie wonder if the countertop would crack. Doubtful. The material was cut-rate, but not that cheap. Besides, her lazy super would probably throw a roll of duct tape at her and wish her Godspeed.

Two years ago, showing Zara how to text message had seemed like a brilliant idea. Josh had been crashing with Callie at the time, and her mom had wanted to touch base. Unfortunately, she thought six in the morning was the absolute best time to talk. Josh might have been up then, but Callie was a firm believer in only rising before nine if you were getting paid to do so. Her mom hadn't offered any cash, so the texts became the preferred way to communicate. She could leave a message, and Callie would get back when she was available.

Fast-forward to today, and Zara had forgotten about the waiting part of the equation. She'd sent six messages while Callie was out with Derek last night.

Where are you?

Where's your brother?
Tell Josh to call me.
Tell me you got this.
Calliope! Call me!!
You do this on purpose.

Callie had read each one surreptitiously while walking from one target to another. They'd collected two more souls last night, and talked with another three people who had seen Tess, but couldn't tell them how to find her. The last one of the night had been a banker who lived on the northern outskirts of Gem City. The fabric of his navy blue starched shirt strained against his belly. He wasn't subsisting on barebones sandwiches. He'd even fessed up that it was his wife who brought Tess into their lives. While the husband rented semi-regularly from the Soul Charmer, his better half sought absolution through Tess's chakra massage. He was trying to get right with more than the Lord, and had produced a new flyer for Tess.

After some not-so-gentle prodding from Derek.

Working magic was exhausting. She didn't have to control the energy within the flask, but Callie's muscles had ached by the time Derek dropped her off at home. She didn't let him walk her to the door—it hadn't been a date—but he stayed on his bike out front until she waved to him from the front window nevertheless.

A scalding shower hadn't been able to singe the phantom tingle of magic skittering beneath her skin, but it had relaxed her enough to sleep. Calling her mother would have undone all the work from the steam. So she'd left it for the morning.

To say Zara was mad as a bull the next day would only disparage bovines.

She'd started with the next round of messages around 6:30 a.m. When Callie finally admitted to herself that she wouldn't be sleeping in, it was 7:15, and the messages hadn't said anything new. Zara worried over Josh and stockpiled all her anger for Callie. It'd only been in the last year Callie understood that was weird. She was the youngest, the little sister. Why was she deigned her brother's keeper? In the last couple years, she'd certainly taken care of him, but their mother had been the one to put them in those roles so long ago. Callie'd been fifteen when Josh had moved out. From that point on, Zara had expected her to know where he was and keep his room ready in case he came back.

"It's not like he's shipped off with the navy," Callie had told her mom.

Her cheek had stung at the fast crack of her mom's hand against it. "Don't you say things like that. You'll jinx him."

Callie had known better than to roll her eyes, but the idea Josh would enlist was asinine to the extreme. She'd mumbled an apology and hid in her room for the rest of the night. She'd eaten three Little Debbie's snacks from the stash behind her bed in lieu of dinner with her mom that night.

At 7:40 a.m., Callie stopped avoiding Zara. More than an hour of buzzing texts and missed calls—no voicemails—had worn her resolve. This was where Josh got his tenacity. It might also explain why she'd agreed to work for the Charmer. Dealing with the mafia and magic were easier than enduring familial responsibilities.

"Hi, Mom," Callie answered the phone. She settled at the end of the couch, pulling her knees against her chest. Fetal position couldn't save her from the spackle of guilt Zara was about to apply, but it was better than nothing.

"I was about to call the police." Zara gasped and wheezed, but Callie wasn't about to let it worry her. Not her first rodeo.

"Why would you call the cops?" Drama queen.

"I've been leaving you messages since yesterday. You could have been dead."

"I'm not dead."

"I didn't know that." Pots clanged in the background.

"Yes, you did."

"With an attitude like that you're never going to be light enough to rise to heaven. How a child of mine gets such pleasure out of worrying her mother—"

"I don't get pleasure from you worrying, but you weren't worrying about me."

The muffled kitchen sounds on the other end of the line quelled. "Of course I was. Now I'm a liar?"

Callie swore. This was going downhill fast. "What are you making, Mom?"

"Making?" she asked, a little dazed. Zara's voice flitted to the soft, curious tone she used with everyone except Callie. She continued, no longer out of breath, "Oh, blondies for the new girl in 4A. She brings me my paper now."

Zara hadn't baked anything for Callie since she was eight. Those double-chocolate cupcakes with a creamy ganache icing were phenomenal. She'd hated sharing them. She didn't bring Zara the paper, though. There was the inherent dig. It didn't matter what Callie did, it wasn't ever going to be seen as selfless. She could only hear, "This doesn't change things," and "You're doing that for Josh, not me," so many times before she'd quit wishing for simple thanks.

It was too damn early for a jog to those emotional scars. Callie smoothed a palm across her face. "What did you need, Mom?"

"Can't I want to check on my daughter?"

"Your messages weren't about me," Callie muttered.

"What?"

"Nothing. I'm fine."

"You sound tired."

"It's early," Callie drew out the word, hoping if she said it slow enough her mom would get it.

She didn't. "Have you seen Josh?"

He wasn't being sent to her in tiny bits, so no. Callie drew in a long breath. Patience was key. "Not recently, but I talked to him on the phone earlier this week. He's fine."

"Fine? What's that supposed to mean?"

"It means fine. As in you don't need to worry."

"Not worry? The two of you are trying to kill me."

Tempting, but no. The less Zara knew, the safer everyone would be. Callie changed the subject. "How's Frankie?"

"He's the happiest cat. That catnip Josh got me for my birthday is Frankie's favorite."

Callie had bought the catnip. She'd bought all the gifts for her mom's birthday, and the cards. Josh couldn't remember the favored feline's name. Whatever. It no longer mattered. She could have handed the present to her mom directly and she'd still give Josh the credit. Callie's boss Louisa told her she didn't have a favorite of her kids, but it'd only made her feel worse. Not everyone suffered from being the least favorite. If such things built character, then she should be the goddamn paragon of character. Erect temples in her name. After twenty-two years of being the lesser child, Callie was fucking done.

She squeezed the couch's arm until the wood beneath the fabric pressed back against her fingers. Deep breaths. "That's good. I've got to go soon."

"No you don't." Zara's over confidence squeezed through the phone receiver like a sneer. What? Callie couldn't make plans on her own? She couldn't change the script?

"I've got work this afternoon, and still need to run errands." Not even a lie.

"That retirement home is running you ragged." Concern? From Zara? Nope, she continued, "That's why you'll never force me into one of those places. If they have enough money to be paying time and a half, then they're bleeding those people dry. You work for heathens."

Would knowing she worked a second job change anything? Unlikely. Besides, she didn't want Zara involved in this whole business with Josh and Ford and the Soul Charmer. If there was one person who needed to be kept out of the loop here, it was Zara. Josh might be her favorite, but that didn't mean their mother was street smart enough to keep her nose out of this. Nothing would complicate their lives further than Zara trying to track down Ford to negotiate. Though, at this point, all she had was her apartment, her cat, and the television Callie had sprung for last Christmas—right before Josh had liquidated all her funds, again.

"Yeah, Mom. Well, I still have to go."

"Tell Josh to call me."

"I will." *Right after I pay off his most recent drug debt.*

Zara hung up before Callie had the chance. She set her phone on the couch cushion beside her, and imagined how it would feel to have her mother worry about her the way she did for Josh. Would it fill her chest with warmth? She shook her head to erase the idiotic idea.

She liked to think her mom hadn't always been like this. Zara had been fun once, back when road trips to Aunt Lily's were an adventure instead of an excuse to ditch the kids. Callie had turned seven just a few weeks before the event and was over-the-moon when her mother had bought her a new swimsuit and hot pink flip-flops. She'd clomped up and down the sidewalk while her mom loaded the car for the drive down to the low desert.

The July sun cranked the outdoor heat to a wicked 107 degrees Fahrenheit, but it didn't matter, as someone—probably Uncle Joe—had crafted an over-sized, homemade Slip 'N Slide in Aunt Lily's backyard. The hill it rested on was subtle, but Callie had been scared once she'd seen it. Josh's pre-teen bragging about how "wild" the slide was had not helped her fears. Zara, though, wouldn't allow Callie to shy away. Her mother had borrowed an oversized shirt from a cousin and took a monumental run at the slide. She'd screamed in delight on her first run. The second time, she'd lifted Callie on to her back. Callie rode down the slide with her mom, bound together by fun.

Zara wasn't a something-for-nothing kind of woman. These days, every word she gave to Callie was in exchange for something else. As riled as she pretended to be over Cedar Retirement working Callie, she was a hustler.

When they visited Aunt Lily's a couple weeks later, though, Zara had spent the entire day on the phone. Her underlings in a pyramid scheme involving five-dollar bills and tarot decks were dropping like flies. Money was short and Zara's temper more so. That was the way of their relationship. The bright spots had become fewer and fewer as Callie aged. She had watched her mother con people year after year. It had just taken a couple decades to realize she was part of a long con herself.

Derek arrived at Callie's apartment at seven on her fifth night as a strong-armed soul collector. It was later than their normal meeting, but she'd liked the change. Not only did it mean fewer hours involved on the darker side of Gem City, but it also allowed her to bypass a visit to the Soul Charmer. The man had already turned her into a human treasure detector. She wasn't particularly game to discover what else he could do to her. That whole humans-to-toads deal sounded fake, but when your hands went Icelandic out of the blue, you started believing in the outlandish.

When she'd encountered soul magic in the retirement home, she should have expected it everywhere else. Her afternoon trip to the grocery store, her first time in a crowd since her quality time with the Charmer, had underscored just how many people dabbled with soul rental. Kristi had done it, sure, but that was one family member, and she was the only soul renter Callie actually knew. But her hands had damn near fused to the cart in every other aisle, passing person after person with either too much or too little soul. At least the flask was with Derek, instead of burning a hole in her pocket. It was irritating, but illuminating. At this rate, borrowing souls had to be close to the norm in Gem City.

Plus, the inability to tell a difference between the freezing cold of a renter in between souls and the wicked chill of those who'd hawked their souls bothered her. If she was stuck with this skill, it'd be nice to know which people were doubling down on souls and which ones had said fuck it—for money or a high or whatever else a rented soul was used for—and pawned their own to the Charmer. She'd never be that hard up for cash. Hawk a television or bicycle to help cover rent? Sure. She'd been there. There was a reason she nodded along when her coworkers talked about their favorite reality show. She caught glimpses of shows playing in the dining area at work, but that had been it for a long time. She was okay with that. Give her a stack of paperbacks borrowed from the library to read, and she was a happy woman.

Which is exactly what she was doing when Derek knocked. He'd offered to pick her up tonight, and taken the filled flask to the Soul Charmer the night before. She didn't get his protective streak, but also wasn't going to bitch about it. She up-ended a glass of water to wash away the sticky remnants of the PB&J she'd just inhaled before opening the door. He didn't need to know she ate like a four-year-old.

His knock had shaken the two framed photos hanging on the wall. Her grandmother's grin in the top photo suggested she was fine with a little jostling. She'd been a strong lady. Callie opened the door without checking the peephole. Even after just a few days, she recognized Derek's knock. She pulled the door open with one hand and snagged her coat with the other. "Hey."

He stepped into the apartment, into her space, thwarting her attempt to bolt out the door. His hulking frame towering over her bumped her heart rate up a few notches.

Three, maybe four, inches separated Derek's barrel chest from Callie's chin. That canal of air grew charged. She tilted her head back to meet his gaze. His locked jaw and slight sneer would have frightened her days earlier, but the air between them was sparking now. Beneath her too-thin shirt her skin tingled, begging for contact to soothe the static sensation.

His hard stare could turn others into simpering puddles of fear. Yes, she was liquid, too, but it was borne more of lust and intrigue. Which did he want from her? She pulled in a harsh, deep breath. He was wearing cologne—a first—and the heady masculine scent had her reeling. She took a half step backward, only to reach for his shoulder to steady herself. The leather of his jacket was supple beneath her fingers. Not bad, though his skin would be better.

"You letting me in, or what?" Amusement laced Derek's husky tone.

He steered her into her apartment, as though he was taking home a drunken coworker. Might as well have been. That brought her to her senses. She shook her head, unable to hide her embarrassment. "Yes, of course."

He gave her one of his pleased grunts. "I liked where that was going and all, doll, but it's gonna be a busy work night and . . . " he trailed off and turned his focus to her bare coffee table. She hadn't been the only one caught up in the moment. Thank. God.

"Yeah." Her tongue had gone thick. She hadn't tipped full-body flush over a guy since she was fifteen. Whether it was all Derek, or maybe a little magic from the Charmer, she was far too in touch with her emotions right now. Locking that shit up was the only way to protect oneself. A few days of stress and magic working alongside a hot dude were fucking with her.

Derek wandered around her living room, searching every thread and hairline crack as if it meant something other than she wasn't flush with cash. He was too big in the small, spartan space. He stood between her chipped coffee table and the equally barren, but better cared for, dinette set. It was a gem of a thrift store find. Loved by many homes. Josh had stained it for her to hide the gouges from late-night bills and after-school homework. She had three chairs, but never used them all. If her mom ever came over, she'd need to pull the table away from the wall to free the third mission-style chair.

"You move a lot?" The question would have been less conspicuous if Callie hadn't witnessed Derek's slow analysis of her furniture. He'd lingered on the uneven couch cushions like he thought she'd stuffed her secrets inside them.

"More than my mother." A little evasion was for the best.

Her stomach didn't sink at his disappointed grunt. He didn't mean it. He turned after realizing he didn't have anything else to take in. He inclined his head toward the coffee table. "You need a book there or a plant."

"You overestimate its sturdiness." She shrugged. She kept her books in the bedroom, but she wasn't about to share that detail. She needed to stop this blurring of lines and focus on business. "If you're done judging my apartment, we should probably get to work. What's the plan?"

"You eat?"

Callie felt a prickling sensation at the nape of her neck, as she realized that he'd shifted back inside his shell, barely talking. But that wasn't her problem, right? "I had a little something," she said.

Another grunt.

"Did you, um, eat?" she added two seconds too late when he didn't say more. "I don't have much in the kitchen, but there might be enough for a sandwich." She still had two or three slices of turkey in the refrigerator, but she'd been saving those for tomorrow.

Harsh lines between his eyes—ones she should have paid more attention to before—eased and faded. "Thanks, doll, but I'm good. We'll be out for a while tonight. Didn't want you starving."

A flush of heat began to rush from her chest toward her face at his thoughtfulness. She bit the inside of her cheek to stop it. He was a colleague. Hell, not even that. He worked for the bad guy. She needed to remember that.

"That your brother?"

She might have yelped, but convinced herself she hadn't. Derek didn't react, but then he was busy running his finger along the picture frame on the wall next to him, near the doorway. She sucked in a quick breath before replying. "Yep. That's him. Josh. I'm about five there."

"Cute dress." She'd worn vibrant purple all the time; that's what little girls did. Now she couldn't remember the last time she wore anything bright or bold.

Pithy responses evaded her, and her initial thought—kids are *always* cute—conjured a nasty taste in her mouth. She shrugged, and it explained her discomfort and wistfulness and necessary secrets better than her words ever could. Derek nodded in response, and shoved his hands in his pockets, as if he was keeping away from her limited possessions now to avoid prying. No, she was reading too much into this. Into him. Into whatever weird magic mojo flowed between them that made her run her hand down the back of his arm. He watched her fingers glide along the black leather of his jacket, but said nothing.

She grazed her fingertips on the exposed skin of his wrist, delighting in the zing of electricity dashing into her hand. The rush of his deep inhale shook her. She should be setting boundaries. She blinked a few times and she stepped away. The pang in her chest was embarrassment, not disappointment. Mostly. "Should we get going?" she asked with the same false confidence she'd mustered when meeting the Soul Charmer the first time.

He cleared his throat twice before his voice became steady enough to reply. "Yeah. Bring a scarf, if you've got one. It's fucking windy."

CHAPTER NINE

Derek had been right about the wind. Callie's cheeks burned by the time they parked the bike north of the square. They weren't far from the art houses they'd passed a few nights ago, but the ticking muscle at Derek's jawline suggested they were seeking bigger fish tonight. He focused on each small task as he packed up the bike, not even meeting her gaze as he took her helmet to stow.

She scurried behind him, doing her best to catch up with his long strides without stumbling on the aged brick sidewalk. Muffled Indian music slipped into the street from an open door a few storefronts ahead. They'd already talked food, so the chances they were about to dig into plates of excellent Tandoori chicken were slim. "So. What's the plan?"

"Information," he answered. His one-word reply may have been gruff, but at least he'd answered. Callie considered that progress.

"Riiiight."

He paused, and she almost crashed into him. He pretended not to notice, but it was likely borne of distraction, and not gentlemanly instinct. "We need to keep a lower profile here."

"So you're not going to break any noses?" The teasing lilt of her voice bordered on flirtation.

He huffed, but a hint of a smile dashed its impact. "Probably not."

"A little variety wouldn't kill us, I suppose."

He threw an arm over her shoulders. Lazy and protective. She stood straighter as the pride of being guarded washed over her. She wouldn't lose herself, or drop the floodgates, but it was okay to enjoy this. Probably.

"We deal in magic, doll. So, let's not tempt fate." He pulled her with him as he resumed his course.

Callie relished the moment. Her hands were normal temperature, her belly was full, her brother was temporarily safe, her mom wouldn't call until tomorrow, and one damn delicious man was at her side. Not fucking bad. Or it wasn't until she saw the sign.

HEALING + RESTORATION + MASSAGE

The words, in an old letterpress font, were painted in deep blue on a closed door. Gold leaf had been applied for accent. Fear slammed a cannonball into Callie's stomach. She ducked under Derek's arm, out of his grasp, and scurried backward. Whether he heard her muttering, "No no no," didn't matter.

He hustled toward her, catching up quickly. "Don't worry, we're not going there."

The strike of panic fizzled as quickly as it had ignited. Now, more than anything, she needed a night without madness. No freezing hands. No fire at her fingertips. No magic tugging at her. No blood. No pain. No tormented people reminding her of her brother. She couldn't tell Derek without letting him see her. The scarred and terrified parts of her. Instead she said, "No soul stuff."

The words eked out as barely a whisper, but her widened eyes told him all he needed to know.

He nodded slowly. "Done."

She pointed at the door. One of the chakra massage flyers was taped to a corner of the glass. "That's her, isn't it?"

His responding shrug read as an admission.

"What if she's here?"

"She's not."

His confidence didn't do shit for Callie. She opened her mouth to argue, but he cut her off.

"I've been working all afternoon. Remember? She owns this place. Her people—her customers—are here, next door, but she won't be here tonight. She's out of town."

"How do you know?" Callie managed not to stutter.

"I'm not trying to screw with you. I told you I'd keep you safe. Don't doubt me. I got you on this, Callie."

Using her name shouldn't have changed things, but it helped. Breath filled her lungs again, and her shoulders relaxed. "Okay," she said with all the confidence she wished she had.

He held out a hand and she accepted it.

"Now, how about I take you dancing?" Derek smiled then, and it was the most rakish grin she'd ever seen. It warmed her body again. Her emotional yo-yo evening wasn't over. Derek might actually be worse for her core temperature than the soul magic detector hands.

He wasn't kidding about the dancing. Derek had brought her to a belly-dancing event. The southwest was rather lacking in Indian culture, but this spot brought it in spades. By day it was a restaurant, but a couple nights a week they hosted belly dancing and live music. The long bench against the wall—where Callie sat—was covered with plush pillows in vibrant shades of gold, emerald, sapphire, and other precious gems. As she settled on a ruby pillow, her earlier reservations wilted further. A thick swath of orange fabric was draped on the wall. Muffling sound wasn't the priority in this place; they propped the front door open. No, this venue was all for opulence. It was miles away from her apartment, but worlds away from anything she'd known. That was more comforting to her than almost anything Derek had said to her. With one exception. He'd asked for her trust. He'd been sincere. She swallowed hard. She'd have to deal with that later.

Derek dropped onto a green pillow at her left. He handed her an open bottle of beer. Any other man, any other night, and she wouldn't have accepted an open container. But if Derek had wanted to screw her over, all he had to do was point her at the nearest soul magic user. Or ask his boss to renege on the deal. She'd trust a beer from him, even take it graciously.

She thanked him, and he tapped the neck of his bottle against hers in lowbrow *salud*. They both took long pulls, but when he lowered his, half the drink was gone. She hadn't made nearly that kind of dent. He was double her size and double the drinker.

Had he licked the brew from his lips in slow motion, or was her brain fucking with her? There had to be some other magic woo-woo at play here. She sucked in a quick breath through her nose and let it out her mouth. A little de-stress breathing would calm her overexcited nerves.

"You been to something like this before?"

What? Were they skipping work tonight or was this the plan all along? Callie's mind was spinning too fast to parse his shift in tone. Had he known she needed a distraction? A *healthy* distraction?

"First timer here. Though, I thought you said you were taking me dancing. Looks like it's all pros here."

Years disappeared when he smiled at her. She could almost pretend he wasn't old enough to buy her that beer. "Right now they're dancing. Later they'll teach people, and usually everyone's drunk enough not to care if they look like an idiot."

"Are you speaking from personal experience?" She leaned her shoulder into his side.

He tightened his arm around her, keeping her in close. The Indian spices in the air mingled with the cologne she'd smelled earlier, combining in a heady mix that made her melt into him. "Of course."

She craned her neck to meet his gaze fully. "For real? You've belly danced?"

"These hips don't lie." He rocked his hips from side to side for effect. Laughter bubbled from her belly. He continued to jostle her and chuckle. His seated dance moves didn't up his sexy factor, but the laughing might.

Callie eased back into the plush cushions, and crossed her legs. Her knee grazed his. "So you can dance. What other skills are you keeping secret?"

Bemusement brought a single dimple to his right cheek. "When I was fifteen I could throw an eighty-mile-per-hour fastball."

"Damn. Do you still play?" Baseball was the only stick-and-ball sport Callie could get into.

"No. Life got complicated in high school. It's been more than a decade since I've been on a diamond."

"You're probably terrifying at a batting cage," she said, picturing him dropping his leather jacket on the concrete and overwhelming the batter's box with muscles and straining cotton.

"You mean because I can hit a baseball like a beast?" A wry smile played at his lips.

The next half hour passed quickly. Derek was better at small talk than Callie would have guessed. His grunts were few and his jokes plentiful. His attention was divided, though. He was constantly scanning the room, watching everyone around them. The lack of his full focus was disappointing, but having experienced both focused attention and neglect, Callie had to say she preferred the latter. Too much attention and you were bound to disappoint, but if you're frequently forgotten, it was far easier to impress when you were noticed. Derek's smile almost made her think she'd be able to make him grin on command.

Or perhaps not.

Derek's eyes narrowed. "One of my sources is here."

"That's good?" His tone suggested otherwise, but wasn't that the point of the night? Callie could pretend it was a date all she wanted—the atmosphere and the beer almost enough to make her forget her job, Derek's job, and the flask in her pocket—but the truth was they were here for information. This was work.

He grumbled and stared so hard at a slender man across the room in a larger group of people, the guy's black cowboy boots should have set fire.

The intensity left Callie's mouth dry and her throat tight. She indulged in a few nerve-soothing swigs of beer. "Should I hold him down while you beat him with noodles?"

Derek scowled. So much for her make-him-laugh-whenever idea. "You stay here."

"So that's a no on the noodles?" she tried again.

He finally looked her way, as though remembering she was there. "I don't want him to know you."

It should have sounded protective, but instead it reminded her how small and useless she was here. Even her newly magical fingertips did jack tucked away at the edge of this restaurant. Had Derek kept her away to keep her fingers from going aglow? The Soul Charmer had stuck him with her, and now he had to be worried she'd fuck up something important. "Sure," she muttered.

His brows furrowed, which only made Callie's stomach sink lower. "He's not a friend." The emphasis was on *not*, as though he thought she might run up to Cowboy Boots, wrap her legs around him, and tell him everything she knew about the Soul Charmer.

"Got it." She took another hard pull from the bottle to give herself something to do.

Derek's source excused himself from a group of people. He was alone, and Derek was ready to pounce. "Don't leave," he said as he stood.

Because she had so many other engagements. "Right."

Cowboy Boots wasn't dressed for a night of Bollywood fun, but then she wasn't either. Still, he would have fit in more deep in the desert than in the middle of Gem City. His black jeans were worn at the knees and tucked into his boots. He'd looked strong, until Derek stood next to him. It was hard to look tough next to a huge man in leather, though. She should know.

The source had knocked his shoulders back and puffed out his chest at Derek's approach. What kind of man wouldn't be scared of Derek? What kind of man was Cowboy Boots? Ford might not run away, but he had a league of hangers on and weapons she'd never heard of in his arsenal. Callie had been introduced to more mobsters and criminals in the last few weeks than she'd ever known existed. Despite her growing circle of associates, Cowboy Boots didn't look familiar in the least. That was a good thing. Right?

She couldn't hear their conversation over the live music and the hum of intermingling people, but with each passing second Cowboy Boots deflated a smidgen. Ford wouldn't have folded that quickly. Callie's scale for who was dangerous had certainly shifted, and under the new ranking Cowboy Boots wasn't much of a threat. As long as he feared Derek enough to talk, she was in the clear.

Everyone else in the restaurant-turned-nightclub was in clusters, groups of friends, couples on dates, while she sat alone at her table with an empty beer bottle. Derek and Cowboy Boots had edged closer to one another, but the latter's wide-eyed expression suggested he was giving up the goods. Derek didn't need her right now. She did, however, need another drink. She left the comfort of the pillows and walked to the bar tucked in the back of the room. The hallway to the restrooms was to the right. Good to know.

Callie had brought her empty with her to the bar. An old boy-friend had once taken her to a place so fancy they got pissed if you bussed any of your table. She'd discovered the hard way when their shitty waiter wouldn't bring him drinks, and she went in search on her own. Her boyfriend had been mortified, but it was more disgusting that they called out her lack of class. Callie avoided that kind of snobbery now. The bartender here didn't mind. He gave her an impersonal smile as he collected the empty.

"Another?" he asked.

She nodded, and he diligently pulled one from the fridge and popped the cap for her.

He'd already moved on to helping another patron as she took her first pull. The alcohol didn't work fast, but the habit helped her muscles ease anyway. Enjoying a night on the town could still be possible. The Charmer, by way of Derek, wasn't making her collect souls tonight, and no one had turned her fingers into icicles in almost twenty-four hours. Hell, she even had a decent buzz going.

But a full day of non-suckage was never in the cards for Callie.

Nate's breath hit the side of her face before she heard him. "Fancy meeting you here."

Callie cringed and hoped he didn't notice. Why would one of Ford's goons be at a belly-dancing bar? Oh right, fate hated her. "Hey," she mumbled. It was better to acknowledge him than risk him reporting anything back to his boss. At least this time it wasn't a secret she was being watched.

"Didn't know you were into shaking that ass. If I had, I'm sure we could have worked out some other deal." Nate spoke as if he, and not his boss, was the one holding her brother hostage.

Sure, he'd been in the room when she'd met with Ford, but not at his side. She struggled to remember if she'd ever heard Nate speak when Ford was in the room. She didn't think so, and she certainly hadn't pegged him as someone who was allowed to make decisions. Then again, she did not know mob dynamics at all. Chances were, angering one angered them all, like bats or some shit.

"I don't dance," she said with all the manners she could muster, trying to shut down the skeeze. She shuffled-stepped to the side and angled herself to better face him.

He grabbed her upper arm and tugged her close again. "Aw, don't disappoint me."

Her stomach twisted. She needed to shift the conversation, and fast. Deflect. Humor. Whatever. "They haven't even made it to the audience participation part of the night. Until then I know nothing."

"I know some girls who could teach you a thing or two."

"Thanks for the offer, but I'm good." Her voice held steady, despite the sensation of liquid lead bubbling behind her kneecaps. Walking away now would be smart, but the desire to be smart didn't outweigh stark reality: If she ran, she wouldn't be the only one hurt.

"You could be better." His eyes darted to her chest. He was picturing her naked on a pole, and she couldn't stop him.

"I should get back." If only her legs would work.

"You on a date?" His accusation was sharp, but it cut deeper because she wished the answer was yes.

"No—"

He cut her off. "You ain't got time for dates. If you got time for dates, then you got time to be getting our shit. Unless maybe you don't care so much about big brother."

She held up her free hand to protest, but he ignored her and continued. "Maybe I should tell Ford you lied about needing time to get the essentials for the job."

"I didn't lie," she snapped. The fear churning in her stomach had coalesced into straight-up fire. "I keep my promises, and when I'm done helping your boss you are never going to see me again."

"Heard that before."

"And once I clear his debt, Josh is done with you."

"Does he know that?"

This was Josh's rock bottom. He wouldn't have involved her in this mess if it wasn't. She almost pleaded with herself that her brother *had* to know it, had to know worse than this meant death, but Nate didn't need to see her desperation. Love was just one more weapon that could be used against her.

As Callie began to sink into a growing cesspool of self-pity, Derek joined the conversation. Because things can *always* get worse.

"I know you?" Nate asked with a scoff.

Derek moved behind Callie, his warm body cocooning her. He peeled Nate's hand off her arm. His scarred knuckles, hovering above Nate's tanned ones, were an inherent threat. "No." That one word held more menace than could be found in the darkest, nastiest biker bar.

"She your date, then?" Nate's smarminess couldn't touch her, not with Derek's torso pressed to her back.

Derek's chest vibrated against her, like he was supercharged and about to explode. His voice rumbled when he spoke. "Not your business."

"Oh, but she *is* my business." Nate rubbed his hands together. Callie clenched her teeth. He was making her sound like a prostitute.

Derek ignored the implication. "Not anymore."

The words didn't sound any scarier to Callie, but Nate took in a big breath. "Ford's going to want to know why she's here," he reminded her again, words full of venom.

Derek stiffened behind her, and then wrapped a possessive hand around her front to cup her hip. "Too bad. You have fifteen seconds to leave."

Nate shifted from foot to foot. "Or what, man?"

"I make you a ghost." A monotone threat could make even the biggest, baddest guy piss his pants, if wielded correctly. No surprise, Derek knew this.

Nate understood, too.

He attempted the quintessential tough-guy nod, but it turned shaky as he met Derek's gaze. He flitted a look to Callie. "Ford's—"

Derek cut him off. "Seven seconds."

Nate had too much pride to run, but he sure got himself to the front door in a flash. He glanced back one final time, to shoot Callie a glare promising repercussions, but in the safety of Derek's hold the fear couldn't sink her.

"Asshole forgot his drink," Derek muttered as he moved around Callie to take Nate's place at the bar.

There's a fine line between fear and lust. Bad decisions were borne of both. Callie fisted the fabric of Derek's shirt and yanked him down to her. She must have caught him off-guard, because he didn't fight her. She pressed her lips against his as raw need flared in her belly. Heat coursed through her body at this little contact. She'd explode if he gave her more.

The pleasure of having his lips against hers was almost too much. The threat of losing it was worse. Any second she knew he'd pull away, to chide her for the choice of time or place. He surprised her when he pushed against her more firmly, opening his mouth to tease her with his tongue. His lips were smoother than she'd predicted, nothing like the rough hand cupping the nape of her neck. She slid her tongue against his in a feverish dance. They weren't in time with the bombastic music surrounding them, but instead synced with their own racing heartbeats.

Derek yanked her against him, and more than her knees went liquid at his hardness pressing against her stomach. Callie forgot where they were, who they were, and slipped a hand underneath the hem of Derek's tee shirt. His skin was fevered over his taut muscles. She grazed a light trail of hair. What would she discover on his chest when he was out of that shirt?

More importantly, what would he do when she removed hers? Her breasts already ached, and that was merely from the ferocity of his kiss. The urge to wrap her legs around him and see if he could possess her lit a fire in her core. It also, unfortunately, reminded her she was at a very public place with a very memorable guy.

The fire in their kiss had burned all the oxygen. She pulled away, gasping. As she sucked in air, her brain slowly resumed its normal functions. What had she just done? Nothing screams pathetic like kissing your put-upon partner immediately after he discovers you're in league with mobsters.

"I'm starting to think you like me protecting you," he said, fighting and failing to hide a smile.

She wasn't that girl. She didn't use relationships or sex to garner good will. She couldn't deny she appreciated the protection, but she could pretend she didn't need his help with Nate. "I had it under control." The lie was foul, but anything would be bitter after the sweetness she'd just sampled.

He cocked a brow.

She tucked her hair behind her ear with a shaking hand. "You did move things along, though, so thanks."

His bemused grunt made her stomach twist in a delicious way, but her brain, now deciding it would start making rational decisions again, overrode any additional sexy ideas. She wasn't using him. "I didn't mean for that to happen."

"For one of Ford's men to be here? Or for giving me a raging hard-on?"

She shoved her hands in her pockets. Better to keep them there, where they couldn't pull Derek back to her. She opened her mouth to reply, not sure how to start, but he cut her off with a chuckle. "Just fucking with you, doll."

Heat coiled low in her belly. Did he have to say "fucking"? Her audible inhale made him smile wider.

"Calm down. No harm, no foul."

"It-it-it wasn't a thank you."

He nodded, but she didn't know if he really believed her. "Then I suppose I owe you one. Haven't been kissed like that in some time."

Heat flooded her face so quickly there was no way to quell it. Derek brushed the backs of his fingers over his cheek. "I like your sweetness."

Callie hadn't been a sweet person in a long time, but trying to form the words necessary to argue was futile at this point. "Should we get out of here?" Oh, Lord, she hadn't meant it like that.

He let the implication slide. "Tempting, but I still need to talk to Bianca. She'll know what Tess is up to."

The change of subject gave Callie's insides a chance to galvanize. "Where is she?"

"Haven't seen her yet, but she'll be here."

His confidence elicited goose bumps on Callie's skin. She didn't rub them away. No need to invite attention to bared flesh. Not when her body was still reliving the pure power of kissing Derek.

"So, you want to tell me about—"

No. God no. It didn't matter which way he finished the question—your connection to the mob, why that dick was acting like you're a whore, how often you go for hot-and-heavy kisses at the bar—she did not want to answer it. "What's Bianca look like?"

He furrowed his brow and stared down at her. The embers of the heated gaze from before were there, smoldering, but now he was measuring her again. Whether it was for the best, he let her off the hook. "Little shorter than you, black hair down to her ass, red lips."

The lust warming her neck sank like a rancid meatball to the pit of her stomach. "Sounds like you know her well." Probably intimately.

His amused huff didn't do much for Callie. "She's worked at Tess's massage joint since before Tess owned it." He frowned, and then mumbled, "Or before we knew she ran it."

Could the alternative healing community be so big as to keep such secrets? Callie could ask Jackie. Her cousin, one of Aunt Lily's kids, was in the business. If roping another family member into the depths of her problems wasn't a terrible idea, she could also ask her about Tess. Instead she asked Derek, "What do we know about her? Tess, I mean."

"Not enough."

She liked his simple answers, but only when he gave them to other people. Had her sexual faux pas put her back into the stranger category? She should want to be there. Distance was smart, whereas Derek was trouble.

Fuck it. She liked courting trouble. "That's not all that helpful."

He cracked a smile, and rapped his knuckles against her beer. "She's never rented souls before. She just snatches parts of ones still in people's bodies. Or she did last time she was working Gem City. Best we could tell she did it for her own high and just used the souls herself instead of pawning them."

Callie couldn't even start to process that. It must have shown because Derek added, "You need a few more of those to be able to handle more knowledge."

"Maybe I'm a lightweight." She took a hearty swig.

His laugh was a deep rumble that calmed her like a double of whiskey. As if he'd heard them talking about drinks, the bartender sat two fresh bottles behind them on the bar. Callie reached for her wallet, but Derek's light touch on her wrist stilled the motion.

"I got it," she said, as if she had more than a lonely twenty in her wallet. She needed to quit knocking the beers back, because she'd need groceries before pay day, and owing Derek only made her look more like the kind of woman she didn't want to be. Plus, this was work. What if the Charmer tacked her bar bill onto her indentured servitude? She liked the Derek part of the gig, but the rest scared the shit out of her. The sooner she was done with the Soul Charmer, the better.

"No. Bartender's thanking us for getting that dickhead out of here."

She nodded toward their server. He didn't stop pouring, but inclined his head in kind. "Okay then."

"But, doll, you're already in a bad sitch, so you're going to let me buy."

"I don't like owing people."

He pulled back like she'd slapped him. "I'm not my boss. This ain't a negotiation. You're a hot girl out with me. I buy. No questions."

She bit her lip.

"What?"

The instinct to clear the deck reared. Did he think they were on even ground? Did she? She swallowed the urge. "Thank you." Funny how hard those two words were when you really meant them.

Lounging at the bar and watching the belly dancers begin to pull random patrons from their seats lulled Callie back into her earlier reverie. Mostly. There weren't souls to retrieve tonight. Only her obligation to the Charmer required her to be out with Derek. Though, the confusing kiss was totally non-obligatory. She vowed to make herself useful tonight, though, in the name of shaking off her nerves. Now she, like Derek, eyed the crowd for a resource. She took in the shaking hips—some far superior to others—keeping an eye out for a signature red lip and dark hair. Men used black to describe every shade of very dark hair. The woman could have a rich brown or a so-black-it's-blue hue. In the southwest both were plentiful, so the makeup was going to be her cue.

Watching swaying hips was not the way to cool one's libido. Derek had leaned back on the edge of the bar with his right arm crossing over her back. She rested against it, telling herself it was a reminder that she temporarily worked for men who frightened Ford's goons. That wasn't the whole truth, though. The pressure of his arm offered the heady rush of possibilities.

Falling for a guy, especially in this situation, was dumb. She'd erected walls for a reason. Sex without entanglements was fun, and didn't damage your heart. Dabbling with a man like Derek was idiotic. Complications abounded. Her brother was being held captive by the kind of men who owned slaughterhouses and chop shops. Yet Derek scared those men. He was in league with a man who could literally steal your soul. She was a lapsed Catholic, but that was some straight-up devil shit. Why didn't her body care Derek was nothing but a bad idea?

"You good?" he asked, pushing off from the bar.

Callie, startled, scanned the room. What had she missed? "Um, yeah."

She quirked a brow at his noncommittal grunt. "Need to hit the head."

Leaving her alone went super awesome last time. "Okay."

"They all—" he stopped himself, and started over. "No one will mess with you."

The implications of his words would twist her insides, so she smiled and nodded. Faking it was her forte. Moments like this, she understood Josh's choices. Well, the drugs part. Not the whole stealing from family, lying, and screwing dudes who carried backup weapons. The booby prize for growing up too fast was overthinking everything. Josh looked for angles, ways to cut corners. Callie was the worrier. How long could the box of Cheerios last? When it was gone, what could happen if they stole extra food at school? Threats of expulsion, juvie, and disownment had weighed on her, but never enough to stop her. She hadn't been the stealthiest of thieves at thirteen, but no one had cared. Now she planned ahead, lest her world came crashing down.

Derek stalked his way to the hallway on the other side of the bar, wearing his edgy mood beneath his leather jacket. But then maybe he didn't want to hide it. Who would choose to mess with a stressed out man his size? He did have a reputation to maintain. Callie was on the verge of falling into a mental spiral, contemplating how he'd earned those wary glances he'd been receiving most of the night, when she spotted Bianca.

The curvy brunette wove through the room, lightly touching a person here, making small talk there. Peals of laughter lingered in her stead. She was petite, but even from several feet away Callie could sense the energy she exuded. And just like that, Bianca turned and headed straight for her.

Derek wasn't there to lead the questioning, and Callie didn't carry the same malevolent aura he did. She would be just another stranger to Bianca. Would they miss their opportunity? Should she try this solo?

Bianca waved to the bartender as she approached, and then inclined her head toward Callie as she spoke. "One of what she's having."

"Pretty sure you could have just said beer," Callie said after a moment. "The selection's limited." Small talk hurt her brain, and she clearly wasn't good at it.

"He knows me, and it's not my usual." Of course it wasn't. Her signature drink was something bright pink and adorned with a wedge of fresh fruit.

Callie took another draw on her beer. So much for not knocking them back. Her hands were warm against the brown glass, which is what usually happened when a bottle was mere swigs from empty. But this wasn't a coincidence. It wasn't the beer in her belly. This wasn't simply nervous energy and pent-up arousal. Her fingers went full-on inferno, and she sat the beer on the bar as nonchalantly as she possibly could, right as the label began to singe. Holy shit. It was nothing like what she'd experienced around someone with a borrowed soul inside them before.

Bianca took a single step backward. "You all right?"

The fire in her hands dimmed. Was she? Why was her reaction so different than before? Goosebumps prickled along her arms and legs, as though all the heat from elsewhere in her body had relocated to her hands and pooled in her palms. "Yeah," she said, curling her hands into fists. She could focus with them clenched. Mostly.

"Right on. I don't remember seeing you here before, and I've got a thing for faces." She winked.

"First timer." Squeeze, release, repeat. She rode the edge of panic, but maintained control.

"Oh, it's a blast."

This had to be soul magic at play. This was ten times as intense as in the Charmer's shop. The heat was overwhelming, but she tried to cling to the Soul Charmer's promise that she couldn't be injured. If she had taken to believing him, the heat must have short-circuited her brain. Callie's thoughts ran over one another, too much input, too much sensation, and too many chances to fuck up. She had a job to do. A job she had to keep in order to get Josh back. She focused on the other woman and not the twin blazes forming inside her hands. What could she learn from this woman? "I was looking at the shop next door. The massage place. Have you been there?"

Bianca started to narrow her eyes, but stopped herself before too much of her skepticism showed. "I work there, actually."

Callie sucked in a breath, hard and fast. Could she get a soul for cheaper here? Maybe Tess or Bianca could help her. Was there a way out from under the Charmer, where she could help her brother more quickly? Ignoring the bundle of flames simmering within her palms—the sensation was alarming, but not painful—she forced herself to be pleasant. "Small world. So what's this 'chakra massage' thing I read about on the flyer?"

Bianca deflected. Her back-alley deal tone would have been more appropriate at The Fall than at a belly-dancing bar. "I just do your old-fashioned massage and aromatherapy. It's great for allergies."

"Oh, okay." She didn't need to have her sinuses tweaked. She needed a bonus soul, a whole lot less violent threats in her life, and . . . holy hell, her hands were stiff. She was able to open them, which was a modicum improvement from when they were frozen, but her skin was akin to a kindled log with blackened pieces curling at the edges and golden embers smoldering beneath. Oh, shit. Immolation was un-fucking-acceptable. Seeing her hands singe and blacken with heat was definitely new. What the hell was happening? The pain wasn't there, but her hands felt impossibly full of dangerous energy, like they were so ablaze they'd inflict serious damage. If it were real, she'd be screaming right? Was she hallucinating? Was this another of the Charmer's tricks? He'd said she wouldn't be injured, but he was also probably a fucking liar.

"You've got some magic in you, don't you?" Bianca's tone might have sounded sultry to those within earshot, but Callie knew otherwise. The fire burning in her hands exploded as the woman edged closer.

Making poor decisions because of her fear was the old Callie. A few years ago, the fear of knowing what Bianca wanted from her would have been too much; she would have melted down. But that was the Old Callie.

"I'm not the only one," she ground out, almost gritting her teeth. Anger and pain fused, pushing Callie into Alpha Cat mode. This fire wouldn't take her. Her hands weren't really scorched. They couldn't be. Others in the restaurant had clearly noticed something was going on, but no one was charging toward them with a fire extinguisher. They had simply given the two women a wide berth. Even the bartender was nowhere to be seen. Which was good, because Callie didn't need another drink. She needed some god-damn useful information. The sooner she had leverage, the sooner she could be done with the goddamn soul-detector fingers.

"Why did you come here?" Bianca asked.

"I heard Tess had something to do with why I keep running into people who set off my magic. Thought she might be able to give me some insight," Callie imbued the words with confidence, but stifled a shudder at taking ownership of the magic the Charmer had forced into her.

Bianca sneered. "Tess didn't make your hands like that. She's not going to touch you."

Callie reached her limit—of the pain, of the bullshit, of Bianca making her hands go firestorm. She clamped a hand against Bianca's shoulder like they were old friends and she'd told a hilarious joke. Bianca's yelp earned a few glances, but no one moved. Her dreams of quick fixes to her soul magic woes were dashed. Callie pressed her hand more firmly against Bianca and the heat leapt from her hands, an acrid scent of melting rayon filling the space between them as Bianca's dress began to smoke under the heat. "Care to tell me why everyone who fails to return a soul to its rightful owner—" she couldn't bring herself to say the Charmer's name "—has your boss's name on their lips?"

Bianca's nostrils flared as Callie's hand funneled more and more heat into her shoulder. "She's doing this city a service. We will be purified," she said through gritted teeth.

Suddenly, Derek yanked Callie's hand away from Bianca. She hadn't even heard him return. Great. This magic was screwing with her mind now, too. She shook her hands as if she could fling the magic away like droplets of water. It didn't work. Derek examined her hands, which were blackened, but thankfully free of melted fabric. He nodded once, some finite decision made, and put his back to her.

"Back up," he said to Bianca.

"You know her?" she spat at him, even as she complied. Callie's brain had fried upon seeing her seared skin, and it was still rebooting. She did her damnedest to ignore her hands and tried to focus on their conversation.

Each step she took in the opposite direction eased the pain in Callie's hands. Her skin slowly faded back to normal, the embers snuffed.

"Yeah, I do, and if you retaliate against her, there will be consequences." Perhaps turning that broad back of his to her had been a way to protect her. Again. He had to be getting sick of saving Callie at this point.

Derek wasn't all threats, though. He had the bartender dig out a first aid kit and told him to tend to Bianca's burn. A fount of information about Tess, the source of his current work stress, was there for the taking, but he ignored the lure.

Callie's ire was ebbing, which let fresh waves of panic and regret crash against her mind. Still better than looking at her hands. Derek didn't avoid them, though. He lifted her hands near his face, inspecting them so closely it bordered on palm reading. She couldn't see them past his bulky fingers. Her skin no longer tingled, and the fires had been snuffed. She'd seen them *charred*, though. Finally, he relinquished them with a heavy huff. All signs of burnt flesh were gone from her palms.

"Let's go." He pitched his voice low.

"H-h-how?" She held her unblemished hands in front of her face, rotating them for full inspection. Had it been a trick? Magic tricks were with cards or coins, not turning women's hands into campfire logs.

"You're okay. It can't hurt you, remember?"

So the Soul Charmer hadn't lied to her. It still didn't make sense. "I *saw* it, though. Felt it. Her—her shoulder . . ."

"She'll heal. I'll explain, but not here. We need to go."

Callie's hushed tone was less about privacy and more about shaky vocal cords. "Don't you need to talk to her?"

His sharp shake of his head was a no and a suggestion to shut up in a single move. Derek wrapped his arm around Callie and escorted her out.

It was for the best; Callie would have made a shitty belly dancer.

CHAPTER TEN

The earlier fire in Callie's belly had disappeared along with the flames in her hands. Bravery came much easier when the consequences of your actions could be ignored. That's what adrenaline was for, to blind us from peering toward the future. The churning worry in her gut shifted its focus from what kissing Derek meant for her future to how big the Bianca blowout would be. Violence wasn't in her handbag. Yet she was the one who'd escalated the interaction with Bianca. She hadn't intended to burn the other woman. Intent required forethought.

She'd melted fabric to another person. Callie's stomach pitched and she swallowed the result of her guilt. Derek parked the bike, and she climbed off quickly. Sucking down quick breaths of clean air had to clear her head, right?

"You're not going to puke, are you?" That Derek, he was all class.

She scowled at him as she shoved her helmet into his hand.

"I'm surprised you didn't take me home," she muttered. She was even more thankful he hadn't taken her to the Charmer. Instead, he'd brought her to the outskirts of Gem City. They'd climbed in elevation, and the thinner air was actually calming her. The empty road and huge spaces between buildings around them would make it a great place to lose someone. Permanently. Her heartbeat started to sprint as her thoughts turned morbid.

Derek's brows pinched together as though to hold back his menace. He scrubbed an open hand against his face, but it couldn't siphon the emotion. "Too much to talk about."

"Talking?" She didn't hide her skepticism. She lit a woman up. Exposed them. If the consequences were merely a chat, why were they out in BFE?

"You took it upon yourself to question Bianca, who you know nothing about, without me." He flung his hands wide, measuring the problem. The hard chest she'd pressed against earlier rose and fell rapidly. The cotton of his shirt strained. She knew the feeling.

"She found me. What was I supposed to do?"

"You couldn't have just made nice with her until I got back?"

"You couldn't have warned me my hands might be on fucking fire when she was around?"

He rocked on his heels, an unbidden reaction to the invisible slap, and then slowly dropped his hands to his side.

"Yeah. Want to explain how my formerly-normal hands—that now turn to ice around soul magic users—pulled some seventh-circle shit next to Bianca?"

He wrapped a hand around his nape. It wasn't going to warm his brain stem or generate better answers, but Callie kept that to herself. The move jutted his elbow in the air like a leather-clad flag. As long as it wasn't a rallying signal, she'd wait. "Well? Any bright ideas there?"

"It's the same thing as last time." Regret twisted his features.

The big man winced, and her chest tightened, but that didn't change the situation. Her voice lost its edge. "I'm going to need more than that, Derek."

He nodded. "Can we go inside first?"

None of the small adobe buildings surrounding them looked particularly inviting. "Where exactly?"

He hiked a thumb toward the building behind him. "Maria's."

The restaurant name was familiar, but she never had reason to spend time in the city's outer edges. The little restaurant was more akin to a home from the outside, but as they neared it she saw there was a hand-painted sign on the door reading: Maria's Cantina.

A woman not much older than Callie led them down two sets of stairs and past whitewashed walls covered with license plates and painting of cowboys with ten-gallon hats to a table with tile inlay. She handed over two laminated menus. "What can I get you to drink? House margarita?"

Callie's stomach rebelled at even the mention. "Water's fine."

The hint of a smile played at the corner of Derek's mouth. "House is fine for me. Rocks. No salt."

The waitress snatched a leftover newspaper from their table and then left quickly to fetch their drinks. She didn't need to see the headline to know police had found another body missing hands. Fucking Ford and his threats. They followed her even to down-home restaurants on the outskirts of town.

Callie fought to stay in the moment. "I didn't peg you as a margarita man." Her judgment was real. Last time he'd ordered one, he hadn't taken a sip.

"It's the best drink they've got. Plus, it's become a tequila kind of night."

In the hierarchy of booze-as-medicine-for-emotional-woes, it clearly went beer, wine, rum, vodka, tequila, and then whiskey. However, depending on your defining experiences, one could, possibly, swap the top three into almost any order. Regardless, Derek was bypassing the beer and going straight to the hard stuff, and that didn't bode well.

Callie shrugged. Not much she could do about it now. "Do I need to wait until you've ingested more booze to get an answer about my newfound magical ability?"

"She'll be back quick." He offered her a quick smile.

Callie glared. His charm wasn't working now.

"Fine," he grumbled. "The magic is functioning as it did before. You're just detecting something different."

"'Different'? Derek, I like you, but come the fuck on."

He grinned at her, more focused on the compliment than Callie's exasperation. "What?"

"You owe me more than some cryptic answer. Your Charmer changed me, and now I'm playing a perpetual game of hot/cold, and unlike you, I'm finding it pretty goddamn unamusing."

"True enough." He paused while the waitress delivered their drinks, nudging the pink and green sugar skulls adorning the table to the side, and nodded when they admitted they hadn't looked at their menus yet. When she left, he continued. "Remember I told you how the people with less-than-whole souls make your hands go cold?"

"Yeah, but it doesn't explain the fiery hands."

"It kind of does." His teasing tone might have made her fluttery another time. However, Callie's bullshit tank was full. Either her unwavering stare would crack him, or the tequila would. Either way, she'd cling to her dark mood until he fessed up.

"The opposite thing is happening," he finally added when it was clear she wasn't about to speak again until he shared more. "I told you before, the heat is a reaction to too much soul magic."

"That wasn't just heat. I swear to God there was literally fire inside my hands. My skin was damn near flayed." She'd have nightmares remembering how true it'd been in the moment, even though all signs of the earlier carnage had disappeared.

He sighed. It was a heavy, masculine sound. She could bewilder this man. Callie softened enough to take a sip of her water and settle into her chair. "That's because Bianca wasn't your normal soul renter," he said.

"What's so special about her?" Did it sound like she was pouting? Callie had to snap out of that.

"To cause that kind of reaction in you? She'd have to have more than two souls in her. Might explain why she's always moving." He tacked on the last sentence absent-mindedly.

Callie snatched it. "'Always moving'? Why?"

"It's hard enough getting two souls to share a single body. Imagine a walk-in closet as your living space. If you had one roommate, it'd be all asses and elbows. Uncomfortable, but endurable. Now shove four people in the same space. Even breathing would get hard in those cramped quarters."

Derek didn't strike her as the kind of man who shared spaces at all. Each time she wrapped her arms around him on the motorcycle, his body stiffened, and not in a "touch my dick" kind of way. Only after a moment and a deep breath could he begin relax into her presence.

Undeterred, Callie asked, "What does that have to do with her moving?"

She'd have nightmares about what she did to Bianca. The more she could diminish her guilt with facts, the better.

"We've got bigger problems than the stupid shit Bianca does," Derek said.

She rolled her eyes.

"What?" Derek asked, half amused, half irritated.

"We were there specifically for her. So, I'm calling your bluff there. We need to talk about her."

"About what she knows about Tess," he corrected in a patronizing tone. He consistently made her blood boil, but not always for the best reasons.

"Maybe the reason why Bianca's been maxing out her body on souls is related." Callie's words were meant to taunt, but Derek eyes brightened.

"You just might be on to something, doll." He scratched his chin, and a few moments later, he nodded. She looked down to finally peruse the menu; an entire page was dedicated to enchiladas. Even in the short time she'd known him, she had picked up that silence often pulled more truth out of Derek than cajoling. If one could base such an assessment on mere days together.

The waitress returned while Derek was still lost in thought, so Callie ordered Christmas-style chicken enchiladas for them both, with the waitress's promise it was the thing everyone ordered. Her sides began to ache as she clenched her stomach. Faking calm and being relaxed were two different things. She could only pretend for so long. Gulping half the glass of water in front of her didn't help, but she wasn't willing to drop her guard enough to steal a swig of Derek's golden margarita.

The restaurant wasn't loud enough to drown all the unanswered questions still bouncing around her head. Maybe they'd learned how to swim. "What's it feel like to rent a soul?" She might be shitty at small talk, but she could offer top-notch random outbursts.

He snapped out of his thoughts. "I hear it's different for everyone."

"What's it like for you?"

He avoided eye contact. "Never done it."

"How can you work for him, if you've never used his services?"

His attention snapped to her. Bright eyes met her questioning gaze. "I'm good at my job. I don't need to dabble in the magic to make people give souls back."

"Sorry. I didn't mean it like that. I'm working in exchange for one, so—"

"—so you can't possibly fathom why anyone would want to be in this world if they weren't hooked on borrowing souls?"

She hadn't meant that. Or had she? His words rang true to her. She sucked in her bottom lip, and he watched it possessively. Heat zinged down her spine. "You've got a marketable skill. You leverage it," she said simply, "I'm not judging." Well, she *had* been, but given tonight's events, she was willing to adjust her view.

His responding grunt rumbled from deep in his chest and he delivered it with a scowl. She was sure she'd dug four feet of her own grave by this point. Olive branch time. "Why does having extra souls—like *beaucoup* extra souls—make Bianca move more?"

Derek indulged in his margarita, taking a long sip. Tequila might actually help this conversation along. "All those souls are looking to escape. You can placate them with contact with others."

Callie thought back to earlier in the night, forced herself to remember Bianca before the flames, before the melted fabric stench had lodged itself in her sinuses. "So that's why she was touching everyone in that restaurant. Did she hurt them?"

"I don't really know," he admitted, as though the words sounded foreign to him. "We'd have to talk to the Charmer. But I wonder if she's picking up some of Tess's abilities."

There had to be a way to do this without talking to the Soul Charmer. Callie racked her brain, attempting to remember what made Tess so special without showcasing yet another inadequacy and asking.

"She steals people's energy," he supplied.

She nodded as if she'd already known. "You think she was taking hits of energy off those people tonight?"

"I don't think anything. Just spitballing."

"Even if she was, that doesn't explain why Tess is ripping off the Charmer." Callie couldn't imagine not being terrified of the man.

She'd held her own only because it was that or die. Badassery came easy when the alternative required a pine box.

To that same end, did the Soul Charmer really need her and Derek traipsing around after this crazy lady and her minion? "Why doesn't he just take care of her?" Callie asked.

"He doesn't have to." He responded so quickly she did a double take.

"Would he make you . . . " she trailed off, not wanting to offend him by finishing the thought.

"It's not like that," he snapped. "I've got hard lines. I don't permanently damage anyone. Ever. I might break a bone here or there, but I won't have someone's death on my record."

"O-kay."

He groaned. "Now I have to apologize. Damn it. Tonight's fucked. Look, magic is crazy complicated. If the Charmer attacks Tess without knowing exactly what's up, the consequences could be seriously nasty. He'll be the one to enact them, though. Plus, soul renting is a small world and people have long memories. We don't know enough about who she might be working with to act."

"Is that what we're doing? Gathering info so the Charmer can know when to strike?" What did that mean? Was he planning to kill her? Every time Callie thought it couldn't get any worse . . .

"Yeah, doll. We're the foot soldiers on this one. Even you, with your magic hands." His melodic teasing voice pleased her more this time. He responded to her genuine smile in kind.

"Well, when you give a girl weapons—"

"We're going to talk about that. Not now, because I'm too exhausted, but I won't forget."

Of course he wouldn't.

— CHAPTER ELEVEN —

ob bosses were supposed to be scary, intimidating men, but Ford looked nothing like the Mafiosos from the movies. His kind features were better suited for the best-friend role in a teen comedy. His lack of imposing stature was part of what made him so terrifying. He stood a few inches taller than Callie, and carried a bit of muscle.

The ones who didn't ring alarms were the most dangerous. Serial killers slipped under the radar the same way Ford did. His vicious side made him unforgettable. Once you associated that slightly upturned nose and dimples with a man who collected severed body parts as keepsakes from those who crossed him, he lost any adorable, best-friend shield one might have mistakenly given him.

Callie's neighbors might not think an early thirties man in a button-down shirt loitering in the parking lot outside was much cause for concern, but Callie had to fight the instinct to scream when she spotted Ford leaning against her car in the morning.

Derek had brought Callie home late the night before. Agreeing to postpone making game plans until the next day had placated Callie's overwhelmed emotions at the time, but in the hazy morning it looked more like a misstep, a rookie move. She'd burned a person last night. With magic. She didn't know if she'd see the Soul Charmer about the fuck up today or if Derek could keep it a secret for her. Her gut sank. Unlikely. Now, in addition to dreading quality time with the Charmer, she was going to have to talk to the man holding her brother.

And with only a single cup of coffee under her belt.

Faking forgetting her wallet inside the house wasn't going to fool Ford. She'd taken the last two antacids in her apartment already, but this anxiety lit her stomach anew. She locked her front door and jogged down the stairs without meeting Ford's gaze once. His appraisal scrubbed against her regardless. She managed not to squirm.

"Think this is the first time I've seen you in normal clothes," he said as way of greeting. She'd prefer he ignored her attire altogether, especially after the insinuations from Nate last night.

Despite her aversion to small talk, she'd do it for Ford. Pleasantries had to be better than the alternatives when speaking with the man who threatened to butcher your lone sibling. "Scrubs are only for work. It's my day off."

"Ah. So you've got time to talk with me then." He didn't bother making it a question. She wasn't going anywhere until he let her, and they both knew that.

"I have errands to run before my other gig starts," she said as a subtle reminder she was working toward helping him. "What do you need?"

"Heard you had a run in with one of my guys last night."

"I saw him, but I wouldn't really classify it as more than that." Mentioning the sexual innuendo and suggestions she should make money on her back to Ford wouldn't help her, but she still wished he'd rein Nate in. She'd pick the weird woman spying on her over a Nate encounter any day.

"Nate would."

She balked.

"You're surprised?" He shrugged. "He said you were on a date."

"I told him I wasn't on a date."

"Said instead of thinking about your poor brother—who, for the moment, I am keeping safe and whole—you were drinking and getting awfully cozy with some guy."

The threat punched her in the throat. Her inhale squeaked to a halt. Would Ford start giving her bits of Josh if he thought she wasn't sticking to their agreement? Would he kill her? Her mind scrambled for the right response, while her lungs pulled several quick breaths to get her breathing back on track. Zeroing in on Nate's fault, Callie asked, "Did Nate tell you who I was with?"

The mob leader arched a brow, but stayed planted against her driver's side door. "Does it matter?"

"It sure mattered to him last night. I was with Derek, the big guy who works for the Soul Charmer."

Acid continued to eat away at her stomach lining, but Callie's confidence grew when Ford let out a short string of curses.

"I was there on business for the Charmer. He's not giving me a soul until I finish out this bit."

"Yeah. I know." Ford had probably talked to the Charmer himself. He was the type of guy who would be chatty with the local soul dealer.

"So Josh is okay?" She couldn't hide her fear anymore. Her mind had never been as abused as it had been in recent weeks. Ford checking up on her was the pathetic icing on the stale gingerbread house.

"He's fine. As long as you're holding up your part of the deal, your brother stays whole."

His choice of words didn't exactly reassure Callie. One could be black and blue from head to toe and still be considered whole.

Saying so wasn't going to make Josh any safer, though. "Okay. Thanks. Is—"

"No more questions about Josh. He's useful, and as long as you're useful, he gets to keep breathing." Ford cocked his head to the right and let out a sigh before continuing. "Have you looked at that police substation yet?"

Thinking about the next part of her parlay with Ford had been low on her to-do list. Stealing when she was younger had meant food and safety for her and Josh. This protected them, too, but there was a big difference between filching perishables from the grocery store or cash from unattended purses at movie theaters, and stealing crime scene investigator files, and she wasn't ready to be a criminal again. "No, I thought you were going to provide instructions. I'm sure there is someone better for this job . . . "

He scrunched his face and sucked his front teeth. "Don't try me. You're doing it. I'll make sure you get the building plans, and we'll let you know where the DNA files are kept."

"What if these files don't show you what you want?"

"You worry about getting us the files. Your face doesn't show on police handouts. That's your skill here. My guys can handle the rest."

Callie didn't normally stand on the moral high ground, which apparently made her prime Soul Charmer bait, but even from her stance of "don't be a dick," what Ford tasked her with was wicked. Helping his crew understand how police were investigating crimes where evidence and DNA had been obscured by soul magic was a cliff dive from her moral middle ground. She and Josh would be cozy together at rock bottom.

Ford hadn't budged from his lazy spot against her car. If she owned a classic car, Ford might have pulled off the signature tough-guy stance against it. Instead she was a little worried his right foot was going to knock off the rubber detailing on her door. It wasn't essential, but there were few parts of her car that held together. She'd like to keep it as intact as possible.

"You seemed stressed," Ford said with sincerity that would have fooled her mom. It didn't fool Callie.

Was he trying to get under her skin? She was almost fed up enough to list off all the sources of her stress, with his threats at the very top, but self-preservation won out. "It's my constant state of being." She wished it weren't true.

"I can hook you up with a little oblivion, to take the edge off." He pulled a small plastic bag from his pocket. She wanted to vomit at the sight of the crystalline white inside it.

"My edges are better sharp." Understatement of the year. If she was going to continue mingling with the likes of him and the Soul Charmer, she needed to be a goddamn honed human dagger.

He laughed and slid the drug back in his pocket. "Maybe they are." The metal groaned as he pushed off Callie's car, but thankfully it remained in one piece. "You change your mind, call me. Otherwise, I'll be in touch once you've gotten that soul."

Sure. As creepy as the Soul Charmer was, he was better to work for than Ford. The Charmer had turned her into a magic tool without her consent. Shitty, yes. But Ford was blackmailing her into using soul magic to break into a police lab. He wouldn't shell out the cash she needed to rent the soul, but he had no problem giving her free narcotics. At least with the Charmer, he didn't hide the fact that he was a scary, shady fuck. Ford, flitting from friend to fiend, cut deeper, and he did it harder and faster. He'd bleed you before you even noticed the bloodied knife in his hand.

Callie hadn't gone into work on her day off since her hospital days. She'd learned quickly that a medical assistant dropping a book off to a friend could get volunteered for an extra shift pretty easily. Her current job was less likely to be short-staffed, but the risk of extra hours without extra pay was still real. However, her morning chat with Ford scared her into the employee entrance of Cedar Retirement Home.

The sooner she completed his task, the better. The masseuse she met the other day did chakra balancing. That had to be close enough to Tess's siphoning of souls—sucking chi, Derek had called it—for her to know the other woman. Tracking down Tess was now her best option. Either she'd snag a soul from her and knock Ford's task out early, or she'd turn Tess over to the Soul Charmer in exchange for expediting her soul rental. Both were nasty options, but another run-in with Ford or one of his goons was much nastier.

"Callie? What are you doing here? Did I goof the schedule?" Louisa's eyes widened as she entered the kitchen, but she didn't miss a beat chopping cilantro and swiping it into a large pot on the stove.

"No, I'm not working today." Her smile was wan, but Louisa pretended not to notice.

"That's good, because I don't think my scrubs would fit you." She pulled a tray out from the oven. The lemon and basil notes of her marinade wafted across the room. Callie's stomach rumbled.

"You know if any of the massage girls are here today?"

"A few of them." She glanced at the clock. "Should still be down at the reception station. Most start work at nine."

"Thanks, Lou."

"You need me to pray for you?" The laughter in her words was false. Louisa would pray for her regardless.

"Couldn't hurt."

Prayers were necessary by the time Callie reached the reception desk. Two of the masseuses were there. Their faces were familiar, but neither were the woman she'd talked to outside the ward. If only asking favors came as naturally to her as it did to Josh. She opened with a "Hey," and it went downhill from there. Her palms grew warmer with each step she took toward them, for starters.

The women replied with rote greetings and returned to their own conversation. Their chatter dimmed when they realized Callie hadn't moved along, but at least Callie's hands hadn't gone inferno again.

"I'm trying to find a woman who specializes in chakra balancing," she interjected. It was as close to the truth as she dared.

One of the women, petite with dirty blonde hair tucked into a loose ponytail, shrugged and said, "I can do that."

"Thanks, but I'm actually looking for a specific woman. She was here the other day, but I didn't catch her name." After enduring a pair of blank stares, she added, "She offered to help me."

The taller massage therapist scoffed. Her thick eyebrows were two shades darker than her brown locks. "That was then. We heard what you did to Bianca."

"B-B-Bianca?" What. The. Hell.

"Small world. You burned our friend."

They knew. People miles away knew what she'd done. Her hands didn't burn now, but the memory scalded her. "I don't know what—"

"Yes you do."

The fight-or-flight instinct reared inside her, but instead of incinerating shirts and skin, Callie ran her mouth. "In that case, I need to talk to Tess. Do you know her?"

The short one piped up again. "Sure. You apparently don't though. She's the chakra balancer you said you knew."

Those simple words packed quite a punch. Callie's solar plexus vibrated as the wind rushed from her. Not only had she already met Tess, but the same woman who was stealing from the Soul Charmer of Gem City also knew Ford. All the bad guys wanted a piece of Callie, it seemed. Couldn't they put their battles aside until after she rescued her brother?

"Can you put me in touch with her?" she asked, ignoring the women's scathing tones.

"If she wanted to talk with you, she'd find you. Right now she's busy taking care of Bianca," the short one said.

"I'd worry about yourself for now," the other tacked on.

If only it were so easy. Returning to Plan A was a whole lot harder after you'd pissed off someone who controlled souls. Tess might not be as powerful as the Charmer, but magic was scary. So was the unknown. Tess was both, and Callie and Derek needed to find her fast before the situation went from awful to unbearable.

Callie had agreed to let Derek meet her at her apartment. Each day she spent with him, the more she understood him. He took his job seriously, and that meant protecting her was paramount. He had no idea how much she needed his protection now.

When he'd dropped her off the night before, he'd referred to her aging vehicle as an eyesore and not-so-politely suggested it didn't fit into the stealthy logistics required for this job. She thought it had less to do with sneaking around—they rumbled up everywhere on a noisy motorcycle—and more to do with control. They'd spent plenty of time talking about that, but hadn't talked about the kiss, even though when she'd wrapped her legs on either side of him to ride home she swore she heard him groan.

The morning visit from Ford and subsequent Tess revelation had stopped her from obsessing over Derek and her flamethrower hands for the better part of the day. Nothing like an in-person chat with the murderous king of local criminals to send you into a panicky spiral of self-doubt and shame. Family woes plus mob bosses equaled stomachaches. She splurged on two bottles of Tums at the store. The extra cash she had to spend was worth it to keep her insides intact.

Derek's thunderous knock at the door was a relief. There wouldn't be dancing and homemade enchiladas that night, but Callie would be one day closer to saving Josh.

"You look nice," he said when she opened the door.

She hadn't fancied up for a night of hunting delinquent soul renters, but she did succumb to the need to put on some mascara and swapped out her standard simple studs for red and white polka dot button earrings. Ford had offered her oblivion by way of powder today. She'd rather reach peak distraction through a different, more natural kind of bliss. The heat of her kiss with Derek might have been one sided for all she knew, but she put a little effort into tonight's look, just in case she was wrong. A few strands had escaped her ponytail, though, and she smoothed them behind her ear. "Thanks."

Derek sat at the far end of the couch, and immediately sprawled across a cushion and a half. It was her favorite place to read books. She didn't ask him to move, though. "I asked a couple of the other guys at the Charmer's about people reneging on their rentals, and then not having souls to retrieve when we get there to collect."

"It's happening to everyone?" Callie sank onto the other end of the couch, pulling one leg up and wrapping her arms around her knee. Hugging yourself was underrated.

"Thank God," he muttered. Derek continued, louder. "Yeah, it's not just us. Weird thing is, they've all been people who have rented from us for a long time."

"And they have to be tracked down?"

"Most of the time," he let a little chagrin coat his words. "Some are junkies, others get caught up in the thrill of whatever it is they do while doubling up. A few are just asshole crooks."

"Couldn't you just let them keep the souls a little longer and bill them for another round?"

"It's a cash business, but that kind of a system wouldn't work for long, regardless. Plus, they get a better fix if we freshen the goods. Rented souls aren't meant to be permanently bound to another's body. Fucked up shit can happen."

Callie wasn't ready to know what those consequences entailed. "So it's a safety thing."

"I wouldn't go that far. It's a maintenance thing." He shrugged, and then continued. "Usually they don't put up a fight about giving it back. We just have to come to them."

"You make it sound like you don't mind." The familiar way he spoke about them reminded her of the way she talked about Josh. A hassle, but one you loved despite the drama.

"They're a big part of my job, and I'm not all blood and broken bones, you know."

"I know," she whispered, as if the non-violent side of him was their secret.

"Not sure why the ones who come to us the most are the ones bailing."

His confiding tone made Callie move closer to him on the couch. She rested her hand on his knee, and he sighed.

"We should find out what Tess offers them," she suggested. Oblivion? It had to be more than her kind demeanor.

"Well, she's making it a lot harder to make them pay their back rent the next time they come in." Derek's sour tone suggested maybe there was lost commission, too. At least the length of her indentured servitude wasn't predicated on dollars earned.

"Sure, but what are they going to do when they need another soul? You said these people are renting all the time from the Charmer." The more Callie invested in Derek, the more she was bound to the Charmer. Danger was becoming normal.

"Tess is already stealing from us. It won't surprise me if she starts selling, too." Defeatism didn't suit Derek.

"Bianca didn't mention selling anything."

His wry smile should have worried her more, but Callie liked seeing him conniving. "Oh, so you're ready to talk about your friendly chat with Bianca?" he asked.

Callie sidestepped the opportunity to talk about her burning Tess's subordinate. "She said the goal is to 'purify' everyone in Gem City. Is that woo-woo speak or does it make sense to you?"

"Little of both. We need more information."

"Then let's go get some." She could help her protector. Did that make her strong? Or at least stronger? Pummeling the bad guys wasn't in her repertoire—as long as some seared skin didn't count—but she could help fix this problem.

"You're damn chipper tonight." Bemused Derek was more fun than the sullen one.

"I'm ninety percent sure Tess selling souls would equate to some sort of magical war. I don't want to know if such things exist. So, yeah, I'm here to help."

He could throw some mean side eye. "Just to avoid seeing more magic?"

And maybe to hang out with him, too. "I'm a shitty soldier."

His belly laugh shook the couch. Callie smiled and squeezed his thigh. "You underestimate yourself, doll. You did light that girl up last night."

She winced, but he smiled and continued. "That's not a jab at you. We do what we have to around here. Keeping her at a distance was the right thing."

Scarring a person wasn't ever going to be right, but she didn't roll her eyes at his sincere attempt to comfort her. Callie's morals might have slid down the bell curve a bit, but she hadn't completely lost her grip on them, no matter what the Soul Charmer suggested. Still, Derek's approval ebbed her guilt. Just a smidge. "Thanks."

"I'm not up for a turf war, either, so we should get going." He checked his watch, and added, "Joey should be getting home in about twenty. His wife usually shows up about an hour from now."

"This is good?"

Derek made the move of raising and lowering his broad shoulders look so simple. She'd had her hands on them. They were much more stone-like than his nonchalant shrug projected. "He's a real pious type. Uses souls to pretend it's not really him tapping hookers."

"I've got a cousin like that."

"We all do. Joey will talk because he doesn't want his wife catching any hint he's been using souls, let alone what they're being used to do."

Derek laid his hand atop Callie's. It still rested on his thigh, and the contact sent her heartbeat into overdrive, the sound pounding in her ears. He gave it a quick squeeze—not the tug to pull her closer she'd been hoping for—and then let go.

Once he stood, he reached into his back pocket. The flask's black stone glinted even in the dim light from her single, 40-watt lamp. She accepted it without a word. When her thumb brushed across the onyx, all her pores expanded at once as a rush of adrenaline coursed through her. Derek helped her with her coat. Its satiny interior was heaven. She wriggled more than necessary as her arms delighted in the sensation. At least, until Derek's fingers brushed the side of her neck. She'd been wrong about heaven. This was more than turning flush—her skin positively danced with energy and heat.

The change in her was obvious, and uncontrollable. Magic was a demanding mistress, and Callie didn't yet know the rules. She rolled her head from side to side, as though she could cool her desire. She needed power over this. Derek loomed from behind. He no longer touched her, but she sensed him regardless. His breath fluttered past her ear in slow, even bursts.

Space from him might allow her to rein this in. She edged a little closer to the door, but not the full step that might suggest an invitation to be pressed up against the cheap wood. Letting go of the flask in her pocket to wipe the fine mist of sweat on her brow was eerily difficult, but once her thumb left the smooth stone, the intense rush left her. Being sandwiched between Derek and the door still held great appeal, but she was no longer on the sexual razor's edge. She swiped the back of her hand across her forehead, and then grabbed the doorknob. Cold wind rushed into her apartment. The crisp air gave her a little more control, the ability to hide her almost-unhealthy attraction to Derek.

He held her scarf out. "You're going to need this tonight." Was his throat raw, or was she imagining things?

He didn't make any extra efforts to touch her as they walked to the bike. He had to have been aware of how close she'd been to making a move. If only he would give her a sign that he wanted her to, it would alleviate some of her stress.

Ford might have assumed her harried appearance earlier was the result of worrying about her brother, and having to deal with his kind of people. Earlier that day was the first time she'd wondered if this attraction to Derek wasn't also playing a big part. She pursed her lips as she strapped on her helmet. Her desire for him was real. This wasn't a trick of the Soul Charmer. That didn't make it a good idea, and it didn't mean the magical world around them wasn't complicating the matter.

Their relationship—whatever it was—was ideal while they rode his motorcycle. They didn't have to talk, for one. As much as Callie appreciated solid boundaries and knowing where she stood, she was terrified of those conversations, of rejection. Derek couldn't reject her over the sound of the motor and the wind whipping around them. They could both take comfort in one another's touch without it getting weird. They didn't need to talk about why her hands were wrapped around his waist, fingers just above his belt buckle. It was for safety. He'd told her to press against him to avoid the bulk of the wind. Maybe it was bullshit, but it didn't matter. His warmth assuaged her fears, and the mix of leather and clean soap was so perfectly Derek it urged her to squeeze her legs a little tighter against his. The vibrations from the bike put them on the same frequency while they embraced. It was a simple joy, and Callie decided on the ride to quit thinking about it and simply enjoy the way his body was melting to hers.

He stiffened as they slowed near a duplex with a manicured lawn on the north side of Gem City. Gone were the tile accents on adobe buildings and the fractured brickwork of downtown. The streets were brighter here, well-lit enough that she could spot the in-ground sprinkler systems spitting water on grass that shouldn't grow in the desert. Derek had always parked at least a half block away from their target. Not this time. He was making his presence as obvious as possible from the outside. Joey would not only want them done talking by the time his wife returned, Derek pointed out, he'd want that hulking black bike off the street as well.

Derek's look—the leather, the motorcycle, the muscles—was inherently threatening, and to a degree it was posturing, but he could back it up. Lord, had he proved that. However, Callie knew he'd rather not if given the out. A softer side was buried beneath all that mean. She was attracted to more than the man's broad shoulders and scarred knuckles, more than the soft way he touched her with roughened fingers. His street smarts were a damn big part of the reason she was locked on him. Callie nodded to the unbidden thought.

If the knock Derek used at her place was thunderous, the bang of his fist against Joey's door was positively booming. She glanced at the eaves, half expecting the house to shake. His knock must have been equally recognizable within the house, as the door flashed open seconds later.

Joey waved them in quickly. He peeked out the door after they stepped inside, as if he couldn't do anything if neighbors were watching. He'd foregone standard Southwestern tile for plush carpeting in the dare-to-drink-wine shade of white. Family pictures covered one wall. Callie ignored the faces in the frames, more focused on the fact her fingers had heated and stiffened as she passed Joey.

He had the air of the type of guy people looked forward to seeing at the high school reunion. His square jaw and overall build made Callie think he'd played football, but if he had, the years away from daily practice had made him a bit doughy around the middle. His time escaping his problems with another person's soul shoved behind his sternum had left its marks, too. The ashen tinge of his skin and the hollow look of his eyes were hard to miss now that Callie knew the signs of soul rental.

"Have a seat," Joey said, extending his arm toward the couch right next to the front door.

Derek ignored him. If their host wanted to be comfortable, he'd have to start talking. Derek wasn't about to let him have the edge. Callie followed his lead, and they walked toward a dining area. An Algebra II textbook rested at one end of the table. That explained the Toros pullover Joey wore. He had a kid at Gem City North High. Callie'd gone to South. They hadn't been allowed to bring their textbooks home. Not that she was jealous. She had much bigger fish to fry than memories of poor school funding.

"You forget something?" Derek asked, without looking at Joey. He ran a finger along the spines of the books on a shelf. The power shift was heady. He was doing it to affect Joey, not her. She needed to remember she was one of the badasses here, too.

"I've been slammed at work. I meant to get down there—"

"You don't look particularly busy right now."

"Sarah's going to be back soon," he pleaded. He was a junkie, only his addiction was to filling his chest with another's soul. Pathetic.

"Give it up, then."

"I don't have time to go now. Tomorrow morning."

"No need. She can take it now."

Callie pulled her shoulders back as pride soared through her. She was essential right now. No one had ever looked at her like she was vital to the job. Louisa appreciated the help in the kitchen, but Callie wasn't the only person who could dice onions. Joey had mostly ignored her presence until then. Just like a rich guy. He hadn't yet realized she had the ability to wield a device that could take his soul. She didn't like the magic coursing through her veins, but she ignored the twin pangs of disgust and fear and pulled the flask from her pocket.

Again her body lit. The slowly rotating ceiling fan pushed enough air at her to tickle the back of her neck. Her fingers warmed against the stone. It was a new sensation, but a welcome one. The raging fire from last night was now more like wrapping her hands around a mug of hot cocoa. She'd prefer to swap soul storage of chocolatey goodness, but was just happy her hands weren't on fire. She didn't know—or care—whether the flask was dulling or channeling the pain. Now wasn't the time to ponder her new magical nature. This was a rare moment of power. She was the woman to be frightened of. She was the one who you wouldn't touch.

Callie strode toward Joey, head held high, and slammed the container's opening against his sternum with more force than she would have thought possible with her slender arms. The muscles in his neck flexed until they were taut bolts that shoved his head backward. His nostrils flared while he stared at the ceiling, but Callie kept the pressure on. When the rush of magic abated, she stepped back and capped the flask. Her motions were quick, if imprecise.

The need to get the flask returned to her pocket before it could flip her magic on again, and make her vulnerable, overrode all other thought. Derek watched her, but didn't speak until she'd secured it and exhaled a steady breath.

Joey also regained his composure, though his face was noticeably three shades whiter. Derek wasn't done with him, though. "Anyone else ask about that soul?" He inclined his head toward Callie, now the keeper of souls, apparently.

"You know I'd never—" Was blathering a side effect of soul extraction?

Derek cut him off. "Yeah, yeah, you're an upright citizen. Just tell me if anyone else asked about taking that soul."

Joey looked around his tidy home, as though spies might pop up from behind the credenza. "Some lady offered to take it. Said she'd fix me."

"Fix you?" Derek asked, nonplussed.

"She didn't seem all too lucid to me. The Charmer is creepy—" he paused, as though wondering if the criticism would earn him a smack. When it didn't, he continued "—but at least he's got all his marbles together. That woman definitely did not."

"What exactly did she say?" Callie asked.

"She offered to *purify* me. Said she could tell I was masking myself and could make me the true person I was meant to be. I told her unless she was offering a billion dollars, she couldn't improve my life that much." Hear, hear for skeptics.

"Did she mention her name?" Derek was on edge, his jaw tightening.

"She gave me a card for when I changed my mind. Not that I'm going to, man." He'd tacked on the last part. The Soul Charmer had cultivated a sincere amount of fear in him. Callie could relate. Joey pulled his wallet from his back pocket and produced the card.

"You kept her card?" Derek was at peak malevolence.

"So, I, um, could give it to you."

Derek rolled his eyes at that bullshit, but accepted the card. It was for the chakra massage storefront. Lovely. "She short or tall, this crazy woman?"

"Tall."

Callie's mind raced. That meant the woman who offered to purify Joey hadn't been Bianca. No one would mistake her for tall. Derek's eyes narrowed. She knew he was thinking the same thing he was: Tess had long legs and the height to prove it.

Two of the three other retrieval jobs they did that night had also had run-ins with Tess, though not a one knew her name. Anonymous benefactors were real, but could Tess be classified as such? They were leaving the final stop, Callie's flask a hot stone against her thigh, filled with another soul. While she'd expected the inherent grimy sensation of being good at something foul, she was surprised how much Tess and Bianca had gotten under her skin. Understanding others is how you avoid getting hurt, and she just didn't get them. That made them the scary unknown.

Bianca had alluded to some masterful plan to cleanse the city. If she were donating millions to city renovation, avoiding credit could make sense. Not everyone said yes to her little proposal—it'd been a fifty-fifty split, half too fearful of the Soul Charmer (and probably Derek as well) to accept whatever she offered. Why not give a name? She didn't hide where she worked. Though, maybe that was just a front. Leave your name and we'll mystically pop up at your house later.

Derek swore under his breath while reading messages on his phone. "We've got another stop to make."

"How many souls can this thing hold?" Callie wondered aloud.

"The most I've heard of is seventeen. So you're good for at least one more, doll."

She'd climbed on his bike expecting a drive to an apartment building. But when Derek pulled into the parking lot of St. Catherine's Memorial Hospital, her stomach dropped to her toes. Only the pegs below her feet kept her insides from dripping to the pavement.

"Why are we here?" Her voice had gone reedy, but Derek had already killed the engine.

He avoided her gaze as he stowed their helmets. "Need to snag a soul real quick."

"From here?" She bit back the urge to tell him she couldn't.

Hospitals didn't scare her. She used to find the astringent-laced hallways comforting. Before she'd been sacked from her gig there because of a brother with sticky fingers. From the *hiss* of the automatic doors opening as they entered, to the muted commotion of heart rate monitors and EKG they passed, to the hearty clacking on keyboards from the nurses' station, every sound inside the building reminded her of what she'd lost. Her plan to become a nurse, her better-than-average pay gig, her escape from being like her mom. She'd lost it all when she'd lost her job at the hospital. Derek couldn't know how much pain walking down these hallways was causing her, but he must have guessed at least part of it, because his silence had grown tenfold.

He paused outside a closed patient room. The nurses had averted their eyes as Callie and Derek passed. He was known here, too. Great.

"This is going to be different." He winced as though waiting for the wallop the words could deliver.

Callie narrowed her eyes. "How?" No point in avoiding bitterness now.

Derek pushed open the door, and Callie's fingers pricked with simmering heat.

He walked in. Curiosity made her follow.

He inclined his head toward the patient's bed. "He's not exactly conscious."

Kapow! There was the punch. Only it smacked Callie square in the stomach. Traction held the man in the bed's right leg and arm aloft, a brace cradled his neck, and an arc of nasty staples left a red semi-circle above his temple. He didn't move when they entered the room. When Callie checked the IV bag, she knew why. Derek reached to rest a hand on her shoulder, but she pulled away. "No," she said, filling those two letters with undiluted determination. "I won't *steal* souls for him. I don't build his fucking collection. There's a line, Derek, a goddamn line, and this is way over it."

"Oh, man, no. It's not that."

The tingle of heat in Callie's fingertips fell to the back of her mind as her disgust rushed to the forefront. She planted her hands on her hips and waited for an explanation that wouldn't make her vomit.

"He—Jerry, this guy—had a bad reaction to the soul he rented. We need to get it out of him." Derek fumbled his words, and while seeing him off-kilter eased Callie's ire, she wasn't about to help him out of the hole he'd dug. "You'll be able to feel the soul magic when you get closer. No stealing."

Callie pursed her lips. It didn't sound like a lie. "What do you mean by a bad reaction?"

"Souls aren't always a perfect fit." He scrubbed a hand against the back of his neck.

"And?"

"When quality isn't an issue for the user, there's always a chance of bad consequences. The rented soul might not be cooperative.

Jerry's borrowed soul fought his own and the mish-mash of all of it had him mentally off."

"You're avoiding details, Derek. Tell me the whole story."

He sucked in a quick breath. Busted. "He drove his car into the side of a train car. His kids were in the backseat."

Bile churned in Callie's stomach. The urge to heave at the horror was there, but important questions had to be asked. "His kids?"

"They're okay. The train was parked. Jerry, though, is in a medically induced coma, and if we don't get that soul out of him he's not going to have a chance at recovery. That borrowed soul wants to die."

Callie hadn't considered the possibility the soul she'd rent wouldn't want to be a part of her. Did unattached souls have wants and needs? "Is the Charmer keeping people's souls from moving on to an afterlife?"

"Above my pay grade, doll. I've got no clue if there is a heaven or a hell. What I do know is the Charmer never keeps a soul for rental for more than six months. He jokes and calls it freshness purgatory. Take it however you want."

She'd prefer not to take it at all. Celestial progression had never been a top priority for Callie, but if her rented soul wanted to move on, she sure hoped it could hold out until after it was free of her body. "Any promises this won't happen to me?"

"You're not going for bottom of the barrel goods, doll. The Charmer will make it a good match for you. I promise."

Could Derek even promise that? She didn't know, but it eased her fear regardless. Callie performed her first soul extraction on an unconscious man. The magic was there, the extra soul ready to move, but the act twinged her muddied morals anyway.

They didn't speak again until they were outside the hospital.

Callie and Derek sidled to his bike. "You mind taking the flask to the Charmer?" She held it toward him, careful to keep her fingers on the silver parts.

He laughed, but it was paired with a grimace. "No can do."

The less time she spent with the Soul Charmer, the better. He didn't only climb under her skin like the unknown—though that was a huge factor—it was as though he tried to take up residence in her body. He'd already coerced her into collecting souls on his behalf (which she had to admit gave her a heady rush) and infused her fingers with magic. Every time she encountered the man, he changed her. She wasn't ready for more.

"I don't know if I can," she said as though she had conflicting plans in her datebook, and not a bone-deep fear.

Derek accepted the flask from her, and she sagged with relief. The feeling was temporary. He stepped close enough for the energy between them to percolate against her skin, and then he slipped the soul holding cell into her coat pocket. "I'd help you on this if I could, but you've become pretty key to this Tess business."

The silver and stone didn't tug on the wool fabric or cause it to sag on one side. It didn't need to. The tremendous weight on her chest more than accomplished that. Derek climbed on to his bike. He sat there, leather clad, with the idling engine emitting enough of a rumble to tickle her sternum, and waited. Would the back tire bottom out when she climbed on? Those two souls, the enormity of what she'd been roped in to, and the mountain of teeming fear settled inside her core had to be more than mere steel and rubber could manage.

She was bigger than her fear, though. Or at least she pretended to be. What was she going to do? Walk home? It was fifteen miles and she was wearing a ratty pair of Chucks.

Not fucking likely.

CHAPTER TWELVE

The Soul Charmer's storefront would forever be creepy. Not that Callie had visited all that often. Derek led them through the front door this time, and the familiar stale scent of long-burning incense lodged itself in her sinuses immediately. She'd been waking in the middle of the night lately, smelling the cheap hippie shit and having to remind herself she was in her apartment and not rooted in the squishy carpet at the soul rental den.

She and Derek squelched their way across the room. What lay beneath that threadbare flooring? Rotting corpses was the best guess, if only because it'd explain the dank tinge underlying the incense.

As they bypassed the counter, the door to the building swung open behind them. The woman who bustled in rushed right to the counter in front of them. "I need a soul for tonight," she blurted. It wasn't clear if the proclamation was directed at Callie or Derek. Dark circles underscored her eyes. Perhaps several days without sleep had made it hard for the woman to differentiate between people. Callie wouldn't know. As long as she got four hours, her body didn't bitch.

Derek took the lead. "Wait here."

"Can't you help me?" When soliciting borderline-legal goods, it was best not to whine. This lady apparently had never gotten the memo to always be kind to your dealer. She was also wearing like-new shoes. Callie couldn't keep a new pair clean more than a week. What kind of person was desperate for a soul, but had time to drop dollars on new shoes?

"Nope," Derek said as he pressed his hand against Callie's lower back and ushered her in front of him and through the curtain portioning the shop from the back workspace.

There was no avoiding the meeting with the Soul Charmer. She'd accepted this. Derek's fingers lingered, a security blanket and a reminder she wasn't going into this alone. Lot of good that'd done last time. He'd stood silent while his boss had forced magic into her body. Her knees now locked, and Derek stumbled into her.

"What's wrong?" He scanned the floorboards and the ceiling, as if expecting an attacker wedged within the rotting wood to emerge.

"Do you have my back?" she asked, both hoping he'd hear her need and hating that she couldn't do this on her own.

"Did you not feel me slamming into you?"

He overstated the situation, and she flushed. "Pretty sure I'd be on my back if you used that kind of force," she said, but the chill of the eerie hallway in the Charmer's emporium smothered the entendre.

The moment of brevity was worth it though, as Derek's cheeks turned a subtle pink. Vulnerability exposed, he answered her original question. "Yes, I've got you."

"You know—"

"I do." She believed him, but Derek continued. "I'll step in if I have to."

Trusting Derek had to be a bad idea. Yes, he'd protected her in bars and diners and when her hands went "flame-on," but he also worked for a man who terrified Callie. One she couldn't say with one hundred percent certainty was totally human—there had to be some reptile gene splicing in action there. And yet Derek worked with him, willingly. The seedy business of soul renting was only a couple rungs up the ladder from the wares Ford shilled.

And yet.

Derek's hand found her back again, and despite the reservations rumbling in her head, she started toward the next doorway without any additional urging.

Like the previous time, she still stumbled through the passage. She scrubbed her hands together, as though it'd remove the oily feeling the Charmer's magic left on her skin. It might have worked, if the oil was something tangible. Derek didn't flinch at the magic—maybe he was used to it, or maybe he didn't feel it the same way she did—but he also didn't acknowledge Callie's obvious reaction.

The Soul Charmer wasn't facing them when they reached the workspace. Callie did a double take. With his shoulders curled forward and his head ducked down, he'd appeared decapitated. Freaky shit was the name of the game here, but Callie had limits. Walking through magical tar was one thing. People literally losing their heads was a whole other.

They moved a few steps into the room, and the Charmer popped his head up. Well, at least people were keeping their heads. That had to count for something.

They edged a smidge closer, and Callie clamped her hand around Derek's forearm. "We have a problem," she hissed.

His eyes widened. Through barely parted lips he replied, "Not a good time."

She squeezed harder, and seconds later he jerked his arm away.

"Shit." Derek was staring at Callie's hands. He hadn't seen the full encounter with Bianca and her abundance of soul magic. He hadn't seen Callie's physical reaction. He'd stepped in at the last minute to stop her from torching Tess's minion, but now he was witnessing the whole thing firsthand. The deep lines cutting across the center of his forehead suggested it was nearly as holy-fuck scary to watch as it was to experience. Why was it happening now, though?

It'd taken a few moments with Bianca for the dull heat to build up to scorching embers. Callie held her hands out, palms up, as though asking for a blessing. They'd already begun to peel and blacken. After the subdued heat with Joey's soul repo, she'd almost made herself believe the fire with Bianca was a one-time deal. She whimpered, the sight harder to bear than the numbing heat. With each second they looked more like campfire logs that had settled to the bottom of a fire pit. She shuffled backward. If this was the Soul Charmer's fault, she needed to put some distance between him and her to slow the burn.

"We've got a problem over here," Derek hollered. The Charmer was only a couple meters away, but acted as though he'd barely heard him. Derek yelled again, louder this time. The Charmer finally turned, looking more absent-minded grandfather than the wicked serpent Callie knew him to be. Focusing on his paternal façade wasn't an option, though, as flames began to lick her palms.

"Oh!" The Soul Charmer clapped in delight, a huge grin taking over his face. What the fuck? Callie wasn't a shiny new toy being gifted to a toddler on his birthday, but that's all she was to him, judging by that glint in his dark eyes.

Her attempt to bite out a cutting response was nothing more than a seething hiss. Callie's body was funneling all its higher capa-bilities, trying to hold it together as goddamn fire tore her hands apart. She'd immediately healed last time, she reminded herself over and over. Mantras weren't effective when you could see your skin scorching. No flames wove up her forearms, though. The sear-ing flames remained contained within her hands and fingers.

"You've really taken to that gift remarkably, my dear," the Charmer cooed as he scuttled toward her.

"Don't think now's the time to call it a gift, boss." Derek spoke the words Callie had been thinking, only far more politely. He stood at her side as she shook and sparked, despite the threat of third-degree burns.

"Nonsense." The Charmer waved a dismissive hand at Derek, and hovered closer to Callie's outstretched arms. "Not everyone can wield this kind of power, you know. I told you your soul was special." His voice trailed off, as though he was already plotting the next awful way he could use her.

Callie tried to scream, but the breathy sound she managed was probably only audible to certain breeds of dogs.

And apparently Derek, too. "Can you cap it while she's in here? If not, I need to get her outside." He moved behind her and cupped her upper arms, ready to steer her through the door.

"Goodness, yes. I suppose my wards really should mute that for you, but it's so rare—" The Charmer abruptly stopped speaking and shot a dark look over Callie's shoulder. Whatever Derek had communicated, Callie appreciated it.

The Soul Charmer cracked his knuckles, and then grasped Callie's wrists. His hold was too close to Derek's for any sort of comfort. He muttered words in a language she couldn't follow, but a half second after he finished speaking, the heat disappeared and her skin looked positively human and unbroken again.

It took Callie fourteen (she counted) deep breaths to pull it together enough to fake being steady on her feet. Derek kept a hand on her. She didn't mind him being ready to catch her if she dropped, especially since the odds were fifty-fifty.

"What. The. Hell. Was. That?" she eked through lips so taut she half expected them to crack as she spoke. Did they do that

Gatorade dunk thing if you survived magical trauma? They should. She'd settle for a gallon of water to chug.

"Excuse me?" The Soul Charmer's dazed response would be more appropriate in the dementia ward at the retirement home, but Callie didn't buy it.

"I did not sign up for magic. I did not sign up for being burned alive—"

"You're being melodramatic," the Charmer said, casting a glance Derek's way. Did he think they'd share a *women* laugh? Fuck him.

"That is the *second* time my hands have looked so completely burnt, I thought I saw bone. And then *poof* it's gone. I can retrieve your souls. I can handle the stiff fingers and the tingly warmth. I cannot handle fucking fire."

Callie was out of breath. Whether from the force of her words or the lingering panic simmering steady in her stomach, she wasn't certain. She hauled in a few more deep breaths, and the Soul Charmer simply stared her down.

"Well?" she nudged.

That genial smile was gone. "I wasn't sure if you were done with your childish tantrum."

She was ready to correct him, but Derek jumped in first. "Did you take the magic from her?"

"Take it away?" The Charmer balked.

Callie opened her mouth to explain a gift-return policy to him, but Derek cut her a look, so she tempered her emotions. She should be choosing her battles, especially when creepy-ass men who can steal your soul or turn you into Fire Girl are involved. With that life lesson in mind, she muttered a few words of gratitude, and edged closer to Derek.

"I assume you brought me souls." The Charmer's tone had soured.

Callie managed to still her facial reaction, but she internally flinched. She'd pissed him off right before she needed to deliver bad news. Would she ever have an encounter with him that didn't result in her making her life worse?

"Of course." She handed him the flask. Despite whatever he'd done to dampen the juju around him, she avoided touching the inlay. Tonight had already crossed into WTF territory. No need to make it more painful.

He moved toward his large desk, lifting one of the black jars from an open drawer. He then popped the lid on the flask and inhaled. Callie hadn't smelled anything when she'd collected them. The Charmer tilted his head from right to left and back again, a soul sommelier in action. After a few tense moments, he turned his all-too-knowing gaze on her. "Only three?"

Innocent words. Cutting words. Was there any safe answer? "Yes," she replied, before Derek could. Speaking up might be the trick to controlling her situation. The quiet and invisible plan had already failed miserably.

His brow arched in question, without twitching another muscle on his face. How could he keep giving her the same passive face with that wicked, questioning eyebrow lifted? Creepy fucker.

"Only three were available," she said. Derek squeezed her arm softly. He remained at her side; he'd help.

"Tess is targeting us," Derek said, trying to steer his boss away from Callie's interrogation.

The Charmer's response was so profane that she'd never heard most of the expletives he unleashed. As his railing ebbed, he finally added, "Tell me what we know."

Derek and Callie reported the basics—the Charmer's frequent customers were being approached with promises of fixing them. She held back her encounter with Tess, because she wasn't a moron. Derek wasn't either, and kept quiet, too.

"She tells them she's saving them, and they believe it?" Incredulity coming from the Charmer was new and jarring to Callie.

She replied without thinking. "If they're using other people's souls for absolution when they sin, why *wouldn't* they be interested in something even better, some sort of full redemption offer?"

"Everyone knows that borrowed souls mitigate any celestial misconduct." The way the Charmer put the emphasis on what the customers knew instead of whether Tess's offer might have some veracity to it, unnerved Callie. She'd often doubted a higher power would be cool with the sin equivalent of a Get Out of Jail Free Card. Either you did right, or you didn't.

"She's messing with repeat business, boss," Derek said, diverting the conversation away from the theological. "She's not after the one-offs, either. Oh, shit, I almost forgot. There was some woman, a customer, up front waiting for you."

"She'll continue to wait then," the Charmer said, in the same tone he dismissed Callie's comments.

Must be nice to not need business. Whatever. She would stick to the script. "Will you rent to those people again?"

"I wouldn't leave them in need." Right, because the Soul Charmer was benevolent.

"How big's the markup when they come crawling back?" Derek knew the game.

"Forty-eight hour wait, and triple price until I'm confident of their renewed loyalty."

Callie couldn't fight the shiver spiraling up her spine. Derek gave her a little squeeze, but he didn't understand. The parallels between Ford's business and the Charmer's were becoming clearer each day. Ford's drugs might drop you down a well faster, but the Charmer leveraged the same kind of business practices. He'd hustle, he'd hunt, he'd punish, and he'd burn those who stood in his way.

"I'm more concerned that our current clientele, the ones who haven't been approached yet, understands the ramifications of dabbling with that conniving woman." The Soul Charmer's monotone whisper belied the barely contained fury dancing in his eyes. Witnessing such restraint should have been impressive. Instead, Callie's temperature dropped, and it didn't have a damn thing to do with magic.

"Understood." Derek was unnerved, too.

The Charmer huffed, and then nodded.

"Next steps?" Derek asked. He bounced his right heel on the floor as though the nervous energy could slip out with a touch.

"You don't have a plan?" The Charmer had resurrected his coy tone. The sound sent Callie's stomach sinking.

"Put current customers on notice. Find our souls."

"Find Tess," the Charmer added.

"To question her?"

"I'd rather you brought her directly to me first."

Derek shot a quick look at Callie, but must have decided to go for broke anyway. "That could mean war."

"Are you doubting your abilities to bring her to me, or mine to handle her?" Simple questions could often be the most threatening.

"If she has the magic to steal our souls, what can I do to nullify her enough to bring her in?" Derek avoided eye contact with everyone. The simple fault of being mortal shouldn't cause him shame.

The Charmer gestured to Callie. "You have her."

"Me? I can't be all magical and stop her," Callie said in a rush.

"Did you not burn her hanger-on?"

Callie's jaw started to drop, but she snapped it closed. Had Derek told him? Did he really refer to Bianca as a "hanger-on?" She packed enough power to set Callie's hands ablaze.

"Word travels," he said with a saccharine smile, exposing his few rotted teeth. He then turned his back and continued whatever he'd been working on when they'd arrived. "You need to fix this. *Both* of you. We will eliminate Tess and move forward."

He didn't ask if they understood, because there wasn't an option not to.

CHAPTER THIRTEEN

"How?" With each step closer to the curb, Callie's repeated question got louder.

"I don't know," Derek muttered. She rounded in front of him, forcing him to stop short and earning her a sour look. "This isn't the best place to—"

Callie cut him off. "How did he know about Bianca?"

"Don't look at me like I ratted you out. I didn't say shit, and fuck you for thinking I would."

"I've known you for a week, Derek. A week. So sorry if you haven't earned the benefit of the doubt."

"I'm on your side here."

"You knew he was going to put magic into me and didn't say a word. How do I know whatever this is—" she gestured between them, the small motion meaning so much more "—isn't something he told you to do? Some kind of con."

"Because he doesn't own me. I work for the man, and he's earned my loyalty, but you have, too." Derek swiped a hand down his face. He took a couple deep breaths, and then continued. "I didn't know he was going to put the magic into you. I mean, yeah, I knew he was going to try. It normally doesn't work though."

"Your excuse is that you didn't think it would *work*? Great. So is that the case with telling him about Bianca, too? You didn't know he'd use it for leverage?"

"I didn't tell him!" Derek turned his back to her and took two steps away before reconsidering, and pivoting back toward her. "I had your back tonight, didn't I?"

"You did," she murmured. At least it had seemed that way.

Callie was in too deep. This world of mayhem was something she'd strived to stay away from. No matter how hard she worked, though, she couldn't escape her destiny to be another lowlife. She'd thought she could be invisible on this job. Her name would be unspoken. The soul renters would be looking at Derek, not her. But the Charmer couldn't let her get away that easily. No, he had to force her to be a part of it. To make her *magical*, like he was some bastardized fairy godfather. Cinderella had mice and a pumpkin. Callie could probably scrounge up some rats at her apartment, but her magic would only work if the rodents happened to be double-dosing on souls. Where was her happy ending?

Derek had proven himself, and she still tossed blame his way like a jackass. She deserved his disdain. What happened with Bianca was apparently public knowledge, which meant her other secrets could escape, too. The ones she told no one. Would people know she liked burning Bianca? Moreover, would they discover how disloyal she'd been in the past? Atonement didn't have an end date for her. Josh played the card constantly. Was he spilling her dark secrets now, too?

"I didn't mean to blame you. I just don't know how he found out." She deflated from her battle-ready, shit's-about-to-go-down stance. There wasn't enough energy left over to conceal the anxiety in her voice.

"Too many people with big mouths." He didn't divulge a name, but she sensed he had an idea who had blabbed. The truth of that knowledge lingered in the air between them.

Callie didn't push, though. "Meeting with him exhausts me."

"The Charmer has that effect on people."

Callie narrowed her eyes. "He doesn't do the same energy suck Tess does, does he?"

"No, he's just an exhausting asshole sometimes." Derek turned Callie around with an open arm. He kept it draped across her shoulders as they finished their walk to his bike.

"My place next?" Callie asked while strapping on her helmet. It was edging toward 11 p.m., and her early mornings at the Home had conditioned her to be in bed at the same time as a seven-year-old.

"You got booze at your place?"

"Not really." The two beers in her fridge were lonely and cheap.

"Then first we're going to the liquor store." Derek revved the engine and cast Callie a look full of expectations. Climbing on meant agreeing to more than a ride home. Her beleaguered mind wasn't game to cull a list of pros and cons. She slung a leg over the seat and scooted in close. Talking wasn't going to do anything about the fear fused to her bones. Not yet. She was still too rattled, but she could find a few minutes' solace in the way Derek's body had acclimated to hers, softening as she cradled him with long legs and a tight hug. She nuzzled against his leather jacket until she could almost taste the rich scent. He waited until Callie had drunk her fill of the moment before pulling out of the space.

Vodka tonics might be magical.

The potato-based alcohol had been the smart choice at the liquor store. Tequila put her on the floor, and Derek didn't need to see her in whiskey riot mode. The clear liquor was the safe bet, and Derek had proven himself adept at making the drinks strong enough for a firm kick, but mild enough to avoid the sense of immolation. Callie'd had enough internal fire for a lifetime.

Her minimal furniture put them in the same places they'd sat earlier in the day. With each round of drinks, he slowly migrated from the far end of the couch toward her.

"You look weird without your jacket," Callie mused between the first few sips of her third drink.

He'd ditched the leather in the kitchenette when he made the last round. The aura of menace he projected didn't disappear without the jacket, but it lessened. Or the booze was working. He pursed his lips for a moment, and looked himself over. "What's so weird?"

The ends of each arm of his fitted tee shirt strained against his biceps as he casually draped his arm across the back of the sofa. His fingers grazed her shoulder and an unbidden rush of heat flocked to her chest. Callie scrunched her bare toes against the thin carpet. "I don't know. You look deceptively normal."

"Deceptive? I can't be normal?"

"You know too much to be normal."

He groaned. "That's probably true." He downed a third of his drink in a single swallow. How many of those would it take before he was drunk? At this rate, she was going to find out.

"It's okay. I'm not normal either." Tipsy was Callie's best setting.

When he chuckled, the low lights in her apartment finally caught the light pink dusting the apples of his cheeks. "You seem pretty normal to me. Hot, but normal."

"Well, as long as hot is a factor."

"Hotness is always a factor, doll."

God, was he right. Allowing him into the apartment had been a bad decision. As was the booze. Last time she drank around him, she'd lit a girl on fire with her freakish hands, and then she'd kissed him. They hadn't discussed the latter at all, which could only mean she'd blown it. Epically.

"You should be wary, man. Didn't anyone tell you the hot ones are always crazy?" Why was she playing into his game here? Sex appeal wasn't really in Callie's repertoire. She could get laid. That didn't make her cover model material. Unless the vodka also put a couple extra pounds on her to hide the ramifications of eating like shit, she was pretty sure she was bringing basic to this party.

He rolled his eyes.

"I'm not lying. You underestimate my level of fucked up."

"Or maybe you overestimate it." He paused and downed another third of his cocktail. "We've all got shit in our past. Baggage. Whatever. Some people hide it really well. Doesn't mean they're better or less crazy."

She took a sip, and another, and another, until her temples began to go mushy. "So you're saying the hot equals crazy equation is false?"

"You always get so math-y when you drink?"

She planted her elbow on her thigh and rested her chin on her hand. His comment was flippant, but she pondered it regardless. "No," she finally decided. "This is special for you."

He skimmed his fingers in lazy circles on her shoulder, and emotions she didn't want to examine percolated in her stomach. "There's more to you than following me around. Tell me, who is Callie?"

The personal question should have stomped on the fluttering sensation inside her. Secrets protected her. If no one knew you, no one could hurt you. She waited for the inevitable fear to rise—that feeling of being stretched so thin that organs were visible—but it never came. "I'm boring," she finally said.

"Not going to buy that one." His palm eased to the nape of her neck. Had he moved closer or was it wishful thinking?

"I serve simple meals to old people at a retirement home for work. I don't sleep enough, and I eat a lot of really crappy sandwiches. Boring."

"Where else have you worked?"

"Are we counting indentured servitude to creepy, soul-stealing men?"

His side-eye glare was impressive.

Lying took too much effort. "I used to work at Southside Memorial."

"Doing what?"

"I'm aces at serving food."

"What else?" He had been paying attention at St. Catherine's.

She didn't talk about her run at being a nurse. Family came first, and that meant hard decisions. It was the right thing to do, but damn if she couldn't remember the knife twisting when that dream had been stolen from her. The memory was enough to staunch the warmth Derek was stoking. He watched her with the patience of Job. No frown touched his face. His fingers didn't press any more firmly against her neck. He just . . . waited. "This is how you get informants to talk, isn't it?"

He shrugged. "I'm a good listener."

She went for another sip, and discovered the glass empty. "New plan. This life story business should be a *quid pro quo* thing."

He raised his eyebrows, but couldn't contain the grin that quickly followed. "Oh yeah?"

"Yep." She sat her empty glass on the coffee table. "I will answer your questions . . . if you answer mine."

"All right." He wet his lips, and continued speaking. Callie didn't hear a word. That tongue, slick and tinged with alcohol, had quickly overwhelmed her the other night. What other things could it do?

"Callie?" He had been speaking. Shit.

"Yeah?"

"I asked if you wanted another." He picked up her glass and waggled it in her direction.

"Is that your first question? Start with the easy ones. I like it. Yes, I'll take another."

He shook his head, but the grin hadn't disappeared. Maybe he found intoxicated Callie charming. If so, it could prove very useful. She could learn more about him. She'd be safer with more knowledge, and that was her only reasoning for playing along. Or that's what she told herself. Kind of.

"My question is still pending, doll: What else did you do at that hospital?"

She hated going first. "I was a medical assistant."

"Why aren't you anymore?" He was pouring drinks like he wasn't also prying into the dark, tar-filled pit of regret she hid between her ribs.

"Don't I get a question?"

"Quit being so pushy or I'm not buying you vodka again." So he was thinking about this being a regular thing?

"I'm not drunk enough to give you details, but I'll say having a meth addict for a brother makes it awful complicated to work in the medical field." Bitterness oozed from her pores, but there was no point in attempting to stymy the flow now. Underneath that acridity overwhelming her body, a tiny anthill of relief reared from saying the words aloud.

"Makes sense."

"It does?" She couldn't quiet her incredulity. Unless you had an addict in the family, it was hard to relate. She'd had friends when she'd worked at the hospital. They'd told her to explain herself, break ties with her brother, and people would understand. But her life was not a made-for-TV movie, and it simply wasn't that easy. In real life, bridges burned fantastically. Your family guilted and blackmailed you. You accepted it, remembered why loyalty mattered, and moved the fuck on.

"When people—mostly junkies—know they have a hook in you, they milk it until you've got nothing left to give," Derek said. "Hospitals and addicts abusing the system go hand in hand."

He handed her the vodka tonic, and then added, "Sorry he did that to you."

Callie's breath hitched while her body vacillated on the appropriate response. This too-attractive man understood her, which was either the best moment in the last month or the worst moment next month, when it inevitably fell apart. Her pessimist side had a long winning streak, but tonight, as the both of them let go of the awful day, she was willing to give in to a little enjoyment. "Thank you."

He nodded, and sat next to her. She leaned against his side, and he curled an arm around her. He lifted her chin with a knuckle. "Hit me with your best shot."

She almost kissed him. Her hand pressed against his chest before her brain realized he meant a question. She blushed at her mistake, but kept her hand on him, because she could. The thin shirt he wore let her almost feel the taut muscles beneath. Derek worked for the Soul Charmer by choice, but this was her chance to understand. Probably. "You understood what the Charmer had done to me."

He nodded.

"Has he ever used his magic on you?"

His arm grew tense against her back, and he pulled her closer. It wasn't for strength, but almost like he couldn't bear to meet her gaze, like he wanted minimal intimacy if he was going to share intense truth, apparently. She understood, but it still cut. Once her cheek rested against his chest, he answered, "Not in the same way he did to you."

The baritone of his voice was clearer when her ear was against him. The forced gruffness he injected may have disappeared when they were pressed together, but the deflection remained. Evasion was never lost on Callie. "What did he do to you?" she asked. Her even voice didn't give away the concern rattling around in her brain. The small circles she traced on his chest might have clued him in, though.

Derek stilled her hand with his own, clutching it against his chest. His heartbeat thudded against her pinky and ring fingers. Silence and tight spaces should have been warning signals to Callie. Danger had found her there before, but while her heart hurried to match his rushed pulse, panic refused to rush in. Her anxiousness was different, milder and intriguing.

"He takes a run at me every so often," Derek said, as if she was supposed to know what that meant.

Her soft *hmm* urged him to continue. "He tests me." He paused, and squeezed the arm wrapped around her tighter.

She wasn't going anywhere. "What do you mean? Like your loyalty?"

"He can read people real well. You found that one out the hard way. He knows I won't screw him over."

"Any man with that much power expects people to fear him, I guess." She feared both Charmer and Ford for those very reasons. The Soul Charmer had the edge now, though, because magic in action, writhing beneath her skin, was goddamn terrifying.

"That they do, doll." He eased his death grip on her.

"So what is he testing?" Pushing probably made her an asshole, but she had to know. It made her rotten to want him to be violated by magic, too, but deep down she did. She didn't want to be alone. Derek might have stepped up for her tonight, but was that out of understanding? Delving into why she wanted this connection to him wasn't something she was ready to explore, but the need wasn't going away.

"Magical ability." Two small, benign words, spat with the disgust of discovering a bone buried in a sandwich.

He masked the morose with vehemence, but Callie was too familiar with that dance as well. Her mom used to pull the same shit. But instead of the normal disgust with Zara, a pang of sympathy struck her. "He's looking for an heir?" Her lightness was fake, but she was trying.

"Yes." Oh. He continued. "You ever notice I don't use that flask?"

"Well, yeah," she said after a moment. They'd just been giving her something to do, she'd thought.

"It's because I *can't*."

How much harder had his repo gig been before she tagged along? Callie had never even considered that.

"The Charmer's tried forcing magic into me, over and over, but every time it just makes me really fucking sick."

"Sick?"

"Worse than a week's run of the flu. How fucked up is that? I want to be more involved in this business, but I'm not good enough *inside* to do it. I physically can't do anything magical." So that was the burn for him. All his physical strength didn't count when it came to the renting side of soul magic. He was the man who could find solutions to any problem, except this one.

"You told me before that it's about being morally ambivalent, right?" Callie asked, trying to soothe his worries. "That's why he could use me. Maybe you're *too* good for this line of work. The Charmer sure as shit isn't good inside. I think it's wonderful you aren't wired like he is. You are good. To me." She turned her face into his side and kissed the thin fabric stretched over his shoulder.

His muscles softened, but he wasn't letting go yet. This tit-for-tat game was too much. "You're good inside. That's why you think that. Flexible morals and that goodness is why you can take the magic."

She pushed against him, until he released her and she could see his face. His brows were drawn and his lips curled. Taking the conversation to a dark place was her fault. As much as she wanted answers now, to find out why the Charmer could force magic on her and not Derek, she wasn't going to extract them. The cost was too high. "Then it's very good I have you to protect me. I didn't want this magic stuff."

The lines on his face faded, and he keened his head to the right. "Why'd you do it then?"

"Agree to be a part of this?" When he nodded, she continued, "You already know the answer there. I'm doing it for Josh." The emotion she packed into his name left no question who Josh was.

"But why? I get he's your brother, but would he do the same for you?"

His hand slid from her back to wrap around her hip. Her body softened as one of his fingers found skin between her shirt and jeans. "It's not about an exchange of sacrifices," she said softly.

"Maybe it should be," he muttered, stiffening his fingers against her side.

The instinct to rally to Josh's defense was second nature, but it was hard to generate much irritation at a man who thought she deserved better. She'd had friends rally at her about ditching Josh, but Derek hadn't told her what to do. He'd earned himself a little more honesty. "It's hard to see it from the outside, but

I owe him. He—" she paused, debating if the vodka was making her magnanimous "—he did what was necessary to keep me safe when I was in high school. He's been my constant. Now I'm doing the same."

Light danced in Derek's eyes. He watched her too closely. It was clear he wanted more specifics, but he held back. Thank God. She'd underestimated how many times Josh would call forward that memory—the betrayal she'd committed, and how he'd sheltered her from the fallout. Those details weren't for others' ears. Not even Derek's. Not even with another fifth of vodka consumed. The job for Ford would get her back on solid ground with Josh, and bury her secret permanently.

Derek pursed his lips. "You're damn resilient for someone so small."

Callie's laugh started low in her stomach, and escaped through a big grin. "You say that like I'm built of steel or something."

She wasn't, but he damn near was. The forearm against her back went taut as he pulled her toward his chest. Her body collided with his, her hand curled over his shoulder. She squeezed the muscle there. She needed a distraction, or she'd lose herself in the sensations assailing her. The hard planes of his chest held firm against her breasts. The pressure had her nipples tightening. She should have worn a bra with some padding. The lightly lined one she had on was more feminine, but it also failed to conceal her response.

Callie tilted her head back, unsure what to say. Energy sparked along her skin, kindling something dark and needy inside. When she finally met his gaze, he looked *angry*. The calm blue of his eyes had turned the grey of a winter storm. His lips were still the soft pink she'd seen moments ago, but he'd thinned them as though he was about to bite out a snarl. Even his jaw line has sharpened, the angles severe. He looked like the brute he played on the job. And she liked it.

She squirmed, and a quick flash of desire passed across Derek's face. His lips lost their tension right before he leaned toward her. Fire. Their kiss sparked pure heat. It washed over Callie in a backdraft. It only took moments for her entire body to be suffused with the bone-melting burn. The Charmer's magic had brought flames to her hands, ones that made her itch to injure others. But Derek conjured a whole other kind of fire within Callie. This she wanted more of.

Derek parted his lips, and she accepted the invitation. Their tongues slid against one another in a needy dance. His fingers dug into her hips as he lifted her and pulled her onto his lap. Straddling him only stoked the blaze. She squeezed her knees against his sides, and he groaned into her mouth.

This desperate need to be closer to him overwhelmed Callie. She wouldn't give him the complete truth about her past. This she could give him though. His hands snuck underneath the back of her tee shirt. His palms spanned her back, and the reminder of his size sent a fresh rush of heat through her. There wasn't a safer place than at his side. She rocked her hips toward his, needing more but not knowing what to do next. Her body had flipped to instinct mode, but her brain was lagging. She edged up on her knees to lick along the outer edge of his ear. He shuddered beneath her. "I need more," she whispered, knowing he'd take care of her.

He groaned. "I got you."

His hands traced down her back to snag the hem of her shirt. He lifted it over her head, and then hissed out a curse at his first glimpse of her without it. "If I'd known you had fucking black lace on, this shirt would have been on the floor an hour ago." He threw her tee across the room without taking his eyes off her barely concealed breasts.

Callie eased back on his lap to get enough space to reach for his shirt, too. The back of her hand glanced his jeans right before she yanked his shirt up. He hissed and helped rip it off with hurried motions. His chest was better than she'd imagined. Shadows highlighted each muscle on his torso, and she wanted to lick every one. But Derek had other ideas, and he was very convincing. Her bra met their shirts on the floor as his hands ghosted up her sides—eliciting goose bumps in their wake—and cupped her breasts in his palms. His lips were soft against her neck and his thumbs teased her nipples. She rocked forward against him, the hardness she discovered hidden behind his denim jeans encouraging her to do it again.

She grabbed Derek's biceps, attempting to pull him closer. His strength might be a turn-on, but it stilled her from getting the closeness she craved. She started to say his name, to tell him what she needed, but his kisses cut her off. A quick, light brush of his lips against her collarbone, a little lick at her sternum, and he began to plant kisses lower and lower until his mouth latched on to one nipple. She whimpered as his teeth grazed her flesh and he redoubled his efforts. He was focused on her upper body, and with each touch he only made her crave him more.

She rolled her hips against his, finding a steady rhythm that spurred her need, but didn't sate it. Derek's kisses turned frenzied. They were both too gone to care if they were making out like teenagers. Maybe teenagers were on to something. She skated her hands down Derek's stomach. Her fingers found the dusting of hair below his navel and traced it to his pants.

Derek pressed a gentle kiss to Callie's lips. Softness wasn't what she was after, though. Her skin was becoming more sensitized by the moment. Her jeans were heavy and confining. His bulky muscles could be heavy, too, but his heated body turned her languid. Hot stone massage via his hands? Hell yes. She hooked the tips of her fingers inside his pant waist, and yanked hard. His eyes widened and a deep rose rushed across his cheekbones.

"You sure?" he asked, his eyes narrowing.

He didn't scare her. Her confidence brimmed as desire welled. "I'm not fucking subtle."

"No, you're fucking gorgeous though."

She was ready to reply with a similar compliment, but Derek was done with banter, and Callie liked a focused man. He wrapped his arms around her, and turned them both, laying her on the couch on her back. He stepped away, and she instantly missed his touch. All she could do was watch as he deftly unbuttoned and removed his jeans and boxers, and then reached for hers. No matter how much of a hurry she was in, she wasn't going to stop him from helping her disrobe. Warmth trailed behind Derek's fingers as he dragged her pants and panties down her legs.

He took a moment to put on the condom, and Callie watched with fascination. Now would be the time for regrets, but she had none. If he'd faltered at the Charmer's tonight, this would have been a bad idea. But he'd come through for her. He'd protected her more times in their short time together than anyone else had. It was nice to have a person who'd rally for her, and it was damn nice to have him naked and all to herself.

Derek's kisses were no longer gentle or tentative. He went deeper with each one, taking control. She didn't mind. He gave her enough of his weight atop her to spur thoughts of being delightfully small, but held back enough so she wasn't crushed under his bulk. She'd expected him to enter her immediately, but he waited. As she arched her body in response to his fervent kiss, his length slowly rubbed against her. The inferno borne of this connection was hotter than any she'd experienced before. She dug her nails into his back. "Now."

He kneeled between her legs. He traced the tip of his length down her sex and back again, his eyes locked on where their bodies would connect. She arched again, and he spared a glance up at her breasts before continuing to tease. She didn't need to get worked up any further; she was already close to redlining, and this was turning her delirious. "Please," she managed to eke out, despite the string of curse words ordering him to act funneling through her mind.

He didn't need any further urging. Thank God. She didn't need an extra soul to mask her from this act. She wanted him marked on her soul. The rushes of need and desire and connection fused in a miasma of pleasure. With each thrust of Derek's hips, Callie slipped further into bliss. She grabbed at him, trying to pull him even closer. His lips found hers again, and she went flying over the edge.

She'd given Derek more than she'd planned, but as his body covered hers, she had no regrets.

CHAPTER FOURTEEN

One dozen eggs, a loaf of bread, grape jam, a pound of sliced smoked turkey, a nearly empty jar of mayonnaise, a gallon of milk, and a family size box of Frosted Flakes. Despite the grocery store trip the day before, Callie's kitchen was significantly understocked.

Correction: it wasn't stocked for company. Derek's lingering presence in her bedroom was welcome, but still unexpected.

His arm had been crushing her when she awoke. He must have gained weight in his sleep, because it took her a good hour to extract herself from beneath it. Though the initial shock of finding him still in her bed—and still really naked—had taken up the first several minutes. He hadn't bailed in the middle of the night, which both baffled and enchanted her. Callie hadn't had a guy stay the night in at least two years. Booting him would have been wrong after how much they'd drank, she started to tell herself, but that justification was so flimsy, her conscience called bullshit.

Derek looked vulnerable laying in her bed. No leather to shield him. No scowl on his face to deter indifference. The covers had shifted low enough to let her see the dimples in his lower back. Callie had peeked below before tugging the comforter up. That ass wasn't even the reason she'd let him stay. It wasn't even that he'd fucked her into next Tuesday. Though, that wasn't hurting the case. The truth was, safety was a scarce commodity in Callie's life. Derek had given her that with a healthy dose of understanding last night. Hell if that didn't mean something to her. Had she divulged enough last night to establish the connection both ways? Did she even want him that close, to see all the muck trapped inside? She undid her ponytail and reset it as a sloppy bun. At least she could control her hair.

Her phone had rung an hour earlier. Yesterday had been her day off. Today was not, and she'd totally forgotten. "Shit, Lou, I'm sorry," she'd answered.

"I thought you might be dead."

"Dead? I already have a melodramatic mother. Give me a bit more credit." She tried to tease. Easier than accepting the fact she might be about to lose her job.

"You come in on your day off, and now you're missing work. You're never late. What's been up with you lately? Everything okay?" Lou's words were truly devoid of judgment.

Callie glanced at the clock above the stove. Ninety minutes was more than late. "I'm really sorry. It's just—" How was she supposed to finish that sentence? Lying to Louisa would wrap Callie in a fresh layer of guilt, and she could barely breathe through her shame swaddling as it was.

"Just life, honey. Don't I know it." Lou knew too much. "Your mama causing problems?"

"When isn't she? I can't believe I did this, though. Do you need me to fill in tonight?" Derek might be able to cover for her with the Charmer.

"No. We're full up. You're all right, though?" The question was benign, but the motherly underpinnings struck hard.

Callie had focused on the towel rack in lieu of the mirror while brushing her teeth earlier that morning. Whatever it took to ignore the faint bags under her eyes. That darkness hadn't been borne in the throes of soul magic abuse. She didn't get it from the emotional battery of gathering vagrant souls from temporary hosts or the hot-cold spectrum her skin had endured the last few days. No, her dark circles were earned the old-fashioned way. "Yeah, Lou. Just tired."

Her boss was quiet for long enough that Callie had to confirm the call hadn't dropped. Louisa's words came slowly, but clearly. "I know that brother of yours is a problem. If you need a few days to sort it out, take them. I'm not going to give your job away."

"Thanks." Callie wasn't sure she could accept. Her bank account wouldn't appreciate the decision.

Lou understood screwed up families and the myriad ways they could destroy your life, but the olive branch only extended so far. "Don't thank me yet. If you ditch on me again, though, I can't keep you. Favorite or not."

"Right." Well, shit. The way Ford and the Charmer were running her, she needed the time. She could take it and ration the food she had in the pantry, or she could promise to show and risk failing and losing her actual source of income long term. "Can I take a few days? When I'm back, I'll be my normal self." God, she hoped she wasn't lying.

An hour had passed and Louisa's offer continued to feel surreal. Bosses being cool about employees not showing was a myth. Unless you were in a ditch, they weren't supposed to tolerate such things. But somehow she'd earned that kind of trust, and now as she continued sweating out last night's alcohol, she had to find a way to keep from fucking it up.

Breakfast would have been a good distraction, if she knew what to make. Lou made those decisions at work. At home it was on her, and she had a naked man in the other room to consider. Was Derek a breakfast eater? Would he expect the big, manly, eggs-and-meat meal she couldn't provide? Her empty stomach gurgled a warning, a roiling notice of eat or puke. Decision time.

Turned out the Frosted Flakes came in a box that big for a reason.

Derek lumbered into the kitchen a little after ten. Despite the extra sleep, he didn't look all that much more rested than she did. He did, however, look far better in low-slung jeans. A break on the bedhead was warranted.

"You got anything to eat?" The rasp of his voice was the deepest she'd ever heard it.

Callie gestured to the big box of sugary corn flakes she'd left on the counter. Her bowl was already rinsed and in the sink.

"Frosted Flakes, huh?" The corners of his mouth began to curl and his eyes danced with mischief. Perhaps last night hadn't ruined everything.

"Best option in the house." With her shrug she let go of the shame of not providing more for him. He'd gotten laid like a pro and she was making him smile the next morning. What more did a man really need?

He nodded. "It's common knowledge they're grrrreat." His Tony the Tiger impression was spot on.

Her laugh chimed throughout the small space. When was the last time her laugh hadn't been weighted with sarcasm or wrought from her gut without glee? As far as reasons for missing work went, Derek wasn't a bad choice. "Bowls are in the cupboard next to the fridge, and spoons in the drawer directly below."

His broad back worked, flexing and releasing fluidly, as he set about helping himself to the best cereal she had. An echo of the heat that had ensnared her before flickered in her abdomen, but she let it smolder. She wanted to believe there was a real connection between them, but she wasn't going to risk botching that potential by leaping at him. He viewed her as strong, and regardless of her position on the matter, she wasn't going to showcase weakness now. Putting her desire above keeping her brother alive would be pretty weak by anyone's standards.

Derek leaned against her counter, cradling the bowl of cereal to his chest and ladling bites to his mouth. He was at home here. Pride flashed through her, making the fine hairs on the back of her neck rise. Her phone made a muffled honking noise as it vibrated against the countertop. Spell broken, she glanced at the screen, and then readjusted her gaze to the ceiling, trying to be patient. It didn't work.

"What's wrong?" Derek asked around a mouthful of crunchy goodness.

She waved a dismissive hand toward her phone. "Just my mom."

"Checking up on you?" He grinned.

"That would be a first." Leave it to her mother to sour her morning-after mood.

He pushed off the counter and sauntered over next to her, still clutching his breakfast. "You good?"

"Yeah." She shook her head, trying to dislodge the unworthiness her mother always stirred within her. "Her cat is stuck in a cupboard and she can't find Josh to come rescue him."

He cut his eyes down to slits, and then at half-speed he asked, "You're kidding me, right?"

"I wish I were."

"You don't look old enough to have an elderly parent." He'd selected those words carefully. It wasn't necessary, but she'd accept the kid gloves for now.

"She's not old, just doesn't like doing things for herself." Bitterness for your family was probably a turn off. She was a real fucking prize. "Josh stops by her place a lot usually. She isn't texting about the cat, not really. She wants to know where Josh is."

"Then she should try texting *him* early on a Sunday."

The lack of judgment from Derek loosened her lips. She couldn't even blame it on the booze this time. "Ford isn't much for letting him carry his phone right now."

Derek stopped chewing the big bite he'd shoveled in his mouth. He lifted his chin and watched her. He read people, and understood her. He would read between the lines. Callie hadn't broken any of the rules Ford had laid for her. She didn't say she had an agreement with Ford. His own minion had spilled those beans. She hadn't said Ford kidnapped her brother, but she had admitted his junkie status. It wasn't a secret Ford was the biggest meth dealer in the high desert. If she could keep from giving specifics about the job, she was ninety-eight percent sure Ford wouldn't send her Josh's foot as a reminder of consequences.

There was no crunch to his bite when Derek finally chewed and swallowed the corn flakes in his mouth. "That's his leverage on you, then. Your baby brother."

"Older brother, but yes."

"Wait? This jack-off lets his little sister clean up his messes?" She'd never let anyone get away with calling Josh names, but as Derek's nostrils flared she recognized he was angry on her behalf. It'd been so long since she'd allowed herself to be mad at Josh, it was a relief to let someone else do it.

"I'm the most capable little sister." She didn't bother trying to fake smile; Derek only deserved real ones from her.

"Lucky bastard doesn't deserve you," he muttered. Malevolence rushed from him in waves, but Callie dove into those waters. He'd broken down her walls enough last night that she couldn't put dis-tance distance between them now. She wrapped her arms around his waist, and squeezed.

"Nice of you to say so," she said as she relinquished him from her hug.

His cheeks brightened to a soft pink. "Yeah. So. This cat. Is it actually stuck somewhere?"

"Probably."

"Is she going to get it out without your help?"

"Probably not." Her groan was too much like that of a sullen teenager avoiding homework. She might be barely out of her teens, but Callie had been on her own for years, and so never had it good enough to bitch about homework.

"You want me to go with you?"

And have Derek meet her mom? "No," she answered, too quickly. The flush on his cheeks brightened, and her stomach sank. "I mean, I wouldn't want to inflict her brand of crazy on you."

He nodded, but her words didn't diminish the hurt she'd clearly caused. He tried to act like it wasn't a big deal. "You don't want to watch me spread the word to the Charmer's regular cli-ents about the consequences of dealing with Tess today anyway, so that's cool."

He wasn't wrong, but guilt washed over her regardless. "I think I'd rather watch you scare the crap out of some idiots than have to be trapped in an apartment with my batshit mother, but she'll start calling soon if I don't go over there."

He placed his empty dish in the sink, and then turned back to her. "In case I need you—for work—where does she live?"

Callie gave him the particulars, swearing she'd be back in a couple hours. She padded the time frame, because she needed more than a couple minutes to normalize herself after interacting with Zara.

They made plans to meet that night, to continue their search for Tess, but Callie's stomach turned sour the second Derek walked out her door. Was instinct rearing its head? She was getting too comfortable around him, and a small part of her was worried. The rest of her kind of didn't care.

The older Callie's car got, the more it sucked gas. She pulled into the fill station, and headed inside to put ten bucks into the clunker. It would have to suffice for the next few days. Thumbing through the cash she had on hand, Callie had to admit that accepting the offer to skip work might have been the wrong move as far as her wallet was concerned.

Sailor-level swearing erupted near the coffee stand inside. Callie cracked a grin. Someone must really need their coffee. When she turned to see what had infuriated the man, her smile receded quickly. Joey, the square suburban dad she'd extracted a soul from, had spilled his cup across the counter. She'd already indulged in her caffeine fix, so she had no excuse for going to his aid. She nabbed a handful of napkins anyway. Her fingers locked around the bits of paper, once again her hands slipping to Nordic temperatures. After all the heat coursing through her body by way of magic and sex, she'd actually started to forget how much this sucked. She should have known a soul renter would set her off. They'd collected his rented one. She shook herself. Knowing better hadn't been her forte for weeks at this point. She sighed, and extended the napkins clenched between her fingers toward him.

Joey's ass collided with the metal counter as he scuttled away from her. A stack of Styrofoam cups toppled behind him. "How did he know?" His eyes darted from her face to the door and back again in rapid succession.

"Know what? I thought you could use some napkins." She extended them to him again. He had to yank hard to get them out of her icy grip.

He dropped the wad on the counter, and then wrapped his arms around his torso. His hands were tight against his upper arms and grated up and down. The soothing motion warped by pressure left red streaks in its wake.

"What are you doing here?" Why was he so scared of her? The grey accent to his visage was new.

Her brows screwed upward. "It's a gas station."

"Ha. Yeah. Sure." His stilted movements reminded her of Josh coming off a high.

Why was she involving herself in this? "What's wrong?"

Joey glared at the floor for so long she thought he'd forgotten she was there. Whatever he was fucked up on had done a number. She wouldn't have pegged him as a user of more than magic, but she wasn't exactly batting a thousand on character assessments. "She came back," he finally whispered.

"Who?"

"The woman who wanted the soul." His voice dropped low, but the words still pierced Callie's heart. Tess.

She fought against her clenching jaw to ask, "Did you give it to her?"

He looked up at her, eyes blazing as unshed tears welled against his lids. "Not mine. She said she needed permission to take mine . . . "

Her knees almost buckled, but she had to ask. "But?"

"I had another one from the Charmer."

That snapped her back into reality. "Already?"

He had the audacity to look sheepish. "I needed it." He let out a mirthless laugh. "I guess she needed it more."

"What do you mean?" Joey'd asked Tess for money last time. Had she paid up?

"When I told her no, she just took it anyway." He met Callie's gaze, the plea blatant. "I wouldn't have betrayed the Charmer. You know that."

She mostly believed him. "Yeah. How'd she do it, though?"

He grasped her arms, and frost surged forward immediately under her skin. He let go before it could bite him. "She dug her nails into my shoulder and then put her mouth at the hollow of my neck. It wasn't like when you took it."

"She sucked it from you?" There was no way to conceal how gross that was. Callie did not say the words "soul vampire," but holy shit was she thinking them loudly.

"I know how it sounds," he snapped. He yanked at the collar of his shirt. No fang marks, but Joey did have three small slash marks at the center of his chest, in the hollow below his neck. The edges were ragged. He wasn't bleeding, but he would probably need liquid stitches to keep from scarring.

"I believe you," she said, mostly to herself.

Joey leaned close, voice dropped low, "She told me she'd be back the next time I rented, but I won't give her more souls. I swear."

Like the Charmer would continue renting souls to a guy who gave them to the competition.

"You'll tell the Charmer then? Explain everything?" Joey continued. The hope welling against his lower eyelids was almost enough to fell her.

Almost. "You want respect from the Charmer, go there yourself and tell him."

Joey gawked at her, despite the lack of a second head suddenly sprouting from her body. "I can't."

"You'll be safe. It's the best option." She didn't know if that was the truth, but she wasn't about to walk into the Soul Charmer's store and tell this story secondhand. No fucking way. This was the price Joey paid for dabbling in soul magic, instead of helping his kid with algebra.

Besides, she had a cat to rescue.

Zara talked a gang of shit about safety, but the screen door of her ground-level apartment was unlocked, and the dilapidated white door behind it left ajar. The neighbors' ones along the row of the complex she lived in were all damn near barricaded. Not that the fifty-year-old construction would withstand a solid foot thrust near the knob. Callie pressed in when her mom didn't answer the doorbell. "Mom?"

"In the back. Frankie needs me." Zara's voice floated, placating and melodic, from the back of the house.

All the damn cat needed was for Zara to quit pussing out and climb the stepladder to get him out. Sure enough, Callie's mom was sitting at the dinette sipping tea. "Your texts said it was an emergency," she said.

Zara pulled her purple robe closed over her exposed thigh. Like Callie cared about seeing her mom's leg. "He's frightened."

Frankie, a ginger fluff ball, was purring so loudly Callie could hear him when she'd passed through the living room. There was no point in arguing with her mom. No matter how many times he'd leapt from shelf to refrigerator to cabinet, Zara hadn't picked up on Frankie's obvious attempt at solace. Callie wouldn't be able to leave until the cat was "rescued" from his favorite hiding spot.

She glanced around the kitchen, but didn't spot the two-step ladder. She only saw three tabloids with recent dates and a tower of empty take-out containers. So much for hoping Zara would learn to solve her own problems. "Where did you put the step stool?"

"Pantry closet." Zara's bored tone rankled Callie more than the dismissive gesture toward the door on her right.

Sure enough, there was the black stool shoved next to the extra laundry detergent on the floor of the closet. Callie'd taken a single step toward Zara when the ice hit her.

God, no. Her, too? Seriously? If their family already had a soul magic hook-up, Josh could have mentioned it. He could have told her what Zara was into. Callie's gut grew heavier the more her brain battered the idea of her mom renting souls. Her fingers grew stiff against the miniature ladder she held. Thankfully, she'd sprung for the pricier wood version.

There were a lot of situations Callie could handle. She had somehow balanced her real job and her dubious night gig, up until earlier that morning. She'd been dealing with a mob boss and his magical counterpart, and was on the whole still in one piece. But accepting her mother used soul magic? Nope. That was one more what-the-fuck on the disaster cake, and Callie was not going to bite.

Frankie chose that moment to start meowing. Callie had no idea if cats could sense magic, but then she hadn't exactly thought people could sense it either. Shit changed, and the fluffy guy knew it.

"Why are you just standing there? Josh doesn't ever take this long. Get him down." Zara's rushed criticisms usually cut deeper. Maybe the numbing sensation crawling through Callie's veins wasn't such a bad addition to her visits to Mom.

She managed to keep walking past Zara and over to the far wall. Focusing on the cat kept Callie afloat, despite the rotting pit of disappointment in her gut. She kneaded her fingers as subtly as she could, and as she moved farther away from Zara, they eased enough she was able to put down the stool, which, while helpful for the task at hand, rather solidified the whole "Mom Uses Souls" front. Frankie was curled in the small cabinet above the refrigerator. Zara kept the door closed, but Frankie had batted it open, like he always did. He was a clever cat; Callie probably would have liked him more if she didn't have to come over and "save him." He didn't scratch her when she pulled him out, but he did flee to Zara the instant his paws touched the floor. Either cats couldn't sense soul magic, or Frankie put family first too. Just like the other Delgados.

"You need anything else while I'm here?" The ingrained need to give and give wouldn't let Callie leave without offering. Not exactly a habit of a highly successful person. Why couldn't Zara be the mom Callie remembered from when she was little? It was a pointless wish, but Callie longed for her mother to go legit. She mentally slapped herself. Josh had a chance to change. He'd already hit rock bottom. Zara still had too far to fall.

Her mom scooped Frankie into her arms, and as she lazily stroked the cat the natural nastiness she exuded softened. "I wouldn't have called, but Josh hasn't come by."

Twinges of guilt overrode Callie's jealousy and nerves. Mostly. Her mom was clearly worried. She wasn't out to make the lady suffer, but telling her anything would only make everyone's lives more complicated. "I'm sure he'll be by as soon as he can."

Zara's gaze darted to her daughter. Her vision too sharp for her own good. "Why are you standing all the way over there? I don't smell."

"Patchouli counts as a smell, Mom." Deflection was better than letting the edge of her mother's words cut her. The distant look in her mother's eyes couldn't be a side effect of using magic. Right?

"Calliope." Only Zara said her name like a curse.

"Yeah, Mom?" Fatigue sacked her. Years of dealing with family bullshit took its toll. Typically Callie could compartmentalize it into safe, easy to manage pains. She could hide the compacted balls of sorrow between her ribs like a squirrel planning for a guilt-filled winter. But now—after night after night of saving face in front of Ford and managing not to crumple in the same room as the Soul Charmer and slamming face-first into a world teeming with wicked magic—she didn't have the energy to detach and manage her emotions.

"I know you know something about Josh. Sit down and we'll talk." Zara looked to the open seat on the other side of the kitchen table, and then back at her daughter.

Callie took a single step toward her mother before her frost began to overtake her fingers. "I can't."

Zara's upper chest was exposed. No hash marks. At least no one was stealing souls from her mother. Whatever concern Callie had for Zara disappeared. "You don't have anywhere to be that's more important than talking about your brother."

"Like you would know." Even as her brain flashed warning lights, Callie couldn't hold back the words. Or regret saying them.

"You know where Josh is. You're just keeping it from me because you don't want me to help him." Zara folded her arms in front of her chest, locking Callie out.

"Yeah, that's me. Never helping Josh."

Sarcasm was lost on her mother. "You're so busy with your schedule and work that you've forgotten about what really matters."

Her willingness to save Josh *yet again* had demolished her schedule. What had Zara been doing while Callie had been putting crime first, in the name of family? Renting souls. And for what? To ease the guilt from screwing over her kids? She wasn't showing junkie signs, so it wasn't drugs. Had she picked up a married dude? Whatever it was, it sure hadn't been making her or Josh a priority. Classy, Zara, as always.

"You're aware I've given over my savings to my big brother multiple times? That I was the one who got him in the treatment program? The one he bailed on? And I was the one who paid your gas bill when you'd given him every last penny so he could get high for a weekend?"

Zara brushed away the truth with a flippant hand gesture. "Helping family out once in a while—"

Pressure throbbed against Callie's temples. Spontaneous combustion wasn't real, but exploding from your mother's asinine version of crazy? Legit. "More than once a year cannot be classified as once in a while."

"Come," her mother beckoned, sweetness oozing all over the room. "You wouldn't be this upset if Josh were okay. Tell me what's going on."

Even when Josh wasn't around, he managed to be the center of attention. Zara's gentle gestures to sit weren't out of concern for Callie. She was merely a means to an end. Per usual. "I'm not coming over there."

Zara lifted one eyebrow, no doubt upset about her daughter's petulance. Too damn bad. "Sit down. You're going to tell me what's going on."

"How about instead you tell me why you've been renting souls?" Well-honed daggers couldn't have cut her mother down as efficiently. Shame tugged her throat, but she batted it away with a swallow.

Zara opened and closed her mouth over and over eking squeaks each time before she finally collected herself enough to speak. "What are you talking about?"

"I know." Those two little words hung between them for seconds or, maybe, years. The truth might not help Callie, but at least it bought her time and space. The sooner she was out of here, the better. Or was it? Was going back to hunting a mysterious woman who possessed the magic to control souls a better option than talking to her mom?

Zara spun a silver ring around her index finger. The light streaming in through the multicolored sheet hung over the kitchen window didn't glint off the metal. Everything here was tarnished.

"We all need an escape," her mom murmured.

Callie had steered the conversation, and now it was careening toward a cliff at ninety miles per hour. Hitting the brakes might be worse, but there was no way she was sticking around for the inevitable plummet. She'd hit her limit. If she didn't leave now, she'd be liable to spill secrets she couldn't claim ownership of, and Lord knew she wouldn't survive the fallout.

She slammed the door behind her, cutting off her mother's platitudes about making herself light enough to rise to Heaven. Arguing with Zara had never worked, and explaining that any deity who was concerned about beating the point spread was a shitty god wasn't going to improve her day one bit.

Theological differences aside, she'd give it to Zara. Maybe she'd picked the right side. At the rate Callie was tanking, there was no one benevolent watching over her.

That might include Derek.

CHAPTER FIFTEEN

Callie had thirty-seven dollars in her bank account and only half a tank of gas in her car, despite this morning's fill up, but after the visit she'd had with Zara, she needed some goddamn pie.

Familiarity in Dott's was a warm blanket. The mismatched chairs in the seven-table deli afforded a smidge of comfort. As the waitress placed the double-portion slice of coconut cream in front of her, Callie tried to pretend her life was full of similar moments of frivolity. Margaritaville? Pssh. Eating pie for lunch was the peak of a worry-free life. The first decadent bite sealed the deal; best four dollars she'd ever spent.

Unfortunately, even homemade pie couldn't stop the what-if scenarios from whirring in her mind. Her mother was a soul user. She might not have been renting while Callie was around—she could have either done it once a decade ago, or yesterday, and Callie's icy hands wouldn't have known the difference—but did it matter? Soul renters didn't need to be strung out and skinny. The more time she spent in this world, the better she understood renting a soul wasn't for those who had hit rock bottom. One needed to care enough to want to protect their soul. That explained the drug addict contingent. Soul rental was a couple steps above rock bottom. Fuck if she knew about rationalizing choices like that.

"How's the pie?" asked a lilting voice that couldn't belong to the waitress.

Callie had been completely lost in the pie-thinking zone. She looked over to see the woman seated beside her. The woman had long, sandy blonde hair, and her pastel bohemian blouse was almost invisible behind the shiny tresses. Callie recognized her immediately, and a knot formed fast and firm in her stomach. "Um, good."

She didn't make eye contact with the woman for more than a moment. It didn't matter. Goddamn extroverts. "Was that the coconut?"

"Yep." Why was Tess making casual conversation? If only Callie's phone would buzz. An excuse to avoid conversation was never around when you needed it.

The uninvited guest reminded Callie too much of her mom. A free-spirit vibe and spacey softness in casual conversation.

"You're Callie, are you not?"

Time stilled as she slowly lifted her head to take in this woman. Her dark eyebrows were pinched together and raised. Great. The lady bro equivalent of "come at me." A shiver spiked down Callie's spine when she met the woman's gaze. Her hazel irises were ringed in coal. Callie whispered her name. "Tess."

She nodded and then waved over the waitress. "A slice of the coconut cream." Tess paused, and inclined her head toward Callie. "Do you want another piece?"

Patronization must be a bonus skill when you gain the ability to snatch and sell people's souls.

Callie shook her head no, not trusting her voice to conceal her fear. She'd wanted to meet Tess before the Charmer's magic had turned her into a weapon. Doing so without Derek had even held appeal before she'd seared the skin on Bianca. Bartering with the other soul magician in town—the one who didn't look like a reanimated reptile—had seemed smart. Only now she knew too much about this world. The sweet, forty-something-year-old woman next to her was a front. She'd ripped a soul from Joey—a dope, but a fairly harmless one—and left him in a well of regret and need. Anyone who secretly snatched bits of people's souls to fuel themselves was shady with a capital S. The Charmer was heavy handed and creepy as fuck, but there was no secret what you were getting with him. He didn't hide his power.

Callie looked at her hands. She was next to another person who could wield soul magic, steal it, and yet her hands weren't going inferno. They weren't doing anything.

Tess's laugh was like wind chimes. Unreal. "Don't worry, I dampened my magic. No need to have you burning down your favorite restaurant."

For a woman who was supposed to be livid with her for lighting up her underling, Tess was being oddly chill. That—combined with her knowledge of Callie's habits and haunts—only served to make her scarier by the second. This would have been the ideal time for Derek to stride in and do his save-the-day thing.

He didn't.

"Thanks," was all she could think of to say. Being polite was Callie's default when she was uncomfortable, and Tess had thrown her too far out of her realm. She searched her insides for reserves of confidence, but they eluded her. Standing near the Soul Charmer had skyrocketed Callie's magic, not the other way around. Was Tess more powerful or was the Charmer able to do the same thing, but hadn't because he was an asshole? Fuck if it were both.

"Of course. I'm not much for fiery dramatics." Was she dismissing Bianca's injuries? Were they cool just like that?

Trusting this woman wasn't going to happen, but Callie sensed a truce. Good pie could do that. "What can I do for you?"

Tess's smile revealed she had all her teeth. One up on the Charmer there. Not that it stopped the sensation of creatures skittering over her skin. "Oh, no. My goal is to help others, and I'm here to help you, child."

"Help me?" Callie had heard a lot of pitches in her life for assistance. Three different priests, her aunts, her case worker from CPS. Ninety-eight of every one hundred were self-serving. Any woman the Charmer called competition and who colluded with Ford wasn't out for Callie's best interest. Nothing helped Callie tap into her fake strength like being underestimated.

"Well, I doubt your recent decision to work with certain people was out of anything other than necessity. You must have been in quite a tight spot."

Callie bit her lip. She could spot a too-good-to-be-true flag from fifty paces. "It's a temporary gig."

"I highly doubt that."

"You don't know me well." Bitch. Stalking didn't count.

"Perhaps, but nothing to do with souls is temporary, and you don't know the man you're working for very well either. Do you honestly expect that the changes to your . . . hands will go away?"

Yes, she had. The Charmer would want his magic back, right? She was only his indentured servant for a couple more days. She'd be done then, wouldn't she? "That's the deal," she said, as though her confidence hadn't just been rocked by C4.

"It doesn't really work that way." Tess patted Callie's forearm.

She didn't need mothering. That ship sailed long ago, and if she did want a new maternal figure, it wasn't going to be anyone teeming with magic and sowing seeds of sedition. "Can you see the future?"

"No." Her chiming voice cut hard.

"Then you don't know he won't take it back."

Tess zapped Callie's arm. Sparks skated up and down, the skin singeing and smoldering in their wake. The desire to slap at the pain and yelp reared, but the room was too full. She corralled the sensation and hissed in agony. Great. Not only could Tess snipe souls, she could also shock people. It edged her up a level on the villain scale.

Tess heaved in a breath, the action full of drama. She knew she was being watched. The sparks dissipated. She exhaled, and then when she spoke her voice was full of charm again.

"Talk to him. When you're ready to help—and I *will* take care of you, Callie—come find me."

She couldn't help herself. "Where would I do that?"

A cheshire grin on a woman like Tess was terrifying. "There's a tarot reading shop north of the city near the Desert Outlets. You know it?"

"I know the Outlets." Callie shrugged.

"I'll be there at midnight for the next week."

Why was she even entertaining this? Oh, of course, because sinking deeper into danger was the Delgado way. She'd had a lifetime to learn it was smart to always keep your options open. "What if it takes longer?"

"Then you'll have missed out on the opportunity to help purify Gem City."

"'Purify'?"

Tess keened her head to the right. "Too many souls are weighed down due to *his* influence. We'll help free them. You can have more details once you've sided with me. For now, talk to your employer, tell him you quit, and then come find me. I can help."

If the last year of her life was any indication, "I can help" were three words that could fuck with your head as badly as "I love you."

Tess was bad news. Callie's bones screamed at the threat of the woman's presence. But was she worse than the Soul Charmer? Maybe it didn't matter. She was already in bed with two nasty men, the Charmer and Ford, no need to add a wicked woman to the mix.

"You want me to talk to him? To tell him about this conversation?" Now she was avoiding the Charmer's name, too.

"I want you to have the truth. You'd be surprised how freeing it can be." Knowledge lay behind Tess's eyes. Tantalizing secrets were being offered on a plate of promises.

Truth was a privilege. One Callie felt like she would forever be excluded from. She *did* want to know the Charmer's motivations, and what he planned on doing with her once she'd worked off the debt, but what was the risk? Tess knew more than she should about Callie as it was. What did she really want?

Truth might set others free, but secrets kept Callie safe.

If Gem City were bigger, Callie would have found a way to get lost. Running from her problems hadn't ever been her style, but the appeal of disappearing was beginning to become clear. Especially when she parked her car outside her apartment building, and spotted Ford's henchman Nate parked a couple spaces over. Was Tess the type to update Ford on Callie's comings and goings? How closely were the two of them working together?

The windows of the black sports car were rolled down. Clean guitar riffs caught her attention, but the music faded into the background as Nate spotted her. His stretched arm hooked outside the window to wave over the top of the vehicle at her.

She shuffled to his driver's side door, knowing she didn't have another option. The passenger's side was closer, but she was too aware of the threat of moving to Crime Scene B to get into this asshole's car. The encounter with Tess had drained her, though she was fairly certain the woman hadn't literally sucked her energy. Though it wasn't impossible. "What do you want?" she asked, not caring about the bratty tone for once.

"That's no way to treat a friend."

"You're not my friend. Pretty sure we established that the other night."

"Don't see your boyfriend here." He sneered at her, but she wasn't about to talk about her sex life with Nate.

Taking the high road took work, but the less-traveled too-tired-to-give-a-fuck bridge was equally effective. "I'm tired. Tell me what you need or I'm leaving."

"You're still pissy about the other night? C'mon."

Ford might have sent Nate over as a test, to see if she'd fall in line. There had to be more to it than that, though. Nate was leveraging a second chance to talk to Callie. She mentally crossed her fingers he wasn't going to be a double dick after the scene with her and Derek at the Indian restaurant.

"It's not about you. It's about me being tired and cold and wanting to go inside." Bad breakup lines were the best she could conjure today.

"Fine." He fumbled through a pile of wrappers and newspapers on the floorboard until he produced a legal-sized envelope and handed it over. "This is for you."

She took it from him with the same care she'd handle a bomb. Reluctant and gentle. "What is it?"

"Oh, now you've got questions for ol' Nate?"

She rolled her eyes, and waited. She was done asking questions, but Ford wouldn't be pleased if she stormed off. There was a lot on Callie's plate, but keeping that butcher happy needed to be a top priority. The memory of his flashing a knife upon their first meeting was still fresh.

"You're really no fun, you know that? Probably why you're going about renting a soul the hard way." He glanced at his crotch and Callie somehow managed not to vomit. If she had, though, she'd have done it right into his lap.

"And yet you keep trying."

Nate scowled at her, but their dynamic had shifted enough for him to drop the subject. "You've got blueprints of the target, code lists, and whatever notes Ford thought you'd need."

This was really happening. Holding documents with the layout of a secure police forensics facility made her officially a criminal. She had literally stepped over the line into conspiring to burgle. Yeah, there was probably a fancier term, and if she was better at this whole thievery deal she might know it. Her cheeks heated, but there was nothing she could do about the sudden rush of anxiety. "Do I really need these?" Her emotions choked her voice to a whisper.

"Yeah, you do. And before you go getting any big ideas, your big, biker boyfriend isn't allowed to do it for you. Ford gave you this job. *You're* doing it."

"I don't have experience with all this. Why isn't Ford having you do it?"

"Your brother made a promise. It isn't about who is best for the job, it's about honoring your word. Well, your brother's word. Ford needs you inside on this job and with the Charmer. Extra eyes on the Charmer don't come cheap, and there's something about you he likes. Don't ask why Ford does something. Just be happy he ain't hacking your baby bro into pieces. Besides, we're not making you do the dirty work with the science people on this one. Simple break-in? Fuck, my mom could do that. Understood?"

She nodded. Nate didn't scare her anymore, but the thought of stepping out of line with Ford sure as shit did.

"Good."

The sense of finality in his voice spurred Callie back into the moment. Thank God. "I still have a couple days before this all happens." That reedy quality had left her vocal cords.

"You got photographic memory, baby?"

It was her turn to scowl. "No."

"Didn't think so. You can't take a cheat sheet to the job with you. Memorize that shit, and be ready. The boss gave you a specific schedule when you agreed to cover for Joshy boy. Don't fuck it up."

As if it were so simple to not botch the job, not get her brother killed, and not ruin her life completely. Breaking into a building that not only had security, but also housed actual police officers—when the biggest score in her life was three outfits from a department store—would be super easy. The urge to puke spiked her stomach again.

"Anything else?" She regretted asking as soon as the words left her lips.

He reached toward his belt, and she spun on her back heel and headed toward the apartment. His laughter followed her, but she didn't look back.

CHAPTER SIXTEEN

"That dipshit from the other night is parked outside." Derek's first words upon arriving that afternoon were far from sweet nothings.

Callie sighed. "I know. He's been out there for hours." Derek reached for the door he'd closed moments ago, but paused when she added, "I think he's trying to remind me of my obligations to Ford."

"I don't like it." The hard set of his lips rivaled the cut of his jaw in severity.

"I'm not particularly pleased about it, either, but he has my brother. So chill."

"It's not just that. They shouldn't be using you for anything."

She'd had the same thought. Repeatedly. Coming from someone else, though, it was irritating. She'd already spent most of the day being told what she should and shouldn't do. Derek's remark, no matter how well intentioned, wasn't needed or welcomed. "Am I not capable?" she snapped.

"Whoa." He took a step backward. "You're fucking smart. You know I think you're an asset."

"An asset? You out to use me, too?"

"No. Fuck no." Derek's voice rose with each word. "It isn't like that, and you know it."

Her mental armor was thin and dented. "Do I? What is it like then?"

"You can't expect me to be okay with Ford forcing you to interact with that guy."

The urge to ask for his reasoning burned, but going down that road required a towering emotional stockpile. Hers was depleted. "Okay."

"Okay?" He didn't trust her quickly deflating anger. She couldn't blame him.

Callie shook her head to dislodge her ire instead of making another fear martini. "If you're really just worried about me, then yeah. Okay."

"I am." He nodded. "Are you going to tell me what you're doing for him?"

"For whom?" She wasn't supposed to answer, but her fuse was nearly burnt out. Talking could help. Confiding secrets to one mostly trusted person was different than exposing the truth to daylight.

His pacing was going to wear a small circle into the carpet near the window. "Ford."

At least he was playing along. Callie certainly wouldn't have been up for this kind of bullshit. "Don't you want to talk about what you learned this morning instead?" The reply a clear sign to back off.

He inclined his head toward her. The miniscule movement put her under scrutiny enough to make her arms itch. "More souls gone MIA, not really any big news. And I wouldn't have asked about Ford if I didn't want to know."

Her forearm was red and angry where she'd scratched too hard. Distractions were failing her, and deep down, she wanted to tell him everything. "Knowing about Ford complicates everything," she said, and it was the truth.

"Do I look like I'm scared of a little drama?" His arms hung loosely at his sides and earnestness wrinkled between his brows.

She dropped onto the couch and beckoned him to join her. "It's more than drama. This is bigger than catty coworkers talking behind each other's backs. There are big consequences involved if I fuck up."

"He's got your brother, yeah?" His nostrils flared in the same way they had before he'd broken a guy's nose.

She sucked her bottom lip to avoid giving voice to the quaking feelings hungry to escape. The cushion beneath her dipped to the left when Derek sat next to her. Oddly that off-kilter motion made her steady enough to nod.

Derek curled his fingers into fists and released them a few times. Silence packed with truth and fear stretched between them. "I'm not going to let him hurt you or yours. Got me?"

"But why? You haven't known me very long." What was wrong with her? Insecurity was bad enough, but caring for Derek made her strip it bare.

"I want to know you more, and that's enough. I don't connect with people often. You and me? We connect. I like that."

"My brother, though. You can't know about it. Or about Ford or—"

Derek cut off her babbling. "Your brother isn't the first person he's taken. Won't be the last. We'll get him back, though. He's important to you, though, and that makes him important to me."

She liked it, too. "You could—"

"I could do a lot of things, Callie," he said, cutting her off. "What I want to do is spend time with you that doesn't require your damn hands turning into torches or you being scared to tell me why you're on the verge of tears, all because of a jackoff like Ford."

"I don't think I'm supposed to agree out loud with you calling him a jackoff."

"See? I'm therapeutic, too. I can call him all the names you're not ready to. I know him, remember? And I'm not scared."

Callie grabbed his hand and squeezed hard. "You should be, though. Don't you know what he does to people?" The word butcher pinged against the sides of her skull, but releasing it would mean stepping over a line she couldn't walk back from.

"You forget I work for the man who can take people's souls— and that's the part he openly advertises. Ford knows better than to poke at me, which is why I'm concerned about his guy staking a claim outside your place when he knows I'm involved."

Did Derek want to stake a claim? She'd let him sleep here. Did that count? Continuing whatever they had was appealing. No question. But she wasn't a possession people could call dibs on. "No one is going to dictate my choices."

He rolled his eyes. "Not trying to take over, but from the little you've told me, Ford's holding your family over your head. Is it so bad that I want to help?"

"No," Callie muttered, refusing to look at him. It was easier to be sullen when she avoided his earnest face.

She still held his hand, and he gave her a light squeeze. "Good. Now what's Ford asking of you?"

"Asking makes it sound so polite." She sighed, and went to retrieve the envelope Nate had given her. "I was specifically told you are not allowed to help me on the job."

"Well, did he say I couldn't aid in preparations?"

"You think semantics are going to cover our asses?"

"Ford might work dirty, but he's a smart fucker. As long as the job gets done to specs, he won't care."

Maybe it was Derek's confidence, or the way he kept protecting her, or maybe she was just sick of having to do this all alone. She'd have to do the job for Ford by herself, but at this point she'd take whatever help Derek could give her beforehand. "I'm sure you already know the police are working to get past the DNA muddling that soul renting creates."

He let out a loud huff of a laugh. "You could say that."

"Apparently Gem City PD is making progress, putting together some solid investigative work that could be used to pass new laws around soul magic. Ford thinks that's bad news for him."

"It's bad news all around, but they'll have enough proof to outlaw soul magic in the next few years either way." Times like this it was hard to forget how immersed in this world Derek was, and how small Callie's involvement really had been.

"Right. Well, Ford wants their research."

"Not saying the cops are rocket scientists, but they've got to be backing that shit up. It's not like you can shred some papers and it all goes away."

"They do, but they aren't allowed to use remote servers because of some state law intended to protect government information. So their back-up servers are in some room at the forensics lab."

"The satellite building off I-5?" He relaxed into the couch, but his lips tightened. His mind was going a mile a minute, she could tell, but sprinting alongside him wouldn't be good for Callie's health.

"Yes, but I can see you're getting ideas. You don't need to be getting ideas. I have a whole pile of where to go and what to do from Ford."

"My ideas might be better than his." He winked.

"This isn't a game, Derek. Yes, your ideas are probably a thousand times better than Ford's, but if I don't do what he wants, I get my brother returned in tiny, bloody packages. If you think I have issues now, imagine me after opening a box with my sibling's severed foot."

Derek's hands were gentle as he pulled her against him. "Sorry. Bad time to try and lighten the mood. Don't let Ford's reputation wreck you. We'll get your brother back. *In one piece.* Let me help you get out of this."

She nodded against his chest, praying she could hold back the tears.

"What do they need you to do this for? His crew is aces at B&E."

She shrugged. It didn't matter why. "My face isn't on a wanted poster."

He arched a brow, but didn't push the subject. "What about the people who did the research? They aren't going to up and forget their projects."

Callie blinked back tears. "I'm trying not to think about that part, but Ford's crew is 'handling' that part."

"He'll probably just scare them." Derek couldn't even make the lie sound believable.

Callie played along anyway. "Yeah. Sure."

"Which night do you they want you to do this?"

"Friday." Her answer was muffled against his worn shirt.

She'd crumpled against a guy, and he wasn't judging her. Her uneven breaths were obvious, but Derek carried on as though it was a normal conversation and the woman he held against his chest wasn't fighting to not lose her shit. At least one person today was worthy of her trust. "That's good. I've got an informant who's a paper pusher for Gem City police. He works Fridays."

She left the safety of his chest. "Why do we need him? Ford gave me all these documents—" she pointed to the papers on the table "—and they detail schedules and locks and where to be when."

"Schedules are good. Having a guy on the inside to make sure people don't change their schedules is better."

It sounded good on its face, but panic lanced her chest regardless. "What if Ford finds out what we're doing?"

"Ricky's never going to meet you. He's not going to know you exist. He's not going to know what you're after. I can incentivize him plenty without him knowing anything specific."

"Are you going to threaten him?" Not that she should care.

"Nah. You forget about my charm a lot."

"I know you're charming." Her smile faltered.

"Plus he likes cash, doll, and I have plenty of that available."

If she had money, Callie would have paid Josh's debt instead of tying herself to the Soul Charmer. "I can't afford that."

"No one asked you to." He began rubbing her back in small, soothing circles. "I like taking care of you. Let me do it."

Ten even, deep breaths didn't slow Callie's mind any, but at least she'd curtailed the fear free fall. If only she'd met Derek earlier, when it was still possible to buy Josh out. It was too late now. It was this, or nothing. "Maybe."

He kissed her forehead, and followed it with a second light one on her temple. She tilted her face toward his and met his lips with her own. The soft touch was sweet and caring and conveyed all that protective talk Derek loved to share. Callie liked it, but the day had left her raw. Acting gently was out for her. She curved her palm around the nape of his neck and pulled him toward her. Hard. He jerked forward and, surprised by her aggression, firmed his lips. He recovered quickly, though, and soon he parted them to let her deepen the kiss. She'd expected him to match her fervor, to push back, but he accepted the onslaught. He met her energy, but let her maintain control.

Callie's hands were shaking—whether from excitement or overload, she wasn't certain—but she brought her mouth to his neck. The heady scent of leather lingered on his skin, the perfect complement to the touch of salt against her tongue. He groaned and she licked the same spot again.

When their lips met the next time, his body had gone rigid with tension. She wasn't the only one shaking. They had big problems to solve and a whole lot to talk through, but she needed an emotional outlet beforehand. He offered an escape, even if just for a half hour.

"Bedroom?" she asked between panting breaths.

His response was fast and firm and what she needed.

An hour later they were both slicked with sweat, stretched out on Callie's bed with only a thin sheet covering them. It was good to be whole again. Or as complete as she could be. Revelations from Zara, Tess, and Joey had shaken her, but Derek had proven reliable.

Thinking about her mom brought more questions to her mind, ones that hammered at her post-coital bliss. Who in their right mind thinks about their mother while lying naked next to a man who looked like Derek? Soul magic wasn't necessary to push her over the edge; she was already certifiable.

"I can hear you thinking." Derek's bemusement would fade if he knew the direction her thoughts had taken. His affection was more than she'd earned.

Callie smiled at the ceiling in a fleeting moment of normalcy. "A lot happened between when you left this morning and now."

"More than what we've talked about?"

"Significantly." This is why she never bothered with snuggling. Vulnerability coupled with honesty transformed her into the ultimate mood killer.

"I believe we've established my good listening abilities. What happened?"

Her mirthless laugh didn't scare him off. It should have, but if he was brave enough to stay, she was bold enough to divulge. He'd discover her next-level fucked-up qualities soon enough. "My hands went icy at my mom's place, for starters."

The black plastic blades of the ceiling fan spun slowly enough she could track each one's rotation. Focusing on inanimate objects was a key to blocking emotions during confession. She locked onto those blades the same way she'd counted beads while confessing at church. If she focused hard enough, she could almost pretend she was alone.

Derek swallowed. "Anyone else there?"

The poor guy was trying to give her an out. It was too late for that.

"Just me and her. She wanted to talk about Josh, and I wanted to know why she'd used souls. Neither of us were satisfied."

The bed shook as he propped himself up on one arm. He reached for her, lightly stroking her upper arm, and despite her nerves she leaned into his touch. He'd cracked her walls, and now she couldn't repair her defenses fast enough.

"It could have been a long time ago. The effects never go fully away."

His attempts to soften the blow weren't working, but the effort was still appreciated. Zara was a shitty liar—one of her few admirable traits. Her reaction had told Callie all she needed to know. She knew she hadn't called her mom out on old behavior. This wasn't akin to a thirty-year-old acid flashback. "It was recent."

"Are you sure?"

The awe in his voice tripped a wire in Callie, one of those gut responses borne out of years of mistrust. The resulting internal explosion sharpened the barbs Callie threw. "My hands don't provide a timestamp on magic, Derek. That's not a skill I'm going to build over time, right?"

His hand stilled on her arm above her elbow. "What?"

"I had a second encounter today. Tess found me. She knows all sorts of shit about me and my life and my deal with the Charmer."

Her emotional shrapnel was filling the growing void between them. Derek was infuriatingly quiet.

"She informed me this little bit of magical infusion in my fingertips isn't going away. Ever." She was tempted to wiggle her fingers at him, but she needed to hold what remained of mind together.

"She's full of shit." God, he sounded so sure.

"How do you know?"

"The Charmer wouldn't give up his magic permanently."

It always circled back to the Soul Charmer. He'd been a part of her life for less than two weeks, and yet his insidious presence had woven itself into everything she touched: her mom, her lover, and even her goddamn skin. He was everywhere. She was right to fear him and whatever he had planned for the future.

"He's still got plenty of magic." Did she sound afraid, or too far gone? She couldn't tell anymore.

Derek's lips curled into a vicious sneer. "Yeah, but he actually put part of it in you. You don't know him like I do. He will want every bit he's given you back."

She wanted to believe him. "How can you be sure?"

"The Charmer isn't much for sharing, and he will want his power back. Always has."

Callie's mind yanked the reins hard. "Has he done this before?"

"This? No, but I've seen him work with others before. I can't explain it, but he never let anyone keep his magic."

Callie could tell he meant the words, but she hadn't forgotten the glint in the Soul Charmer's eyes when she'd last visited.

Derek continued. "I am not going to let him control you." The possessive tinge was inherently sexual. Their mutual nudity didn't help matters.

"I trust that." He didn't want to share her, and perhaps that could save her. There was just one other problem. "Though, I need to know if you knew about my mom."

"No." His fierceness rocked the bed. The sheet slipped to her waist, but his gaze remained fixed on Callie's eyes.

Even the single squeak of a bedspring wouldn't deter her. "You've never seen her in the shop?"

He hesitated. "What's her name?"

"Zara."

He shook his head slowly. "I don't know her. I can't promise you she never bought from the Charmer. If she was good about paying her debts and returning the goods, I might have never seen her. But I swear, Callie, I would not have kept this from you."

Biting the inside of her cheek didn't clarify anything. The pain was barely a distraction. "Do you think he knew?"

"The Charmer?"

She nodded.

"I can't say, doll." He tucked a few loose strands of her hair behind her ear. "He might have, but I doubt it's why he hired you."

That shouldn't have calmed her, but it did enough that she didn't get hung up on his use of the word "hired" instead of "black-mailed." She rolled on her side to face him. His eyes were lighter now, a rich sky blue. "What *was*, then?" The need for insight clawed past her insecurities.

"It could have been a lot of things." Could he tell how badly she needed this? Perhaps, because he continued, "I think he knew you could handle the magic. I told you before, it's not exactly a common deal. The wrong person with that magic would go manic."

"And you still think he's going to take it back?" She almost said "let me go." Where had that come from? Callie's barter with the Soul Charmer had clear terms. She worked for him for fourteen days, and that's it.

"If he doesn't on his own, I'll convince him." Flashes of Derek pinning marks and punching men rushed to the forefront of her mind. His muscles seized. His pecs flexed a hair's breadth from her face, presenting the gift of a loaded weapon at her disposal. The violent streak still stirred unease in her gut, but the potential safety it promised simultaneously lured her in. A double-edged sword could be mighty shiny.

"Okay," Callie said, hoping the sense of finality she'd imbued the word with would actually help her let the issue go.

"Okay. Good. Now, can we talk about Tess?" At least he had the good sense to wince.

"We probably should," she admitted, "but we need to talk about Joey first."

"Joey?" He angled closer to her, as if hearing another man's name while lying in bed with her stirred some natural territorial instinct.

Smiling was out of the question, but it was oh so tempting. "The boring guy we retrieved a soul from the other night. The one who was freaked his wife would see us."

"I know Joey." His shoulders relaxed. "What about him?"

"Tess stripped him of another soul." That was the nice way to put it. Derek sputtered for a moment, but eventually let her explain the encounter.

"And there were cuts on his chest?" His questions were focused. He knew what to ask, but didn't explain why.

"Yes."

"Did Joey give her the soul?"

"He said he refused to give her permission, but she took the rented one he had inside him anyway. How is that possible? To straight up rob someone of a soul?"

"It's possible, but not good."

"Obviously. Joey looked like one of those corner tweakers, ready to start rocking."

"There's that, but the cuts and the theft sure sounds like she's pulling the souls into her body instead of collecting them safely." Oh, fuck. So what Tess had done wasn't weird because of the whole stealing business, but because she didn't put it in a goddamn jar in the process?

Her incredulity couldn't be contained. "So it's cool she robbed him?"

He flopped on to his back, shaking the bed. "Of course not. It's just when you extract a soul without tools—like your flask—it's dangerous."

She imagined the Charmer's creepy claws at her neck, ready to snatch her soul, and she shuddered.

"We'll take care of this. Of Tess. She's probably batshit because of all the souls she's holding in her body, but if she doesn't have the power to create her own tools, it means she's weaker than we originally anticipated. The Charmer can take her out. Easy."

She'd believed all but that last word. There was nothing easy about this. Tess knew too much about Callie and her relationship to the Soul Charmer already. "Tess is on to him." She winced as she spoke.

She didn't scrimp on the details of her awkward meeting with Tess, though she left out the size of the pie slice she'd devoured. It wasn't the time to talk frivolity, or coconut.

When she was done, Derek raked his fingers through his hair and rolled onto his back again. "She wants you to work for her?"

"That's what she was after. Though, I'd trust her about as far as I could throw her."

"You believed her about the magic thing, though?" Perhaps it was easier to insert his foot in his mouth when he wasn't wearing his boots.

"I believed—and still do—that the Charmer is a liar."

He pursed his lips before agreeing. "Fair enough."

"She puts on a better face than he does, but she still made my skin crawl. There's something not right about her."

"Feeding off souls will do that to a person." No matter how causally he said it, the truth rang clear and hollow.

"Feeding off souls?"

"She's doing more than siphoning energy at this point. It's like she's hoarding souls to create an internal armor. The more souls squished in a single body, the crazier the person becomes."

"She talked about saving the city. Pretty sure the lady has a god complex, and enough information to freak people out with what she knows." Callie totally meant herself.

"She has power. That's normal. She wanted to meet you, though, and that means we know where to find her."

"I really don't want to see her again." Especially now that it was clear to Callie the soul vampire business was an everyday thing for that lady. "But I know you're right. The longer she's out there, the bigger threat she's going to become."

"Agreed. The sooner we bring her to the Charmer, the sooner you're done with both of them."

"Do you think we can talk him into going himself? Like give him the information, and let him handle the rest? What else could you or I possibly do at this point?"

"You were in the same meeting I was. He wants this done by us. That's not going to change."

"That was before we knew she could nullify her magic around me."

Derek's sullen smile made Callie's stomach sink. "He probably knows. I bet with the right motivation you'll still be able to bring the heat, though."

Motivation? She had more than enough threats and life-or-death balance shit in her life. "I think I'm full up on motivation."

"Well, then, it'll go fine."

"You're bad at this pep talk thing."

He kissed her. "Nah, you just haven't been properly pepped before. It can be hard to recognize. You'll do fine once we're there."

CHAPTER SEVENTEEN

The desert had a way of swallowing construction. During the day, the Desert Outlet Mall stood out like a shimmering mirage amid the sand and rogue juniper bushes. At night, though, without sunlight to cast the squat adobe buildings' shadows, the entrance to the frontage road leading to the shopping cluster was practically invisible. On the third try, Derek managed to spot the cutover. "Would a streetlight kill them?"

Callie shrugged. "Just because it's outside the city doesn't mean they don't have the same light pollution ordinances."

Riding as a passenger in her own car was weird. The vehicle took on new tones from the other seat. The rattle of the muffler wasn't as bad here. The gouges in the dash Josh had sworn were there *before* he'd last borrowed the car weren't nearly as deep.

"It makes even less sense out here."

"I would have thought you'd like it."

"Why? Is all this dark and mysterious doing it for you?" He waggled his eyebrows. He'd been playful most of the afternoon and evening. It had to be a guise to calm her nerves, but it had worked, for the most part. He'd even agreed taking the motorcycle to a meeting with Tess was a bad decision. The only problem was, that left her riding bitch in her own car.

She cast him a side eye glare, but softened it with a sweet smile. "No, but isn't it easier to do business in the dark?"

Derek stiffened his spine. The comment wasn't meant as a jab, but she'd put him on high alert. Needling at unknown touchy issues shouldn't count against her, right?

"I didn't mean—" she started to apologize.

"Oh, no, that's fine. Though you do keep forgetting I do a lot of my job by *talking* to people. I'm starting to get the impression you think I'm far more nasty than I actually am." He grinned at her before she could get self-conscious over that comment, too. Her neuroses placated, he continued. "Tess was smart to pick this place. Yeah, it's dark like everywhere else, but these buildings have a lot more space between them. More alleys mean more hiding places."

"Hiding places work for your half of the plan." Callie injected as much enthusiasm into her words as she could muster.

"We could have waited until tomorrow," he muttered. An extra twenty-four hours worth of planning might have been nice, if Derek was right, but Callie couldn't handle another day of worry. He eventually acquiesced, and anyway, his mere presence had been enough to calm the tense situations they'd been in so far. Callie didn't have that same talent. Being fast and hiding her emotions were basically her top skills. And neither was particularly useful in this situation.

What she really needed was a healthy dose of fake confidence, but Tess had knocked Callie off her game. Placing all bets without knowing the odds was just asking for someone to take your cash. Derek's money was on mental agility. He thrived there. She'd witnessed the way he could assess a room and leverage his lethal grace. She didn't pack a stash of secret weapons.

"No need to wait," she finally told him. Fear of the unknown shadowed her words.

He nodded. "You know the plan."

Ah. The plan. "Yeah, but it's too simple. How do you know it will work?"

"Just don't let her touch you first." The plan—if they had to call it such—consisted of keeping Callie's magic in play until Derek could take action. But she'd demanded to rush the timeline, which meant they were mostly banking on luck.

"What am I going to do if she dampens my magic again? If I need to defend myself, I'll be screwed."

"Kick her in the bits."

Derek laughed at her you've-got-to-be-kidding-me stare.

"You've never been kicked there," he added. It wasn't a question.

"You're aware I don't have balls to crush, right?"

"Intimately. Still, if you'd been kicked there, you'd know: it's a fucking vicious thing, regardless of your parts."

"I'll trust you on that one." She'd rather not find out if he was telling the truth.

Derek parked the car outside of a furniture store. Before he cut the engine he asked, "You're sure the tarot spot is on the other side?"

"Positive." After racking her brain as to why the address Tess had given her seemed so familiar, she finally realized: her boss Louisa actually frequented the place. Her stomach tightened until a pang forced her jaw to clench. Lou'd had a rough life, and Callie wouldn't accept Tess mooching energy from her friend.

She unlocked her phone. Five minutes past midnight. Hell. This was happening. Forcing herself out of the car was so much harder than she wanted to admit. Walking into the Soul Charmer's shop nearly two weeks ago and bartering for use of a soul had been the lowest she thought she'd ever sink. She couldn't say the same anymore. The steel in her spine had held resilient that day because, in the end, she was there to protect her brother. "Family first" carried her through nearly every shit situation. The guiding forces of guilt and loyalty kept her moving forward even when she'd been petrified. Pretending seeing Tess was the same thing as stepping through the Soul Charmer's door the first time was such a bitter lie she couldn't accept it. God knew she wanted to.

The walk across the cracked concrete toward the neon TAROT sign with its burned-out T would have been a hell of a lot easier if it were for the greater good. If the final act would absolve her of past sins. If it were about keeping her brother whole. If it could make her mother give a shit about her. Meeting with Tess again wouldn't do any of those things. It pleased the Soul Charmer, but he was going to give her that soul tomorrow regardless of whether she helped capture Tess.

The disgusting truth was she was meeting with Tess for herself. It made Derek's life easier, and she wanted to help him. She hadn't wanted to help anyone this deeply who wasn't family. Ever. It could have been the magic, or maybe the joint journey through darkness. She didn't know and, frankly, didn't care. Whatever fucked up thing bound her and Derek together, she would respect it. At least he'd never held her biggest mistake over her head like Josh had. That already put Derek ahead in the loyalty ledger.

Her resolve to see this thing through steeled, Callie opened the door and stepped inside North Side Tarot.

Bells jingled as the door closed behind her. Small lamps sat on every flat space around the cozy room's perimeter. The shades—each a tone of purple or black—were lit with soft twenty-watt bulbs. Their illumination was swallowed by the dark rugs layered atop one another, and the plush chairs stacked with velvet pillows wedged in the remaining space. For other-worldly ambiance, it wasn't half bad. The floor was clean and dry, which already put it twelve steps ahead of the Soul Charmer's place.

A woman in a pale purple maxi dress sauntered into the room from the rear entrance. "How may I assist you tonight?" she crooned, the tone all too reminiscent of the voice Callie's mother used when she spoke to the neighbors.

Fresh irritation helped keep her steady. "I'm here to meet Tess."

She dropped the pretense with a shrug. "Oh. Sure. I'll let her know you're here."

Did this woman know why she was here? Had Tess told her she'd be in tonight? Psyching herself out was not helping. Customers might come here to see Tess. Callie hadn't considered the fact she probably looked like any regular person coming in and seeking emotional relief through magic and massage; the truth was she fit the profile as well as anyone else.

A wingback chair upholstered in black leather was wedged in the far corner of the room. It didn't quite fit with the tarot shop's velvety vibe. So, naturally, Callie took a seat there. It reminded her that however calculated Tess's façade might have seemed, nothing was ever perfect. Not even when you could wield magic.

"I expected you'd need more time to think." The melodic over-tone couldn't disguise Tess's wariness.

Callie wanted to relish in the thought that she'd put Tess on her heels, but she wasn't an idiot. If she knew anything, it was that emotions were easy to fake, given the right motivation. "It was a long day of bad shit."

She swaddled herself in as much honesty as her mind could manage. A good lie was ninety percent truth, after all.

"Talking with your former—" she paused letting the question dangle for a breath "—employer could ruin anyone's day."

Callie nodded. The Charmer was a ninja-level day ruiner. He just hadn't been the primary source of today's frustrations. And, well, she hadn't actually talked to him. Tess didn't need to know that though.

"Did he confirm what I told you?" Tess's hard-on for the Soul Charmer kicked Callie's heart rate up a notch.

"Does it matter?" Playing disgusted with the Charmer was easy when Tess's need to feel superior to the man was so plain.

Tess barreled right on through the trapdoor. "He's quite conniving. I'm glad you were able to look past his lies. We can't purify anything with his deviation blocking the path."

Communicating with these soul magic wielders became more difficult the longer she was involved. Tess sounded like she should be screaming on a street corner and clutching an end-of-days sign. Parsing out what was insanity and what was part of this complicated, magical world was way out of Callie's pay grade.

She did, however, need to move things along. As part of their plan, Derek would be in the back room by now, but he'd still have to sneak past the other woman who worked there. Keeping Tess distracted was Callie's job. Fuck it. She could indulge the crazy a little longer. "How does the Charm—"

"Don't say his name in here!" Tess spat. Would she react the same to Ford's name? Best not to go there.

"Sorry. How does *he* stop you from purifying the city?" The bitter aftertaste of talking purification clung to her tongue like an accidental swig of week-old milk.

"His slime blocks the path."

O-kay. Tess might actually be legit crazy. "What do we need to do to clear the path?" Lord, forgive her, she sounded like a member of a cult.

Tess held her forehead and closed her eyes, as though wearied by the mere thought of answering Callie's basic question. Callie shot a glance toward the door to the store's back room. Derek needed to speed the hell up, because placating a cult leader wasn't really a skill in her stockpile.

With a heavy sigh, Tess finally answered. "Additional souls can do wondrous acts in the right body. He has access to a wealth of good, but insists on handing them out to any person who comes in off the street. Those people aren't using them like they should be, to change the world. They're using them to break from their celestial contracts. That was never the intention of our magic. He knows better."

Callie had to admit, Tess had a point about the trivial way society viewed rented souls like get-out-of-hell-free cards, and avoided talking about the bigger picture questions about using them, like where the souls they were borrowing had come from. Kind of like hot dogs. "What's the real intention of soul magic then?"

"The magic itself doesn't have intent, child."

Stalling was harder than people gave it credit, especially when the person you were trying to stall was speaking in riddles and could probably kill you with her mind. "Right, but what's its purpose?"

"To elevate us." The incredulity in her tone implied the answer should have been obvious to her.

"That sounds an awful lot like raising our souls to heaven." Callie couldn't resist quoting her mother's favorite line of scripture.

"If you're suggesting what *that man* is doing with souls is God's will, you can leave."

"No!" She answered too quickly. After a moment she tried again. "Not at all. I recognize you're doing something more important and valuable."

She scoffed, but was clearly flattered by the remark. "Saving society is vital. We can't let him corrupt them all."

Callie played along. "So you're saying we need to get his souls?"

"'We'? So quickly you've come aboard." Tess beamed, but Callie couldn't tell if it was genuine.

Callie held up her hands as though they were living grenades with the pins pulled. "I don't want this magic."

"I can't make it disappear. I was clear about that." Why couldn't she? Because she wanted to use Callie, too?

"Are you willing to help me, though? Control it at least?"

Tess took a step toward her and the first inklings of warmth buzzed at Callie's fingertips. When her hands began to glow, she asked, "Can you stay back for now? Trying to avoid flame mode." Like avoiding carbs, though, it was futile.

"I can't teach you anything if you don't accept the magic." Tess closed in, leaning over the chair where Callie sat.

She held her hands below her face in the space between them. They lit like Roman candles, ready to start firing shots of riotous color through the room. Callie turned her palms away from Tess, hoping it would cool the blaze. The desire to touch Tess welled in Callie's chest. Where was that coming from? It wasn't her normal fight-or-flight response. It was darker. The magic inside her—her magic— wanted to be fed. Callie just wanted to protect herself, but would touching Tess burn her, or further ignite the power roiling within Callie's open hands? This job was officially too damn dangerous.

"How do I accept it?" The question came out as a sob.

Tess's nails sank into Callie's right shoulder. The sharp pain was rapidly replaced by a swell of flame, as the fire in her hands began to lick its way up her arm. "You need to feel it."

Burn victims often passed out from the pain of the heat, but the fire didn't actually injure Callie. Her head swam, regardless. "It's too much—"

"It's because you fight it. Accept the purity of the magic. Pull it in. Embrace it, and the pressure will subside."

Pressure. Shit. That was the word. Flames licked at her skin, but beneath the surface her muscles throbbed, as though the magic was treating her like a dollar-store water balloon. She was going to pop. "I can't keep it." It was too much. Too scary. Too wrong.

"Not a choice. Accept it and ascend—"

"You Tess?" Derek's growl raked over sandpaper.

Tess jerked her head in his direction, but he'd already shot. She grabbed weakly at the dart protruding from her shoulder. "You . . ."

Her body fell on the floor in a heap. Derek shot her again, this time in the chest.

"Was the second one really necessary?" Callie asked.

"Too many surprises today." Blood smeared his neck and the back of his right hand.

"Agreed." Callie slumped in the chair as the fire within her quieted to a simmer. She ignored the niggling thoughts of embracing magic. "Are you okay?"

"Fine," he said. Liar.

"The other lady?" Callie swiped a hand across her shoulder. Blood marred her fingers, but the flames had cauterized her wound. There was probably a bright side buried in all this, but she couldn't spare the energy to searching for it.

"Snoozing. We need to book." Derek hefted Tess's limp form over his shoulder. If they hadn't just tranquilized the woman, Callie might have fantasized she was dating a firefighter instead of a debt collector for one of the bad guys.

Their paper-thin plan was working, but that didn't mean they were solid. "Are you going to walk across the shopping complex with her like that?"

"It's dark. Didn't you say that was beneficial to my kind of work?" He waggled his eyebrows at her, but she still saw the strain in his neck. Something more than the deadweight on his shoulder was hurting him.

"Let's not screw this up. I'll bring the car over." They should have done that in the first place. Shitty plan.

Derek attempted a shrug. "She's not dead. So technically everything's going according to plan."

Tess sure looked corpse-like. Was it getting to her? Probably. "You sure?" She was going to quit agreeing to poorly constructed plans . . . starting next week.

"Stay behind me, and get the car's back door open when we get there. I'll handle the rest."

The two of them and their unconscious prize held to the shadows. Callie's hands were just visible as they worked their way through the alleys to the darkened lot they'd parked in. Tess didn't need to be awake for her surplus of souls to have an impact, even if it was a small one. Callie decided the dim glow and the edge of heat were worth it to stay within arm's reach of Derek.

The moonlight highlighted the drops of blood he left as they moved. The mounting pressure of the magic threatened to fell her, but now wasn't the time to wuss out. If she had any real control over the magic, she'd offer to cauterize his wounds, too, but burning the guy you were screwing seemed like a recipe for failure.

The proof of their presence was scattered in a DNA trail behind them. The good part of working with criminals, though, is they weren't likely to call the cops. Unfortunately, she still needed to get Tess to the Soul Charmer without further incident, and the man with the plan was bleeding too much.

—— CHAPTER EIGHTEEN ——

allie should have known toting an unconscious woman through Gem City wasn't going to be easy. It *shouldn't* be easy. Kidnapping was probably some sort of criminal art form. Derek's natural ability there was unsettling, but fortunate, given the circumstances.

Or at least it was until she noticed his chin dipping.

"Derek." Panic lanced her through the chest.

His grunt of acknowledgement lacked energy. A second later his hand slipped from the steering wheel. Callie yelped and grabbed it just in time to correct their path before the car veered into oncoming traffic. He hadn't reacted to her scream. Just great. She nudged his foot off the gas and edged the vehicle to the shoulder. Callie wedged a foot onto Derek's side and hit the brakes. The car slowed, but thanks to their circuitous route there weren't any streetlights to expose them. Once the car was safely in park, she spread the lapels of Derek's jacket.

Blood was like any other bodily fluid: gross in all but the correct context. The right side of his shirt was soaked, in the darkness it turned black. She skimmed her fingers across the damp fabric, the tacky substance on top clinging to her fingers. There was a tear in the tee, hidden by the saturation, above his nipple. Contemplating how someone got a knife under his leather jacket to slash him there wouldn't help anyone. Thinking would lead to panic, and she needed to be in nurse mode. He needed stitches, but she didn't have the necessary tools here. She slapped his cheek and called his name until he roused enough to look at her.

"Can you hear me?"

He gave her more than his standard grunt, but the words were unintelligible.

She swore internally. "We need to get you patched up."

"Charmer's," he muttered. It made perfect, twisted sense that the Soul Charmer would have the tools to fix Derek's wound.

Callie scanned the car for a spare bit of fabric to staunch the bleeding. Nothing but a—wait, had Tess moved? Maybe not. Great, now she was psyching herself out. She shrugged out of her coat and yanked her own cotton tee overhead, wadded it up, and then placed it just so against his wound. Managing to get Derek to keep his hand on top of it was a whole separate task.

As she finished the last button on her coat, she heard a groan from the backseat. She didn't have the energy to fight Tess. Snagging Derek's tranq gun and plugging the woman with another dart was far simpler. With their hostage back in Dreamsville, Callie hopped out of the car and came around to the driver's side, nudging Derek across to the passenger seat. A big man like that shouldn't be so pliant.

She drove as fast as the aging engine would allow, and hoped it was fast enough.

"Most people would mention getting stabbed," Callie muttered. The two unconscious people in the car weren't listening, but she wasn't talking to them; she was trying to distract herself from the fact that with Derek out, she was now on the hook for the safe delivery of both of them.

"I was wrong. We should have waited a day and made a real plan."

She spared a quick glance at Derek. He sagged against the seat, and his hand had begun to drop from his chest. Callie grabbed it and pressed it firmly against his wound. "Keep it there."

He sucked in a harsh breath, but at least he wasn't dead.

"Just because my car is a piece of shit, doesn't mean bleeding all over it is acceptable. You're cleaning it when this is all over." Maintaining control now meant he'd be okay. She could crumble once she made it to the Soul Charmer's shop.

She glanced in the rearview mirror. No red and blue lights were flashing at her, but damn if she didn't expect cherries to pop behind her any second. How would she explain Derek's knife wound, or the green darts sticking out of the woman slumped across the back seat? Were licenses required for tranquilizer guns?

Balancing the need to get to the Soul Charmer's fast against the extreme desire to avoid the Gem City Police, Callie pushed the car to five miles above the posted speed limit, but no further.

Ten minutes later, she parked her car outside the Soul Charmer's storefront. She didn't bother with safe distances or worry about being inconspicuous. Tess's face was planted in a pool of drool. It didn't get much more conspicuous than that.

Callie rushed around the car and opened the passenger door. Jostling Derek was enough to make him open his eyes. Steady feet weren't going to be found, but his legs weren't total Jell-O. Callie managed to get him standing. The bastard was heavy, but she wedged her shoulder in under his armpit and steered him the few steps to the door.

Once inside she yelled, "Charmer, you better have some medical skills!"

"I don't remember offering you such services. Are you looking for another barter?" The Soul Charmer sauntered out from the back room. He deserved to be punched in the throat for his ambivalence.

She was about to tell him what he could do with his propositions when the Charmer caught sight of Derek. "What happened to him?" he asked in a rush, concern snapping to his face in a flash.

"Knife wound. You any good at stitches?"

The Charmer lifted a stool from behind the counter and brought it toward them. He sat it next to a wall, and Derek dropped onto the wooden seat immediately. The Charmer investigated the injury, holding up Callie's wadded shirt in question. She shrugged and he gave Derek's wound a closer look. "I can heal him," he said finally.

"He's going to be okay?" Her throat was tight and raw, but the Charmer didn't pounce on the vulnerability. Maybe he cared about Derek, too. Huh.

"Of course. A little blood loss."

"Tess is out in the car," Callie blurted.

The Charmer's lips pulled back. Too bad a smile and a snarl looked identical on his face. His eyes hardened, and that wicked glint appeared a moment later. "Stay with him."

"Where are you going?"

He narrowed his eyes, but Callie was beyond caring about how the Soul Charmer *felt*. "To get tools for him, and to send someone out to retrieve my prize. Where is your car?"

"Right outside the front door."

He huffed, but scuttled to the back without any further comment.

She squatted next to Derek, her shoes sinking into the carpet as her weight shifted toward her toes. His eyes were barely open. Blood loss could act a whole lot like a concussion. Callie would rather compare it to a normal injury than the real memory his dazed demeanor pulled: Josh, on his back in the middle of their mother's living room. He'd been so high he hadn't bothered to close the front door, much less lock it. Zara's jewelry, what little there had been, and her TV had been stolen along with Josh's shoes. Callie'd taken Josh to the emergency room for the first time that night. It was the same night she'd discovered her big brother wasn't simply dabbling in the occasional pharmaceutical, but had developed a sincere love affair with methamphetamines.

Derek's skin was feverish when she pressed her hand against his cheek. He wasn't her brother. He wasn't an addict. That fact only got her so far. The gouges in Callie's heart were more than deep ravines; they were black holes. Opening up to people was hard enough. Her emotional scars tainted every new memory, every sight. Derek hadn't been injured for her. This wasn't some heroic wound. What happened in that back room was a mystery, but odds were it wouldn't have made her proud. But Derek's allegiance to the Charmer could be just as much a motivation as getting Callie out of Tess's sights.

Guilt shook her hard enough she rested a hand on Derek's knee for stability. He hadn't done anything to earn those thoughts, so Callie crammed that thought down with all the other uncomfortable pellets.

"You still with me, big guy?" He needed her and she'd gone asshole in her mind. This was why she didn't do relationships.

"Mhm."

"The Charmer will be back in a second. He can fix you up." She almost believed it herself.

"I'm already here," the Charmer said from behind her. He shooed her out of the way with a frigid hand.

Expecting a first aid kit was a newbie mistake. The tray the Soul Charmer carried had a few normal medical supplies, like a needle and thread and gauze. The black, pulpy concoction with flecks of red filling a small dish at the center, however, gave Callie pause. "What's that for?"

The Charmer kept his focus on his patient. Probably a good idea. He prodded Derek's cut, drawing hisses and groans in equal measure. "Someone cut you deep."

The words were meant for Derek, but they hit way closer to home then Callie would have liked.

The Charmer scooped the pulp into his palm and pressed it to Derek's chest. Again Callie asked what it was for.

"I liked you better when you were quiet," he hissed. After a moment, though, he told her. "It will stop the bleeding."

The pressure from his scrawny arm had Derek's swaying. Words that held no meaning for Callie flowed out of the Charmer's lips and filled the room. Her fingers began to warm, but the magic never ignited a spark.

"Aren't you going to clean the wound, at least?" Why was she letting this man care for Derek? *She* had the medical training, not him.

The Charmer ignored her again and wiped his hand on his pant leg before picking up the needle and thread. Biting back the offer to help squeezed Callie's throat. Emotions were dangerous, especially for people with too much pride.

People like Callie.

The Soul Charmer busied himself behind the counter after stitching the gash in Derek's chest, tinkering with jars and boxes like she'd seen the men at the retirement home do.

Derek had slipped out of consciousness, but remained upright against the wall. The Charmer didn't cast him or Callie as much as a glance for more than twenty minutes.

"How much longer until I can move him?" she finally asked.

"Who said you're going to?"

Callie walked to the counter, a woman with purpose. "I did."

The Charmer's guffaw rattled into a cough, but before she could press the matter, another man entered from the back of the store. He was Callie's height, maybe thirty, with slicked back hair.

"She's awake," he reported to the Charmer. He projected menace, though not as much as Derek. Probably another soul repo man, but his vibe was a little more of an ex-club kid who had decided to bulk up and become the bouncer.

The Charmer turned his wicked gaze to Callie. Dark, insidious intentions danced within his dilated pupils. "That's your cue."

She managed not to choke. "Excuse me?"

"Finish your job, and you can take him home. Well, to your home."

"What's left to do? Did you not catch the part where I tracked, tranquilized, and kidnapped a woman on your behalf tonight?" Saying it aloud did not make it sound better.

"Find out why she thought it wise to steal from me." Venom should have dribbled down his chin.

"I don't know enough to do that. She'll be scared of you."

"You're scared of me." The lack of inflection or accusation only made the bald truth starker.

Agreeing wasn't necessary. "My hands—"

"—will be an asset. You may go get my answers, or you may leave. Without him."

She shot a look to Derek. The bleeding had stopped, but he needed observation from a person who gave a shit.

"He stays until I have answers." The Charmer's hiss coiled around Callie's abdomen squeezing like the boa constrictor he'd likely been in a past life. "Your choice."

"Fine. Where is she?"

The Soul Charmer's henchman didn't flinch as the rickety steps descending into the shop's basement swayed under his weight. He didn't bother to introduce himself, but the Charmer had made it clear she was to follow him. The headshop scent from above didn't filter through the floorboards. The wood and sandstone of the lower level cocooned them in dank depression. Her guide unlocked a door and gestured for her to enter.

"She's inside," he rumbled.

The pellets of anxiety she'd hidden between her ribs rattled. Her breath quickened, her lungs pressing hard and fast against her bones to keep her steady. "You coming with?" He wasn't Derek, but they both technically worked for Team Creep.

Her hope for aid was dashed with his scoff. "She's your problem. I'll be out here."

Not much comfort, bucko. Could he hear the tittering clacking of her fear inside her torso? He pointed to the door again. That was probably a no.

This was for Derek. She repeated the mantra in her head with each step toward the doorway. She might have hesitated at the precipice, if it were an option. The force of the magic the Soul Charmer had placed on the room sucked Callie forward, almost like she had no will of her own. Which sounded about fucking right. The Charmer was holding someone she cared about upstairs. Agreeing under duress was simply what she did in his presence. Naturally the barrier of his makeshift prison would yank her inside.

The walls were bare and the concrete floor smattered with sawdust. Below fluorescent lighting, Tess sat in the center of the room, bound to an aluminum chair. The darts had been removed from her chest and shoulder, but small bloodstains remained. Rust-red reminders. They'd doped Tess significantly, and yet she was awake. Was Tess a horse in a former life, or did magic supersize one's metabolic rate? Callie shook the thought away. She needed answers, and fast. Tess would give her the information she needed, she'd update the Charmer, and then get Derek the hell out of here. Right. She nodded to herself and took two steady, boss-lady steps toward Tess.

The woman lifted her head. Tess's cheek was swollen, likely thanks to Mr. Friendly outside, but the developing bruise didn't diminish the cruel, knowing look she cast Callie. It worked, too. The cache of fears between her ribs exploded. Buckshot of terror, worry, and weakness assaulted her core. Organs were bruised. Bones were fractured. Muscles were torn. Her heart double-timed it. But pumping blood faster wouldn't slow the pain or ebb the rising tide of worthlessness.

Who was she kidding? Interrogating Tess was so far out of her wheelhouse she'd need a plane ticket and two boats to even see the thing. This was the woman who had tracked her to the retirement home, and to the diner as well. She'd watched her. She'd *known* an awful lot about Callie's life. She'd bet Tess even knew about her deal with Ford, though how well she knew the mobster was anyone's guess. How could Callie turn the tables on her? Tess was batshit, but could playing into her ego work when they were locked in the Soul Charmer's basement? Not likely. Her chest burned. Derek would have had an answer here. He'd have known what to do. Unfortunately, he was busy sleeping off a knife wound upstairs.

How was this her life?

Tess's laugher did more than get under Callie's skin; it separated the chest wall, tearing muscles and ligaments along the way. Callie coughed in response. It was obvious which of them was in charge. This was going to suck.

"I overestimated your worth, little bird. You're far too scared to be of service."

Callie had been called worse, but it still stung. Pretending you didn't care about failure was difficult. She'd mastered it to avoid Zara zeroing in on her. Tess wouldn't get the joy of seeing her flinch. The truth was: failing now wasn't an option. Callie gritted her teeth until her jaw ached. The soreness helped hone her mind. Derek had protected her time and again. Now it was her turn to return the favor. How could she succeed at saving Josh if she couldn't even walk out of this situation a winner?

"Or maybe you're underestimating me now." The threat of disappointing Derek kept her tone even and cool.

"I don't think so," Tess sneered. "You let the boys shoot me with sedatives and tie me up. I thought you'd want something better, but I was wrong."

Tess knew the buttons to push, and Callie wished she could ask how. That wasn't what this was about though. She baited the line. "You didn't actually offer me anything better. I don't need a new person manipulating me."

"I offered you a chance to be out from under him. I wanted to help you."

"He gave me magic. What were you going to give me?" Had she just implied her flame hands were a gift? Ugh. She should punch herself for that.

"Help," Tess said, as if it were so simple.

"No, Tess, you were going to use me, just like he wants to." Callie sauntered closer, ignoring the heat coiling in her palms. Uneven burners on an aged electric range were destined to short circuit.

Tess pursed her lips. Hurting another person on purpose wasn't in Callie's DNA, but the temptation to remind Tess of the magic she and the Charmer fought over was too tempting. She tapped a finger against Tess's bound hand. The sparks from her hand lit the small space, but faded before reaching the floor. Tess winced, but remained silent.

Callie circled her. "That's the truth of it, isn't it, Tess? The Charmer wanted me to find you, and I expect you wanted me to find his souls for you."

"I found plenty of his souls just fine without your help." *Touché*.

"Then why *did* you want to help me?" Contempt drenched each word.

"Magic takes time to master. Even more so when you didn't seek it out yourself." She was playing nice, but Callie couldn't let herself buy it.

"You sound like you aren't a fan of magic, but you wield it pretty freely, lady."

Tess fought her bonds to stiffen her posture. Callie had hit a nerve. "I would never speak ill of such a gift. I trained for years to learn to pull the energy, found the right people to help, but now . . . "

Damn, Callie really wanted her to go into monologue mode. "But now?"

"It doesn't matter. You're not interested."

"Convince me. Tell me what's worth all this. What could possibly be worth stealing from the goddamn Soul Charmer and purposefully getting involved with all this nasty?" Callie kept her tone light, but she needed an answer. Why would anyone choose this?

"It doesn't have to be nasty."

"But it is." Callie edged away from Tess. The cool wall behind her offered strength.

"I could fix all that." Words of false promise from a fanatic.

"That's a tall order."

"You've witnessed my magic." Tess paused, waiting for Callie to nod. She had. Tess's eyes were wide as she continued. "I've siphoned sin from thousands in the last year. Sipping a tiny portion at a time. They got euphoria for a few hours, and I gained power. Imagine how much sin we could purge with the power derived from the collection of souls he has. Just imagine."

Tess's god complex made a little more sense now. Not that Callie was buying into the rule-the-world shit, but she understood the ability to affect such change could go to one's head. At least something made sense. "Why does purging sin matter to you so much?"

"This magic—" her eyes danced with manic joy "—is beautiful. It's meant to help. We can cleanse people. Everyone will understand they'll be happier without the need to sin, without the guilt of it. They will adore us for saving them from themselves."

Callie groaned. "Pretty sure that's the church's job."

"They let their people do anything. We won't let that happen. Once we've touched their souls, we can keep them from making such poor choices. You'll have the power to protect your family from bad decisions."

Callie had to give it to her. It was a good pitch. If it was even legit. The Soul Charmer certainly wasn't interested in the mundane lives of his clients. That man liked a lot of peeking at souls and cold, hard cash. Tess's brand of crazy might make this real to her, though. If it was true, shit would only get worse. Who wouldn't want to keep everyone safe and happy and keep their loved ones from the dangers of the world? Only, who was Tess to make those decisions? What if the church was wrong? What if people weren't going to be punished for living freely? If the church had its way, having sex with Derek had damned Callie. There was nothing abhorrent about what happened between them. He didn't judge her for her baggage, her family, or even her situation with Ford. He smiled when they were alone together. She smiled, too. He made her feel whole and worthwhile and special. The idea of Tess as the arbiter of acceptable behavior dug at Callie. This was probably why the Charmer wanted her for the job all along. Callie was a good person—Derek told her as much—but she gave little fucks about what others' moral measurements were.

Callie couldn't help herself. "Who put you in charge?"

Tess's arms strained against her bindings. After a moment she hedged. "Does it matter?"

Goddamn it. "Yeah, it matters."

"I am the one who will purify this city. That's all you need to know."

Talking to a crazy lady was about as much fun as scraping your shins on a brick road. "So while you're stuck down here, the poor people of Gem City are generally fucked? That's what you're saying?"

"The purification will happen regardless."

Callie placed her hands on Tess's thighs, and leaned forward. She needed this answer for Derek. "Are you working with someone else?"

The smell of burning fabric hit her before she recognized the fire beneath her palms. Her frustration with Tess had overridden the pressure of the magic. Derek had been right about motivation. She should have let go. She wasn't the kind of person who would torture someone, but her emotions were flowing through the flames. Her breathing eased with every second she let the twin torches flare. It wasn't right. It wasn't fair. She needed to care about that.

Tess cried out. Callie tried to pull back, but something was stopping her. Her desire to save Derek and herself from the Charmer had screwed with her magic. She needed to let go. It was the right thing to do, and yet her hands didn't budge.

"There are others," Tess screamed between gasping breaths.

Callie finally won the struggle and jerked her hands away. She took all seven layers of Tess's skin with her. She didn't have enough space in her torso for the ball of guilt and horror that formed at the sight of the exposed muscle and tissue underneath. This is what magic did. It turned people into crazy, awful beings. The Charmer and Tess were both power hungry. They used twisted justifications to avoid accepting they were slaves to the rush. Callie couldn't let herself become that.

Her voice wavered as she asked the next question. "Who are they? Names."

The metal chair ground against the concrete floor at the force of Tess's shaking body. Callie couldn't ever swear a medical oath again. She no longer had that right. "I don't know who will be here. I wasn't the only one recruited."

Recruited? Come the fuck on. "Who recruited you?"

"Fire won't get that one out of me, little bird." A wry grin spread on her face. She had to be in shock. The pain had somehow blanked from her brain.

"Give me names." Would Ford be on her list?

"Your mother will be able to find one." She laughed.

"What?"

"Zara is always in need of a fix. She'll find another of mine."

CHAPTER NINETEEN

Blaming a lack of sleep on Derek's injuries was what a weak woman would do. Callie wasn't weak. She had given the Soul Charmer the information he wanted. His henchman had told him about Tess's injuries. Callie had winced, but the salacious way he licked his lips at the news had been replaying in her mind for hours. She'd ignored the Charmer as he laid out his plans for his new prisoner, and had held steady long enough to claim Derek.

She had rescued him from that den of depravity, and then tucked him into her bed. Now her battered brain flitted between worry for the man she cared for and dread that he'd reject her once he knew what she'd done to collect him.

Trading one worry for a lesser one wasn't healthy, but she wasn't about to become a yogi anyway. Digging into her task for Ford should have been terrifying, but her nerves were fried. The blueprints Ford had provided seemed straightforward. At least *something* was. Callie pinched the bridge of her nose. Easy plans didn't exist. Their extraction of Tess proved that.

She headed to the bedroom at the sound of a muffled groan. Derek was sprawled across her bed. She'd stripped him of his jacket and shirt when they'd returned from the Charmer's. He'd curled into a ball and fallen asleep quickly. Now, though, he'd opted for a starfish position. She sat in one of the two open spaces on the bed, her hip next to his.

"How are you feeling?" She hadn't soothed anyone in a long time. Was she doing it right?

"Like someone stabbed me in the chest." His road-rashed voice made her wince.

"At least you weren't shot?" Probably not the right thing to say.

He gave a single laugh, but the force made him cough. Tears welled in the corners of his eyes. Callie didn't wipe them away. Tucking him into bed and offering him pain killers was one thing, but drying tears was another.

She glanced toward the bathroom. The fact that he was conscious meant the pills were wearing off. "Sorry."

"No need, doll," he croaked.

"You want another Vicodin?" He hadn't asked why she had a stash. It was nice not to be questioned.

"In a few. I'll be functional tomorrow."

She shook her head. "Blood loss is warping your sense of time. It was a deep cut, too. You'll be out of commission for a bit."

"Charmer's stuff works fast."

His blackmail sure got her into that basement lickety split. She stowed her guilt. "Says the man groaning in bed."

"You like when I groan in bed." Even injured, he could get her blood pumping. Like sex was a good idea right now.

"I only like it if I'm the one making you groan. Now, seriously, you need rest."

Derek grabbed her hand as she started to stand. "I'll be on my feet in the morning. Don't worry about the shit with Ford. I'll still be there to help."

She needed to work on her poker face. "You can't go with me anyway—"

"I can't go *inside*. We talked about this. I'll be there."

"You need to heal."

"His magic has fixed more than a slice of my flesh before. Trust me."

God, she did, and it turned her stomach. What other injuries had Derek received while working for that man? How many times had he been revived by magic? He wouldn't let another soul touch his, but there had to be consequences to this type of thing as well.

"Why work for him?" she whispered as the thoughts coalesced.

"It's what I'm good at, and my loyalty is valued there." The hardness in his voice was full of pain, but it had nothing to do with the stitched wound on his chest. It slammed the door on the conversation, but told her more than enough. He owed the Charmer. She sensed it wasn't an indentured servitude like hers, but whatever it was, it was big. And he did not want to discuss it.

Letting it slide was the adult thing to do. Being an adult sucked. "Understood. You still want that pill?"

He gave her a weak smile. "Yeah."

Once Derek was snoozing again, she returned to memorizing her heist plans. The petty crimes in her past hadn't prepared Callie for a task of this magnitude. The closest to on-site police she'd gotten was a mall rent-a-cop, and it wasn't exactly difficult to evade a man who was forty pounds overweight. Desk jockey police might not be in their prime, but they'd catch her or shoot her. Guns were a factor she hated having to contemplate.

What kind of favor would the Soul Charmer demand in exchange for healing a bullet wound? She'd be indebted for a year, at least. One would think the fear of being shot would be at the top of her terror list, but it's what would happen *after* the bullet hit her that scared Callie the most.

If she designed a government building, she'd make it a maze. Gem City Police apparently didn't agree, or maybe they didn't expect bad guys to want to break into their facilities. Either way, the path to the server storage room was simple. She'd walk one hallway until it ended, take a left, and the door would be there. It was in the center of the building, but not exactly hard to access. Blueprints were deceptive, though. The printouts on their own wouldn't show all the opportunities for things to go to shit.

Ford or one of his men, however, had been kind enough to outline those helpful notes onto the page. Locked doorways and keypads were marked, as was the main desk where she'd have to check in. They'd included a card in the envelope that would gain Callie access first to the building and then into the forensics storage room, but not a script for what to say to the cop at the entrance. There also weren't instructions for a contingency plan. At least Ford was confident the access card would function. The server room required a six-digit code to enter. They changed it weekly, but supposedly the one on the sheet from the mafia king would work.

The numbers meant nothing to her, though, and her mind didn't want to commit them to memory. They weren't from a song and didn't include any former addresses or lucky numbers. She swiped a hand across her forehead, displeased to discover she'd worked up a sweat like she was back in middle school studying for an American History test.

Memorizing every sequence of numbers in the world wasn't going to guarantee the job would be a success. The soul part— which she strived to pretend was totally normal and not terrifying—would mask her DNA and fingerprints. Unless she became the first person ever to pull off inconspicuously wearing a black ski mask inside a police station, cameras were going to catch her face. Ford had been confident the soul was necessary. Hopefully her face would blur while she was doubled on souls. She hadn't heard of that being a thing, but she was only an "insider" on this magic shit for a couple weeks. She had to cross her fingers that'd work, because the chance of spending the next decade in an orange jumpsuit wasn't calming Callie's nerves.

Derek didn't need to know about her camera fears, because then he'd offer to help her. When Derek learned what she'd done to Tess, what it'd taken to get him out of the Charmer's for the night, he wasn't going to want to be in any deeper with her. He'd liked that she was morally good, and that couldn't last when you seared the skin off another person. Best to make her own plans now and save him the additional hurt.

Callie jumped when her phone rang. Nothing said you were definitely, totally ready for a master break-in like being scared of your phone. She silenced the ringer, then answered. "Hello?"

"How's it going, sis?"

She peeked in on Derek. Once she was confident he was still sleeping, she pulled the door shut and replied in a dark hiss, "Dangerous question, Josh."

"You're still going through with it, right?" Panic made him squeaky.

"Don't be ridiculous. Yes, I'm still going through with it." Did he think so little of her?

His sigh muffled all other sound on the line. "Good. I mean, thanks."

"Are you being taken care of?" Concern began to twist in her chest.

"I'm still whole and they're feeding me. No worries. As long as they get what they want, we'll both be fine."

Callie frowned. That didn't sound like Josh at all. "Are you reading from a script?"

"No, but everyone's real clear on what needs to happen. I need to know you're clear, too."

"Crystal." Her throat squeezed.

"How's Mom?" His question startled her.

"Fine. Fucking cat hid in the cupboard again. She wanted you to rescue him."

"She does better when she's around family."

What the hell? He loved laying the bait out for her. "Since when? She's batshit around me."

"She isn't good at expressing it. I'm more like her, you know?" His words underscored the hidden message: but you take care of me.

He did this needling when he wanted guilt hanging like heavy chains around Callie's neck. "You didn't call to talk about Mom."

"I wanted to make sure you were ready for tomorrow. Soon this will be over, and I'll be back home."

"And done with that junk?"

"I'm done with all this. But I don't have a chance unless you hold up your end."

Alarms flared in her mind, but her mouth didn't care. "*I'm* the one who always follows through, Josh. Don't forget."

"I'm so much like Mom. I just need to know you have my back."

An invisible knife cut deep into Callie's waist. "I've always had your back." She spoke slowly, like it could actually cool her anger. It didn't work.

"Sure. I've just never fucked up this bad." His nervous laugh did nothing for her.

He wanted to go into the past. She followed him, like always. "I called them on her because she was a danger to me. You were gone."

"I know," he said, repeating those placating words. She'd heard them so many times they no longer held any meaning or sincerity.

"Sure." Child Protective Services had been happy to separate her from her habitually neglectful mother. Her brother hadn't stepped in after he'd moved out. He'd been busy working or, at least he'd said he was at the time. Later she realized he'd just been getting high. Zara went off the deep end when Josh left. She stole the food Callie brought home and left her alone for weeks. So, yeah, Callie had made an anonymous tip about her mother. Josh had agreed to sign the papers to be her legal guardian. He helped save her from Zara, and let her be an unofficial emancipated minor. He'd kept the secret of how CPS got involved from Zara, but his own guilt over what they'd done sent him begging at their mother's feet for love (and secretly, forgiveness) every chance he got.

"We've got each other's backs when it's most important. I know you'll come through, baby sis. I believe you."

He was right about that. No matter how much he drove her crazy, Josh would have her back. He simply hadn't had the capacity to do so lately. Sober Josh, though? He was a man you wanted in your corner. Derek could be friends with Sober Josh. Callie bit her tongue. No need to share that thought with either of them. One step at a time.

CHAPTER TWENTY

"You've got to take that thing in for me." Callie foisted the soul-filled flask at Derek. She couldn't face the Soul Charmer again. She didn't want to know if Tess was still in the basement. She didn't need to see the burns on the woman's legs again. The Charmer wouldn't resist taunting her in front of Derek. She might not climb out of the well of shame after that.

He stepped backward. "Nope."

"The Charmer likes you better. It'll be easier for you."

"He likes you just fine."

"You wouldn't be fit to collect souls today if he hadn't worked his mojo on you. Clearly, this means you're his golden boy—which, ew—but go with it."

Derek pulled her close and his laugher shook her chest, too, lightening her thoughts. "Fine. I'll take it, but not because it's easier for me."

Tilting her head as far back as she could, Callie met his gaze. "My feminine wiles got to you. Finally."

"My desire to keep you out of jail trumps your wiles." The quick squeeze he gave her rear was possessive and flirty. Whatever concoction the Charmer had used on him, he was top-notch Derek today. Much of her leftover regret at going to the Soul Charmer's shop evaporated with that realization.

"Though, feel free to seduce me at your leisure, doll," he added.

Derek was determined to collect souls that morning. Wounds be damned. He would have found a way to go even without her blessing, so she had agreed in the name of keeping him whole. She needed to balance out the heals/hurts scale after last night. The Railyard District made Callie cringe, but ostensibly the soul renters there were artists, and were quick to give up their borrowed souls so they could get back to blowing glass and welding metal. Derek had suggested she meet him there for brunch, but she was not going to try vegan omelets, even on someone else's dime.

Despite the magic and everything that had happened with Tess, the mood was light. Derek's healing deserved the credit. His chest was still tender, but the wound was already closed. At noon all that was left was a dark magenta streak. No matter her stance on soul magic and the bastards who used it, Callie had to admit it was pretty badass.

The levity from his recovery couldn't overshadow what was to come hours later. Taking the step from petty thief to legit criminal hadn't ever been on Callie's life agenda. It was going to happen, though. Tonight. And she still needed a way to halt Derek's involvement. His feelings for her were destined to implode when he learned she'd tortured Tess. He let people think he'd kill them, but he didn't leave scars on his marks. Callie had done real damage. It'd be doubly disastrous if he had guilt from helping her with a police break-in. Joy receded from her body, seeping from her bared feet and burying itself in the thin carpet. She probably needed to vacuum.

Callie shuffled the police documents Ford had provided. She recited the access code to the server room, and then peeked at her cheat sheet. This morning, on her way back from the handoff with

Benny, she'd remembered the code correctly for the first time, and now she had the numbers down pat.

Three quick raps at her door echoed in her empty apartment. Why was Derek back so soon?

"You forget something—" Speaking while opening the door turned out to be a rookie move. Her hands began to cool immediately.

"Tell me what you did." Zara shoved past Callie, clocking her shoulder hard enough a bruise would develop by morning.

"Nice to see you, too." She didn't bother rubbing at her stinging shoulder. Zara didn't deserve the satisfaction, and it wouldn't ease her pain or warm her hands. She gave her mom enough space to keep the icy sensation in check.

Zara's fingers were curled into little fists that she slammed on her hips. The move might have frightened ten-year-old Callie, but she'd had a decade to get past her mom's scare tactics. Zara's blouse—a peasant top whirled with mish-mashed colors—fluttered as she huffed. As though an angry sigh would explain anything to Callie.

"You're going to have to be more specific, Mom." Josh wouldn't have divulged about CPS. No way. Not when he was still on the chopping block, damn near literally.

"I went to get my . . . relief today, and my masseuse was missing. Tess. I guess you know her, and ran her off with some thug."

A cartoon anvil could have dropped on Callie's head right then. She locked her jaw and counted to ten before responding. "You know Tess?" Her words were shaky, but the underlining fury rang clear.

"Yes!" Zara was a petite woman under normal circumstances, but as she threw her hands skyward she morphed into a colossus in the one-bedroom apartment. "She helps relieve my stress, and now I can't get her help because of you."

Callie shook her head. Tess hadn't lied. It'd be damn dangerous for Zara to start telling people about Tess and Bianca's under-
handed dealings or their rocky relationship with the Soul Charmer.
"What makes you think I have a thing to do with you not being
able to get a massage?"

"Her assistant said to talk to you." The accusation was
empty. So she didn't know as much as Callie had feared. Zara no
longer overwhelmed the room. In fact, from the few inches Callie stood taller than her mother, she spied Zara's roots beginning
to show.

If her mother knew, who else might have details about Callie's
involvement in Tess's capture?

"Mhm, and what else did her assistant say?" Years of playing it
cool around her mother paid off.

Zara's nostrils flared. Funny how calm confidence could make
the bullies quake. "She said you knew where Tess was." Her voice
trailed off, her power diminishing.

"You can throw a rock in Gem City and hit a massage therapist. Get a new one."

Zara took a seat on the couch. Not that she'd been invited to
make herself comfortable. Or steal Derek's spot. Callie clenched
her jaw, but parried her blows for what mattered: getting Zara the
hell out of her house.

"Tess is so much more." The ethereal allegiance in Zara's words
was too much.

Callie cut her off. "She's not good for you."

"She helps me!"

So that's where Josh got it. "Lots of people can help you."

"You've never understood. Not everyone is as well-adjusted as
you. We can't just be okay."

Be. Okay. Was that even a thing? "Are you new? Since when am
I living the choice life?"

"Please. You lord your stability over us and then have the audacity to bitch about your bills."

"I haven't said shit about bills to you since I was fourteen and you decided the gas bill was less important than a bar night with the girls." Callie needed to be in a Zen state of mind to pull off this bullshit for Ford tonight, and Zara was not fucking helping.

"Josh told me about how you couldn't help your own brother out because you owed money."

"I don't 'owe money,' Mom. I have bills, and, yeah, I don't have a bunch of cash for him because I've already given my savings to him twice. I'm wiped. He's been using us for years."

"He's getting clean. He called me earlier. Said he's detoxing."

No, no, no. "Josh called you today?"

"He did, and he asked for my help. He cares about his mama."

Callie was breaking more laws than she cared to count, working double shifts—first at the home, and then for the Charmer—and to Josh it still wasn't enough. "What did he ask for?"

"He'll need a place to stay when he gets out."

Callie would have provided that, without the added anxiety of some weird reverse Oedipus shit. "And?"

She waved away the question, but still answered under her breath. "A little cash, to get him back on his feet."

Pretending big favors were little wasn't about ego with Zara. Guilt filled the bones of every member of the Delgado family. Zara atoned for her self-loathing and shame with her son. In sitcoms the baby was always spoiled, but in Callie's house it had always been the boy. Josh was where Zara found redemption. There and, apparently, a soul-siphoning masseuse/crazy cult lady.

This conversation was futile, and Callie didn't have time for it anyway. So she went for the kill strike. "You don't have cash, Mom."

"How would you know? You barely visit me." Zara threw the jabs while getting up from the couch and moving toward the door. She didn't want to travel this road, either.

"Okay. Whatever. Let me know when you hear from Josh again."

Zara paused near the door and her shoulders rose as she pulled in a rallying breath. "You find out what happened to Tess, or I'll—"

"You'll what?"

"I'll find another way to make this happen. I need the relief a couple times a week, Calliope. I have a life to live, you know."

It sounded like a threat, but then most conversations with Zara ended that way. "What do you mean?"

"You know." If she could have underlined her words with a black marker, she would have. Zara was barely the right side of classy to be above using his name, or admitting she knew him.

The Charmer. Of course. "You can say his name, Mom."

"I only said her name so you'd help. I'm not going to say his name. You shouldn't either, or the fallout of messing with him is on you."

She'd been buried under the Delgado family fallout for years. At this point, what was a little more rubble? Soul magic was already in Zara, and the obsession was enough to send her to Callie's door instead of waiting until the next time the cat got stuck somewhere.

"Go see Father Gonzales." Callie had to try something.

Zara's eyes widened. "Excuse me? I see him plenty more than you do."

"The soul magic doesn't really fix anything. Work it out with Father Gonzales."

"Her massages work. They ease the . . . " Zara trailed off. When she sniffled a moment later, Callie recognized it was true emotion.

"It ruins you. I can't explain everything, but you're chasing highs just like Josh. Don't fall down that hole, Mom." She pled like her eight-year-old self would have. That was before Zara slid into total selfishness.

"So you're saying I'm ruined?"

"I didn't say that. I'm saying you're better than letting some hack mess with your soul."

"I'll rise up to heaven." No matter how devout the phrase sounded, the shaky breaths beneath it belied her fear.

"You can do that without Tess."

"Fine. You're clearly not interested in helping your own mother. I'll just have to find someone who can." With that last barb, Zara slammed the door behind her, and Callie hung her head. The sight of the chipped pink polish on her toes blurred as tears welled in her eyes. It'd been years since her mother had made her cry.

How did you get someone clean from the rush of soul rental? There wasn't an additive you could just remove from the blood-stream. Callie's tried-and-true method of hiding from her feelings didn't make her the expert, but Zara would have to deal with her guilt to get free of that need. Callie wasn't Zara's biggest fan, but family came first, and there was no way she'd allow the Soul Charmer to rent to her mom.

"You don't have to do this," Derek said for the eight hundredth time. He'd parked his motorcycle in the same alley where they'd first met. She'd spent the afternoon worrying over how to keep her mom from the Charmer's doorstep, and now the sun had set and she was the one slumming it downtown.

Callie rolled her eyes. "We both know I do."

"Why not just—"

"There's no 'just' anything. Not with this. Ford was clear this was a requirement. He's right. I'm not having this traced to me."

"I don't like it." His lips pulled tight, and every muscle on his face hardened.

"I've never liked the idea of renting a soul, and now that I know so much more my distaste has quadrupled, but guess what? The whole reason I agreed to work for the Charmer was for this soul. So I could do this job and save my brother." Case closed.

Derek nodded, accepting he would lose this battle. He stowed their helmets on his bike and took her hand, and then led her in the side door of the Soul Charmer's shop. She stayed in the hallway with a million picture frames while he went ahead to get the Charmer.

The anteroom was smaller than she'd realized. The black ceiling soared above her, but she could touch both walls simultaneously if she stretched her arms airplane style. Focusing on any one frame set her skin crawling. Every feature except for the eyes was blurred in the portraits. They watched her. There wasn't enough magic in this room to turn her hands painful, but she didn't feel alone. Hopefully that didn't have anything to do with the woman she'd left in the building's basement. Everything the Soul Charmer touched unnerved her, and she was about to let him touch her again. Josh owed her. Big time.

Derek peered in from the workroom and nodded to her.

"Ah, Calliope, dear. Is it already time for this?" There was no way she'd told the Charmer her full name. Her skin continued to crawl, but it had little to do with magic.

"Can we get this over with?"

He beckoned her with a rheumatic finger. "In a rush to get your first taste?"

No, she was exhausted after dealing with every egotistical, jerk-faced person in her life in a single goddamn day. Add in her general fear of shoving another person's soul into her body, and the fact she was on the verge of stealing from the police, and she wasn't really in the mood for his insinuating tone. But she needed the damn thing, and she needed it with as little commentary as possible. "Let's just do this."

The corners of his mouth pulled downward, cutting deep grooves in his cheeks. "You're no fun today. You wanted an unsullied soul, yes?"

She nodded. Why was she doing this? Oh right. Family.

"It's more fun when the soul is less like your own," he taunted.

The memory of the man in the hospital rushed to the forefront of her mind. "The less of a mess we make of my soul, the better."

He arched a brow. Was she not supposed to know it would mangle her soul? Had she broken Derek's trust with that comment? Fuck.

The Charmer began to extend a hand toward her, but Callie stopped him. "Wait. Just whose soul is going into me?"

"You worked two weeks for this. Do you think I'm going to provide subpar wares?"

"No, I just . . . what kind of person?"

The Charmer's lips thinned, but he answered her question. "I don't do this normally, but, fine: mid-forties woman. No kids. Worked for the Church. That's all I'll say."

Callie nodded. It was better than nothing.

The Soul Charmer pressed two fingers against the hollow at Callie's neck. He better not cut her. When she flinched, he whispered, "Close your eyes and breathe. It won't hurt."

She noted he hadn't said anything about not injuring her, because they would have both recognized that lie.

Despite the magic swirling in the room, none of Callie's flared. His cold fingers traced down her sternum to stop between her breasts. Derek huffed at her side. She held back her smile. No need to let the Soul Charmer get any more glimpses of their connection.

"Deep breath, girl."

She ignored the condescending tone and did as she was told, and then the air rushed out of her. He hadn't hit her, but her rib-cage vibrated like she'd taken one hell of a wallop. She staggered back and Derek caught her. "You good, doll?"

"Not sure," she muttered, low enough for his ears only. The experience of soul renting had been touted as euphoric; a coworker once said it was better than the relief of every religious confession combined.

"Is that it?" she asked the Charmer.

"Is that it?" He beamed, as though such a question tickled his scaly heart. "Don't you feel her mingling with you?"

Callie searched her mind. Should there be another voice? Was she supposed to feel like a different person? Did she suddenly want to tell Josh to save his own damn self? Nope, nope, and nope. "Should I?"

Nothing had unnerved Callie more than hearing an elderly creep like the Soul Charmer giggle. "Perhaps not."

"It worked, though, right, boss?" Derek asked the question Callie was too scared to pose.

He stared at her chest. The perv. "Oh, the second soul is in there. It's less bright than her own, but it's still quite visible."

"Mine's brighter?" Even after what she did to Tess?

The Charmer grinned, clearly on to the direction of Callie's thoughts. "Yes, it's still quite pure," was all he said, though.

Her mother had barged into her apartment in search of this high. Joey had gone and gotten another one even after being threat-ened. People blew paycheck after paycheck on this. Callie didn't get it. She'd witnessed the high in others. She's glimpsed the glassy-eyed indulgence. All Callie got was a heavy ick factor at the idea that there was a bonus soul inside her and she'd let the Charmer put it there.

Callie cast a skeptical look toward Derek. "And people get hooked on this?"

He shrugged.

"My magic does change things, but I expect you'll still rather enjoy the benefits of the soul. Bring it back when you're done," the Charmer said, effectively dismissing them.

Business with him had never been this easy. He had to have some plan in play, but Callie's mind had been run too ragged to recognize it.

She didn't have time to spare either; she was due at the police station within the hour.

"We need to check your wound." Callie rushed Derek into her apartment.

"I can handle a little soreness. We shouldn't be risking you being late over a damn healed injury."

She waited for him to meet her gaze, and then rolled her eyes. "Healed injury? You were *stabbed. Yesterday.*"

He stripped his shirt over his head. "Fine."

After he'd sat on the edge of her bed, Callie ran her palm across the angry red mark on his upper chest. It was raised, like scar tissue, but the healing process had been so fast that the whole thing didn't make a lot of sense. The area around the healed gouge was still warm, though. "You're still running a fever."

He gave her a look that said he'd bust out a thermometer to prove her wrong. "A fever isn't going to stop me from getting you to that job."

Did he know what she was trying to do? No, he couldn't know. The Charmer hadn't been alone with him long enough to tell him about Callie's scalding meeting with the queen of soul massage. In fact, the entire time they were there, the Charmer hadn't cracked a single joke about her being beneath their feet. Which in hindsight seemed a bit weird. . . .

"You need to stay here. Ford didn't want you involved anyway, and I don't want to risk you getting hurt a second time on my account." It was the truth, foreign and real coming from her lips.

He launched to his feet, but wobbled when he got there. "I choose what I risk and for whom."

Her heart squeezed twice, once because he clearly cared about her, and second because of how guilty she felt about it. The Charmer might say her soul was still pure, but she couldn't take it if he were wrong. If Derek saw how fucked up she really was. She had to do this alone. Burning bridges now kept him safer long term. She swallowed back her fear and accepted that he meant something to her, and that she was doing this for his own good. "Will you at least take something for the fever? Just a Tylenol or something?"

"To make you happy. Yeah."

The Vicodin she handed him was too big to pass for a pain reliever, but he didn't even glance at it before tossing the pill into his mouth and swallowing. "Better?"

Her hollow voice shook. "Yeah."

Callie adjusted Derek on her bed a few minutes later. That shit worked fast. He was still conscious enough to talk, but not to do much else.

"Why?" he eked out, having figured out that she'd tricked him. She was such an asshole.

"You're too good to be involved with all my crazy."

She leaned down and kissed his forehead. "I'll be back as soon as I can. If you stay, you can be mad at me then."

Callie didn't wait for his mumbled response. She didn't expect him to still be at her apartment when she returned. Drugging the dude you cared about tended to be a relationship killer. But better that he severed ties with her than get pulled in deeper with Ford.

Enough people she cared about were already under the gangster's thumb. She wouldn't pull Derek under just so she could escape.

—— CHAPTER TWENTY-ONE ——

Crossing a street turned out to be more difficult than making a deal with the Soul Charmer. Wasn't there supposed to be some sort of carefree nature that came with having an extra soul wedged inside you? It wasn't helping Callie one iota. She reached for her cache of false confidence, but found it empty.

She gripped the still-open door of her car as though letting go would send her into a freefall through space. "I can't do this."

She looked to the passenger seat, and could almost imagine Derek sitting there, encouraging her.

Her shoes sank into the concrete. Her mind raced through eight dozen different scenarios, but entering that building and failing? She refused to picture the consequences. She unlocked her phone and checked the time. According to the schedule Ford had given her, she still had fifteen minutes of empty corridors inside the station to make her move.

She'd haul ass down those hallways and be out as fast as possible. She sucked in a steadying breath. This bonus soul stuck in her chest better do its part.

Josh. His shaggy black hair and goofy grin stole to the forefront of her mind. She could do this for him. And, fuck it, she could do it for her, too. Resolve firmly set, Callie released and closed the door, and made a beeline to the Gem City Police Department Sub-station Eight's side entrance.

The grey slacks and blue polo she wore—an IT person costume—shifted to muted oranges under the bulb at the access door. The camera mounted above the door didn't pan at her approach. That had to be a good sign, right? Ford's key card slid from her pocket with ease—at least the inanimate objects were on board with this mission—and after a quick tap against the electronic plate the door buzzed in approval. Was it wrong to hope Ford's card wouldn't work? He couldn't have blamed her for failing if the tools he'd given her were fucked, could he? Didn't matter; now it really was on her.

Focus, Callie, she thought to herself.

She stepped into the empty hallway, and the door slammed behind her with an echo that must have carried for miles. The hallway was blessedly empty, so no one caught her jumping at the sound. Dropping her guard because the police wouldn't have forensic—and hopefully not photographic—evidence of their burglar wasn't an option, though. Refocusing, she pictured the blueprints in her mind.

Callie hurried forward at the speed of a mall walker: clearly not running, but moving fast enough to make people wonder what was wrong with her and didn't she know they had gyms for that kind of shit. IT people always seemed like the high-strung types who'd run to solve problems anyway, so maybe she was doing a good job playing the part. She'd never seen one at the retirement home, but made-for-TV movies had taught her a lot.

This couldn't be a real police station, could it? It was too quiet, even at one a.m. While reviewing plans last night, Derek told her the four cars she'd see in the parking lot without police signage belonged to the medical examiner's team members and the on-duty security. The dead bodies were in the basement, he'd said. Avoiding the living was going to be hard enough, but knowing there were a bunch of dead people just mere steps from her was an aneurysm waiting to happen. And with Derek out of the equation, the planned distractions he would have provided were gone, and they wouldn't have been able to cover her for passing out and twitching on the floor anyway. Why didn't she let him come with her again? Damn sense of honor. It better not get her killed.

It didn't take Callie more than twenty seconds to reach the security checkpoint after entering the building. Despite Ford's initial description, though, it wasn't the front desk. There was a small Plexiglas door, about hip high, partitioning the entrance from the main working area. The door was open already, but there was still a policeman sitting at the table adjacent.

He rubbed his right eye as though it'd remove the evidence he'd been desk napping. "What can I do for you?"

"Oh, I just need to pick up a couple files."

"Isn't a little late for paperwork?" His question wasn't cutting, but instead was full of unsuspecting sympathy.

"Not my choice, but you know how it goes." The truth sprang to Callie's lips.

"I do, honey. Head on back. If you need anything, my name's Vic."

"Thanks, Vic." She might have said more—to be more friendly or normal or whatever—but fear and elation at having not yet fucked everything up would have made her sound manic if she'd replied. Crazy, squeaky women were probably memorable, and Callie was determined to be nothing more than a figment of his late-shift dreams, the kind he'd forget by the next morning.

Once she walked past Vic's desk, noting the frat-boy comedy flick he had playing on a phone propped on his desk, the end of the hallway was ten feet ahead. Peeking around the corner would be weird—she'd survived her first face-to-face encounter, hadn't she?—but going into this blind was too stressful. She slowed near the corner, and leaned around the edge as surreptitiously as she could. There was no SWAT team waiting for her. Hell, there wasn't even one of those slow Romero-type zombies. She righted herself and made the left turn.

The placard reading SERVER ROOM made the door easy to find. Gem City PD was not bringing its A game to protecting its citizens' data. The servers inside stored court case data, police records, and research. Lots and lots of it. Once she returned to the side of the lawful, she would totally be writing the governor about this kind of lax security. Provided she didn't get caught, of course.

The keypad above the door's handle lit as she pressed the first button. Six numbers later, she was still outside the door. Shit. This was Zara's fault. Callie had the numbers memorized forward and backward before her mom blustered into her apartment. Now the sequence was like one of those words that was right on the tip of your tongue, but no matter how hard you focused, you just couldn't remember. Such bullshit.

Callie sighed, and checked both directions in the hallway before trying again. She was still alone, but for how much longer? Would a movie keep Vic from checking on her? She had ten minutes to work with when she left the car, but her dumb ass hadn't checked the time again when she got inside. This was why the mafia should have used a professional. An expert would know to synchronize watches, set an egg timer, or something else useful.

Thank God the keypad didn't have one of those three-strikes-on-your-code-and-you're-permanently-locked-out "security" features. Eight tries later, the door finally opened. 5-0-9-7-2-9. She slipped through the open doorway, letting a quick sigh of relief escape her parted lips, and closed the door carefully behind her.

Callie walked to the third server rack on the right and plugged in the little black drive Ford had provided into the port on the side. When the light started blinking green, she moved on. Technology had a touch of magic. It didn't matter how that drive worked, she was going to leave it there until the light turned yellow. In the meantime, she needed to find the right paper files. Luckily the city had doubled up on storage, and the left side of the room was stacked with grey file cabinets like the ones they'd had at her high school's principal's office. Not that she'd been there often.

That's where her good luck ended though. The administrative assistants for the police force weren't all that organized. In the fourth cabinet's third drawer, Callie found a hefty folder labeled "DNA Soul Pairing." Sounded accurate enough. She pulled the two-inch thick folder free, surprised it took both hands to lift out.

Her focus was trampled as what sounded like a stampede thundered past the storage room's door. It was so startling she almost dropped the papers she was holding. Masculine voices called to "get the gurney" and "rally at door four." Their words didn't mean anything to her, but she needed them to go in the opposite direction of her exit. Not that she knew which door number that was. The footsteps echoed for days, or maybe it was just seconds, she was too scared to tell. She needed out.

An invisible hand squeezed her throat. She ignored her tightening airway and ran to the servers. Pinning the bulky file under her arm, Callie extracted the drive from the rack and mouthed a silent thank you at the yellow light that had greeted her. The heat the device generated as she slipped into her pocket was too familiar. She wasn't extracting souls from delinquent clients, but she was still taking something important, something that wasn't hers and would greatly be missed. Was this who she was now?

She stepped outside the storage room, the snick of the lock barely registering in her ears as the door closed behind her. She needed to get her ass out of the police station as fast as possible, and without attracting the attention of whoever had stormed past a few minutes earlier. She rounded the corner, the one leading back outside.

"Hey!" a male voice called out. Vic wasn't at his desk. His phone wasn't on the desk, either. *A smoke break now, Vic, really?* The exit at the end of the hallway now felt much, much farther away. Her muscles twitched as the flight-or-fight instinct surged inside her.

Callie managed to make herself pause, though she couldn't control the subtle shake of her knees. "Yeah?" Containing the squeak of her vocal cords was impossible as well.

She was almost to the guard station. To where Vic should have been. How many steps until she was back outside? Twenty? Twenty-five?

"Where are you headed with that?" The short-sleeved white button-down the man wore strained over his potbelly. The sight was both comforting and unnerving. He didn't look like a cop. Who was he, and what was he doing here?

"I need to review these notes for my boss," she fibbed. It worked with Vic. She should have stopped there, but her ballsy attempt at confidence made her talkative. "You know how he can be."

The man narrowed his eyes at her. "What's your name? Have we met?"

Should she lie or tell the truth? Both had the potential for disastrous consequences. Plus the threat there might be an actual police officer in the building chipped at what little swagger she had left. "I don't know if we've met before." She took a step toward the exit. If she sprinted, she thought, doing the rough math in her head, she could be there in five seconds.

He followed her movements. His strides were longer than hers. He was too close. "What's your name?" he prompted again.

"Eve," she blurted. Not entirely a lie. IT Girl Callie would have gone by her middle name. Probably.

"Doesn't ring a bell." He stepped toward her again, and she backed away until her shoulder blades bumped against the cool wall. He edged in close, and glared down his nose at her. She hated when assholes used their height to get all bossy.

Her fingertips began to sizzle. Great. He was a soul renter to boot. Even in the goddamn police station, she couldn't avoid them.

"If you were reviewing a file from that room for a boss, *I'd* be that boss," he hissed. Spittle landed on her cheek and turned to steam immediately. His eyes widened. "And I don't remember giving *anyone* an assignment like that."

Callie had managed to keep the file pinned against her ribs with her forearm and elbow, which was wise, as her hands had gone full on molten. Only three inches separated their torsos, but she lifted her left hand between them. She could feel the heat radiating, and the quiver in his voice suggested he could as well. "What are you doing? What's going on?" he sputtered.

She slammed her palm into his chest and shoved him as hard as she could. It wasn't much, but when one wielded pure fire, force wasn't a big factor. The man stumbled back a few feet, smacking open palms at his burning shirt. The outline of a black handprint was charred into the fabric. Like he'd been touched by the devil. Her lips pulled away from her teeth in a feral smile.

The door at the end of the hallway flung open, and Callie turned to face whatever backup had arrived. She just hadn't expected it to be *her* backup.

"Doll! We need to go!" Derek's voice pierced her adrenaline-addled mind. She ran for him, her mind reeling at how he could even be at the station. Was the cocktail of adrenaline and guilt making her hallucinate?

Within ten steps her magical flame had been fully extinguished. The flames on her attacker's shirt had gone out, too, but as for the extent of the burns? Well, maybe he shouldn't corner unknown women if he didn't want them to buck back. Derek looked past Callie at the man. He didn't say a word, and the two of them ran out of the door, across the street, and hopped in her car.

Smart guy. If he didn't flinch at that, and still wanted to save her, maybe he wouldn't judge her for torturing Tess. If he could get past that whole slipping him a narcotic thing.

Each heartbeat throbbed in Callie's neck, as though it pressed against unseen bruises. Only her own mind could conjure enough fear to attempt to choke her out. Maybe it wasn't loyalty that ran in the family, but insanity. She leaned her head against the headrest of the passenger's seat. Her pulse was too quick, and no matter how many deep breaths she took it refused to slow.

Derek had already put the car in drive and was pushing the gas pedal down by the time Callie gasped in a few lungfuls of air. She finally asked, "How are you—"

"How am I here?" Derek's words cut.

She nodded, keeping her gaze straight ahead of her.

"You mean after you tried to drug me?" There it was, the verbal knife he deserved to use, pressing deep between her ribs.

Squeezing her eyes tight wouldn't make her problems disappear, nor would cradling her legs against her chest. She did both, anyway, and hoped her self-hatred might cocoon her in invisibility. She barely parted her lips to speak. "I needed to save you from me."

His laugh could have punched a hole in a wall. "Did I ask you to save me?"

She popped her head up from her knees. "No, but I didn't ask for it either, and I can't let you fuck up your life on my account."

"We talked about this. I make my own decisions." A breeze of comprehension had cooled his fire.

"Well, I'm a shit choice. The last thing I want to do is pull you into Ford's mess."

"He won't touch me."

"You sound confident, but I never thought I'd be in his world, either. Then he kidnapped my brother and threatened me with knives. Things change, and I wasn't going to let you fall into that, too."

"Have I not proven myself trustworthy?" He slammed his hand against the steering wheel. "Fuck. How many times do I have to say I've got your back until you believe it?"

"It's not that I don't trust you. There are things about me you don't know, and once you find them out, you won't want to have risked your life on my account."

His large, heavy hand landed on her knee. "Baggage is part of who we are. If I knew your secrets already I'd be some sneaky fuck. I'm not, but I'm also okay with you keeping some secrets until you're comfortable."

"Oh."

"But I am not—seriously, Callie—*not* okay with being drugged."

"Right. Won't happen again." She winced and let her words drip with sincerity. "How'd you come to so fast anyway?"

"Charmer's healing stuff is still working. Burned it off fast."

They were quiet for a moment. The matter wasn't closed. He'd need to talk more. She needed to talk more. They weren't dissolving just yet.

The bonus soul didn't make her feel any better about her behavior. It didn't mask her pain. Perhaps one had to *want* to accept its benefits for it to work. Its power depended on how much you believed in it. She'd let part of another person inside her, to forever taint her, to cover up her crime. To blur the evidence she'd left at the crime scene. She had to trust it had worked, because the other promises associated with soul renting, like feeling moral freedom, sure as shit weren't legit.

Derek's fingers thrummed on the steering wheel.

"Why doesn't this—" she tapped her chest "—absolve my guilt?"

He pursed his lips. Was he locking away secrets she'd have to earn back access to, or contemplating the question? The muscle in his jaw ticked several times before he finally spoke with the gravelly timbre she was accustomed to. "No clue. I mean, I don't know the metaphysical shit that goes on with the Charmer, but normally there's—I don't know—an added energy, I guess."

"Like Bianca?" Life had practically shot from that woman's pores.

"That was like soul energy on steroids, but yeah, kind of."

"Oh." The extra soul in Callie's body wasn't yielding any exuberance. Her attempts to look inward and channel her inner monk hadn't resulted in new energy or life, or even a scrap of vitality, as far as she could tell.

"The other magic might override it." Derek acted like it was a long shot, but he understood how quickly Callie's life had gone from moderately to fully fucked. He was grasping at straws, just like she was.

"That guy saw me. He's going to remember me."

"He's not going to talk."

"How can you know that?"

"It'll be handled. Besides, he's going to remember the injury and not your face. They always do."

So he had seen the burn she'd given the man. "My real fingerprints and DNA could be back at the police station."

Derek's eyes narrowed at her nonchalance. "No, the soul rental hasn't failed before. It won't fail now."

"I don't buy that, but nice try." She wanted to be rid of this soul, the magic, and the information she stole for Ford. The sooner she cut ties to it all, the better.

"Press your thumb on the screen of your phone and see what it looks like." He punctuated his instructions with a "just do it" look, as if to say that if Callie wanted to salvage things between them, arguing wasn't going to help.

"People don't memorize their fingerprints. How would I know if it's different?"

"Indulge me."

She picked up the phone, exaggerating the action, aware of her petulance but unable to help herself. After pressing her thumb against the glass, she tilted the screen to catch the light. "Okay, that's fucking weird."

"What?"

"Look."

"I'm driving," he growled. They were a block from her apartment.

"It's all zigzags."

He opened his mouth, and then closed it again. "No swirls?" he finally asked.

"No. It looks like what some kid would make up for an alien. Like Charlie Brown's shirt as fingerprints." It had actually worked. Falling down the magical well hadn't been for nothing. She'd escaped without leaving fingerprint or DNA evidence. Now all she had to do was get her brother back, ditch the soul magic, and hope the douche from the police station couldn't identify her. Callie let out a little laugh.

Derek didn't miss the weird, maniacal tinge to her voice. "You going to be okay?"

He gave her hand a quick squeeze, and it helped to ground her.

"I have no idea how to answer that question." At least she was being honest.

He nodded, but it was more like he was sussing out his own thoughts and finding them agreeable. "Fair enough," he said.

The faint buzzing in her ears dulled and then disappeared as her panic level dropped to the safe-and-rational zone. "All the cameras were turned away," she reminded herself.

The corded muscles lining Derek's forearms eased. Her frenzied edge had cut him more than he was likely to admit. When all this shit was properly handled, she would do her best to make it all up to him. "I heard you called in a favor. I made sure the tapes are now gone, too."

Callie's eyebrows shot up. At least it was a pleasant surprise.

"Just minimizing risk," he grumbled, the low pitch suggesting it was no big deal. A soft pink color tinged his skin, slinking up from the collar of his jacket. By the time it had reached his cheekbones in a full blush, her abdomen had unclenched and her breathing returned to normal again. Leave it to Derek to distract her from her fears with his own discomfort.

How did one thank the person who'd protected them to such ridiculous extremes? You didn't see loyalty and care like that outside of blood relations, and yet he'd done it for her. Despite the drugging incident she wasn't sure she'd ever live down, he'd come through for her. He was still at her side. She wasn't his family, and she wasn't deluded enough to think it was all because of her badass bedroom skills. Nobody was a good enough lay to warrant committing multiple felonies and earning the ire of a mafia boss. And yet. How had she earned such devotion? Tonight she'd risked the life she'd carefully crafted to help her big brother. It's not like she was unfamiliar with behaving idiotically for the sake of others. Only family, though. Was this what happened when you let people in? No, she'd tried that at the hospital. They'd wanted her to dis-avow her brother. Derek guarded her.

This time it was she who reached for him. His thigh muscles twitched when her palm rested atop his jeans, as though jumping to greet her like a Labrador left at home all day. "Thanks," she whispered.

"A little to the left would be a really nice thank you."

CHAPTER TWENTY-TWO

Outside of Callie's apartment building, Derek parked her car in the closest space. If they'd been on his motorcycle, she would have had the extra time it took to remove all her gear to figure out what to say next. Instead he cut the engine and that 4 a.m. silence crept in, the kind only ghosts and the highly inebriated could withstand.

He walked to her apartment with her. He stayed three steps behind her, quiet steps that squashed her nerves like spiders on a sill.

He edged inside behind her, and locked the door. The silence followed them both, filling her one-bedroom.

"How did you get to the substation?" she blurted out, realizing that the chrome and black of his bike had been missing from the parking lot.

"Rode it to get you." He punctuated the phrase with a thanks-for-reminding-me grunt.

"You left the bike back there?" She couldn't bring herself to say either police or station. She hovered near the kitchen counter.

Derek didn't move toward the couch. He remained rooted to the threadbare carpeting at the center of her living room, a living totem of muscle and fury. "Few blocks away at a friend's place. Ran the rest."

She didn't conceal her wince. He had done all that for her? While recovering from being stabbed?

After she'd tried to knock him out with narcotics, too. Fuck her. "I'm not worth this trouble," she said with a sigh of accepted rejection.

He rounded toward her. A big man giving her the side eye was not something Callie ever wanted to see again. "You don't get to do that."

Her lower back bumped against the counter's edge. "What?" she asked, even though she knew.

"You betrayed my trust. You tried to drug me. You do not then get to make this about you." With each sentence he took a step closer to her.

"I'm so—"

He towered over her, anger cutting grooves between his eyebrows. The powerful breath behind his words grazed her cheeks when he cut her off. "I want to be pissed at you, and your 'I'm sorrys' and your habit of throwing yourself headlong into danger because you think letting someone help you means ruining them. It doesn't do a damn thing for me."

Wisps of leather and soap made Callie's chest burn. The scent of him triggered a cascade of comfort, desire, and guilt. Her eyes welled with tears, but to let them fall would only be putting her emotions first. "I get—"

He cut her off again, hands slamming against the countertop at either side of her hips. "No, you don't get it. I get you, though. That's the problem. I haven't lied to you, Callie. I can handle a fucked-up family. *Trust me.* I can deal with guilt and secrets. What I can't deal with is you making my goddamn decisions for me."

Even caged between him and the counter, her flight response refused to rear. She was a hypocrite, and he deserved more. "You're right."

He sucked in a deep breath. His flushed cheeks puffed as though he prepared to rail at her again. Instead he let the air rush out. "I'm what?"

Her weak smile didn't solve anything. "You're right. One of the few things I have going for me is that I make my own decisions. It's part of what's made dealing with Ford and the Charmer so hard. I can't do the one thing that's always ever comforted me: I can't control my life. I can't say no to them. Choices are made without me and I'm forced to just deal. And I went and did the thing I hate so much . . . I did it to you."

The deep creases in his forehead smoothed, but he didn't back away. "You did."

"I know you don't want my apologies, but fuck, Derek, I owe you more than a sorry." She pressed her fingers against her lips, because no words were going to fix this.

He nodded, and when Callie moved her hand from her mouth to tentatively rest on his upper chest, he closed the gap between them. Her hand pinned between them, his lips slammed against hers. This kiss wasn't gentle or protective, but he wasn't laying claim either.

His hands gripped her hips and he deepened the kiss. Derek wouldn't tell her he understood why she did something so idiotic. He wouldn't say he forgave her. Not yet. He wouldn't promise to let her try to repair the broken trust between them. He didn't need to use his words. The fire and need igniting between their lips covered it.

—— CHAPTER TWENTY-THREE ——

Callie and Derek found their footing the previous night. She'd revealed one of her darkest fears in the midst of an atrocious act. Anyone else would have ditched her. Derek got it, though. Now she'd have to earn back enough trust to learn what it was in his past that made him understand her. It was early when they stepped out of Callie's apartment, and headed to recover Derek's motorcycle. Plenty of time to gently push for answers, she thought.

Fate, as always, had other plans.

"You're in one piece. That's got to be a good sign." Ford had already started up the staircase as Callie and Derek were approaching the edge of the second-floor landing. Ford slathered himself in boyish charm, but, especially in the ochre light, he couldn't mask the cruelty beneath.

"Can my brother say the same?" Taunting the equivalent of the jock who hazed the new kids might not be wise, but she'd run out of fucks to give.

The dick rolled his eyes. "Yeah, he can. Though after all this, I don't understand the value you see in him."

Derek's grunt, as if he had finally found something in common with the dirtbag, earned him a nasty side-eye from Callie.

Ford ignored him. "Do you have what belongs to me?"

Belonged? Why was everyone around her so interested in ownership? Who had the rights to the souls? Who could claim their magic? Discussing all this with a mob boss in the stairwell to her apartment the morning after she'd snuck into a police station and stolen investigation files was right below cleaning a stranger's bathroom with a toothbrush on her to-do list.

Derek interrupted her thoughts. "You couldn't wait until later?"

The sun was high and bright. She used to enjoy that. Not now though, with winter stampeding down the mountains. Exhausted and cold was a bad combination on its own, but adding in her general sense of dread put Callie mere inches from crumpling into a puddle of anxiety. Doing so in front of Ford was not an option. Not now. Not ever.

"Governor's moving faster than predicted, and we've already disposed of the research's human component. Besides, no need to have our girl stress over that information any longer than necessary," Ford said with a genial smile.

A deep rumble filled the space. Derek. They'd have to rediscover their footing, but there was no question whose side he was on.

Ford shook his head slowly, relishing the patronizing action. "You're only here because I've allowed it, Derek. Don't forget that."

Derek doubled in size. His presence overtook the concrete hallway. His towering frame keeled toward Ford. The man didn't flinch. "You seem to be forgetting how easily your soul could disappear." The dark promise tumbled from Derek's lips, a smooth waterfall with a wicked undercurrent.

But Derek couldn't wield magic. He'd told her so. Was he bluffing? Callie had never heard him use magic and his connection to the Soul Charmer as an open threat to anyone before, but, in that moment, she believed he could make Ford's soul disappear, and, more importantly, so did Ford.

The mafia man's hands were stuffed in his pockets, but he hurried backward three steps. Was it wise to strike fear in dangerous men? Only if one could back it up. Callie's fingers curled into fists at the thought. Bringing the heat, literally, had saved her ass earlier. Hurting Ford would be worth a hidden scar or two on the rented soul buried beneath her sternum. If it came to that.

"Let's get this over with inside." He jerked his head toward her door. "Too many eyes out here."

As much as she did not want Ford inside her apartment, she wanted her nosy neighbors to see her handing over confidential police files even less. Once they'd stepped inside, Ford rocked his weight from one foot to the other. He didn't peer at the family photos hanging next to his shoulder. He didn't look toward the fridge and suggest she offer him a drink. He didn't try to sit on her couch. Hell, he was a better unwelcome guest than her mother.

Derek didn't sit, either, instead preferring to loom at Ford's side. He was practically begging for an excuse to use his fists. For his part, the mob boss looked completely unimpressed, wearing a look of calm confidence that, if it was a bluff, was damn convincing.

"You get both?" He meant the files and the data.

Callie nodded. She retrieved the bulky file folder from the countertop and shoved it toward him. He accepted it with a single hand, and didn't show surprise at its weight or heft.

"The drive?" he prompted.

"First, how do I know my brother is safe? That you'll free him? That you'll hold up your end of the deal?"

His exasperated sigh should have earned him a swift kick to the shins. Instead he retrieved his cell phone—under Derek's watchful gaze and occasional snarl—and dialed. He clicked over to speaker mode.

"Yeah?" a male voice answered.

"Have Josh say hi."

"What's going on?" Josh said after a second. He sounded weary, but still very much like her brother.

"Roll down the window and look up, Joshy," Ford directed. Then he nodded to Callie and her window.

Derek's subtle nod, the infinitesimal sign of security, was all it took for her to rush to the curtains. Her brother's too-pale face peeked out of a black SUV in the rear of the parking lot. Callie needed several calming breaths before she was able to turn toward Ford again. He'd already ended the call. Anxiety and relief warred within her. Again. It was supposed to be over now, but her gut didn't believe it.

Bastard gut.

She wadded her concerns and squished them beneath her stomach. Distracting emotions were best buried. She tossed the small drive onto the coffee table. It skated a few inches and stopped near the end closest to Ford. He snatched it with a scowl. She'd given him everything the police had, and he had the nerve to glower at her?

"You plugged this into the third rack, right?" He emphasized the number. Nothing like the douche who kidnapped her brother doubting her competence.

She nodded. The risk of saying the wrong words when she was so close to being done with Ford and having Josh back safely was too great.

The quick salute he gave her smacked with condescension, but it also meant they were done. "Stay here. We'll send Josh up." Then he turned and left.

The door snicked closed behind him.

"Creepy fucker," Derek muttered.

Her hands were shaking, and Callie wiped a fine coat of sweat from her forehead. "Understatement."

Derek hadn't closed the distance between them. "You want me to stay?" He wasn't ready to leave. "I mean, do you want some time alone with your brother?"

He wasn't bothering to conceal his need to care for her. Another day she might analyze that, poke at why he wanted to be near her, contemplate if she was his way to atone for the dark secrets in his own life. Save the girl, make up for the bad. Today she didn't have the energy for such drama. She'd spent years working to remain under the radar, to be the girl no one noticed. Now too many people knew her, and the stress and the fear and the pressure of it all was congealing in her stomach. Derek had reeled her in before. She'd let him keep her from the edge now, but she couldn't afford to say all that. Yet. "Can you?"

One corner of his mouth pulled upward. "Of course."

She'd taken a single step toward him when her front door flew open. Derek lurched around to block the man who'd burst in.

"It's okay," she yelped. "It's Josh."

It was, but it was a sickly version of her big brother. Derek released him, but remained angled between the siblings. Callie swallowed her fear.

"You okay?" Falling back on the words Derek had offered her after the break-in steadied her. Distracted her from the changes before her. Her brother had never been bulky, but he hadn't been classified as lean either. In the weeks since she'd seen him, his face had gone gaunt and his hair, once the same rich brown as her own, was darkened to near black with grease. A raspberry scrape on his left cheek was the only mark of brightness he carried.

"Yeah, yeah, I'm going to be fine." He'd licked his lips between every word, shooting questioning glances one after another at Derek.

"Good?" The package of anxiety she'd hidden in her stomach quivered.

"I can stay here, right?"

So much for Zara's proclamation about Josh crashing with her. What else had her mother lied about?

"Tonight, sure." Callie moved toward her brother with open arms, ready to hug him and let this drama be finally over with. It wasn't though. She stopped mid-step and dropped her hands to her sides. Frost built beneath her nail beds and her hands turned icy.

"Goddamn it," she swore.

Josh's confusion didn't help matters. Of course he'd used souls. Of. Fucking. Course. "You alright, Cal?"

"I'll be fine," she said through gritted teeth. She backed away until her hands regained warmth.

"Look, I'm going to need to stay here for awhile. Mom isn't going to handle this well, and I need time to recover before I see her. You do kind of owe me, after all."

Derek's anger snapped before Callie's could, which said something. "You want to try that again?" he rasped.

"Who is this asshole, and why's he in your apartment?" Josh asked to Callie, and then turned to Derek. "Charmer's business is done. You can get out, Lurch."

"You've got fucking nerve, kid, I'll give you that," Derek said.

Callie pressed her hand against Derek's back. He softened, and moved to her side.

"First, Derek's a big reason as to why you're alive and not in tiny pieces all over the city right now. Be nice. Second—"

"I'll take care of you now. Family does that." The same words her mom, her aunts, her cousins, and every other person in the Delgado family threw around, were now coming from Josh's mouth. He punctuated them by reaching for her, his hands grazing her forearms before Derek shoved him away.

The hailstorm raging inside her was agony. Ice licked up to her elbows as she stumbled backward, and her skin darkened. Frostbite. Her brother had given her frostbite. The terror of the previous night, the unending worry over her temporary abilities, it all came up. Literally. Her stomach revolted. She ran to the bathroom, barely making the bowl as her stomach spasmed.

The white bathmat did little to protect her knees from the Saltillo tile below as she knelt in front of the toilet. She hadn't exactly wanted the guys to follow her in here, but she thought her upchuck move would have at least killed the conversation. Wrong. In between heaves she heard the two.

"Don't know what you've threatened my sister with, but it ends now." That was the Josh she'd saved. The perk of family was that you knew each other's cores. Yeah he was a junkie and a thief and an on-and-off liar, but when it came to choosing between people in the family and those who weren't, he always sided with her.

"You're one to talk." A thread of possession laced Derek's derision. He understood her core, too, and had accepted her despite her special brand of crazy.

Goddamn men. Arguing on her behalf while she puked in another room.

"Pretty sure you and the Soul Charmer shouldn't be involved." How well did Josh know Derek?

"You're the one who threw her to Ford to pay off your fucking debt like a coward. You're the one who foisted her on the Soul Charmer. You're the one who risked her goddamn life." The floorboards creaked. One of them must have edged toward the door.

Derek. He continued, "So I'd point that finger elsewhere if you don't want me to snap it off."

She pushed up from the floor. The first person outside her family to have her back was now yelling at the one other person who had regularly stood up for her. As if one couldn't feel worse while leaned over the commode. Derek wouldn't actually injure her brother. Probably. Intervening would be smart, regardless, but she didn't make it far before her stomach roiled again.

Josh chuffed. "You don't know anything about me or my sister. She's done with the Charmer anyway."

Callie wished that were true. Derek must have agreed. "She's done with him, but she isn't done with me. And I'm not about to let you make her feel like shit."

"Wait. What? Me?"

"Yeah, you." The edge of a wicked growl sliced Derek's voice, a tone she knew he saved for uncooperative targets. "How ungrateful can you be? She risked everything to save you. Not saying she shouldn't have done it, but that kind of dedication deserves your respect and never-ending gratitude. If you were anyone else, I'd have already broken your face for the shit you put her through."

Josh's voice had gone tight. Callie couldn't tell if it was out of fear or guilt. "I appreciate her, and I know her a lot better than you do."

"It's not a contest, kid, but I'm the one keeping her safe, so quit being a dick. Sit on the damn couch, and when she gets back out here thank her and then shut the fuck up."

Josh didn't say anything more. Glass clicked as her refrigerator door closed. That reminded her: the empty vodka bottles sitting atop the fridge needed to go in the recycling. Focusing on the mundane steadied Callie. The dry heaves had finished—she hoped. She quickly brushed her teeth and rinsed her mouth a few times before wading into the tension of her living room.

The magical layer between the Soul Charmer's rooms was thick, but the energy in Callie's living room rivaled it. Josh sat on the sofa, taking up as little space as possible. Derek was on the other end. He took a deep swig from a glass of orange juice and tried to project a controlled aura. She wasn't fooled.

"Stomach settled?" He pushed off the couch and walked toward her. He placed his glass on the kitchen counter, and then wrapped his arms around her.

Being angry took more energy than she had. Indulging in a hug was simply easier. "I'll be all right." Her words were muffled against his chest.

He pulled back enough to look at her. "Water?"

Were her eyes still ringed with red? She shook her head. "I'm exhausted."

He nodded and gave her a quick squeeze.

She leaned around him to speak to Josh. "You eat anything recently?"

His gaze darted to Derek before answering. His nerves were showing, but his voice was solid. Faking confidence was a genetic trait. "Not much. You guys already eat breakfast?"

Callie's eyebrows drew together. Before she could point out his idiocy, he answered his own question. "Right. Sick. Never mind."

She was going to get high on oxygen at the rate she was taking calming breaths. "Kitchen's pretty bare, but feel free to make yourself some toast."

"Thanks." He got up and started toward her. "Thanks for letting me crash and, um, for everything else."

She took a couple steps backward, but smiled.

"It's what we do." Her DNA might be muddled at the moment, but despite the outside influences, at its core it held the same traits as Josh's. Family loyalty was locked in, right alongside their brown eyes.

Her brother moved to hug her, and Derek intervened.

"What the fuck, man?"

"You can't touch me." Callie couldn't hide her wince.

"I know I made things hard for you or whatever, but I still love you." He edged forward again, and Derek put a hand on his shoulder.

"It's not that." Couldn't Derek explain this? She gave him a pleading glance.

Earning his care this quickly was scary, but that didn't temper her gratitude when he took over. "She can't be near people who have used soul magic right now. Part of the shit with the Charmer. Hurts her," Derek explained.

Josh's face scrunched like a lemon had been shoved in his mouth. All he said was, "Oh."

Callie scrubbed her hand on the nape of her neck. The skin had cooled from her earlier sickness, but she was still off. "We're going to take care of some business. Couch is yours."

"Cool." He wasn't arguing and that was good enough for today.

His eyes stayed on them until Callie closed the front door behind her. He might not trust Derek, but then again, her brother's taste in people was questionable.

She trusted Derek. Officially. And that was fucking scary.

CHAPTER TWENTY-FOUR

The day before, Callie had become a criminal. A real one. Not just ganking makeup at a drugstore. You could fit an entire ocean between that and appropriating confidential police research. She couldn't even call herself simply a thief anymore. That title was lost when she'd burned a man's chest. Thinking about it, semantics suggested she could say it wasn't assault with a deadly weapon, since it was her hand that burned him. Though that argument would not likely hold up in court.

Her reunion with Josh hadn't gone quite to plan. She couldn't hug him, which she wanted to do badly enough it hurt. She also couldn't shake the feeling he didn't understand how dangerous saving him had been. Resenting him wasn't something she wanted, but her mind kept flashing back to the conversation she'd overheard earlier that morning. Like Josh's attempts to defend her while simultaneously demanding she give even more. She mentally booted herself for the thought. He deserved her help not because he had kept her secret all these years, or because he covered for her with Zara. He was her brother. Taking care of him was what she did.

But Callie was still struggling to accept that Derek wasn't sticking around just to screw her over. Although, even with a bonus soul inside her, he was a better person than she was.

Derek parked his bike near the Charmer's rear door as usual. "You ready for this?"

She wasn't. Inside that door the Charmer would take back the soul. She wanted that, but her muscles turned to bow strings with each step toward the entrance. "Today has to be better than yesterday, right?"

He grinned at her. "Don't tempt fate, doll."

She nodded, but rapped her knuckles against the wooden doorframe they passed through. Just in case.

"How did it feel?" the Charmer crooned as soon as they were inside. His delight churned her stomach.

She wasn't prepared for up-chuck round two, though. "No big deal."

"Did you wish to keep it then?" The words were playful, but the menace behind his eyes was anything but.

"No," she said too quickly.

He beamed. "In that case, sit." He pointed to a stool next to his bench.

"Why could I still use magic when the soul was in me?" She wiggled her fingers.

"My magic isn't negated by a single soul. If it were, this business would not be nearly as successful. It all worked as planned." He was half ignoring her while digging through drawers like some aged apothecary ready to cure her ails.

She mouthed "as planned" at Derek, but all he offered was a shrug. It was time to be done with the Soul Charmer. If she never returned to this overtly sterile and creepy room again, it would be too soon.

"Ah!" The Charmer held up a flask, but it wasn't the same as the one Callie had used. While inlaid with dark stone, there was no mistaking the green hue.

"Why are you using a different flask?" she asked before her brain could quell her stupidity.

"It's gentler." He put zero effort into concealing the lie.

"Let's get it over with then." She gritted her teeth and wondered what kind of pain she'd inflicted on others when her position had been reversed.

The flask's opening pressed up against her sternum, her breastplate vibrating from the impact. She jerked forward, tits first, as the container created an industrial-grade vacuum. Her head swam, but nothing hurt. Or it didn't until she blinked and found herself sprawled on the floor. Derek's rough hands were under her arms, lifting her. Random black spots obscured her vision of him.

"Apologies, Calliope." The Charmer's patronizing fake grandpa voice grated against her already throbbing skull. "It seems the rented soul rather liked you."

"Liked me?" she groaned.

"It's rare, but then again, you're a special one."

"You got it, though?" Derek's husky voice was the balm she needed.

"Yes, of course."

Once she was sitting on the stool again, her faculties returned. If that was finished, then there was only one more bit of business. "Let's go ahead and get the magic removed now, too. I'm up for it."

"I'm not." No shame with this one.

"What do you mean?"

"I can't very well take the magic out of you now."

"Why the hell not?"

"Watch your tone." His obsidian eyes flashed. Powerful lightning cutting through a cloudless night.

She closed her eyes, but it didn't improve anything. "Our deal is complete. I don't work for you anymore. So, *please*, take back your magic."

Saying please had almost killed her. It was far worse than the goose egg forming behind her ear.

He sighed like he was indulging her, and she bit the inside of her cheek so hard she tasted blood. Now was not a good time to piss the Soul Charmer off. "I still need you."

"For what?"

"Tess is contained, but she—"

Ungrateful asshole. "You already have her. Remember, Derek was bleeding all over the place as a result of our capturing her? Remember that I . . . "

It's like the bastard had baited her. "That you what, Calliope?"

Callie caught Derek's gaze and let him see the hurt and shame and guilt roiling inside her. She couldn't voice her regrets here. Her secrets were to be laid bare. The Charmer cleared his throat. He wasn't going to be denied her humiliation.

"I already got the answers you wanted from Tess for you," Callie said, keeping the patronization level at one hundred percent. "We know she was recruited to take souls from you. Just not by who. We know she's batshit and thinks what she's doing is going to make Gem City a better place. We know she's a big believer in group think. What more do you want?"

He cocked his head to the right, like a hawk eyeing its prey. "You forget your role."

"My role?" she gasped. She'd already collected souls for him, and then captured his enemy and burned answers out of her. What else did he expect to squeeze from her?

The Charmer ignored her, his beady eyes locking on Derek instead. "My business is threatened. That means your life is, too," he told him.

He had to mean livelihood, not life, right?

"You said Tess was the threat." Derek's measured tone kicked Callie's heartbeat to a hummingbird pace. Why was he acting like he knew what the Charmer was talking about?

"She isn't the true threat." Bottles clattered and toppled as the Charmer slammed an open hand against his desk.

"She was taking souls, boss," Derek cut in.

Callie resisted adding a very unhelpful, "Yeah!" She needed Derek to see she was on his side.

"She was, but she was not, as you say, in charge. She refused to reveal who recruited her, someone else who is now targeting us." The Charmer's vitriol slid, unseen, down Callie's legs like broken egg yolks against a house on Halloween. Was she being battered for another magical invasion? She wasn't soul French toast.

"Then is it really an immediate problem?" Derek pushed boundaries, but at least it felt like she and he were on the same side. And it wasn't the Soul Charmer's side.

The man who could steal their souls took two, fast, tiny steps toward them. "What's mine is being taken, destroyed. That will not stand." He swiveled his head, again, more birdlike than usual, to glare at Derek. "How would you feel if you were robbed of that which you loved?"

Derek had never suggested the Charmer had anything on him. He'd never spelled out the reason to Callie why he was so loyal to his reptilian boss. It was a mutual relationship, he'd said, but as the threat clogged the air, one thing was clear: their dynamic had changed. Was this on Callie? Or was this part of why her idiot move with the pills made sense to him?

"I can investigate," Derek said, his voice quivering at the end.

"You'll do it together." Final words from the Soul Charmer, the man with all the power.

Callie fought the urge to curl in on herself. Skipping breakfast was the right call. "I already did my part. Why does this involve me?"

His eyes widened. Had she gone too far? "We need to find the person who wants to steal my power. They're stealing all my souls and ruining their value."

Whatever the fuck that meant.

Callie licked her lips. He was already screwing up her life, so there was no reason not to push harder. "Again, why does that involve me?"

"What needs to be done isn't possible without you. You, my dear, are the only one capable of sensing this person. I can't very well lose such an asset right now." Three feet separated them, but his words wrapped around her throat like a cold, scaly hand.

Her jaw dropped. What. The. Fuck.

"Now, child, it won't be forever. The sooner you complete the task, the sooner I'll unburden you."

"No," she muttered.

He ignored her. "Tess did mention your mother was a client of hers. Frequent client. You failed to share that tidbit. Seems the taste for the dark side runs in the family?" He grinned, aware Callie was too angry to speak.

Real nice, Zara. If one family member wasn't in debt to the mafia, it was another who was dabbling with soul magic. Callie needed to get out of the Charmer's store. Like now. The sooner she resolved this, the better. "We find out where this other soul magic person is, and then you and I are done?"

"I am not in the mood for negotiation."

"It isn't a negotiation. I want answers," she bit out.

"Yes, when you've helped quell this coup, you can ask me again to take the magic." His even tone wasn't what threw her, and it wasn't his magic floating beneath her skin either. Callie put it together: he didn't think she'd want to lose the bothersome gift he'd so graciously endowed to her. Ego the size of Texas on this one.

"You will take this magic back." If she could figure out how to actually make him do anything.

Derek took her hand and squeezed it. They left the Charmer's shop together, and she hoped he planned to stay at her side for more than the drive home.

Derek hadn't spoken a word since they'd left the Soul Charmer's shop. The black and silver flask was back in Callie's pocket. Even its heat and the realization she'd continue to work within the world of soul magic couldn't distract her from the tension between them. She should have spoken as soon as they exited the building, but words failed her.

Derek had treated her like she was special. He'd told her she was a good person, and he'd meant it. Now, he'd know the awful truth, and she ached with the thought of losing his trust. She wanted to keep him, but she'd known this would happen from the start. Now he would understand.

He followed her up the stairs to her apartment.

Once inside, though, he didn't beeline for the bedroom. The shower was running and the bathroom door closed, which left them brother-free in the living room. He strode to the couch and plopped onto a cushion. His cushion. "We going to talk about this?" His voice scraped along gravel.

Rubbing her palm against the side of her neck didn't soothe any muscles. The nervous act only telegraphed her emotions. He'd broken her walls, and now she couldn't muster a decent poker face. This was going to hurt. "This is why," she whispered.

"Come over here." He patted the couch cushion.

She did, because sitting would limit the mess when she melted into a puddle of shame.

"Tess." He didn't spit her name, like Callie would have. There was no inflection in that four-letter word.

"I had to—"

"Why?" There wasn't any judgment in his tone, but the curiosity was obvious.

"He wouldn't let me take you unless I did." The image of him crumpled and bleeding flashed in her mind and she winced.

"You're going to have to give me a little more here, doll. Why wouldn't you wait for me to come around?"

Wait, what? He wasn't mad?

"You were out from the blood loss and the Charmer wouldn't let me take you home until he had answers from Tess," she said. "He said I had to get them. I couldn't leave you with him. They weren't watching you. What if you'd stopped breathing and I hadn't been there?"

He smiled. "He wouldn't have let me die."

"I couldn't risk that."

Derek reached forward and ran two fingers along Callie's jaw before placing them on her lips. "Thank you."

She started to speak, but he pressed his fingers more firmly against her mouth.

"Did you really think I'd judge you for getting answers?"

He pulled his fingers away.

"I did awful things at the Charmer's, and then to protect you from them I did awful things here. I couldn't imagine you wanting to be with me after you knew I'd done that. And if you'd helped with the break-in, too? I didn't want to force regret onto you. I have enough of it, and I wanted you to be safe."

He nodded and the simple act conveyed more understanding than she'd been allowed in her life. "We protect what's ours. I didn't want that for you, and I'm sorry you had to do it. But if you want me to be mad at you for looking out for me, it's not going to happen."

"You're not pissed?"

"Just tell me next time. We all have to make hard choices, do shit we aren't proud of. I wouldn't hold that against you. That said, I'm still not going to take so much as an aspirin from you for a very long time."

She had the good sense to look chagrined.

He pressed a light kiss to her lips. "It's hot to have a woman protect me."

"You think everything is hot."

"Only on you, doll."

Reaffirming their relationship in the bedroom strengthened Callie. Her muscles were sore after their activities, but the ball bearings of stress and fear hidden in her torso relinquished their hold on her. Trust was fucking weird, but nice enough.

"I think Tess was right about my magic," Callie blurted, then paused. She'd startled herself by claiming ownership of the fire teeming below her skin.

Derek skimmed his fingers along her hipbone, his trajectory never faltering. "You sure about that? Woman was crazy."

She nodded. "Totally batshit. Agreed. The Charmer isn't taking the magic back, though, is he?"

"No. I don't think so." Disappointment crushed her with those five words.

"Tess said he couldn't take it back anyway. So I guess I already knew I wasn't going to be able to go back to normal. I've been thinking a lot, about us, about me, about what's happened in the last two weeks. Maybe this is some fucked up sign I need to learn how to use the magic for now, and go from there." Hope lifted her voice an octave.

"That sounds smart . . . " Derek narrowed his eyes as he met her gaze. "But you're about to use the good sex we just had to make me agree to something, aren't you?"

"No. First of all, it was better than good." She waited for him to smile before continuing. "Second, I'm not asking you to do anything. Well, except to be cool about it."

"And what exactly is it you're about to do?" His hardened gaze sent a shiver down her spine. Goosebumps prickled her skin in its wake.

"I think I'm going to tell the Charmer to fuck himself."

Derek had made several strong arguments as to why changing her relationship with Gem City's Soul Charmer was an awful idea. He was probably right. His ardent need to keep her safe warmed her heart, but the trust deal went both ways, and he had to trust that she was making the right decision for herself.

She'd texted her mom from the street outside the Charmer's shop. After all soul magic name drops and the way Zara had stormed out the other day, it didn't hurt to touch base. She didn't receive a reply. That was okay. She'd deal with one family crisis at a time. The way she always had.

She'd rescued Josh. He might not stay clean, but she'd do her best to help him try. Derek helped her understand that, which was why she was striding into the Soul Charmer's store with the most confidence she'd carried in years. Derek had remained at her apartment when she left, proving he was really in this relationship for her. She didn't need to worry over him now. It was time to push the Charmer in a new direction and see how greedy he could really be.

She tugged her sleeve down to cover her palm and tapped the ancient brass bell. The Charmer's head poked out from between the back entrance's curtains in seconds.

"Ah, Calliope. You already have my answers?"

She ignored the condescension coating the Charmer's words. She was in the dank storefront for a single reason. "No, I've decided I need more from you if you want more from me."

While Callie was eager to go back to her real life. Back to mornings with Louisa. And nights with Derek that didn't involve a magic flask. She was a realist. The magic wasn't as terrifying as it had been even a week before. If she had to carry it, she wanted to get more than a "good job" from the greasy old man who strong-armed her into wielding it in the first place.

"Not your decision," the Charmer hissed.

"Wrong. We made a deal. You changed the terms, and now I'm doing the same." His bone-melting stare wouldn't break her. Her need to reclaim her life was too strong.

He skittered toward her.

"My magic is inside you." His gaze assaulted her, but the pervert hadn't stabbed a flag in her torso in the name of God and country.

"If it's inside me, then it's mine now, not yours." Every stutter-step the Charmer took toward her cranked her internal flight response another notch higher, and dialed back her confidence level with equal measure.

"Is that what I should tell the police officer who was here this morning?"

Her hand collided with the counter as her balance faltered. "What?" she choked out.

"Someone—a petite woman—broke into a police substation, and she burned a crime technician. Horrible business, really. The police came to me for help, as the perpetrator's fingerprints were illegible." His nearly toothless grin turned Callie's stomach.

Her hands began to heat as he moved within a few feet from her. The flight response was on lockdown. Her feet had melded to the grimy floor under the Charmer's threat.

Prison. Felon. Criminal. The words blazed her mind. She had saved her brother, but the cost? She turned into exactly what her mother told her she would: a failure.

The Charmer watched closely as tears welled in Callie's eyes. He continued speaking as though they meant nothing to him. "At the time I couldn't remember providing my services to any women. I don't keep written records, you know. But after the officer left, something jogged my memory. Do you think I should I call them back, tell them I've suddenly remembered something?"

"No." At least she didn't sputter. Callie hauled in a behemoth breath and quelled the impending tears. Regaining control of her life was too important to let fear get in the way. "I think you need to hear my revision to our arrangement."

"You do, do you?" He was practically laughing in her face.

Her earlier bravado might be squished beneath her soles, but she had enough pride to push her goal: "Make me your apprentice."

That got him. The Soul Charmer's jaw dropped enough to give Callie a too-long look at the man's silver teeth.

His silence allowed her strength to grow. "Will you teach me how to use this magic in exchange for my continued services in finding your competition?"

"Apprentice." The grin was back. Fuck. He stared past her breasts, clearly seeing the soul beneath her sternum. He seemed lost in thought for a long time. "Yes," he finally answered. "While you obtain the information I need, I will help you understand that which you wield."

"Okay." Such a mild word for the roaring conflict in her belly.

She'd entered his store in the name of regaining control and power. She'd gotten what she'd asked for, but didn't quite feel like she'd won. Magic offered strength, but the taint wouldn't wash off when she was done. Callie refocused on what was important: Her brother was safe and she'd found someone outside her family who earned and respected her loyalty. She could survive this.

If it took learning his craft and finding his enemies, she would find a way to escape the Soul Charmer.

She'd play his apprentice.

For now.

ACKNOWLEDGEMENTS

Writing is a solitary endeavor, but getting it done is a whole lot easier with a great support system. I can't say how much Amanda Bonilla and Megan Frampton helped me make this book happen, but I can tell you they are the best cheerleaders and probably love Callie and Derek as much as I do—maybe more. Thanks to Jo Hoskinson for her beta skills, and generally being the other half of my brain for VBC. To Marcia Koehler, Stacia Kane, Jeff Farrell, Windy Aphayrath, Bree Bridges, the VBC girls, and so many others for your enthusiasm and excitement.

Also, big thanks to my agent Cheryl Pientka and my Talos editor Cory Allyn for helping make this book happen.

Finally, the biggest thank you goes to my husband Matt for understanding deadlines means we order pizza or other food "they will bring to us," and being the biggest champion for my writing. Matt, you're amazing and I love you.

Chelsea Mueller writes gritty contemporary fantasy. She founded the speculative fiction website *Vampire Book Club*, blogs about TV and romance novels for *Heroes & Heartbreakers*, and is co-chair of SF/F charity Geeky Giving. She loves bad cover songs, dramatic movies, and TV vampires. Mueller lives in Texas, and has been known to say y'all.